# Jessica Lucky

by

V. S. Cawthon

ISBN-10: 1-4961-8458-0
ISBN-13: 978-1-4961-8458-0

# DEDICATION:

*To Sweet Loraine*
*And Brother Joe*
*My Fabulous Beta Readers*

# ACKNOWLEDGMENTS:

*Jonathan Swift, Quentin Tarantino, Alex Russo,*
*and above all*
*The Immortal Oscar*

*Our lives begin to end the day we become silent about the things that matter."*

Martin Luther King

# I

*I don't believe in fate. But I do believe in luck.*
*Woody Allen*


*Ghost Posse,*
*Tomorrow —*


*Popopopopopop!! Popopopop!*
*Moonrise and gunfire over the Western Hemisphere's richest island palace — a shining, six story faceted Xanadu, gleaming in the August moonlight, visible from every watery horizon.*

*The island's midnight tranquility suddenly vanishes into an acrid staccato flicker of golden muzzle flashes, lighting up the windows of the King's lavish study, sixth floor north corner. Then there is a pause in the shooting. The windows go dark again.*

*This lofty castle rises above, and presides over, an island that might once have been the template for Eden itself.*

*Popopopopopop!*
*Again, abruptly, automatic gunfire cracks open the night, popopopopopop...pop...pop! And again abruptly ceases.*

*Lights suddenly blaze from every bulletproof window up and down the temple's vast facade. From every direction, turbaned Sihk guards race toward the giant shadowed titanium entry doors...*

*With a single desperate roll of the dice, an assassination of a King has been attempted.*

*And failed.*

*Strike at the King – you'd better kill the King.*

*In the womblike sanctuary of his office, stands, trembling, one of History's richest financial barons. Tall, pale, eternally young, this gentleman has just survived attempted murder. He stands stunned and instinctively frozen in the bright reality of the moment.*

*He is alive. He cannot believe it; neither can the four men sent to kill him.*

*If you track Huffpo, if you have a laptop or television, read People Magazine or have a friend who does, if you skype, text, FB or Twitter, you know his name: Anthony Perkins.*

*Having been surprised by this preposterously bold attempt on his life, Perkins is garbed now only in a black silk robe, hastily half-tied, nothing underneath.*

*He is a youthful, attractive man, but his face is now ghost-white, his heart pounding wildly, his breathing now almost under control again, his narrowed eyes taking internal inventory of his body for possible unfelt wounds. In shock, he feels nothing.*

*He reaches first between his legs. He and his brother are both, according to anecdote, endowed in the extreme, rumored by the starlets and socialites both have squired down through the many years to be in the same category as Howard Hughes, Don Johnson, Liam Neeson. And for five hundred years, these two brothers have ridden the magnificent crest of immortality, as owners and discoverers of the Fountain of Youth, a mythic place that is in fact real.*

No one believes it. Fine with the Perkins' brothers, formerly named Costa, when they'd arrived as lowly conquistadores with Ponce de León on this little gardened island Paradise in 1513, and had stumbled across this treasure...

*Surviving pirates, Indians, runaway slaves and land developers, down through the centuries, the brothers now quietly rule the hemisphere in anonymous gentility. They are easily trillionaires, though no one really knows.*

*Now, truly fearful, Tony Perkins carefully reaches inside the robe, then downward, feeling for the wetness of blood...*

*What kind of luck would it be to rule eternity from this perfect gardened sanctuary, only to have one's manhood shot off, when everything else, for the last five hundred years, had proceeded so swimmingly? The ultimate in mixed emotions...*

*The slightest gasp of relief.*

*"Well, thank the gods — my horoscope was right after all," Perkins whispers to himself. The shooters have missed everything but the chandelier, and a Fabergé decoration, and the priceless Picasso behind his desk.*

*Half - destroying his office study and its incalculable wealth of decorative art, are dozens of ugly bullet - gashes, whose near - misses most noticeably fracture a priceless Fabergé egg on his desk, rip open a wild, ragged pattern of holes across a Picasso original. Destruction of the Picasso would scarcely trouble Perkins. He hates it anyway. Just another Foundation investment. The collage hangs behind his desk where he never has to look at it.*

*Deep splintered pockmarks form erratic blast patterns upon the thick mahogany and oak walls that, until moments ago, seemed to provide perfect protection for this slender, youthful Master of the world...*

*Now, he is trembling, his dark silk robe threatening to fall open, confirming he is only human, after all. His relief at complete survival is supplanted by a deep, growing anger. He looks down at the would - be killers, on their knees before him.*

*And Anthony Perkins is not alone.*

*Kneeling only a little more than an arm's length away from Perkins, and trembling also, breathing hard, are four young African American assassins, their mission now a ruinous and possibly lethal failure, their hands are atop their heads per command, fingers interlaced, eyes wide and white with fear, their weapons scattered in the rich pearl carpet around them — four Tec - 9s, machine pistols inexplicably chosen for intimidation.*

3

*For accuracy, fortunately not so much.*

*The would - be killers now kneel surrounded by a dozen sleek black snarling Doberman Pincers, a squadron of palace mastiffs, King Perkins' last line of defense, the growling cadre of grinning, thirsty, gleaming tan and ebony Death that has saved his life.*

*"Who let those dawgs out?"*

*"They let themselves out." Perkins smiles. "They've been trained to know when to come. Gosh, so sorry they knocked you guys on your asses. They've been trained to do that too."*

*"Will you — can you show us mercy?" Nothing got hurt but that ugly - ass painting…*

*"Before I tell you what's going to happen, could you answer a couple of questions?"*

*"Anything, sir. Anything!"*

*"How much were you paid for me?"*

*"Five million."*

*"American?"*

*"Yes sir. Not a dime til the job got done. God damn it."*

*"You want mercy? What would you do if you were me?"*

*"Best case? I expect I'd hang my ass out to dry."*

*Perkins laughed.*

*"Did Ghost Posse send you?"*

*Silence.*

*"For me alone? Or for me and my brother. Answer or die."*

*A long moment's silence. Then:*

*"Sir, I'm ready to die. I've made my peace."*

*"The rest of you?"*

*All nodded in defiant agreement.*

*"Considering inflation, I should be worth more than five million. It's a damn insult."*

*"Wasn't nothing personal, sir."*

*In the distance, Perkins could hear the cries of the platoon of huge, heavily armed Sikh security personnel racing closer, their shouts filling the arched hallway.*

*"You gonna kill us, man? We're just the messengers."*

*"Don't move. The puppies will rip your throats out."*

*"We won't move."*

*"They'll be sending others, sir. There's a fatwah."*

*"Ghost Posse." Tony Perkins murmured, almost to himself. "Five million. Ghost Posse. So typical. Cheap bastards."*

*"It wasn't nothing personal, sir. The money was just too good."*

*"Don't move, damn you. Now I'm in a bad mood. So are my puppies."*

*"We won't. move. We just want to get out of here alive — if you can show mercy."*

*"Pinkie promise?"*

*"CALL 'EM OFF!"*

*Within moments, the shooters were being flex - cuffed. Despite his still - elevated blood pressure, Perkins had begun to feel a certain affinity, even affection for the clueless killers on their knees before him.*

*In his own long life, Perkins too had hunted men. And his mere physical survival contained within it a spoonful of the most precious medicinal sugar of all — forgiveness.*

*"Sir, please, don't end our lives..."*

*"We all got kids. We needed the money."*

*"Sir. you own the world. It's easy for you. My house is about to be foreclosed."*

*"You the King. We bow to you sir. We wanted to be rich like you — it's the American way. We won't come back. If they send others it won't be us. We're done. Clemency, sir. Please sir, leniency...mercy."*

*Tony Perkins stares at first one, then another, of the young men, restrained before him, awaiting their fate.*

*In the bullet - shattered office, time pauses, then seems to stop, the only sound the terrified beating of their hearts.*

*Five seconds pass. Then five seconds more. Perkins' breathing has relaxed. Almost shyly, he has tightened the belt of his robe. He is most notably a very shy man. But now his dark eyes are bleak, angry, and cynically cold. In his half - millenia of existence, he's faced far greater terrors than this one.*

*His composure returns. In the bright room, each moment seems an hour. The encircling Sikh guards await instructions. Perkins looks thoughtfully into the fearful faces of first one, then the next of these youthful killers.*

*"Please, sir. Mercy...mercy..."*

*Their target allows another five seconds or so to tick off the clock. He watches them sweat.*

*"WOOF!" Perkins shouts, then gives an irritable laugh as he watches the young killers jump in fear. The Doberman cadre does not flinch.*

*"Get 'em out of here." To the leader, he gave a further word of advice: "You jokers need to go back to community college and learn how to code. Crime ain't your natural line of work." If it was, you'd all be millionaires at this very moment.*

*"Yes, your majesty," The leader answered sardonically.*

*The three are led from the office to a PERKINS FOUNDATION helicopter, already warming up below in the palace courtyard to return them to the tender mercies of a central Florida Sheriff, back on the mainland...*

*"One other thing," the lead gansta said, almost over his shoulder. "Can we get the Techs back? They ain't ours. They were fronted."*

*Perkins laughed in disbelief.*

*"Samir, make sure those weapons are clear and return them to these geniuses at the end of the flight."*

*"Thank you, your majesty."*

*And as quickly as they had come, they were gone. Perkins laughed again in disbelief.*

*"Damn, what balls."*

*Now Please Allow me to Introduce You to the Youthful, Lovely, Protagonist of title — Jessica, (in the hours before she gets lucky): She lives two hundred miles north of this just described, early morning, bullet - ridden drama out in the Gulf of Mexico.*

*Jessica lives in a gated McMansion, rich and privileged, in oak - shaded Tallahassee.*

*Brainy, leggy, horny, this fifteen - year old girl is an Everyteen, not to be judged, any more than Youth can ever be judged.*

*She spends a lot of time with her 'i' phone and her laptop Diary, which is where we find her, perfectly manicured fingers flying, on the very same hot moonlit August night after Master of the Universe Tony Perkins has escaped assassination, on his enchanted, beleaguered island paradise down south.*

*These two are destined to meet.*

*Frantically, excitedly, exhaustedly, Jessica is writing… and writing… and writing….*

*Jessica's emotional profile? Let's see: Lazy? Yep. Grumpy? Sarcastic? Uh - huh. Horny? Well, she is fifteen. Almost sixteen. Another noteworthy personality trait, mentioned often by her bitter, troubled, emotionally distant Mother: Jess, you've got quite a mouth on you…Quite a mouth.*

*Leggy, beautiful, pre - MIT whip smart, possessed of Old South ruling class charm inherited from her equally sexy, ice - cold lawyer Mom, Teen Angel is currently fighting off an obsessive, lustful* crush on a classmate, the black Student Body president – Barry, who swears he feels the same way about her.

Oh, Teen Angel! Among her other talents, Jessica sings like an angel, starring in last year's school production of <u>South Pacific.</u> So cynically indifferent to the world beyond herself! To her friends, she is junkyard dog loyal. To her enemies? There are none.

Jessica and her clique rule the Cheer Squad, the student council – the high school realm entire. Her besties are Angela and Phong. This teenaged Troika rules the school. Rare for juniors to rule the school. Yet somehow, stunningly, against stereotype, these girls are not evil bitches.

For all her dark self - obsession, her anger and wounded heart, her resentment at her Mom's banishment of her beloved father from her childhood castle of dreams, Jessica is struggling meantime to emerge from the cocoon of childhood, into an almost amazing moment of gawky, clumsy, blinding teenage beauty.

She loves to party, has tried cocaine and liked it and said no to any more, steals her Mom's Scotch – a few jiggers stops Time. Or at least sends it sideways.

This is important. Why? Because Teen Angel wishes most of all to never lose another moment of Youth.

Jessica, Phong, Angela have formed a group dedicated to the worship of Oscar Wilde. They call themselves 'Daughters of Dorian' in his honor, and the club's slogan is one of mighty Oscar's most famous aphorisms: <u>Youth is the only thing worth having.</u>

But, pre - eminently, Jessica wishes merely to accomplish "six impossible things before breakfast."

From all adult authority, Jessica hides her Slacker consciousness behind a Machiavellian disguise of Volunteer service every weekend and straight A's on the six week card. A beautiful smile for every face she faces.

In a high school world jammed with posers, slackers, suck - ups and up - crawlers, Jessica and her friends are Masters of the Game.

*They rule. Yet if youth is the only thing worth having, every day, every hour, these rulers of high school's hive - like teenage universe watch and feel another tiny sliver of it vanish for ever. It is a hateful fact of Jessica's existence.*

*3 A.M., silver moonlight shining on the big windows of her Tallahassee bedroom. Now she types:*

*So funny how Barry forgets half the time he promised to call...Mom would hate him because he's black even though she'd never admit it. So politically correct. It could be the best thing about him. A way of striking back at her. I wonder. Hard to sort it all out, D –*

*I've noted how guys generally are about three years emotionally behind us. In maturity, responsibility, self - control. In general they're idiots, and I keep wondering why. My guess? It's the presence of my monthly bloodfest, what we Daughters of Dorian refer to as 'La Visitora' – we were all into Spanish when we got our Surprise, within three months of each other.*

*Since then, merely due to the monthly arrival of La Visitora, the certainty of a monthly bloody wound and the pain accompanying, has taught us all what Reality was capable of doing to you. These are no playground scrapes either, like the football team suffers through and brags about.*

*La Visitora really explains why we're so far ahead of the boys. We young unlucky maidens learn the hard way how dangerous, unpredictable, unfair Reality can become in a midnight cramping moment, how your own body can turn on you, in a single brutal snap.*

*It's a different, deeper fundamental awareness guys never even dream of. So what do we do about it? We learn to suck it up. Why? Well – We have no choice. Not complicated. And that's the beginning of adult wisdom.*

*Oh, Phong, Angie and I are years ahead of the guys in class. La Visitora is why. What else could explain the distance between us and them?*

*Why am I even writing about this? Trying to understand why the guys are such children, yet I keep dreaming about Barry... I think about him all the time. Don't think Mom has anything to do with it.*

*So tired Dear D, time to hit the feathers —*
*Peace Out. Jessica Out.'*

*3:20am Aug. 2 Jessbaby99signoffgmail*

*Jessica shares the same bright August Florida moonlight as the two legendary brothers she will soon be privileged enough to meet personally — the beginning of her lucky streak.*

*Two hundred miles south of the Tallahassee McMansion bedroom where she and her laptop ruminate on all the troubles and challenges, the woes and miseries of her fifteen year old life, on the island known as Crystal Lagoon, sharing the same moonlight, the same late night hour — the brothers are calming down from the recent assassination attempt.*

*Priceless, three hundred year old Turkish brandy is having a positive medicinal effect in this regard.*

*In the wee small hours, Xanadu again slumbers in near - darkness. Though invisible, Island Security now hums with hyper - vigilance. Yet one by one, the lights in the huge front windows are extinguished. The Sikhs had again silently vanished to their posts. The Dobies had been fed, rewarded, bedded down.*

*"All I was worried about was whether those jerks had shot my d\*\*\* off," Tony remarked to his movie star/ lawyer brother Tommy. "Shows you the depth of my moral focus."*

*Tommy laughed.*

*"I'd have checked down there first too. Isn't that what counts? It reflects the title of that Malraux novel: 'Man's Fate.'"*

*Tony laughed too. "I'm the Man With Two Brains – hate to lose either one of them."*

*"Well, they missed. Drink to it."*

*"Well, they missed. This time."*


*In the last moments of moonlight, balancing the vast castle's stately spires, battlements, towers and minarets, are a series of wild Frank Gehry gull - winged cornices, swooping, curving, caressing, giant hammered silver scoops that so soften the medieval muscle of this massive fortress, architectural genius both ancient and modern melded in ingenious harmony, the past and the future interwoven to form a dark, looming fantastic silhouette that rises high over the island like that of a tremulous, ominously predatory Phoenix...*

*And central to the castle's magnificent courtyard, Crystal Lagoon's defining, supernatural feature: a two hundred foot tall tree of undetermined origin and charismatic singularity, the most amazing tree in all History.*

*It is legendary, known to all who have seen it as The Tree of Knowledge of Good and Evil. Everything on the island utilizes this iconic sticking point, this mysterious, supernatural totem, as the psychological and physical starting point.*

*It is as though the island could not exist without the great tree at the center of everything. A low wall surrounds the gigantic, oak - like trunk.*

*No one ever steps over that wall.*

*Now, under smiling moonlight, only a single narrow golden glow lights the castle, shining down from the fortress's highest, turreted minaret – a slim vertical gleam of candlelight, mocking the darkness and silence surrounding.*

*This tiny, sky - high panic room is ablaze with bright fire from a multitude of fiery candelabras.*

*Old habits die hard. The brothers grew up in rural Spain, five hundred plus years earlier, in the time of candlelight.*

*At that time in their young lives, both these country peasants were still illiterate. Stupid and obedient. Good, conscripted soldiers of the Queen. Everything else has changed since then. Yet as for the candlelight, they prefer it still.*

*Tommy plays solitaire in silence. His older brother Anthony, the murderers' intended target, stands by the narrow vertical window, gazing down at a sliver of his empire through a sliver of bulletproof glass.*

*"They'll come again," Tommy notes finally, flipping over another card from the deck of cards in his hand, and tucking it into place. "And they'll keep coming. They'll try for me next time."*

*"Yes, you're my lawyer," His brother replied. "They get you, they get me."*

*Tommy turns another card. He stares at it.*

*"The Queen of Spades. The Death card."*

*"Kammi."*

*"My exact thought."*

*"That Curse. One way or another, she's behind all this trouble."*

*This apparently innocent remark seems to remind the older brother of something.*

*"I wish I hadn't fallen in love. Actually – That's what's behind all of this."*

*"'Of this matter is little Cupid's crafty arrow made'..."*
*Tommy yawns, quoting Shakespeare — once a contemporary, although*
*the brothers never had the good fortune to meet him personally.*
*Tommy studies the Queen of Spades. "Who reads the tabloids? I*
*didn't even know who she was."*

*"She lied to me about everything. Why did I tell her about the*
*Water, Tommy? Why did I run my mouth?"*

*Tommy shrugged. "Because you were in love. And let's face it*
*— the girl is funny as hell. Even when unintended. Beauty and charm,*
*the twin serpents entwining the surgeon's staff. What was it Orson*
*Welles said? 'Show me an actress and I'll show you a devil.' Kammi's*
*whole life is a breathing, golden Academy Award ceremony. I may*
*hate her guts, but she makes me laugh every time. Only the great ones*
*have that gift."*

*"Why didn't somebody on the staff alert me I was living a*
*lie?"*

*"Who among our entire corporate staff would have dared*
*question the choices a King makes? Don't question yourself, brother.*
*Kammi's the best liar I've ever seen in ten lifetimes of liars."*

*Tommy hesitated a moment before adding, almost murmuring,*
*to himself, "But I wish you hadn't told her about the Water. It could*
*be our doom."*

*Gorgeous, clever, lying witch. Tommy understands his brother*
*is crazy in love with this Demon. He says nothing more.*

*"What do we do now?"*

*"What we always do. What we've done for the last five*
*hundred years. Or is it a thousand? It seems like a thousand. Find a*
*way to survive somehow. Immortality comes with a few challenges —*
*remember when we spent five years hiding from the Cherokees?*
*Eating RATS? Nothing could be worse than that. We have more*
*power than God now." At least that gives us a puncher's chance in*
*this fight...*

*Far below, moonlight and summer breezes ripple within the languid gardened paradise of Crystal Lagoon, a dream - world sufficient to satiate any rational man or God.*

*King Perkins looks down upon the distant, dazzling panorama for some time. He gazes across the courtyard at the somber, impassive presence of The Great Tree. The castle's girding forests, gardens and fountains seem lit with the glimmering refraction of silver coins flung by the millions everywhere under clear, breezy moonlight. The beauty of the world he overlooks is mesmerizing.*

*The problem is, Tony Perkins is no longer rational.*

*He is in love. Desperately in love.*

*And he sees not an empire, nor Paradise, nor the immortal world that blind luck, and a world - altering discovery on a routine patrol – of a half dozen sweating, pewter - clad, comically helmeted conquistadores 500 years ago – stumbling upon a little trickle of gleaming purplish Water, and his current riches that ultimately flowed from that gentle little trickle, affording him and his brother Tommy's immensity of time and treasure, now and for all the many centuries previous.*

*His comrades on the routine patrol had been so awestruck by the overwhelming magical power of the gigantic tree rising above them, they had overlooked the little trickle of sparkling purple water. All later died of cholera. The two Costa brothers survived – and had remembered about the Water.*

*Now – King Perkins would trade it all for one more single night with the mesmerizing Kammi Kay.*

*Oh, the things that he has seen, the tastes that he has tasted! Every appetite fulfilled, endlessly over the more than intervening five centuries, to the point of boredom.*

*It all means nothing now.*

*He sees, hears, thinks, feels, breathes, only a single thing, a name worth more than all of it, more than everything in sight, more than everything within the command of his all - powerful signature. The memory of the girl who told him No. Who walked out of his life without a word of warning, and married another man.*

*Kammi Kay.*

*Beyond his island's fantastic shores, the pre - dawn moonlight spins out a last achingly romantic silver glimmer upon the broad black silent perfection of the Gulf of Mexico. The island called Crystal Lagoon is once again silent and safe.*

*"Top of the world, brother." Tom turns another card. The nearby narrow titanium vault - door is secured by six case - hardened steel bolts. Their world is momentarily impregnable. The brothers try to calm themselves down.*

*The priceless Turkish brandy helps.*

*"Top of the world." The brothers toast the future. And the past.*

*Tony Perkins tightens his silk robe about himself. The candelabras blaze warmly, comforting globes of fire. The brandy blazes too. He reaches down between his legs, just to make absolutely sure. Anthony Perkins has survived assassination. And that's the good news.*

*Yet the lover, the Beauty who has driven him to the edge of madness, has left him. She has fled in the arms of a bitter rival.*

*And that's the bad.*

*Kammi Kay. The most sexually exciting Regent since Cleopatra.*

*Kammi Kay. The greatest liar and whore since Delilah.*

*The girl who said No to a King. Mere weeks before their planned nuptials.*

*That's gotta hurt.*

*Worse still, she has instead married a musician.*

*Worse still, a black musician.*

*Worse still, a rapper.*

*Worse — A gold - toothed, Revolution spouting rapper tatooed like the Illustrated Man.*

*The founder, father, El Presidente and leader of Ghost Posse. That's really gotta hurt.*

*Worst still, a contemptuous, gold - toothed, world - famous Genius of the genre, a charismatic powerhouse who has become a towering figure in both the worlds of entertainment and politics, perhaps the most talented and authentic voice for the aspirations of black America since Malcolm X – Dr. Felix Munye, aka 'the Doctor'.*

*Kammi Kay, the planet's reigning Reality star and the most beautiful woman in America, if Huffpo clicks are any indication, had met Dr. Munye by coincidence backstage at one of his sold - out concerts, and had fallen into the Doctor's powerful arms like a stunned, very lucky groupie – the luckiest since Desdemona, yet unstrangled.*

*Only weeks later, Kammi's marriage to Dr. Munye in Aspen made world headlines.*

*And instantly they had become, the planet - wide, in every headline, in every breathless news cycle, forged together in the fiery hot flashbulb world of the Paparazzi, a single transcendent entity...*

*<u>KamYe!</u>*

*"I guess we got married in a fever. I know I did." Kammi Kay had later explained to Babwa, or perhaps it was Katie – Tony Perkins was drowning in priceless brandy the night the surprise interview aired. Oddly, during Sweeps Week. Thus, his memory of the horror is sketchy.*

*"We were so hot for each other," Kammi was bragging. "I wouldn't let him touch me till after our vows. You wouldn't believe our wedding night. There must have been a billion rose petals. From one end of the suite to the other. And, of course, the bed. We had every kiss videotaped from three different angles, every...every...well, you know."*

*These universal, star - bright names — brothers Tommy and Anthony Perkins, Dr. Munye, and his Reality bride Kammi Kay — KamYe as these two are now universally known — are among the most instantly recognizable on earth, heavenly baubles hanging from the distant unreachable twinkling Christmas tree of planetary social media, where TMZ fame is like the very best Christmas gift of all, even if it only came to others, to only a Godlike few in an entire world of desperate, fascinated envious nobodies.*

*The Christmas stockings of the whole world might be stuffed with coal, but it made the misery easier to bear, to watch through our glimmering electronic screens, just as the hungry children of Charles Dickens's London watched from outside firelit mansion windows a hundred fifty years ago, to gaze at the spectral gleam rising from the palms of our hands, at the wondrous Christmas joy experienced within by the so very lucky few, and fantasizing, and dreaming of the fantastic banquet ongoing, so near yet so far away — the paparazzi - mobbed red carpet of planetary celebrity, the Heavenly champagne - and - caviar kiss of all - forgiving fame that could be held and admired and envied and hated but never, ever be shared, never experienced except in dreams...*

"Did I tell you I offered her a billion dollars to stay with me?" Tony now asks his brother. "In Swiss gold."

Tommy is wise enough to say nothing about Kammi Kay, whom he despises.

"It's Munye who sent those assassins," Tony adds. "Ghost Posse. A little blood doesn't matter. He wants this island."

"She told him about the Water. She told her bitch mother too. Just like she promised not to."

*"I doubt he believes her. How can you believe anything she says? Especially something that sounds like science fiction anyway."*

*"I believed every word out of her beautiful lying mouth. Like a goddamn fool."*

*"She was singing about Love, not Eternal Life."*

*"What's one without the other?"*

*"Relax, brother," Tommy replies. "We've still got all the world, all the money, and Time." <u>Time to figure something out. Time to figure a way to fight our way out of this. Not a lot of Time. But enough. Probably enough.</u>*

*"She's all I can think about."*

*"Oh, come on. Stop feeling sorry for yourself." Tommy lifts his glass in a toast. But he is still gazing at the Queen of Spades, the Death Card. Kammi's card.*

*"I wonder where she is tonight?" Tony murmured, gazing down at the vast moonlit beauty below. "Probably in Europe at some huge concert blow - out, running toward a Lear jet with flashbulbs blazing and paparazzi and thousands of screaming teenage girls chasing them both… Going to some all night drug orgy in the mountains… And she's no doubt paying for all his drugs… His hot little love slave…Oh, that incredible booty…" The cameras of the world, and the eyes of the world, could simply not look away from her. Tony's memory could not look away from her. Kammi Kay has the magic. Kammi Kay rules the hive. The hive of Reality.*

*"Stop torturing yourself."*

*Reluctantly, Anthony Perkins responds to his brother's toast.*

*"And I almost got murdered tonight." Tony laughs. "They shot the Picasso instead. Everybody's an art critic."*

*He lifts his glass. The Turkish brandy helps.*

*"Look on the bright side – They missed."*

*"Yeah. They missed. This time. And she's gone. Oh, God."*

*"That may be another bullet you dodged."*

*"Don't you dare say a word against her."*

*"Apologies."*

*"Top of the world, Ma," Anthony Perkins nods. "I hate her too." Now he whispers softly, sadly, almost to himself, "I hate her with all my heart. With all my heart."*

*"Top of the world, dear brother," Tommy gently repeated. "Accentuate the positive. Don't mess with Mr. In - Between."*

*<u>And thus, a week later, give or take....</u>*

*Dear D –*

*It's Jessica, bitch*

Cannot believe it! *Barry* will have a cow. My *mom* will have a cow. *Angie* and *Phong* will have a cow! *I'm* about to have a cow. *In a minute it's gonna be raining cows up in here!*

And what a break this will be for Daddy's journalistic career!

I hear the King's brother is the really hot one. Tommy I think his name is. He was in a movie. These guys are the most mysterious players in the state. Rich, young, evil, pretty – *what's not to like? What's not to hate?*

How did Daddy even get this gig? OMFG! I CAN NOT believe it. *I'm going to get to meet Anthony Perkins!*

So anyway here's how I've decided to introduce myself when I meet him, Diary: *Hello, Mr. Perkins. So nice to meet you. You're so rich and famous! I read about you everywhere. But I've never seen even a photograph. Very mysterious. So secretive. Is the IRS after you? Was that impolite to ask? My Mom says I've got a mouth on me. You're very handsome. Oh, you like the way I look in this little black dress? You'd like to see me again later? You'd like to spend some quality time later alone with me in your billion dollar castle? I'm almost sixteen years old – that's not too young for you? Are you sure? Why am I not surprised? Oh, my name? Do you really want to know? You do?*

*Okay. So...*

*It's Jessica, bitch.*

*It's Jessica, bitch.* *That'll take the King down a notch, I'm quite sure. Then I turn my back on him and fantasize him watching me walk away, I'll make sure this cute little black dress fits like it's painted on, his tongue hanging down...He'll be sweating through his tongue like the Dog I'm sure he is...Youth's the only thing worth having, but he'll never have me. I wonder what his brother looks like? Tony and Tommy. Tommy the movie star. Damn, Jess, is it all you ever think about? Boys? And their brothers?*

Just like Britney would have done it. Sure, she's a granny now, and sure it's a golden oldie but I still love that lick! Time ate her Beauty, just like it does with all of us. Britney's lick, but I endorse it so...*It's Jessica, bitch.* Ha. Reverse Robin Hoods. These trillionaires can go f*** themselves.

So there.

Cool down, J girl, it's just another interview job. Dad and I do these from time to time. I'm the Scout. Except this time it's the richest boy on the planet, not just some dude who plays for the Dodgers... I can't believe Daddy finessed this one. He's been so far down, for so long...

...and I love my Daddy. And I pray he'll be better again soon. If anybody can find out the truth about Crystal Lagoon and all the drama down there, it's my brilliant dad... He'll have to sober up a little first.

He can do that.

Diary, let me catch you up. Someday I'll want to read back over this, and remember, not so much how it was, as how I *thought* it was, in these sort of stressful, teenaged times...

When I asked Dad what strange course of events were in process of leading us downstate to Crystal Lagoon, to interview the secretive royalty who rule the island down there, in his usual succinct way, he replied:

"One of the brothers was nearly assassinated recently. They are in dire need of some good publicity. Their whole Empire is under pressure. I think it's why I got summoned. They know I tell the truth. One thing is sure, dear daughter – there's a lot at stake going on down there." He paused. "You ever hear of an outfit called 'Ghost Posse'?"

"Of course. One day they'll rule the world." *Their music is changing America's cultural history. They drew a crowd of a half - million at the HBO AIDS / HIV Rap - a - looza.*

"They're the killers." *Ghost posse is behind that whole botched - up assassination, I know that much.*

"Don't be racist, Dad."

He laughed. "Yes, dear."


Dad hasn't been doing all that well since he and my Mother broke up. That should never have happened. It pretty much destroyed them both.

Their paradoxical curse? They were, and are, too much in love. It's come down to smoking ash, and yet they're still nuts about each other... Love's funny.

Once we had such a great family; I'm fifteen years old now, almost sixteen. A lot has changed since 'the good old days'.

Then, I lived with two beautiful, brilliant parents, in a gated McMansion with scads of money, toys, playmates, and dogs and cats and turtles and goldfish and even a couple of rabbits here and there. We had what seemed like an unlimited, happy future together.

Okay, so the rabbits were a learning experience. But otherwise, it was a dream of a childhood – our family's good old days together.

As childhood was ending, I vaguely remember a stretch of silence and tension. Something very bad had happened between them. Then Dad moved out, about three years ago. No screaming, no whispering.

All very civilized. *Rich girl with looks, bad boy with skills. The story of the world.*

And then the world ends.

A lot of kids can't wait to grow up. Not me. I just want my family back together again.

And then, *to never get a day older.* Like Peter Pan. Like Dorian Grey. I know there's a way. *There's got to be a Pause button in space - time.* I spend my free time in our high school library and on the net looking for it.

But every time, I wind up reading Nancy Drew or sexting B. It's tough staying focused at my age, when so much is coming at you moment by moment...

And it's difficult absorbing the punishing unhappiness of my parents' split - up. What I wouldn't have given to have a big sister, to help me sort through everything.

But as an only child, the weight of it all comes straight down on my head.

And, of course, every month, my awkward too - tall body is getting its ass kicked. I won't describe it; less said tha better. Awful. Mood swings? _What_ mood swings!?

"All the love we had, your father and I, in creating you – it goes to you now, Jessica, just like a deposit of money in a bank." That's so typical of how my mom would put it…"Don't think about our split - up. Just remember how much we love you. Always remember that. It's the first truth."

_All I want for Christmas is my family back!_

_So tired, bright moonlight outside, Can't wait to tell Barry about my upcoming trip down to Crystal Lagoon. He's not calling – again. Jerk. I am so hot for him. Another of love's paradoxes. He hasn't got me yet. But I'll be sixteen soon. That's when it will happen. I think about him all the time. He says it's that way for him too. He's a good liar. Florida in late summer the most beautiful…_

_Time to hit the Click, D – Time to hit the feathers._

_Peace out, Jessica out._

"Jessica, clean up your room."

"In two shakes."

"In not even one shake. Now."

Mom's a high - priced corporate lawyer. I love her, don't get me wrong, and I admire her. God, I just hope I'm that good - looking when I reach her age.

But the insomnia, her relentless unspoken ambition, the restlessness that causes her to chop veggies into salads at midnight and cover them with cellophane three meals in advance, her amazingly lovely face bathed in the glow of her laptop when husband and daughter were just trying to get a little sleep, for heaven's sake – I think it finally wore Daddy out.

Mom comes from a pioneer family in this state – read, 'rich'.

Her family is really rich. Daddy was broke as a bug when they met. But it didn't take long with those two. *Rich girl with looks, bad boy with skills: the story of the world.*

She came out of the gate at a hundred miles an hour. Mom's the ultimate fast - tracker in this slow paced north Florida burg. She's out of place here, but I don't think she is really even living here.

She's living in the future, and that is a place without a geography. I think she wants to be Florida's first female governor. As mentioned, that kind of ambition takes its toll.

Once she had the greatest sense of humor, and between Mom and Dad, our house rolled with laughter.

Forget that. She and I don't hug much these days either. She goes to power meetings, political dinners, and works eighty hours a week. I just take orders and occasionally scream back.

I spend most of my weekends with her. When she's not heading out the door.

Brutal.

She lives in the McMansion, Daddy rents a single - wide.

He's fallen a long way. Once he was a top - flight journalist. Hard to believe now, given his current circumstance, but once he even won a Pulitzer Prize.

He's so talented, it must be why he landed this once - in - a - lifetime Anthony Perkins interview out of nowhere. Just in time, too.

Because now sometimes Daddy has reached the point where he has to sell things at the flea market to make ends meet.

Blame vodka. Blame Mom. As mentioned, he's still crazy in love with her. And she won't admit it for the world, but I know she feels exactly the same. That's why they're always fighting. I know he only blames himself, but we don't talk about it. I help him. We have fun. But it's been a long fall.

On these interview trips, I'm his Scout. I do a good job too. The jobs have been getting rarer. This Perkins' invite is an incredible break for him. I guess they read his stuff. His reputation always precedes him.

Smirnoff aside, Dad's the real deal.

Mom listens to that radio talk show guy, Lush Rimbaud or whatever his name is, the fat dopehead, and has adopted a real Trog outlook politically. I use fake names for the famous losers in this memoir in case I want to publish it some day. They sue you for anything in modern America. As Mom always says, everything has to be run by Legal first. Everything.

This is a part of the country that has been having a lot of race problems.

And Ghost Posse is a really big reason why.

Back when we were still a happy family, when Daddy started carrying a flask in his journalist's bookbag, I knew he wouldn't be around much longer. Then one Sunday he just moved out. Mom didn't even know he wasn't coming back until late that Sunday night.

One of the few times I've seen my mother cry. And mean it. She cried her beautiful damn eyes out that night, and I found myself crying right along with her. Dawn came, and we were both still crying, first her, then me, then both. But it didn't bring him home.

My dear, dear Daddy is still as sweet, handsome, talented and kind as ever, just a lot quieter. But you don't f*** with him. Once he and Mom were such equally stubborn, determined winners in this life.

I pray he'll get better soon. He always took such good care of the pets, and took such good care of Mom and me too. A sweetheart. The whole thing's sad and ridiculous.

But the most ridiculous part is, my parents are still crazy in love with each other. Theirs is one for the Ages. All they have to do is open their eyes and see the Obvious.

But, as mentioned, love's funny. Teenagers know about stuff like this long after adults have forgotten the fact. And sometimes when Mom looks at me, she sees him.

That's when I catch the hell.

"Jessica, I couldn't help noticing your bedroom hasn't been cleaned up since Hurricane Katrina passed through it some innumerable semesters ago."

"I'll get right on it, Mommy dearest. Just finishing a text to Phong."

"That's what you said two years ago."

"In a sec."

"Why. Don't. You. Go. Upstairs. Now. And. Fix. The. Problem. Please."

*And why don't you go — !*

"Please stop picking on me!"

"Stop being so antsy. Clean up your room!"

"I'm not being antsy!"

"Your room! Now!"

"Yes, Mommy dearest."

"Don't call me that – Carrie *dearest.*"

"Yes, Mommy dearest." *And stop calling me Carrie! I'm unhappy, not crazy!*

"Oh!"

"Oh!"


Our school has two Barrys, Red Barry, who proclaims himself a teenaged Bolshevik and is president of Student Council, and black Barry. Black Barry gets elected president of everything else: *see, we're cool, our school is cool.*

I like black Barry. In fact, I fantasize about him.

It just clicked. We haven't done anything yet but the lord knows, we talk about it enough. B. is so sexy, so different than anything in my gated, whitebread world – he's exotic. Our texts are so sexy they could put us both under the jail. When we get going, we practically peel paint off the walls. I think words can be hotter than actually *doing* it.

But how would I know?

I will know on my sixteenth.

This isn't about love, it's about growing up, and I like pissing off the jocks and soshes too, truth be told.

At school I'm caught between two worlds, but there's a balance to it that's currently missing in my home life. No cliques for Jessica.

Mom's rich. But I'm no Goth, no hippie, no jock, no sosh, no psycho, dagger, Mook or Gourd. I'm not in the band.

That makes me cool by process of elimination.

But the utmost reason is, I've got the two coolest bffs in my class. The three of us bonded over a mutual fascination with Oscar Wilde, and even formed a kind of informal club in his honor, *Daughters of Dorian.* My friends are Angela and Phong.

Angela is smart, sweet, somewhat naïve. She's also beautiful, platinum - haired, a cheerleader, a whale - saver and treasurer of the Student Council. Phong's her opposite, a skinny, sexy, spikey - haired little Asian ass - kicker whose parents made it out of Viet Nam on the last helicopter back in the Day. Phong's a second - generation stranger in a strange land.

Whatever, we blend together splendidly. On one subject we agree relentlessly: Oscar Wilde is God, and we agree with his axiom, *'youth is the only thing worth having.'*

None of us have tattoos yet though. One small gold belly jewel, that's as much as I've been penetrated.

So far. As mentioned, I fantasize about it. And about Barry. Just another part of the Tweener, Coming - of - Age burden. Barry and I still talk on the phone more than we text, a rarity these days. Our i's are kept on vibrate.

"Florida's a messed - up state, B. The comedians say our state bird is the mosquito, and our state flower is a .38 Smith & Wesson revolver. That's really hurtful – it's *so* unfair to our state's reputation, and *so* not true."

"That's ridiculous," He laughed. "Couldn't agree with you more, Jess. Haven't they ever been to Miami?"

"You do? So glad you see that! You're so evolved for a guy. Love it that you and I see eye - to - eye. The gun nuts are turning us into the Alamo! A .38 revolver? Oh, *come on!*"

"Ridic."

"What *is* the state flower? I don't even know. Magnolia?"

"Glock Nine."

Barry knows how to make me laugh. Barry's smart. Mensa smart. Barry's the reason I started paying attention to politics. That's why I started this chapter with a reference to Ghost Posse.

For those of you who have been on the moon, or in Branson, Mo. for the last two years, Ghost Posse has become a nationwide African American political movement that started out as a rap group with about five fans on the West Coast, and, overnight, just blew up.

Reason? As mentioned, a guy named Doctor Felix Munye, who is like a combination of Elvis and Malcolm X and MLK and Joel Osteen and Obama and M&M. When he sings, when he raps, when he speaks, when he sermonizes, lectures, conversates – walls shake, and the columns of another Trog temple fall down.

Throw in Gandhi, Moses, Socrates, Elmer Gantry, and some of those other ancient oratorical wheezers, and you've got the profile.

The Doctor is the amazing ebony, tattooed dragon who swooped down and swept away luscious Kammi Kay from the castle of the King. And that Beauty was not exactly low - hanging fruit when he got her. Just the opposite.

We still don't know how he finessed it. But he did. The Doctor's another bad boy with skills.

Loosely based on a series of speeches and lectures Dr. Munye gave at Harvard and Brandeis a year ago, the outlines of his proposed racial separatist colony, 'Africa

America', is what's got this country so all hot and bothered lately.

His vision is still a little inexact, but the power and appeal of his anger, and that of his followers, is unmistakable.

It shows you the power of his charisma to see this gorgeous black man wearing hornrimmed glasses and a professor's elbow - patched sports coat in front of all those academic Trogs, while he's telling them what time it is, using five dollar words that so impress the Ivy League's *professorate,* and hearing their cheers of approval, at this separatist dream whose time may just have come. Dr. Munye is the reason why.

Like I was saying about Daddy – The Doctor's another bad boy with skills.

*Ladies and gentlemen of Harvard University! Friends! Citizens! There's an island off Florida that is ours, stolen centuries ago from our runaway slave forefathers by rich white men. I hereby notify you we are seizing that island on behalf of the ghosts of our forefathers – we are the guardians of their dream, we are their posse! And this evil island will be taken back from its bondsmen, and become the political center of our new world, the capital of the emergent internal colony of Africa America! Fellow citizens, give us your hands! Your help! Your hearts!*

So Dr. Munye has already stolen the King's prized lady faire, and now he wants his island too? That's really injury to insult.

And what the Doctor wants, the Doctor gets.

But The Doctor rarely wastes his time lecturing academics.

Dr. Munye is usually sweating, bare - chested Black Jeesus, with a ten - piece horn band and hot back - up singers behind him. And the number one Reality Queen on the planet, Kammi Kay? Those enigmatic, lovely, seemingly empty dark eyes? That amazing booty, that makes JLo look like Kate Moss? You can't go through a supermarket check - out without saying hello to those two doing kissy - face in *People, US, Globe* mags.

*KamYe!*

The photo - shoots they grant always seemed to occur coincidentally during Sweeps Week.

Kammi always looks glassy - eyed with love. She looks at the camera all slack - jawed, worn - out and smiling, like she's spent the last three days on her back, and he's always wearing that half - sarcastic, half - ironic smile, gazing down on her. He's got a huge stubbled jawful of beautiful white teeth that look like he could rip your throat out if you ever did him wrong. The whole package. Mmm.

Doctor Munye is awesome. I still remember the headline in the *Democrat:*

\* \* \* \* \* \* \*

*KAMMI, MUNYE IN ASPEN VOWS;*
*RECEP ENDS IN BRAWL, 81 ARRESTS...*

\* \* \* \* \* \* \*

Wow. Some wedding! Mmm. So distant from my Mom's dollar - dominated whitebread world — seventy - two hours in a Colorado slammer... Now *there's* an education.

Even when he'd married white, Munye's popularity and his mission's strength remained unaffected. The ratings only went up. Dr. Munye's political instincts were unerring. He'd picked the right white girl. *Kammi Kay.* The most famous, and arguably the hottest, female television star in America. And, for that matter, on the planet. *Dr. Munye's Reality bride instantly joined the long list of female sexual*

*immortality: Eve, Delilah, Helen of Troy, Cleopatra, Guinnevere,*
*Ann Bolyn, Princess Diana… Kammi Kay.*

Huffpo proclaimed them reigning Media royalty with
the bestowal of a single appellation: *KamYe.*

This rap group, *Ghost Posse,* currently rules popular
music in our troubled nation in these Dystopian times. The
vast political movement of the same name arose out of the
message in those merciless urban beats. Eighteen months is
a long time in a troubled democracy.

And the girls all go nuts for The Doctor.

Ghost Posse sells out 80,000 seat stadiums, and
when they come to town, riots happen. But this group has
become a lot more – an aspirational iconic Doom Machine,
Mom's hero Lush Rimbaud calls them… A really scary
political force, with explosively growing support the nation
wide.

This is pretty fierce music. I get it, I really do, and
every time Barry jams the headphones on my head, I
succumb to the beat of Ghost Posse like we all do.

It's irresistible. It's the Future. It's infectious,
hypnotic, pure jungle. Doctor Munye's genius is in taking
things back to first principles.

Of course my mother puts it another way, *Ghost
Posse and the esteemed Doctor Dumye, are leading America's great
cultural Dumb - down. And let's not forget about his internet porn
queen superstar wife! The future of America. Raise a glass to the
future – Here's to your Future, Jessica. It's a Drum.*

*"It's Munye, Mom – not Dumye."*

*"He married that idiot big - assed Reality star, didn't he?
Have you ever heard her trying to count to ten? On 'Counting From
One to Ten With the Stars?' Did you happen to watch that show?
The absolutely brilliant Kammi Kay? I think she made it as far as
seven!" Oh, the irreality of Reality television, the iceberg that the
Titanic of our culture is heading straight toward – and your beloved*

*Dr. Munye and his beloved Kammi Kay are steering the great boat, the ship of Fools, as far from reality as you can get in this voracious fame cannibal of a Nation! Daughter, put down your damn phone and read a book!*

*"Whatever." Mommy dearest....*

*"Ghost Posse meets Reality television. Little blonde Money Hoo Hoo tosses her first dwarf, live, tonight, only on A&E. My God, where will it end?"*

*"Well, Lush Rimbaud is the worst of the lot. Mommy, could you at least turn down the radio? Your Fuehrer's voice is giving me a headache!"*

*"At least Lush knows he's a comedian. Oh. Don't forget to take out the laundry from the dryer, Jess. I've got a meeting. Be sure to lock up."*

Remember the old joke, what's the difference between a fox and a pig? Two stiff drinks. That's my Mom. Massive Trogette. She's so beautiful she gets away with it. Every time.

Besides, what teenaged girl doesn't hate her Mom? At least five minutes of every day, I don't care how close the two of you are. Even fathers and sons aren't so... *contentious.*

Having just trashed her to hell, I now have to qualify it – Deep down, way deep down, my Mom's got a beautiful, even mystical, soul. An old soul. And, despite her recent cra - cra, the lady is pure class.

I've seen it. I grew up with it. A deep soul to match her physical beauty.

Tall, with a Nicole Kidman flame of red hair practically to her butt, ex - beauty queen, volleyball star, top five in her law school class at UF, Phi Beta Kappa... Oh, and let's not neglect to mention a year modeling in New York and Italy, before starting her legal career – she was even a judge for a while. The whole package. Grr.

When she met Dad, she went absolutely over the moon. That's what gets me. They both were – and are – absolutely over the moon about each other, to this very day of silence and recriminations...

So whatever went so wrong with her? One of my parents must have had an affair and the other one found out about it. But who?

They were so in to each other, a betrayal like that is serious. Utmost serious. I know she can't make Daddy come back to her, and that drives her crazy. I've given up trying to figure it out.

Ridiculous. And I don't even know why I still care. But it's killing me.

*Jessbaby99*

*Text, Barry to Jessica, 3:35p, Friday Aug. 6*

*Barry: hey J what up*
*Jess: Depressed..out by tha pool*
*Barry: ? hot teen like you owns the world*
*Jess: i'm getting old*
*Barry: u trippin'... u r 15!*
*Jess: exactly... soon they'll make me go in for drivers license*
*Barry: crazy girl..u snuck moms lexus out last weekend..Its the memory of my black life, ridin' dirty next to a naked teenage white girl in flip - flops with a bottle of Scotch between her sexy legs, leanin' on the gas lke fg danica patrick .with lights off on the freeway,*

*doin'at least a hundred...No white Sheriff is ever lettin' this N outta that traffic stop alive...nxt time I drive*

*Jess; sometims i'm a little wild ..get it from my mom ..don't lie playa u had fun...I liked it when u were kissing my nipples..It wasn't the booze that got me wet baby u so sexy*

*Barry: 120 mph on I 10 w lights off.. seriously?..hella one way never to get older ..jus what i need.. to die w a crazy white girl... w/ u.drinkin scotch out th bottle..15 yr old hottie like u ? white cops catch us they lock my blk ass under jail.. i was scared and i don't get scared...nxt time i drive*

*Jess: i'm just mad a the world rt now...u r a pssy it was a full moon i could see for miles lol...like the song says, I could see for miles and miles and miles*

*Barry: nxt time i drive*

*Jess: ur a pssy lol*

*B: I was hard and soft all at once — felt like love*

*Jess: .. wish i could make a selfie that would keep me young for ever .. like the Dylan song For Ever Young...like Dorian's portrait*

*Barry: yeah i liked that book .. let's start again...What up?*

*Jess: Nuthin' what up wid u*

*Barry: u talkin black again?*

*Jess: Yeh. Hate th whitebread world I'm caught in. straight up Compton baby ..from now on... like it? Tryin to learn..gettin more natural at it .. anything for u baby*

*Barry:...I turn you out yet grl*

*Jess: Talk's cheap..where u*

*Barry: Home tired. Whut up*

*Jess: got a pedi this a.m.*

*Barry: Can i see? Where u*

*Jess: Gettin a tan out by the pool..*

*Barry: Which bikini?.. send selfie*

*Jess: Uh uh.... I'm naked. well except for the pedi.. think it's called cobalt blu... and the silver anklet and neck chain you gave me....big gobs of lotion on my nipples etc. i'm baking in oil. like sardine.*

*Barry: Selfie! Now!*

*Jess: i love this feeling. feel like i'm in the garden of eden except for the pool chlorine. Eternal Eve...nobody in Florida should wear clothes in august. if Mom shows up she'll have a cow. don't know why, she does it too. Should i put on a thong? i think a tan line looks good on white girls...just wish it could be like this forevr..melancholy J..boo hoo*

*Barry: i'm comin over*

*Jess: LOL...Gettin browner too..20 mins more in this heat, i'll be a sistah..fine w me.. won't have to go to the country club no mo'...ruling class is overrated..just rednecks with dough*

*Barry: Selfie! Damn girl*

*Jess: If something happened, too much sun and the pool chemicals caused my skin to turn chocolate, u wouldn't give me a second look u only like white girls... what would u do then? My body's gettin so dark....i see th way u look a Angela*

*Barry: still hit it*

*Jess: covered in sweat too i'll be a sistah soon*

*Barry: u been reading sci fi again*

*Jess: No, it happens sometimes! called Epidermal Regression*

*Barry: epi — whut?!*

*Jess: happened recently to African women in sun... stop watching porn a minute and follow this*

*Barry: how u know what I'm doin*

*Jess: Iku. read this in Huffpo. 4 African women in a cornfield outside Johannesburg see a stream .... they drank from it... purplish in color, tasted like flowers — the women got a sense of power and awe .. hugging each other. One held back from the others. In moments the women who'd been hugging became ALBINO! The woman who held back experienced no change in epidermal coloration. Stayed exactly the same. Still wid me?*

*Barry: don't believe all the s\*\*\* u read on net*

*Jess: Huffpo... the women are albino .. shunned ...witches. the stream just vanished... Scary huh... like a curse reached up and grabbed them. Like Carrie. That's what mom's started calling me.. Carrie! the teenage movie psycho?*

*Barry: Ik who carrie is*

*Jess: my mom's nuthin but whitebread fun...it's all about the benjamins...she thinks w enough paper she can stop Time*

*Barry: Them bitches better off dead than to be polar bears in Africa ..curse.*

*Jess: wish we could stop Time...how hard could it be? Wish einstein was still around I'd write him a letter beg him to figure it out fast*

*Barry: selfie ur pretty smile.. th rest of u 2*

*Jess: u have seen that already*

*Barry:...no i'll come get it*

*Jess: I'm brown enough right now to be your cousin, another 20 minutes your sistah.. evn sunshine causes a form of Epidermal Regression.. see whut i mean? It Happens!*

*Barry: I still hit it*

*Jess: Okay, further proof, i'll scan you the whole article — 'this is the first confirmed occurrence of the syndrome, known medically as <u>Epidermal Regression,</u> in the 21st century. <u>Epidermal Regression</u> is a clinical condition characterized by transferring skin color to another person by touching that person, a phenomenom first documented in New Delhi India in 1891 by M. Cannady... considered responsible for the rise in social and economic isolation of so - called 'untouchable' castes in urban areas of India in late 19th and early 20th century.' see? I never even heard of that before. just thought you'd want to know .. <u>Epidermal Regression</u>...Google it, dawg*

*Barry: I still do u grl...I turn u out, black or white.. all i think about is our frst time .. u r hurting my grades...not to mntion my b**** lol*

*Jess: ...in another five minutes we could be brother sister...nevr thought incest could be so hot ..fantasize about our 1st time..so hot*

*Barry: baby..u makin' me ache down there.. want u so bad*

*Jess: For our first time i'm getting a Brazilian... already*
*promised u ..i want 2 take all night w u think im a little bit in love*

*Barry: u put on that thong yet*

*Jess: yeh... thong makes my legs look so long ..stole it from*
*mom...can barely see my pedi from up here... lol*

*Barry: Selfie! Rite now! Do what yo' pimp say bitch*

*Jess: Uh uh. Might wind up on net like Kammi Kay's sex*
*tape. 2 young for that infamy*

*Barry: i'm coming over..don't say no...Kammi's doin*
*okay..Queen of the damn world...that tape made her goddess of the*
*'net....she almost broke the net*

*Jess: Look who she married..that didn't hurt*

*Barry: Didn't hurt either of em..com on baby just one*
*snap..gimme somethin to live for..or I'm on my way ovr I mean it*

*Jess: NO! lol .. better not. she could be home any time. If she*
*caught u here i'm on my way to Catholic girls academy... (sp i think)*
*then you'd never get whut u want*

*Barry: neither would u*

*Jessica: lol*

*Barry: u and your mom sunbathe together?*

*Jess: Why u care*

*Barry; milf. super - milf. be honest.... see where u get it from..*
*2 bad she's such a bitch*

*Jess: She's the go - to Trophy trogette down here.. she only goes*
*out to make my daddy jealous. she alwys makes sure he knows about*
*it.. i don't think she cares about other guys*

*Barry: u the hottest, grl...when u 3 babes walk down the hall,*
*th waters part*

*Jess: Charmer...u wil say anythin*

*Barry: I'm serious, seen it too many times, u phong angela,*
*they all get out of the way, jocks, mooks, gourds, bitches, soches,*
*daggers.. all bow down the killer trio, u bitches rule the school... u*
*don't even try*

*Jess: oh ur silly*
*Barry: Seriously*
*Jess: Charmer... what r u after let me guess lol*
*Barry: get your looks from milf? still want selfie*
*Jess: from both parents. dad's sexy too.. he's sort of dangerous,*
even now that he's down and out... they r both sensualists
*Barry: ?*
*Jess: they both like to f\*\*\* each other. Only not no more*
*Barry: Hot as u r, they had fun the night they made u*
*Jess: charmer... from what she told me it happened early a.m.*
just as the sun was coming up.... Mom spent a fortune making this
pool area like a jungle grotto, like Eden almost. I feel like Eve in
Eden. Ready to be bred. think about u inside me...makes me
lightheaded.. Okay, thong's off...Wonder if Adam and Eve were
interracial? want our first time 2 last all night ...finish as the sun's
rising...like when I was created...baby...B... i'm having such sleazy
thoughts about u,....this feels like more than a teenage crush... heat's
got me....what u wearing?*
*Barry: Comin over. Nuthin will stop me ...i'll take my*
chances .. 2 hours from now u b my baby's momma
*Jess: Wait. I think she's home. She'll make me go inside.*
Gotta blaze baby. so sorry if i got u worked up...I am too blieve me..
2 bad about the tan line. its her. see u @ yr party...hope u like cobalt
blu... i'll try to work it so i can stay late yeah that's her, she's here
mlos. Aww. Damn. Just whn it was gttin good.. sextus interrupus lol
:-( yours (soon), J*

The foregoing sext was written, on my part, while
lying in my bedroom in my sloppy flannel pj's eating
Krispie Kremes with caramel mint ice cream dumped on
top and watching a re - run of the *Money Hoo Hoo Hour.*

No apologies for watching that junk, the dumber it
is the easier it is to concentrate on important stuff. Like
sexts. I like teasing Barry.

He'll be more fun when we finally get together if I can keep him in a state of sexual insanity.

But Barry's got a mean side to him. I like to punish that side. Besides, Barry writes s*** like that to me too sometimes.

Take my word for it, he knows how to get me hot and bothered. We know how to push each other's buttons. All's fair in love and war, at least in this summertime teenaged, curfew - choked wasteland... Somehow I feel I'm being watched every moment.

I wonder if someday it'll reach a point where nobody ever actually sees anyone else, that we do it all, have sex, even breed, through these screens somehow?

And if there is a Higher Consciousness capable of controlling the Pause button in space - time, isn't it plausible that THEY are watching US? That we are being observed from Beyond through the very same omnipresent screens we ourselves so obsessively view Reality through, all day every day and every night, till our eyeballs practically fall out?

So who's watching all the billions of Watchers in our planet of lonely voyeurs? Who's watching the Watchers? Maybe THEY are. Once we've got the screens held up to our faces, it would be easy for the gods to track our every move. Cue the eery music, Maestro.

Later, Diary.

Peace out, Jessica out.


Coming in from class next day, I was greeted by my mother's screaming, frightened voice at our front door:

*"Out, you bloody bastards!* Get out of my house this instant. Next time I'll show you a gun instead of the door! Out!" *Who the hell are you guys? Who do you work for? I'm calling the cops god damn it, right now – who ARE you?*

"We're leaving, ma'am – just a routine security check, employee background. We work for World Health Corp. Apologies for the inconvenience."

"You work for the *Perkins' Brothers?*"

"No ma'am, we're just background researchers for a food wholesaler. Again – Sorry for the inconvenience."

*"Inconvenience?* You were photographing our wedding album when I walked in on you! What the hell!"

"Mommy?" Two big intruders were coming toward me as I stood at the threshold, listening to mother screaming from behind them. I was just home from school. Both villains wore expensive suits and ties, sharp shoes, and were only scary and gnarly - looking because of the heavy black sunglasses. Kind of looked like upscale cops, Miami Vice types... Actually kind of sexy – *oh, damn it, Jess!*

But Mom was freaking.

"Out, damn you!"

I waited for them to stumble out before I jumped inside and slammed the front door behind me.

"Mommy, *who in hell are these randoms?"*

"I wish I knew!" My mother replied angrily. Her eyes were still fixed on the front door, now closed behind the departed.

Something in her voice jarred me, because I'd heard it from her so infrequently over the years: fear.

I'd just been coming in the front door as the two guys in business suits – in itself an odd and somewhat sinister attire for Tally in the summertime – rushed by me, pushing me aside, not running but not exactly strolling either. My mother's anger has that effect on people generally.

A moment later I heard the *clang* of the steel front gate slamming emphatically behind them. Behind their sunglasses, both dudes had been dark - featured, serious looking, one smaller, one bigger, that's as much as I was able to glimpse as they fled by.

If I had to say, I'd say they both looked like cops. Spies. We discovered later they'd gained access through a basement window. Later Mommy explained to me the intruders were photographing a family picture album when she'd walked in on them. And they were reluctant to leave before they'd finished; but her screaming did the trick.

Now my mother and I faced each other. I could see she was still shaken. Mommy said later it was like a scene out of 'The Matrix IV.'

"Those guys were pretty well - dressed to be working for Wal Mart."

"Believe me, Jess – it's not Wal Mart that's employing them."

"Who then? Because they were scary!"

"Oh, that was so weird. Every day it seems there's something like that lately."

"Are you okay?"

"Jessica, your father – what has he been up to? Is he in some sort of trouble? He tells you everything."

"He tells me nothing."

"Is he in trouble with the gamblers? Cheating on his taxes?"

"Taxes!" I laughed. "Oh, come on. He's so broke!"

Emotionally, mother and daughter were facing off physically, both of us secretly dying to be close, to confide, hug, comfort, yet instead we were as confrontational as mortal adversaries.

There was an elephant in the room – Dad – and each of us stood on opposite sides of it. Later I looked back on the convo as I always did, with my mother and I like two scorpions in a bottle, tails raised high, underneath the lofty beams of her big fancy lonely echoing livingroom.

"Those two men are part of a team that's looking for information about your father. Something's wrong."

"How do you know that?"

"How do I know? My office computer and laptop have been hacked. My credit card accounts have been accessed and copied. My insurance and mortgage people have called me in the past week to verify inquiries I'd supposedly made. But I hadn't. My whole existence is under scrutiny. Even the trash keeps getting combed over. Your dad…"

"His only vice is Comrade Smirnoff; you should know that. You caused it. You know how he loves you. You broke him, Mommy. You've fractured his soul!"

"He's reduced to drinking *Smirnoff?*" My mother's astonishment reflected the dream world she'd been living in since their separation, the emotional blindness of her life behind the paneled walls of her law offices, and the gated isolation where our days passed in silence and tension. *"Smirnoff?"*

"Well – he says Comrade Smirnoff gets the job done. He never goes out. I never see him even use his i. Daddy's a straight shooter. Maybe it's *you* they're investigating. You're the one with the fat bank account, the political future and the shady big shot friends…"

"I thought that. But it's your father the inquiries keep turning to." *The spider - silent inquiry was widespread, subtle and deep,* She added. *There have even been a couple of beauties floating into town, snooping around, spreading a web, arranging drinks with male members of my staff, after three martinis a guy will tell a beautiful woman anything. But the subject always focuses on Jack, not me.*

"You broke his heart, Mommy D. Yeah, he may be on the ropes, but you know as well as I do – he has integrity."

"Maybe... that dog track series he got the Pulitzer for? Yes. It was so long ago! The Mafia had an interest in that, maybe? Yes. That's likely. He's friends with that mob boss down in Chiefland, Pauley Vee? This background check isn't an everyday credit pull, Jess. I just know it. There's more to it. Something's very wrong here."

"Oh, I know Pauley Vee. He's no gangster. He's only a sweet old retired guy with a big belly. Sweet as sugar. He just runs a bar down there."

"Oh, if you only knew!"

"What do you mean?"

"Pauley Vee – child, he's not *in* the Mob, he *is* the Mob. I thought he'd retired. Don't kid yourself about Pauley Vee, honey. Believe me, when sweet gentle kindly old Pauley Vee is hauling somebody down to the river, it isn't to baptize them in the Faith. Take my word for it."

"He's the sweetest, nicest man! You're so wrong!"

She gave me a sarcastic half - look, half - laugh.

"Half your dad's friends are on the run from somebody."

"You're just still in love. You're always saying mean things about him. That just proves it."

"Jess, I'm going to start keeping a pistol in the house. But first you've got to promise me you'll never touch it."

"What if *my* life's in danger?"

She laughed ruefully. "Other than that. Besides, you don't know how to shoot a pistol."

"Oh yes I do. Daddy taught me. He taught me really well too."

"I'll show you where I keep it then."

"What a thing to bond over." We both laughed. "Besides, Mommy – you don't know how to shoot a pistol either."

"Yes, I do. Your father taught me too." We laughed together again. The huge livingroom suddenly didn't seem quite so empty and lonely, as a spark of the old family warmth flashed between us. "Just promise me you won't hurt yourself with it if I keep it in the house."

"I promise. It's ridiculous, but I promise."

"Alright then." *Funny how it took Smith and Wesson to spark a moment's friendship between us...*

"I'd rather do my damage with a frying pan anyway. Old school."

"And you can tell your father…" And here my mother's face, so permanently affixed in a liar's smiling high income professional grimace, softened suddenly, and for the first time in forever she seemed both human and vulnerable right there in front of me; and her lovely grey eyes held, very lightly, tears of some mysterious origin. I wish I could have known their origin, but with Mommy you never really knew.

"You look so beautiful, Mommy, when you're crying…" I blurted out.

"…Just tell your father…tell him if he needs an attorney, I can get him the best in the state, and not to worry about cost. We're still a family – even yet."

"Oh damn it all, Mommy…what *happened* between you two? I live my life around here, it's like my heart's buried in a grave of stubbornness and lies! And let's face it, all three of us are buried in that grave! What good is revenge if we're all buried under it? So just tell me – *what happened between you two!?"*

"Ask your father!" She snapped, ice cold suddenly, again, as always. And, as always, that was the end of that.

# II

*Daddy*

Now, as to Daddy. The thing everybody knows about him is that, seven or eight years ago, he won a Pulitzer Prize in journalism for an investigative series he did on a dog - racing scam ripping off the public down in mid state. A lot of crooks went to jail on account of it. Maybe it's a remnant of that gang that's been poking around Mom's life lately – the Mob has a long memory, according to the movies...

So I'm sure that's why the Perkins' brothers selected Daddy to do this first and only exclusive feature on their ordinarily extremely secretive island world – that terrific Pulitzer series. Eight years after, that Pulitzer could still save his career.

Not to brag, but my Daddy is brilliant. But ever since Mom started going all corporate on us, my Dad's been skidding.

He calls vodka 'potato wine' and sometimes it's a funny joke, but he's fallen a long way in the last few years. He's not a bad drunk, just quiet and contemplative, and we've had some nice conversations in bars and saloons he takes me to, when he's on a case. He's been reduced to doing journalistic piece - work, and I'm kind of his scout...

We play word - games when we're out on the road together – like making up headlines for famous historical events. One I remember especially that Daddy wrote, was the headline in the Democrat notifying the world of the arrival of the Ten Commandments:

\* \* \* \* \* \* \*

*MOSES ON SINAI; OFFERS TEN PT. PLAN*
\* \* \* \* \* \* \*

"What about it, Jessica? Not bad, eh?" *Ten point plan? The Ten Commandments? Get it?*

"I'm like your Dr. Watson, Dad," I remember laughing, referring to the great detective Sherlock Holmes. "I'm your scout. I can't wait for our next case."

And guess what? Out of nowhere, that case had fallen into our laps. *Small world, big coincidences.*

Now, even though we were at summer's end, when Daddy announced he was coming over the next day, I could instantly visualize the wide road stretching out again like a promise of the first day of endless summer and adventure ahead, beyond the battered red hood of my Dad's Toyota. Just wide road in front of us, and Mom's stress in the rearview. I hadn't even asked where we were going.

*"Your mission, Jessica, should you choose to accept it..."*

*"I accept it, I accept it! Dude, I'm there! Come get me!"*

*"Dude?" My father replied. "Dude? It's come to this? Dude?"*

*"Come get me!" I laughed. "Fast!"*

*"Better pack for three days. Informal."*

*"Hurry."*

*"See you tomorrow at noon promptly – dude."*

*"Now you've got it." Click.*

I just threw a change of summer clothes into my overnight, and off to a meet - and - greet with the two most evil, richest and sexiest men in the Western Hemisphere. How do I know? Because Dr. Munye said it was so. And the Doctor never lies.

Well, I threw in the part about 'sexiest' – goes to show you what a perv I've become.

I don't care.


Anything to skip another weekend with Mother.

No more Lush Rimbaud blasting through the upstairs, with his warnings that America was already in the throes of a low - level race war, and no more listening to Mom's new favorite, the horrid suicide blonde Trogette chubette Fancy Lace, shrieking nightly for retribution and the blood of the guilty no matter who and where they might be, for the guilty were everywhere, and she was everywhere on Court TV. America's, and Reality tv's, Red Queen. One phrase this Prosecutor has never learned, and never will: *'I'm sorry, I was wrong.'*

Rimbaud's sneering voice followed me into the laundry room.

"That's right, Mr. and Miz America, the statistics tell you it's a race war we're in right now. A low - level race war. This is Saigon, 1964! For every single instance of white on black violence – *there are 114 instances* of black on white violence in America. Sound like racial progress to you? Five percent of the population cause seventy percent of violent crime in America. That five percent is African American males under the age of 35! Lambs to the slaughter, that's what's going on, Nutto - heads, stay with me, we'll be right back... *Color of Crime.com, check it out, the numbers don't lie. We'll be right back..."*

I fire back with the Rev. Jeremiah, even louder, on my Sirius XM stereo, his fire - and - brimstone rhetoric rising from the laundry room to shake the timbers of my mother's Troggy conservative whitebread fantasies.

"... and the world of black America is more isolated now than in the cotton field days of old, my people. Oh, my people! How does white America interface with black America? You think slavery was ever really abolished? Ha. Ha. They see us only as extensions of cash registers at Wal - Mart. At the Dollar Store. Or behind plexiglass, as extensions of drive - thru cash registers at McDonalds! Those cash registers are where our people are chained to, just like the ball and chain of plantation days. How can our people make up the distance between the races, close the gap? We've been displaced twice, first in the slave journey, and again in the forced integration of our people into a world where we still have no chance. Close the gap? Not in my lifetime, and not in God's lifetime.

"So that's where you'll find us, White America, if you were ever to care enough to bother come lookin', and if you can't find us chained to your nation's cash registers, if you can't see the truth of our desperation in front of your own eyes, go out to the prisons, see the slaves caged by possession of a silly, harmless weed, once again into a world not of our making, a – "

"Jessica, turn down YOUR RADIO!"

"Turn *YOURS* down, Mommy dearest. It's giving me a splitting brain freeze."

"You're turning into Carrie," She screamed. "Next you'll be telekinetically causing knives to fly around my house!" *And it's still MY house!*

"Don't call me Carrie. I'm angry, not crazy."

"Are you sure about that?"

"Well, who drove Carrie crazy anyway? Her crazy *mom,* that's who!"

"Don't you dare call me Mommy dearest again! Am I clear? *Carrie?*"

"Stop calling me Carrie!"

"Fine. Turn it *down* – Carrie *dearest!*"

"Yes, Mommy *dearest!*"

"Oh!"

"Oh!"



"Hop in, daughter. Mall's out. Balls out."

"Balls out, dad."

I flung my overnight into the flatbed of his dirty red truck and climbed in fast, snapping my fingers and singing to the Temptations' music on his FM:

*Poppa was a rollin' stone, hey hey hey –*
*Wherever he hung his hat was his home....*

"Damn, child – you sing like an angel..."

"Oh, and Momma said to tell you how much she misses you and how you'd better take good care of her daughter –"

"She said that?" He brightened.

"Hell to the no. That bitch will never give an inch."

"You're such a pretty little prick."

"Wonder where I get that from?"

We laughed. And off we flew.

"So. What's this big assignment?"

School would be starting in five weeks. For once I was looking forward to going back. I missed Phong. I missed Angela, (aka Princess Cantaloupes, a nickname you'd understand completely if you ever saw her leaping up and down leading cheers on the sidelines). But most, I missed Barry. This was starting to feel like a lot more than a teenage crush.

"Ever hear of Tony Perkins, the trillionaire? Crystal Lagoon?" Dad asked, once we were a half hour south of Tallahassee.

"Who hasn't."

"Know anything about him?"

"Tony Perkins? I know something. Daddy, I can't tell you how excited I am to meet these guys! That island was the subject of Dr. Munye's lecture at Harvard last Spring.

A feature of this Evil Empire had especially seized my youthful imagination, the continual rumors that the population of this fabulous island of billionaires never aged.

I liked the sound of that.

Oscar said it, and IMHO it's the truest of the true: *Youth is the only thing worth having.* I wanted to keep having it. No doubt the island rumors were just a jealous waste of air, but my fantasies have a reality of their own.

"Have you heard that the Trogs down there never age?" I asked.

"It's a world of myths on that island. Still, I seriously doubt that."

"Maybe I can meet Madonna?"

"Maybe."

"That's her favorite vaca spot, according to *People.*"

"I just hope to God I can pull this off. Game changer."

"That island is all they were talking about at school last semester. What's it got to do with us? Did you know that Perkins guy almost got assassinated recently?"

"That's why we're going. It's why I got invited. So. I do the interview, you take the photos, just like last time. I pay you in Krispy Kremes..."

"You pay me in Krispy Kremes? Oh, no."

"Why not?" He protested cheerfully. "You love Krispy Kremes. It's fair!"

"It blows."

"Okay. Maybe you'll see a few dollars out of it too."

"Tony Perkins? I still don't believe it! You're actually going to be interviewing *Tony Perkins?*"

"And his brother."

"I heard the brother was in the movies back in the Day."

"I know you like Krispie Kremes more than life itself. So. We good?"

"Pay me in cash and let me buy my own Krisps..."

"This is a profit deal."

"You're a greedy Trog."

"Well, I *do* provide the camera."

"I have my own camera. Better than yours. It's in my i."

"Impossible!" He acted stunned. Dad was always playful after a pull from the flask. "You're saying you have a telephone with a camera in it? Out of the question! That could never happen."

"Oh, Daddy." It was so silly and endearingly troggy when he started trying to tease me.

"A phone with a *camera* in it. Ha. That's more unbelievable than a ten dollar hamburger!"

"They have those at Applebee's now."

"Not a chance, daughter."

I sighed.

*Tony Perkins! No way, José!* One of Daddy's favorite phrases formed a sudden thought bubble above my young head, and I'd have occasion to contemplate this phrase often in the near future: *It may be a small world, Jessica, but in it there are a lot of big coincidences. That's what journalists live off of, those strange coincidences. Like a spider weaves a web, we wait and watch, and if we're lucky, something will fly in.*

We would confront many big coincidences in the future, and on the mysterious island, awaiting us.

"Maybe if they throw in fries and a coke," He grumped, "I could see it then."

"Nope. Just fries. No coke. Ten bucks plus tax."

"Damn it! Are you saying I can't even afford Applebee's now?"

I sighed again.

"They say he's a vampire. That it's a vampire island."

"Who's a vampire?"

"Tony Perkins!"

"Did I tell you, he may be offering me an actual job? So be sweet. Curb that mouth of yours, Watson."

*And bust wide open, if he's as crooked as they say... If he's a vampire we'll put a stake through his heart and post it in Bulletin form on the UPG website...*

I could almost read Daddy's mind. *Another Pulitzer might be enough to bootstrap me out of that single - wide, save the soul of a washed - up paperback writer... take me up the ladder from Smirnoff back to Stoli before my liver becomes a pickle...*

"Anthony Perkins – The guy who won't let his picture be taken? The guy who was about to marry Kammi Kay? Before the Doctor flew down from Olympus in the midnight hour and swept her away? Before *KamYe*? The guy all the black people say stole their island from them? Ghost Posse?! Oh, I've gotta text Barry! Are you sure we'll be welcome? That we're actually going to be allowed to meet this Trog?"

"Who's Barry?"

*Oops.*

I finished my last Krisp.

"Yummy."

"Daughter, how do you consume those donuts without even chewing?"

"I chew them. They're just yummy good. So I chew 'em really fast."

"Those donuts will give you a heart attack."

"I don't give a good god damn."

He glanced at me.

"Jessica – be still."

I was blushing.

"All I'm saying is, is they're yummy good."

"Daughter, you're getting quite a mouth on you."

"I'm sorry, Dad. That's how Mom and I quarrel sometimes. She's got a mouth on her too."

"Tell me about it."

"Mom's lost her mind. She's gone cra cra. I'd rather live with you in your singlewide."

"You're ruling class and you're going to stay ruling class. No daughter of mine will be raised in a trailer park. We'd have fun, but it's a dead end. Anyway. According to the UPG agreement, Perkins asked for me personally. By name. Believe it or not, there was even a job offer. They were a little vague about that though. They're familiar with my Pulitzer series. I was honestly flattered. There are no conditions to this interview and visit. I got eight hundred dollars up front, and a per diem contract."

His voice took on a stern, serious tone. *Shut up and pretend to listen, Jessica: A grown - up was now speaking.*

"Look, sweetheart – at this stage in my so - called career, this is a big deal. We may need both our cameras before this one is over."

I hesitated just a moment. Daddy was sticking his flask back into his book bag. We were doing seventy, the Toyota had drifted once, just a little, out of our lane - line, but Daddy was always careful, and we'd never been stopped, in all our travels together.

But even I, unlicensed Jessica, knew that pop - up showers plagued the highways of our fair, sweating state at this time of the summer, and once we started drifting, the danger was hydroplaning – actually, the danger was getting killed.

Daddy was always careful, but I found myself keeping an eye on the speedometer, and an eye on the yellow lane stripes racing by underneath us… I knew he was falling.

I just wasn't able to assess exactly how far.

"Do you know about Ghost Posse," I asked finally, "and what's going on with that?"

"Of course I do. I may be a greedy Trog, but I'm no Mook." He glanced over, uncertainly: *Am I?*

"Well, you are quite old. Ghost Posse only started to make a real impact about five minutes ago." My i was on vibrate. I felt it now. It had to be B. "That's an outfit that's going to change the world, Daddy. They want their island back. It was a runaway slave hide - out before the Civil War. It really belongs to them and they want it back. They call it New Haiti. I wouldn't bet against them."

"I know. I'm not a Mook."

"And they are NOT killers."

He laughed again.

"Yes, dear."

Mooks were always the last to get the word. It didn't necessarily have anything to do with age, just general cluelessness. Trogs were out to get you, sometimes they were laughable, sometimes dangerous, and they were always adults. Mooks were merely non - denominational idiots. Oh, don't forget Gourds. Gourds were Mooks without the math skills. My high school was Gourd - heavy, faculty and student body alike.

Daddy laughed. He didn't mind giving me a lot of rope.

"As long as I'm not a Gourd."

"You're not a Gourd." *You may be ancient, but you're no Gourd.*

"That's a big relief."

"You're actually very good - looking, father. Even if it does look like you just flew in from Honolulu."

"I got a new shirt for this interview. At the flea market."

"Love the palm tree motif."

"Well, Jessica, anyway this weekend we're going to get to see how the other one thousandth of one percent lives."

It was hard to hear Daddy sometimes. He has a soft voice, and the a/c in the Toyota was roaring for its life in the early afternoon Florida summer heat.

"We'll never see Tony Perkins anyway." B. had put it this way: *Tony Perkins is so secretive, he's Howard Hughes without the Kleenex boxes.*

"His publicity office promised me full access. He wants to try to improve his image. That will happen when you realize people are trying to kill you. Actually all this political tension over the future of Crystal Lagoon is the reason I got the invitation to go down and interview this crazy recluse. His brother's name is Tommy. He's the lawyer. The power behind the throne."

"I hear the brother's really cute."

"How the hell would you hear something like that, daughter?"

"Language? If you please?" *Dad, you're getting a mouth on you.*

"Apologies. Now answer."

"Just gossip that's been going around. You know how teenage girls run their mouths. It makes the brothers better villains if they're hot."

"They're on the wrong side of the Narrative at the moment."

"What do you mean?"

"It's a bad century to be a rich white guy. Don't you read the newspapers?"

"Online."

*Two years ago I know Perkins was a finalist for Time Magazine's Person of the Year. What can I say? I'm a journalist's daughter. I still read newspapers. Electronically is all.*

*I know about things like Howard Hughes, and Epidermal Regression, which Barry doesn't believe happens but it has and does, mostly in India but at least once in Africa too — and ten - dollar Applebee's hamburgers even though I don't even eat there...*

"Well, that's what United Press Group is paying me the big bucks to find out. Tony Perkins is finally granting an interview. I think they realize down there on his private island that it's time to polish the old public relations image a little. He recently survived an assassination attempt... The bullets missed Mr. Perkins by about one inch."

Throughout the trip down to Pauley Vee's Saloon, I would occasionally, grudgingly perform my Dr. Watson's tasks by studying the headlines that tracked King Perkin's rise and fall in the eyes of America's dominant media.

Daddy liked to remind me that the Romans had a saying, 'the voice of the people is the voice of God', but in our troubled nation the voice of the dominant media – God – had gradually become the voice of the people. *Bow down masses, look on our words, ye mighty and beware!*

\* \* \* \* \* \* \*

*PERKINS TENTH RICHEST,
RECLUSE ALL SMILES
AFTER PRESIDENTIAL MEDAL*

\* \* \* \* \* \* \*

*PERKINS REACHES TIME'S
PERSON OF YEAR FINAL CUT*

\* \* \* \* \* \* \*

*CONGRESS LAUDS BILLIONS IN PERKIN'S
GIFTS FOR COLD FUSION HIV/AIDS,
EPIDERMAL REGRESSION STUDIES*

\* \* \* \* \* \* \*

"Check it." Dad said, handing me another sheet of paper. "This is where the narrative starts to mysteriously shift – about this last mid - summer... Right after Kressa Kay and her daughter Kammi's genius rapper husband, your hero Doctor Felix Munye, suddenly take an interest in that island – "

"I admire him. I never said he was my hero. Necessarily. He's just a game changer, that's all..."

"And Kammi Kay? A game changer too?"

"The hottest reality star on planet earth! Don't kid yourself, dad. That took genius! A million girls want the cameras on them. But they're all on Kammi Kay. She is Queen of the Hive."

"Why? Because she has the biggest ass on planet earth?"

"Pretty much." I had to laugh. *At least she didn't haul us into war in Iraq!*

\* \* \* \* \* \* \*

*PERKINS BROTHERS REFUSE KAY KORP. 'GENEROUS' BUYOUT BID FOR CRYSTAL LAGOON; KRESSA KAY 'FURIOUS' WITH 'SEXIST DISMISSAL' OF FAIR OFFER*
\* \* \* \* \* \* \*

*KORP. JOINS FORCES WITH GHOST POSSE TO LIBERATE PRIZED ISLAND*
\* \* \* \* \* \* \*

"Like those headlines?"

"It's a lot quicker than actually reading the stories below."

"Well – now you write one."

Now we were doing seventy - five in the shade. And the blazing sunshine too. Daddy seemed to be holding the Toyota steady, even as we kept picking up speed. But I could almost feel the invisible film of rainwater under our tires.

"Could you speak a little louder, Dad? You need to get the a/c fixed."

*Small world, big coincidences,* and here we were, on our way to a destination that was currently in the historical crosshairs.

Barry had mentioned Crystal Lagoon a couple of times, during his diatribes about the unification of the African American Diaspora, but I guess I was the Mook on that one.

I hadn't even been clear on the island's geographical location, just that it was out in the Gulf of Mexico somewhere, southwest of Cedar Key...

"Is that true, Daddy? I have a good friend at school who swears Crystal Lagoon was once a runaway slave sanctuary. And that it became a slave republic, even before the Civil War!" *The island really belongs to the descendants of those ex - slaves.* "Ghost Posse is just redressing a historical grievance – one of many."

"Then why are Kressa Kay and her big - assed daughter Kammi so interested in the place all of a sudden?"

"Well – I don't know. I mean, she's married to the Doctor..."

"There's more to it."

"Like what?"

"I've researched this." The look on my father's face showed a deep concern. "That little chunk of limestone is the big prize, for whatever reason."

A beautiful island, a broken promise of a land where the American dream could be redeemed for its slave population, a dream which Time, Propaganda, and Jim Crow caused to be eventually forgotten...

But who knew if that were actually true, if the convenient historical narrative had the slightest degree of fact attached to it?

Nothing had been written down, no records kept.

Only legend and rumor and superstition kept the memory, and the dream, and the vision of *New Haiti* alive.

Like so much of the history of black America, it was all passed down by word of mouth, and by white historians with agendas of their own, whether pro or con, not to be trusted – which made race - baiters, right or left, like Sharpton and Jackson and Rimbaud so malignantly poisonous, turning History into fear just to stay famous and rich.

It didn't matter. White America had struck the first blow, centuries earlier, in the endless national bloody no - win Knock - down games, ever ongoing.

The memory of, and retribution for, that evil surprise attack from so long ago, would follow white America relentlessly, all part of the long bloody apology...

*Small world, big coincidence.* Soon Crystal Lagoon – or New Haiti, depending on which side of the Divide you stood on, would come under mortal attack.

Daddy and I would be among the witnesses to one of History's ironic turning hinges, perhaps the tiny hinge on which the future of a great nation would swing back into some degree of social equilibrium at last.

And Epidermal Regression would be why.

As Daddy had said, choosing his words with the utmost care, *like everything else in America's racial history, there are at least two versions to be sorted through – anything could have happened on that island. We'll try to find out.*

I'd just finished reading 'Heart of Darkness' by Joseph Conrad – pretty good for a fifteen year old, yes? And I remember thinking of the mysterious Mr. Tony Perkins, crazier than Howard Hughes and richer than Hearst – richer than Croesus, actually – as a kind of Mr. Kurtz, hiding out on his gorgeous island with guards and guns and all the money...

We'd all heard Madonna lives there part of the year. She's my real heroine. I'd give anything to meet her some day.

So does the wife of the president of Syria. Also Jade Jagger. Wives of hedge fund managers and fat cat diplomats. Saudi Arabia and Hong Kong are disproportionately represented, I have since learned.

Other famous types whose names I won't mention in these pages. Huffpo notes every time a jet lands or departs, and another billion bucks, in cash, in suitcases lands or departs, with it...

And they land, or depart, every hour of daylight. Every day of the week. Every week of the year.

"Daddy – I'll bet Perkins is running a drug empire. All those Hollywood types – jets in and out every hour... It would be very possible to bribe a sheriff or two down here."

"Very possible."

"The game's afoot, Dad!" I was bouncing up and down in his old Toyota, mad with teenage excitement.

I'd seen a picture of 'King' Perkins once, in a Florida Features class, walking next to John Gotti, the famous Dapper Don. No one could be sure this sinister silhouette was really Perkins, but –

Dad tossed me a notepad, and a ballpoint pen.

"Based on what I've told you so far, write me a headline that sums it all up. Pressure's on, daughter."

"I can handle it."

The game's afoot!

Daddy smiled gently, this time taking only a small sip from his ever - present steel flask. Then he stuffed it back into his journalist's book bag, as we outraced the brutal afternoon August sun down 27 South, toward Oz.

A moment later, I read back to him my Pulitzer - Prize winning headline:

\* \* \* \* \* \* \*

*PERKINS SURVIVES SHOOTING; 4 ARRESTS;*
*LAGOON IN LOCKDOWN;*
*PERKINS 'SHAKEN' SOURCES SAY*

\* \* \* \* \* \* \*

"That's not half - bad, Jess. I'd even call it Krisp - worthy. You may have a future in print journalism after all."

"It's print journalism that doesn't have a future," I yawned. "I'm hungry."

# III

*Spanish Swamp*

Florida, for the most part, is as flat as the Gulf of Mexico that surrounds and embraces it. As we flew southward, even on the modern six lane 27, I began to sense an eery convergence of space and time as we descended deeper into the pre - history of a Florida that had existed before Time...

With every mile, the jungled swampland gathered density nearer the roadbed, and as the Yota's engine roared further toward the past, turkey vultures feasting on the concrete lifted lazily away from lunch, and water moccasins traced pretty, curving patterns in the endless expanses of black water stretching the forty miles from highway to Gulf. The huge black snakes carved smiling patterns on the swamp water within inches, it seemed, of the roadbed.

"Kind of a scary world," I remember remarking to Dad. Overhanging the highway, and blocking out great swaths of sunlight, great grey clouds of Spanish moss reached outward and upward from walls of kudzu, dying cypress, and a thousand tall, limbless oaks that seemed to guard the past like sentries, eagles' nests topping them all.

"Once we hit the Gulf, the sun will come out again. Till then, we're entering the land before Time. If you can relax, there's quite a beauty to it. The land before Eden."

"It feels like being in the deep end of a birth canal, with a long way to daylight…"

"Unbuckle your seatbelt, sweetheart. At least till we've cleared this part of the trip."

"Why?"

"It's just a kind of good luck thingie. We'll buckle up again at Cross City."

I eventually got the point.

There was eery evidence along the trail. Small white DOT crosses every few miles noted where the deadly, languid swamp had claimed another inebriated motorist who'd awakened upside down, and only eight feet below safety, too disoriented to disengage the seat belt in the moment before an unheard last scream met the first surging, gurgling indifferent *russshh* of the brackish black water. I glimpsed dozens of those crosses down the forty miles of wide, bad road.

Every cracker knew better than to wear seatbelts along that silent, gloomy forty mile gauntlet, where dense shoulders of kudzu, poisonous vines and Spanish moss form a corridor of eerie, enigmatic impenetrability through which four - lane 27 is civilization's only narrow north - south sanctuary. Doing ninety now, we fled down it toward Cedar Key and Crystal Lagoon beyond.

As we drove, we half - expected, and even talked about, the possible surprise appearance of the gracefully swaying slender green neck of a full - grown dinosaur, it's friendly prehistoric head perhaps stretching itself forward toward us above the black water, appearing through the foliage and bearded Spanish moss.

Nor did it take much imagination to visualize pterodactyls parked in nests high above the swamp amidst the turkey buzzards, falcons and eagles dwelling there, and in the black water below, herons wading, turtles sunning, bullfrogs leaping for their lives, water moccasins gliding, gators grinning, vultures circling, garfish rolling over in the brackish water, a forgotten world, a world trapped in the nightmare of history, a world unable to escape itself, a bleak and ruthless world, living and dying unlike any other.

Old Florida.

I'd heard Crystal Lagoon was Old Florida too, but a kind of Eden - like paradise – of course, money can buy any kind of improvement on the past, but even before seeing its phenomenal beauty, I couldn't help mentally contrasting paradisiacal Old Florida the Perkins' brothers ruled with this dark, prehistoric world that had grown out of the darkness prior to the dawn of Time…

But even this primitive glimpse of jungled pre - history felt somehow near and dear to my heart, the palmetto and scrub pine, the water moccasins tracing curving wakes in the black water below the pavement, the buzzards lifting slowly off the highway moments ahead of the roar of Dad's Toyota…

Old Florida. My home, whether manicured Paradise or cypress - choked blackwater jungle… *my home, my heart's home. Always.*

As you may remember, Daddy's the Pulitzer Prize winner, I'm the fifteen year old. No doubt you figured out he has a big influence on my descriptive passages. No apologies, Trogs, all my friends say I'm really gifted. Dad just sticks in an adjective now and then. *Believe it, Trogs – lol!*

Along this stretch of highway, Old Florida seemed to emerge out of the prehistoric past.

Dark, bordering swamps pressed up against the edges of our four - lane. Groves of cypress, oak, sycamore, poplar, gum and pine rose out of the swamp's single unifying feature, the haunted inland sea of black water that spread over hundreds of square miles of impassable jungle, black water flowing up to within yards of the roadbed underneath our Toyota's humming tires. *The antithesis of Eden...*

The water, darkened further by tannins from thousands of cypress knees, flowed away from 27's concrete four - lane sanctuary into depthless, scarred, sawgrass - choked marshes. I tried to see something, anything, beyond the first brambled, vine - strangled tier of jungle walling us in. I could sense, as well as see, the frightening black water waiting silently just below. It made me go a little breathless with anxiety.

*Be careful Dad... Our tires are skimming across rainwater...*

No matter how hard I stared, beyond about ten yards from the highway, there were only walls of decaying darkness.

"This stretch of old 27 always reminds me of the land that Time forgot," Daddy remarked, keeping both fists firmly on the steering wheel as we hugged the concrete, speeding south. I tried to remember how many sips he'd taken. The water below us looked evil, dark and deep. I felt the Toyota accelerate. I glanced at the speedometer: *85.*

"Be careful, Dad. The highway's wet."

"Yes, dear."

*When I'm with Daddy, I'm never afraid. Nervous sometimes – but never afraid. He's just got that quality about him that settles your fear... He won't let anything happen...*

"I'm convinced the real Fountain of Youth is back in that swamp somewhere."

"Why?"

"It sounds silly," My father replied, "I grew up near Gainesville. I know in my heart it's down here in coastal north central Florida somewhere. Of course Freud would call that wish - fulfillment."

"I'd swim that swamp to find it," I told him seriously. "Phong and Angie and me have a club we call 'Daughters of Dorian'. It's dedicated to eternal youth."

"...Angie and *I,*" He laughed. "And yes, eternal youth is what the Spanish conquistadors were willing to give their lives for, just before they drowned in all their fine armor."

"Having eternal youth is all Angie, Phong and I talk about."

"Oh, that's right – 'the 3 Oscar - teers'?"

"Yup. D'you think Indians might still live back there in that swamp somewhere?"

The close, brooding shoulders of the swamp scared me. I kept babbling while I powered up. The presence of my i helped me not be scared. The black swamp raced by below.

The power of the future, in the electronic device in my hand, began to prevail over the primitive power of the past.

My eyes left the highway's frightening panorama of pre - history and focused on the lighted i screen in my lap. I heard myself babbling. I couldn't help myself any longer. The i had found its way under my thumb.

"I saw ghosts one night on this highway." Dadster remembered. "Could have been Indians. Or Conquistadors, trying to find their way back home, through the mists, through the five hundred long ago years, back to Spain and their homes..."

"....Or Zombies! Zombies would thrive in a place like this. They wouldn't have to be afraid of snakes."

"Why wouldn't they?"

"They're already dead!" I hate pointing out the obvious.

"Anything's possible." Dad glanced down at my evil i, but only smiled. "How about the Spaniards who died searching for the Fountain of Youth? Strangers in a strange land. This swamp would be a bad place to die. So far away from home..."

He couldn't resist glancing down again.

"I'm texting Phong. Just a quickie. I swear."

"You're a teenager," He laughed, as though trying to remind himself. "It's what you do."

"It's just a hi bye."

"Ah – Old Florida." My father reminisced. "Sometimes I try to imagine it the way the Spanish first saw it, back in 1513. It must have seemed like a magic world to Ponce de León when he first got here. He was searching for the Fountain of Youth.

"Men will do anything for a chance at immortality... And even if they'd found it, how long could they have kept the secret? The lure of eternal life, of immortality, produces its own lethal poison, buried in the promise of living to infinity. Just like in that movie you and I watched on TCM, *The Treasure of the Sierra Madre*. 'The gold lies just over them thar hills.' I think the fountain of Youth exists. I really do – buried under the bones of those who once discovered it, and murdered one another trying to keep it to themselves..."

"You're too cynical. What if the good guys had found it? Used it to do good?"

"Anything's possible," He laughed. "Except ten dollar hamburgers."

"I'd give anything to stay fifteen forever. Even aging another day is *unacceptable*. Phong and Angela both feel the same way. We're at the top of our game right now." I looked over. He was locked onto the road ahead. "There's all kinds of rumors about that island, y'know. They never get older down there. That's what all their wealth goes to. Scientific solutions to aging. That makes sense anyway. The whole world should be focused on this single predicament – to defeat mortality."

He laughed. Ahead of us, a flock of buzzards lifted languidly away from their roadkill lunch in the outside lane, a bloody routine buffet in the corridors of this dark world.

"I brake for buzzards," He laughed. "They mess up your grill."

"Just think, Dad – the Fountain of Youth, maybe fifty yards from this highway, and we'll never know…"

"Anyway, this swamp has outlived its time. The developers will never be able to drain it though. It's too big and too deadly. I've driven this road at night. It's so black you can't even see the stars. But I've seen ghosts in the road. Maybe they were the ghosts of Indians, maybe Spaniards. They were moving fast. Almost dancing. I thought I must be hallucinating. I kept thinking how much History must be trapped inside this water." He was yawning. "How much time. I'd been doing a story down at Cedar Key. Anyhow, that's a night I felt lucky to make it home."

"Dad – *look out!*"

"*Damn!*"

Death. Three seconds ahead.

Death — in the almost comic, misshapen hump of a
huge, tusked hog — had suddenly galloped up from the
slope of the swamp yards in front of us.


In the next split second the front of the Toyota's
bug - spattered garnet hood shuddered visibly as Daddy
suddenly, violently braked left, and my astonished, uplifted
eyes widened as the blurred highway beyond the windshield
lurched dangerously right.

*Wham!*

If the palm of my right hand hadn't slammed into
the dashboard protectively, my face would have. The front
tires started to screech leftward, skidding toward the
terrified fleeing animal and the deep median. *Pitch, yaw.
Reduce velocity, oh God, Daddy, don't oversteer!* I felt the yota's
rear end begin to slowly, uncontrollably rotate counter -
clockwise against the friction of the concrete road surface.

Only later did I notice the remembered stench of
smoking tire rubber and brake pads scorching. The sense
of weightlessness was terrifying, literally heart - stopping.

In a single moment — life or death.

The silent water moccasins, the grinning Gators —
The black swamp water seemed to rise upward toward us.
All reality soundlessly hesitated in mid - movement, the
gods deciding whether to let the writer and his daughter
live or die, daddy gently, expertly steering into the 70 mph
near - spin, the tires skidding into the indifferent wetness of
the concrete, then a cautious, perfect maneuver that
probably saved our lives, the shimmering stubborn hood,
and front wheels underneath it, slowly veering mercifully
right again as Dad balanced, more than wrestled, the wheel
in his beautiful hands, ten degrees of control less or more
and the next names on the little white crosses would have

been his and mine, and now I felt our treacherous leftward momentum relent, the yota's velocity slowing further as he managed to stabilize the trembling veer of the machine into gradual, tortuous alignment once more toward the mid - point of the grey, sun - kissed lane straight ahead. *Speedometer: 40…35…*

And grinning Death had let us go again deeper into Life. Into the past. Into the Future.

*Horseman, pass by…*

The closest call of my life, three seconds from first glimpsing the appearance of a dark bristling hump scuttling across the concrete only yards in front of us, to the bullet - dodging gasp of exaltation at the certain gift of survival. Three seconds. Perhaps four.

"I think I busted your dashboard, Dad – "

"That's one lucky razorback," Daddy breathed, glancing only for a moment into the rearview. "Whew. Almost as lucky as us." He was ghost - white.

"God, that was close. You didn't miss him by a foot. That hog was huge. Big as an oven. We would have flipped."

We took a few moments to get our breathing back under control. Daddy didn't touch his flask again for the rest of the trip.

"Beautiful driving, Dad."

"Just lucky. The first thing you always do, Jessica – *decelerate.*"

"Got it."

"And above all – try to get lucky."

* * *

*Barry to Jessica, 2:45p*

Barry: Yo hey J

Jess:.. Finally got a signal...in the middle of a hell swamp .. almost hit a hog back there would've been killed. i mean it

Barry: to die a virgin. the worst.

Jess:. so glad u care. lol

Barry: No seriously, don't die a virgin, there are terrorists up there in heaven just waiting for u..could be one of th few the proud th 72

Jess: lol

Barry: Read that one on FB

Jess: Needed the laugh so scared still

Jess: Funsies .. no sexting tho

Barry: Why? no fun?

Jess: 2 much fun. D on board...he can see screen

Barry: Lets make a porno

Jess: u been doin coke

Barry: yeah a ton my cousins in town..sex on my mind baby

Jess: I can tell..u r hyper... u r obsessd by KK & Dr.. . ghost posse meets reality tv..irresistible n this cultur

Barry: London Astoria... first queen of the electronic Hive. Clinton impeach changed all the rules... that girl knew how to give a bj

Jess: The tall blonde – the heiress? barely remember her now.... u just like blonds dawg

Barry: Kammi's different than London Astoria.. sees herself as a Queen but no one feels inferior to her. Its magic... why she's lasted

Jess: ik...the net married lonely crowd to electronic village.. live inside our screens now.. virtual love safer than graveyard love

Barry:..coincided with rise of Reality television.. perfect 21st century genre .. reminds us what authentic humanity is, out there beyond our screens, even if fake

Jess: My hrt's stil racing seriously dude almost rip

*Barry: Kammi's London Astoria's Reality successor…Queen of the Hive…. She just had to let us watch her have sex… English kings had to go thru ritual whipping by priests to prove fealty to their subjects… all the fight for power over Hive, more ruthless than Mary Queen of Scots and Elizabeth I, millions of pornos hit.. market, the struggle to rule Hive…but Kammi outmaneuvered them all. And Dr. Munye, her king… weird culture we're inheriting … they've even got their own media hyphen name, KamYe, only most famous get that designation…KamYe*

*Jess:…God save KamYe lol – I can tell ur coked so wired*

*Barry: famous jazz line 'the Creator has a master plan/peace and happiness through all the land' – thought we followed the master plan the Big Man forgive us – all the races*

*Jess: At least God loves Kammi Kay…and Kressa The Queen Mother*

*Barry: built KayKable empire off that one single sex tape her daughter made… Pimp - ess. Right up there with Hefner..worth a bil or more now*

*Jess: u r too smart for Harvard*

*Barry: Just snorted a ton of coke. Sex and history on my mind. Ik this sext all over the map u care?.don't want to stop*

*Jess: me neither. time goes so fast this way this swamp truly freakin me out*

*Barry: okay. when u back? finish this then*

*Jess: really luv u when we talk about deep concepts u r so smart..luv u..i love u…Take u for another ride naked in moonlight let u kiss me everywhere*

*Barry: .. Ghost Posse gonna take that island.. take u on our honeymoon there… whut u got on?*

*Jess: Dawg. lol STOP*

*Barry: Kiss u everywhere twice on Monday*

*Signal lost.*

*(Signed off 4p)*

"Are you going to hammer on that damn screen all the way to our motel?"

Like all adults, Dadster is jealous of my iphone. They know their world is being left behind.

These tiny, lighted screens are the tombstones for everything that happened in the twentieth century, you just can't point it out to Trogworld. It's just that sexting makes road time pass so fast.

Didn't want to look at the highway again. I checked my Dad. His face was impassive, but his eyes had been glancing from 27 down over my screen!

Dad watched me re - pocket the i.

"Lost the signal."

"You and your friend – you were debating the paradox of the Heisenberg Uncertainty Principle?"

"Something like that."

"Know what the two hardest things are in the world to catch?"

"I imagine I'm about to find out?"

"A major league fly ball on a sunny afternoon..."

"That's one."

"And a teenage girl telling a lie."

"*Daaa - aaad,*" but I couldn't help laughing. He knows me too well.

"Dad. A growing girl needs to be fed in a great while!"

"We'll be at Pauley Vee's in about half an hour. Sound good?"

"Oh, I like that place!"

Some of our best talks had been in that cypress saloon, on Saturday mornings in autumn on our way down to Gator games.

"Pauley Vee always gives you a free Stinger, Daddy – why?"

"For old times sake."

"That's what you always say. Someday you'll give it up. I'll get it out of you."

We drove in silence a while.

"Mom says Pauley Vee is all mobbed up."

"Nonsense. Absurd. Ridiculous. He's just a sweet old bartender."

*Thou dost protest too much...*

"We've had intruders in the house. Somebody's been going over all her records and contacts. She thinks it has something to do with you and Pauley Vee."

Dad wasn't about to rat out his mobster buddy, but he wasn't up to totally lying to his darling daughter either.

"Well, back in the Day, it's true – when Pauley Vee took a guy down to the river, it probably wasn't to go swimming."

"That's what Mom said too. We had intruders. She freaked."

"I expect they were working for the brothers," Dad reluctantly explained. "They've been vetting me for this job I've been offered. These guys are super - careful. Getting your head nearly blown off will do that."

"Those scary suits – It's like a *job* thingie?"

"Don't sound so disappointed. Did you think it was the FBI?"

"Damn."

I gave a resigned sigh.

"You and Mom better get back together before I go all delinquent on the two of you. As it is, I'm already going to need a lifetime of therapy."

"I'm afraid your mother's moved on. I heard she's dating the lieutenant governor lately?"

"Oh, no. She hasn't moved on. Not at all. That guy's just her beard. I think he's gay anyway. She still loves you. I don't care what she says, it's all a lie."

I watched, out of the corner of my eye, his face relax noticeably.

"She hates me," He said.

"Take it from a little birdie who knows. I hear her cry herself to sleep all the way down to the end of the hall."

He glanced over at me, trying to see if I was going all Parent - Trappy on him.

"Well, Jessica, Hemingway had a phrase, 'the world breaks everyone, and after, some are stronger at the broken place...' Not verbatim exactly. But you get the point. That's my deepest prayer. That somehow Humpty Dumpty can be put together again, stronger at every fracture than ever before. I've actually prayed for it, and I don't pray." *I never have given up...*

"Well, you'll have to make the first move. She never will."

"No. Absolutely not. Never."

"She's a stubborn bitch, Dad. If you wait for her to give in first, you'll die alone in that singlewide."

"You're fifteen years old. Do you even have a boyfriend? Have you ever even had a boyfriend?"

"Yesssss."

"This Barry?"

"Don't change the subject."

"I'm changing the subject."

"Very troglike of you, Daddy. Very troglike."

"Tell me about your boyfriend."

"The most important thing?"

"Yes."

"He's a Virgo."

"Jessica."

"Well, just one other thing…"

"Let me guess."

"Would it bother you to find out that my boyfriend is black?"

"Is he?"

"Would it bother you?"

"Is he?" Daddy laughed. "I'd be thrilled."

*That's supposed to be half the fun, driving the parents crazy…*

"Why are you so cool with that? It would drive Mom to the wall! Actually, she might approve of it. It would help her political career…"

"No doubt."

"…As a matter of fact, why *are* you so pro - black people, anyway? Where does that come from, Daddy? I thought you said your parents were crackers."

"I've often wondered about that myself. But maybe here's a clue. I have thought about it a lot. I was watching *Animal Planet* recently, and it brought something back. This may have been the Rosebud moment…"

"Excuse me? *Animal Planet?* Is this another change of topic?"

He spoke so softly I had to lean almost across the console to follow him…*No, it brought back a memory, a memory that I think had a real impact on my life….*

…"When I was little, probably about four years old, our maid at the time used to bring her daughter, who was about my age, to work with her.

"That damn episode of Animal Planet brought it all back, every sad little memory of this friendship I had...

"Little Angela. Her name was Angela, and we just hit it off immediately, and we became the most wonderful of friends. Closer really than brother and sister. I hated weekends because Angela wouldn't be coming to our house.

"We must have shared about a year together. With all respect to you and your Mom, I've never loved another human being so innocently and completely with all my heart, as I loved little Angela.

"That year together was like ten lifetimes. We were one. She was black as night, I was albino - fair. Too bad you can't bottle that kind of pre - racial innocence in us all, and sell it. It would be priceless.

"So my parents noticed. Race - mixing in that back - assward part of the world was still frowned on then, so all of a sudden, my parents had a talk with our maid, and the next week she wasn't allowed to bring Angela with her to work any more. Eventually the maid had to quit, and my parents never could explain why. Not even the way we explained to you when your rabbits went away, that they found a better home on a farm. They didn't even have that...

"Just: 'she had to go away'.

"Jessica, I was thinking about all this recently, when I was watching an episode of 'Animal Planet' featuring a young leopard whose mother had been killed, and the leopard keeps looking for its mother, in all the places where they used to hunt and play together, just kept looking and looking. You could see the grief in its eyes, in its body language... Even animals feel loss... you could sense an especially deep sadness because the loss was incomprehensible. The young leopard would never know where its mother had gone. Never.

"It brought back the same kind of memory for me, looking for Angela after she was gone. And never knowing what had happened to her. I was just like that young leopard, looking for her in every room, every closet, in cabinets, even under the house. I looked, now and again, for weeks. I even managed to get up in the attic somehow. I remember feeling so desperate, that she might be hurt somewhere... Believe me, I didn't stop looking for weeks. A week is a long time for a little kid. My parents wouldn't discuss it. That's when I think I first realized that wisdom begins with loss.

"The emotional memory of her left me slowly. Then one day finally my sister was gone. Then, a while after, my Shadow. But not my Rosebud. Are you familiar with that allusion, from 'Citizen Kane'? Angela was my Rosebud, and at some level, the subconscious memory of her remains with me to this very day."

Just then I really wanted to reach across the console and give my dad a hug. I could hear the past, unhealed, in his voice.

"You couldn't – well, find her again some day?"

"Of course not. They lived on another planet. We only knew the mother as Lessie. They came at dawn and they left at dusk. We never knew them and never could have known them. That's how it was back then. They probably moved up north. It was impossible, in those days – it was as though they never existed. Just a dream in childhood..."

"That's a really sad dream."

"Maybe that's why I share your fascination with Epidermal Regression, Jess – I know it is rare, but it happens, and I've often wondered, what if those two little children had been consecrated with Holy Water, Blessed Water from the Church or wherever you might find it, Magic Water, just splashed with a few drops...whether Angela and I, touching each other, could have switched colors, sort of like a racial version of 'The Prince and the Pauper'...or even better, we could have become one color, it wouldn't have mattered which, and put all the rest of this nonsense behind us, and grown up as brother and sister...

"And I wonder if, somewhere, even today, Angela – if she's still even alive – I wonder if she still remembers the time when the little white boy she used to visit, climb the trees with, tickled each other, took naps with, chased through the rooms like two halves of the same being, a ghost and its shadow, trying with a tag or a tickle to perfectly merge, unite for life – I wonder if she even remembers? I was just the towheaded little boy who spent his days following her around with utter innocent devotion, and loving her with all his heart and soul? I've often wondered whether, in her adult moments alone, she ever even gives a thought back to that beautiful secret kinship we shared? Its freedom? Its purity? Ah, she's probably not even alive any more." *That damn young abandoned leopard on tv brought it all back, searching for the rest of its life to rid itself of an incomprehensible loneliness that would never quite go away. Wisdom starts with loss.*

I glanced over at Daddy. His eyes were filled with tears.

He quickly laughed them away.

"Ok Princess Flying Thumbs – so who's this mysterious black Barry who keeps blowing up your screen? And when am I going to finally meet him?"

# IV

*The World's Fattest, Baddest Solar Ballpoint Pen*

Pauley Vee's saloon doesn't look like much from the outside, a wide low brick box set on a packed sand parking lot with pick - up trucks and decade - old American made rust buckets parked every which way, with blazing central Florida August sunshine pouring down, melting ambition of the tatooed constituency of losers hiding in the air conditioning therein, waiting out the summer on Florida's central coast.

It's by no means unusual to see the Finance company's tow truck loading up one of these masterpieces and holding shotguns on the former owner till the re - acquisition is complete. That invariably leads to an alternative transportation modality known as 'barefooting it' till the back payments are caught up, and meantime Pauley Vee always pays for the first cab ride home.

Daddy had such a cute way of describing this time - honored tradition I tried to repeat it here, as close to verbatim as memory provides...

The sand parking lot arcs three quarters of the way around the low brick temple. Scraggly palms throw indifferent shade over the building. Daddy calls the architectural style 'red neck remorse', but it's the inside of the saloon that makes it one of my favorite places Dad and I ever visited together.

It's a dark, exotic neon - lit refrigerator, perfumed with bourbon and cheap womens' cosmetics, the fragrances of seduction and surrender, whether real or only promised...

When I was little, Daddy would fill my fists with coins, and every time I look now at the corner jukebox, I remember barely being able to reach the coin slot even on tiptoes, much less read the names of the songs.

I measured my growth by that jukebox, and still always first play the first song I ever played, *Don't be cruel/ To a heart that's true...*

Every year as I grew, I could read more and more song titles, but I always played Elvis first.

We parked the Toyota in scalding August heat, and stood outside the brick watering hole just for a moment.

"How could it look so small from the outside and be so big inside?"

"Pauley Vee built it that way to keep the tourists out," Daddy had explained with a laugh. "He doesn't need the money anyway. He's sitting on half of Ft. Knox."

It was like being inside a wonderful cypress - lined barrel, the walls golden warm and soft, the light smoky and kind of deflected, day or night, always the same. Icy cold. Like entering a meat locker. Booths along the long brick walls, bar chairs with comfortable backs for all day drinking, a long shiny bar, and there you are.

The interior of the bar was crowded and smoky, but even so the a/c was cruising at about 40 degrees Fahrenheit.

"It keeps them sober longer," I remember fat wonderful old Pauley Vee explain the thermostat once.

Immediately I felt my tiny twins stiffening inside the slightly sweaty T, and goose bumps blooming underneath the down on my neck and forearms. It was a sweet thrill chill, summer and fall, always the same, and the wonderful dry cypress scent over all this exciting, shadowy world.

The mood always reminded me of the dangerous atmosphere of Rick's Saloon in *Casablanca,* in redneck re - make. A shining jukebox full of golden oldies took Sam's place. But I always had the feeling every one of the shady exiles along the bar would have given their fortunes for letters of Transit out of the region's purgatorial grip.

As we made our way into the bar, a big argument was already ongoing.

"Okay, so in that case, who's the greater actor? Jeff Bridges? Or Michael Douglas?"

"Bridges."

"Bridges."

"Douglas! What about 'Wall Street?' 'A Perfect Murder?' 'Falling Down'?"

"Bridges! What about 'Blown Away?' 'Fabulous Baker Boys?' 'True Grit'?"

"What the hell do you know? Okay, which of these cougar goddesses is hotter? Sharon Stone in 'Basic Instinct'? Or Marisa Tomei in 'The Wrestler'?"

"Marisa."

"Marisa."

"It's close, but – Marisa!"

"Al Pacino? Or Dustin Hoffman?"

"There'll never be better acting than Hoffman in 'Tootsie'."

"Okay, here's an epic struggle between two gods, *two cinematic Sumos enter the cage, and only one will leave* – Robert Mitchum? Or Steve McQueen?"

"Jack!" Pauley Vee roared at us. "Dawg! Welcome back!"

"Now I'm home, Pauley. You look good. You've lost weight."

"And Jessie James," Pauley Vee's cement - mixer voice rolled over. "You growed up, girl."

"Hello Mr. Pauley Vee."

"This is the best saloon in Florida," Daddy said. "I speak as an authority."

"Why isn't the tv ever turned on?" I asked Pauley Vee as Daddy and I sat down at the bar.

"Too many Reality shows for a rural central Florida barroom," Somebody down the bar said. "Day and night. Every channel. There's no escape. You see the new one? Sheep grazing at that mansion in Beverly Hills? Even Spielberg can't make them stop it."

"To hell with Dr. Pill," One of the drinkers cursed.

"To hell with Orca and those Chrysler give - aways!"

"To hell with Jerry Springer and Fancy Lace!"

"...the creep Methany..."

"Somebody needs to smother Money Hoo Hoo with a foam pillow..."

"Impeach Judge Trudy!"

"See the problem?" Pauley Vee growled. "Nobody agrees on anything any more. Reality tv has destroyed our culture. And two more weeks til college football."

"CNN sucks," Shouted about five voices along the shiny bar.

"Well, there's some agreement," Pauley laughed.

"How about a stinger, Jack?"

"Sounds delicious."


This is where I first learned, to my amazement really, the hatred of The Great Unwashed, unleashed toward this form of current popular television entertainment – *Reality TV*. I had always enjoyed that stupid stuff. Money Hoo Hoo was one favorite, Judge Trudy another.

But I hated Fancy Lace, the bleached blonde prosecutor who'd been kicked off 'Dancing With the Stars.' Even Mother laughed at that refugee from "Alice in Wonderland" – *Fancy Lace is the Red Queen, Jess. Verdict first, trial after...*

Now Pauley Vee's long bar roared with intemperate anger at what we were being forced to accept as legitimate entertainment, and it gave me an idea of the degree of lonliness in the big low dark room. Television was more to these guys than an electronic fireplace. *For many of them, an only friend. A friendship turned bad, all wrong.*

"These days it's either reality – or Reality Shows. God knows which is worse."

"It's so wrong. So wrong. A capsule expression of everything that's gone wrong in America."

"The whole nation has become so relentlessly franchised, any gesture at authenticity draws us like moths to a flame. Anything that doesn't have golden arches attached to it – it's like a memory from American Graffiti. It all started with the Jersey Shore series...and just metastasized..."

"They produce that garbage for a penny on the dollar, and since it's on every channel, what choice do we have?"

"The Housewives of East Amarillo. Somebody had that piece of s*** on the other afternoon. Somebody else threw a beer bottle at the screen."

"I haven't had the tube on since then," Pauley Vee growled. "This is a civilized house. A proper house."

"'Keeping Up With Kammi Kay!' Ever watch that one?"

"At least the bitch is hot. Undeniably sexy. God, that booty!" *I mean, I heard she's got an 18" waist — that's what makes the rest of her so unbelievably voluptuous...*

"Those eyes, Tiffany quality polished obsidian, huge and empty as hope itself..."

"You know Tony Perkins is missing that — "

"Watch yer language. Ladies present."

"Sorry, Pauley."

"When she married that crazy rapper, it was a day - long event. They arrived at the church in carriages, like European royalty! Divide the number of tattoos by the number of gold teeth, and you've got the average IQ of the groomsmen... The cops came and threw the whole reception in jail. What the hell?"

"That was Ghost Posse at its finest. Those assassins at Crystal Lagoon." *The Gangstas that couldn't shoot straight.*

Daddy nudged me and got a teenaged frown in return.

"Judge Trudy — Jesus Christ! The worst. How can you be a Jew and a Nazi at the same time, and nobody even notice?"

"Goose Garrison! What the hell? Even worse!"

"And that moron, Money Hoo Hoo — Just kill me, God."

"Don't forget Jerry Springer, the ex - mayor. His audience attacked him! Last month. He was nearly torn to pieces."

"That got ratings – *big* ratings."

"Methanny – she doesn't even wear panties. She keeps opening those scrawny legs and flashing the camera. *Look at me! Look at me! Look between my legs. Make me feel human!*"

"Crab Grabbers."

"Pawn Boys."

"Cheetahs."

"Lendra."

"Towing Town."

*Hhhiiiissssss,* the bar cursed when this last program was mentioned.

"I hate Fancy Lace," I broke in. "The ex - prosecutor on Court TV."

"Yeah. Verdict first, trial after," A woman, down the bar, half - laughed, half - cursed. "She's right in tune with the rest of this damn country – modern America, straight out of Alice in Wonderland – the Red Queen. She rides the prevailing media Narrative like it's a donkey on the way to Bethlehem. The mob screams, and she goes to work. She still owes them Duke LaCrosse players a quart of her blood. She ought to have had her ass whipped in the public square."

"That's exactly what my Mom says about her," I interrupted admiringly. "My Mom's a lawyer up in Tallahassee."

This boisterous Fancy Lace hating lady bore a striking resemblance to the comedienne Roseanne Barr. Her big bare arms were absolutely technicolored with tattoos, and she was wearing a Gator National Championship blue t - shirt. And she hated Fancy Lace. I loved her.

Looking down the line of drinkers filling every chair in the long bar, I suddenly had the eerie feeling that every face in Pauley Vee's that afternoon resembled, to some extent or other, somebody I had seen on some TV show or other.

That's when it hit me, *Jessica, you've been watching too much tube. This could easily be a psychosis. You could already have crossed a line and not even know it. Next you'll imagine you're Napoleon Bonaparte or some deceased wheezer like that...*

"Well, I don't care what anybody says – I *still* like 'The Reformed Prostitutes of the Bunny Ranch'," another voice offered.

This came from a hopeless looking old bald guy in a wifebeater, who came closest to the cartoon character Bill Daughtry, from *King of the Hill.*

Nobody answered him, and for a moment the bar fell silent.

"You can tell they all want to quit being whores, only they can't say no to the money."

He sighed sadly. He looked down into his beer.

"It's like a metaphor for all the rest of us."

"They're not really reformed. That's the plot hook," His friend explained. "See, the focus of the show is on their moral struggle."

"And Gator Wrasslers! Have you seen what they do to those poor reptiles? That should be a class one felony! Those bastards should be in Raiford! Tyin' 'em up and tickling their bellies like that!"

"It ain't nothin' 'Bama didn't do to us last season..."

"What? *What?*"

"No fighting over football till the season starts," Pauley Vee warned them.

"'Bama didn't use no *hand grenades!*"

"They didn't have to," replied his wife quietly, unwilling to let it go. "Our defense rolled over voluntarily, with our little feets up in the air, all cooperative - like. There wasn't even no sense of shame!"

"F– the Crimson Tide!"

"Knock it off, you two." Pauley Vee always had the last word.

Roseanne waved off their quarrel and her voice rose above the low murmur of discontent along the bar. And suddenly she didn't seem like a lady mechanic.

She sounded like a college professor, giving a lecture.

"Reality TV is just a bunch of jerks so self - involved they're supposed to make the cultures they represent seem authentic. Distinctive, in an era when everything in this nation looks, tastes, feels and sounds exactly the same, from McDonalds's to the CNN news. Everything is an echo or a copy of everything else. We peer out past our screens for a glimpse of anything new, different, original, and God knows, of quality.

"But we no longer know the difference, and hence, the clowns have won by default. Every voice that is not a scream is instantly driven from the stage. Excellence and moral optimism – things of the past. All that American culture can do now is lower the lowest common denominator. It's like a brain - eating virus that cable TV is absolutely overrun with...

"Reality? Or Reality TV? It's all equally f****** unreal. Pick your poison. To hell with it. Football season starts in a couple of weeks. We'll turn the goddamn TV back on then. *And it's all Kressa Kay's fault.* That monster pimped her own daughter out, just to make a billion dollars... I know Kammi Kay personally. It ain't her fault. She's just an idiot. Her brains are in her ass, that's all. She made that one sex tape. And her mother got hold of it and ran with it. It's the mother who schemed up this whole Reality empire... The American Empire is like that saying about individuals… you're born with the face God gave you, and you die with the face you earned.

"Our Empire will go into the grave wearing the stupified, slack - jawed face of Money Hoo Hoo, with drool all over us, trying to remember why we existed in the first place…"

I couldn't resist interupting Roseanne.

"You know Kammi Kay? The *Reality* Star Kammi Kay?" I asked. "From 'Keeping Up With Kammi'?"

"This coast is crawling with famous types. It's Crystal Lagoon, after all. I know her. Yeah. I know her. Not well, but I know her. And she ain't as dumb as she acts. She's sneaky. Shady lady."

"I like you, Roseanne," Pauley Vee said admiringly. "Smart, smart lady."

*I love you, Roseanne,* I smiled.

Pauley Vee turned to Dad and me.

"That sweetheart used to be a professor. At the junior college. Every so often she lets it show."

"You know Kammi Kay *personally*?" Somebody down the bar roared in disbelief. "The sex tape queen? The fox with her brains in her big ass?"

"I gave her a ride in my boat the other day!"

"Sure you did!"

"Don't believe me? See if I care! I hauled her back from Crystal Lagoon. Tied up inside an oyster sack. She's *persona non grata* over there. And that's putting it mildly."

For a fifteen - year old girl, I know a lot about bars. For instance, the lady who looked like Roseanne was drinking margueritas. She'd had more than five and fewer than twenty. Just an educated guess.

"Whenever a politician gets shot, we turn it on then," Pauley Vee answered me. Daddy said he has a voice like a cement mixer set on low. "Gives us something to cheer about."

*Woke up this mornin*
*Got yourself a gun*
*Got yourself a gun*

*"Don't worry, Dad,"* I heard myself stage whisper, *"that's called a ringtone.* From the Sopranos."

"I *know* what it's called!"

"Excuse me, guys. I gotta take this," Pauley Vee turned away from the bar. He reached for his i.

Pauley Vee. A face like a shovel, a slow, gravel voice with a New York City note still noticeably defining it, thin, slicked back Tony Soprano style brown hair, a Hawaiian shirt mostly covering a great appetite of a belly. I'm sure you can tell, Daddy's been helping me editorially with some of my imagery...

Pauley finished his call right quick.

"We heard Tony Perkins got shot. But there wasn't nothing on the news about it. Of course them billionaires control the information coming out of Crystal Lagoon pretty tight. Otherwise, it's just August in Florida. Keep the blender running on high, after a while it sounds just like Parrothead music."

Pauley Vee was beautiful because he was authentic. Not a false bone in his body, Daddy assured me. A bar owner straight out of Central Casting – Pauley Vee and Dad go way back, and sometimes I see them chatting and laughing privately. You can sense their friendship then.

I'm never invited to join them. Nobody is.

And nobody – ever – messes with Pauley Vee. Daddy laughed off his friend's reputation for mayhem in the old days, saying only, *when Pauley gave somebody a ride to the river, it wasn't to go swimming...*

I knew that was probably just guy talk.

"Pauley, you remember my daughter Jessica?"

"Beautiful girl," Pauley Vee murmured. He winked at me. He's a hundred years old if a day, but I had a crush on him when I was ten.

"The usual, Jack – a Stinger?"

"Thank you."

"And for you, beautiful?"

"Oh, I suppose I'll have a beer." I put my hand seductively on his huge hairy arm. That always worked for subtly sexy Mom. Why not me? I tried to be subtle. "Anything imported."

I hate it when adults laugh at me, especially men. *TROGS!!! MOOKS!!! GOURDS!!! ALL OF THE ABOVE!!! Check appropriate box!*

"A Shirley Temple, Pauley. And – Watson – you said you had an appetite?"

I hid my embarrassment behind a menu.

"Tuna sandwich on wheat."

"Coming right up."


Everybody seemed to have heard about a shooting on the island...

"It's all fourth - hand rumor anyhow. Them billionaires don't share their champagne and caviar world with us, all that much. Must be nice to hang out with Elon Musk. And Paul Allen. And Mick Jagger. Heavy dudes."

"Bill Clinton was down here last month with three women," Somebody noted. "Vegas blondes."

Football hadn't started yet, so the topics *du jour* as the liquor flowed more freely, swung between America's low - level race war, the curse that the Reality TV industry had visited on what remained of American culture, and most vocally, what it meant to have, in this neighborhood of trailer parks and flea markets, the presence of a colony of famous billionaires only a dozen miles off the Central Florida coast.

The mysterious Perkins' Boys had mesmerized the bar the way the daily reading of the Lottery numbers might.

Their existence was causing everybody to dream a little of what it would be like to be Tony Perkins, one of the richest men in all human history.

"We're going over to the island tomorrow," I advised Roseanne, five minutes later after we'd become bff's. "Dad's a reporter for UGF."

"Since the shooting, they've tore down the dock. You can't hardly get there anymore except by plane or chopper."

Dad looked up from his stinger.

"How can we get to the island then?"

"I might can help you with that," Roseanne smiled. Daddy glanced at Pauley Vee. Pauley only nodded.

"Why does everything get blamed on Ghost Posse?" I heard my mouth demand. "It's *their* island, after all. They've got the fame so they get the blame."

"Spoken like a true teenage Libtard."

"I'm just saying, don't be so quick to judge. That's what courts are for."

*Well, Jessica, you just can't shut up, can you?*

"And another thing – I just read this, and it's a fact! Crystal Lagoon is outside the twelve mile limit – not even a part of the U.S.! Satellite technology has established the legal location. What's the justice department got to do with it? It's political pressure!"

"Ghost Posse." Muttered Barney Fife, *sans* badge and pistol with one bullet. He was wearing an 'I'm With Stupid' t - shirt. The arrow pointed straight up. "I will guarantee you they're behind it. They announced they're reclaiming the island for their ancestors – going to name it New Haiti. Put their own government in place."

"F****** Ghost Posse. Just when tourism was starting to turn around."

Pauley Vee's voice rolled down the bar, and every face turned toward him.

"They got a giant tree on that island that's immortal. Jack, when you and your daughter get over there, you'll see it. But you won't believe it. You can't kill it. Supposedly God put it there – the Tree of Knowledge of Good and Evil. They say it's a conduit straight to God. Only God ain't listenin' no more."

"Ah, come on, Pauley. We thought you'd quit drinking."

"Yeah, boss man. We've heard this one before. It's a legend in this bar. The Tree of Knowledge of Good and Evil. There's supposed to be bottles of Jack Daniels hanging off the limbs. Everybody's heard about it."

Pauley looked down the bar at the faces foolish enough to express skepticism. You had the sense he had a good memory about such things.

"I know this *personally.*"

"Sorry, Pauley."

"Yeah. I made the mistake of doubtin' you once before. Sorry, boss."

"I know the guy who bulldozed down that tree. When they was building the Perkins' castle, by mistake this old boy bulldozed the tree flat. And it's huge, a two - hundred footer. Taller than a football field is long. The root structure, according to the dozer driver - same dimensions."

Every soul at the bar, including yours truly, was mesmerized by the narrative rolling out of that concrete gravel truck of a mouth.

"So sometime during the night, clouds obscured the moon for maybe two minutes or three. That was the only time the magic could have happened. But the next morning the great tree was right back in place, completely undisturbed, bigger than glory."

"Naw," Don Knotts protested.

"Yep. Completely undisturbed. There's a kind of music that comes out of it. I mean – the music, you can't hear it, but you can. It's sad, like the wind. What I'm saying is – there's some kind of very old curse on that rock... The Perkins' brothers built their castle with the tree as the centerpiece. It's the island's central feature."

"It's the most beautiful place I've ever seen," Roseanne murmured to me. "If there's such a place as Paradise, Crystal Lagoon is it."

"Money can buy anything," One of the drinkers grumbled.

"It has nothing to do with money," She replied with a shrug. "You'd have to see it to understand."

"The magic tree – You got that from the horse's mouth, Pauley?"

"From my cousin's husband. He was the driver. He won't go back there. Became a Christian. Quit drinkin'. Before he worked on that island, nothing scared the guy. He's done state time – *Raiford* time. Ballsy dude, and his hair practically turned white overnight. Damn tree cost me my best customer! He used to spend three hundred a month in here, easy. See, that's the thing about religious miracles. Always so unfair to the innocent."

"I hate Tony Perkins," I blurted out.

"How come you hate old Tony," Gator Roseanne teased me. "Did he break your heart?"

"Bet he made his fortune selling cars. Bad cars."

"Nah," Kid Rock interjected, from behind a big glass that looked like Pepsi but I knew it wasn't. Rock n' roll must be going downhill. Kid Rock had a BEST BUY nametag on his pocket. "It's dope. Dope and hookers. It's what keeps 'em so young over there. They make every dream come true. Wouldn't that keep anybody young?"

*Everybody in this bar looks like somebody famous. But I don't think they are. Famous. They're not. Who they look like, I mean.*

The lead guitarist from Bono's band, U - 2, only wearing a dirty housepainter's jumpsuit and without the Irish accent, had a different take, which he now expressed in a slurred redneck twang.

"I got this from the horse's mouth. The Perkins' brothers won that Cay in a crooked card game with a bunch of Cherokee Indians. Then they discovered oil on it."

Roseanne laughed and belched. "Behind every great fortune, a crime, as the Frenchman said..." She laughed again. "If it's oil, how come there's no derrick anywhere on the island?"

"That sweetheart is always coming up with quotes like that, Jack," Pauley said admiringly. "She used to be a teacher at the junior college. Till alcoholism cured her of sobriety. Anyway, she can help you get over to Crystal Lagoon tomorrow. Just be sure to say Pretty Please."

Jack raised his stemmed Stinger glass in Roseanne's direction.

"Pretty Please?"

"Any guy's got a daughter sweet like yours has got to be a right guy," She laughed.

"I can speak to that, Jeannie," Pauley said. He nodded in Daddy's direction. "This is a good man to have for a friend."

"Sure. I'll haul you over. I got a boat. Dawn tomorrow, West Bend marina. Pay me gas and a case of beer to get over the hangover I'm going to have. 12 oz. Bud in cans. Any other brand, we don't ride. And fifty bucks."

She waved for another marguerita. "We'll have to call ahead and have security meet us. Nobody but me would even try to get a boat up that close in these currents."

"Thank you so much. We'll be there at sun - up. That marina just up the road?"

"Yep."

"Jack, lately that island's getting a little hairy." *A colonial war could break out at any minute. That island's worth a lot of money to somebody. I think even the Russians are helping out Ghost Posse, the way they helped Castro in '59...Just watch your back, you two....*

Pauley Vee disappeared behind the bar, then re - appeared, holding what has got to be the baddest, fattest - barreled ball point pen I've ever seen, you could barely hold it and write with it. A steel connector held the two halves of the pen together. I could half - read, half - imagine the complimentary advertising on the pen's fat barrel: *Pauley Vee's Selling Booze in Central Florida / Since Before You Was Born. 1989 —*

"Those are weird looking pens Pauley Vee's giving away."

"They're solar. Prototypes. They don't run out of ink for a long time."

Pauley and Daddy went into one of their private caucuses, obviously discussing the merits of this stupid looking so - called "Solar" ballpoint, and once again I was left alone to finish a delicious tuna sandwich and brutally soggy fries. Pauley was probably trying to talk Daddy into selling his pens on commission at the flea market. That's how bad it has gotten in my father's life.

Now the whole bar was one long murmur of argumentative laughter.

"Ain't no oil on that Cay. Where's the derricks? It's drugs, I tell you. Why else would there be a landing strip? For *jets?* Nah. He's handling for the Peruvian cartel."

"It's drugs. What else could it be? Half of Hollywood visits there."

"It's drugs. Gotta be drugs."

"I've heard Hitler's hiding on that island. They've got make - up specialists over there that can make you look fifty years younger – or older."

"Nobody likes Perkins," Pauley Vee agreed. "Who cares when you've got four billion dollars and live in a castle surrounded by worshipful slaves?"

"Oh, he's got more than four billion," Somebody disagreed. "A lot more. Him and that brother of his. A lot more. Those two have more dough than Mother Russia."

"He has a brother?" My father acted only mildly surprised. "Is that the movie star?"

"Well, he's the corporate attorney now," Roseanne corrected. "Good looking dude. Those two are like Jack and Bobby – you never know who's pulling the strings."

"You know them?" I asked her.

"Sort of," And she looked away, ending that line of conversation abruptly.

"He's selling drugs out of that thar castle," A rather unpleasant looking trucker tossed in. I didn't like the way he'd been mean - mugging me. "No way he gets that rich selling granola and teaching yoga to a bunch of trust fund (expletive deleted) babies..."

"First job of a good journalist," My father lifted his Stinger in a toast. "Go in innocent. Let the interview establish guilt. It usually will."

"My Dad won the Pulitzer prize, catching crooks," I pointed out. "He's good at it. Really good."

Roseanne was standing beside me, and now looked up at me appraisingly.

"I know I'm just a gumdrop, but look at this child — she's as tall as a boy! How old are you, honey? Twelve? Thirteen?"

I blushed in anger. "Fifteen years old. Almost sixteen!"

"I bet your Mom's a looker. A *real* looker."

This time it was Daddy's turn to blush. Without turning, I could sense his neck burning red a little, and the color in his face rise. I could imagine the brandy in his Stinger glass tremble a little too. Just a little.

That's how Mom and Dad still are about each other, still, like two high schoolers, each trying to steal a first kiss from the other. *Rich girl with looks, bad boy with skills. The story of the world.*

Laying awake at night, thinking about each other. Hating each other. All that stupid obsession stuff. Even now, whenever Mom goes out with some superpowerful political Trog, she makes sure Daddy knows all about it. Brags about how good it was. Ridiculous. Sometimes she's such a bitch. Daddy hates that too —

*Of course I hate that about her, Jess — but it's part of what makes her so goddam interesting. She's all girl, the good, the bad, the...*

This is something kids know a lot more about than adults. Our emotional IQ is higher because it's all intuition. But what difference does any of it make? My parents love torturing each other. And torturing me too, right along with them! Barry and I, at our worst, can't touch those two.

"Hey baby," the unsavory trucker Trog previously referred to, seemed to be addressing me. "Don't worry about yo' Mama. You're the looker — and quite a looker, too."

"She's my daughter," Daddy said without looking around. We were a few chairs away down the bar. "She's fifteen."

"What the hell do I care?" *I didn't ask for no ID, pal. I've been on the road a straight month. Time to dance.*

As soon as we all heard that, I happened to notice Daddy carefully tucking away Pauley's fat ballpoint in his shirt's front pocket, then carefully setting down his Stinger glass. I couldn't see Daddy's face. I guess he knew what was coming. He was already starting to remove his wristwatch.

"Sir, I said my daughter's fifteen years old."

"I wasn't asking for no ID, pal."

The area around us went quiet.

"She's too young to be dancing in bars."

"Ah, f*** you. Come dance with me, baby. I been on the road a month."

"No thank you."

"Oh, come here, dammit..."

*(Jessbaby99 to Phong, 940pm Friday)*

*Jess: You would have loved what came next, Phongie, it was right out of the old West. Daddy came off his chair...then Mr. Trog tries to shove him to one side to get to me*

*Phong: Okay so then what happened next*

*Jess: A shot to the dude's solar plexus. My soft, sweet Daddy! I didn't see that coming! (Neither did Mr. Trog) Hit him so hard...Dude bent over like he was gonna vomit*

*Phong: Your daddy smacked a guy? No way.*

*Jess: Way...framed him up and hit him square in the chest...I heard it...bone on bone*

*Phong: Wait while I get a ciggie, this is getting good*

*Jess: Shut up you don't smoke*

*Phong: Your dad's like, like — he's an intellectual! They don't hit dudes*

*Jess: Xcept in movies and that's what this looked like. The whole day looked like a movie. Oh so much to tell u we drove back in time a thousand years from the city...u should have seen this swamp we went through...it's where the fountain of youth is probably. so daddy clipped this jerk so hard! A shot to the chest, pow, upper cut, pow, right cross, and this jerk hits the canvas. Phong I swear. And it was just that quick...if i'd blinked would have missed it*

*Phong: Liar!!! No way!!*

*Jess: Well u know i couldn't believe it either*

*Phong: Your dad's the sweetest adult i know*

*Jess: Pauley Vee (bar owner) told me Daddy was SEC middle - weight boxing champ at UF a million years hence...two of them once fought their way out of a brawl in Chiefland...he wouldn't have made it out alive if it hadn't been for Dad...I always wondered why daddy gets his first Stinger free every time we're there. It's Pauley's way of saying he remembers... Pauley's an ex mob big boss accordin to rumor and nobody to ever mess with, totally fearless and dead - eyed, but when i asked him were they in danger of being killed that night he just nodded... 'your dad saved my life. it's worth a few* stingers...' the look in his eyes...wow if a scary crocodile could shed a tear I think I saw one

    *Phong:* Your dad the prize fighter!

    *Jess:* Now. This you really won't believe. But guess who's in the motel with me right now?

    *Phong:* Gandhi? Elvis? I think you've been huffin' anyway

    *Jess:* nevr mind... u will never believe it anyway – did i tell u we almost got killed 27S big ole hawg

    *Phong:* Tell. what stray u pick up this time

    *Jess:* Promis u won't mock... It's so real, this whole trip cant wait to tell B

    *Phong:* ok...watch him J, he's sketchy i kp tellin u shady

    *Jess:* suspicious minds

    *Phong:* luv is blind grl just watch it...he's dawgin' Angie. Hard

    *Jess:* lets dont go there

    *Phong:* ok jst promis dont trust me right but imho he a dawg...u deal...so tell m this stray?

    *Jess:* it'll sound weird...we're a dozen miles away from an island full of billionaires and the bimbos who love em

    *Phong:* Tell

    *Jess:* Swear u won't laugh. u can be an edgy little b sometimes

    *Phong:* tell me Oscar Wilde walked in the door wearing a velvet cloak and i'll believe u

    *Jess:* Kammi Kay

    *Phong:* Kammi Kay what

    *Jess:* Kammi Kay's here in the motel with us...other bed, texting her Tiger Mom

    *Phong:* u lie...Oh, liar! u had me so sucked in

    *Jess:* See? Told u

    *Phong:* Oscar Wilde's one thing. but Kammi Kay...she lives in another dimension from us...what's this, Matrix 6?

    *Jess:* She's broke ass and kind of cra cra... it's her...

*Phong: Sure ...And a hog killed you too... then Elvis appeared*

*Jess: She won't let me send a selfie — something about her image being proprietary - legal*

*Phong: Martians don't like selfies either*

*Jess: okay fine*

*Phong: Carbon monoxide fumes in your dad's yota...?!*

*Jess: she looks like forty miles of bad road but it's her. When daddy said its a small world big coincidences, i never had any idea how far that theme could stretch...*

*Phong: Liar — oh I get it, the tv's on, and her and that dumb ass Reality family of hers is on Channel 13...w 40 million twitter followers, she's in your motel...sure thing*

*Jess: Earth to Phong... real deal...One half of KamYe is parked on the other bed of this cheap motel and we've got to give her a ride to Crystal Lagoon tomorrow at dawn. And she's sucking down tequila like she lost a bet... the island's a babe magnet. She came up to me outside this bar we were in where the fight happened... She's tied in with this guy who owns the island, Tony Perkins. love connection. they met in LA...Perkins is the guy she left to marry KamYe, ok. Perkins is the world's richest guy...sex must have been out of this world to turn her back on that*

*Phong: No...its like shroud of turin...i want to believe....but. Also she doesn't drink. Its well known. She says it all the time, she doesn't drink to set a good example for her millions of fans. so your lies have caught up to u at last*

*Jess: she doesn't drink? really? Really?*

*Phong: She drinks?*

*Jess: Ah how can i put this to persuade u...she's slammin' shots like Spring break in pc beach...remember how u were puking? like that*

*Phong: KK...in the flesh?*

*Jess: In the flesh!*

*Phong: Her sisters? Where they?*

*Jess: Dunno. She was on the island and got kicked off...wife got mad. KK wants us to help her get back... She's txt her mom right now*

*Phong: Kressa. Tiger Mom*

*Jess: KK scared to death of her*

*Phong: King Perkins has a wife? didn't know...u sure?*

*Jess: heard the Diva broke his heart when she married Doctor...now sh want back in...that island a babe magnt*

*Phong: Pretty as on tube? As rich?*

*Jess: Yup. It's her... prettier in person not brighter tho... and not a dime on her. Pimples. Tiny. Kind of looks arabic. Straight on, she looks like a cobra. She made some people mad on that island. Says Tony's brother hates her...She's used to getting her way. Headstrong and flirty. Thought she'd grab daddy by the b\*\*\*\* when he said he couldn't help her. always worrying about her wrinkles too, a mirror every five minutes...more obsessed with gettin older than i am*

*Phong: No bleeping way! swear to me its really her*

*Jess: Way*

*Phong: The girl in the sex tape? the girl whose first marriage only lasted four hours... the girl who couldn't count from one to ten on national tv*

*Jess: Same.*

*Phong: No way...im jealous*

*Jess: Way*

*Phong: Her ass*

*Jess: Yep. Definitely it's her*

*(Jessica signs off 950p)*

Now, returning to the afternoon at Pauley Vee's for a moment, once that trucker had gotten to his knees, to avoid further awkwardness Pauley Vee very gently suggested Sugar Ray and I leave before the cops showed up.

"There's a grand jury down here looking at me," Pauley Vee apologized. "I'd rather skip the publicity just now. Y'all are welcome back any other time."

"That mfer broke my jaw," The trucker was spitting blood.

"If I'd broken your jaw, you wouldn't be able to keep running your mouth."

"Why do we have to be the ones to leave?" I had protested. "We didn't start anything."

"This jerk has kin back here." Pauley almost tenderly patted my shoulder. "In these parts it's like Sherwood Forest. The sheriff down here has a lot of power." Pauley Vee threw a bar towel at the kneeling, beaten redneck warrior. "No need to poke the bear. Sheriff's on the payroll – but still."

"I think my jaw's broke, god damn it."

"Mop the floor and mop your face, Darryl. Then get out of my bar and don't never come back. Jack – you and Jessie James might better book too. You're always welcome back. And just let me know if you need me. I'm there." Pauley Vee gave a mirthless laugh. "Just write me a love letter."

Dad nodded and patted his shirt pocket. Where he'd stuck that fat gift ballpoint.

"Never question Pauley's wisdom, Jessica."

But then Daddy did something that amazes me to this day. The bloodied trucker kept shaking his head to try to clear it, and wasn't showing the ability to rise to his feet again.

"That's okay, Pauley. I'll clean it up. Sir, let me help you up."

"Mfer."

Then my father reached down, extending his hand toward his bloody opponent.

"Sir, I'm apologizing for my part in this. We're two grown men and we're in a bar. It's so unfortunate everything went south like it did. For my part – I apologize."

After several extremely awkward and uncertain moments, the trucker shook his head hard once more, and reached up, allowing himself to be pulled upright to his feet. The bar was so quiet you could have heard a glass touch the counter.

"I boxed in the Marine Corps," Darryl said to my father. "Never got tagged like that." He was rubbing his jaw very lightly with the palm of his hand.

"Lucky shot."

"I been on the road eighteen hour days a solid month. I was out of line. I was wrong in the moment. You get kind of crazy on the Interstates... All them civilians have their Cruise Controls set on 80... You can't get around 'em..."

"We're worn out too. We came down 27."

"Through Spanish Swamp?"

"Yes."

"It's been a long day."

"Yes."

"My apologies, young miss." This time he didn't try to reach out and touch me.

"It's okay."

"Thanks. Well, I'm on my way."

"Good luck."

"Thanks. Sorry. Thanks."

Pauley was already around on our side of the bar with a mop and a bucket.

So 'Darryl' left. And about five seconds after the front door swung shut behind him, the entire smoky, golden room erupted in solid applause, interspersed with raucous Gator chomping from all the famous nobodies up and down the line.

I learned a lesson from my Dad that afternoon that remains with me still. And I learned something wonderful about him too. Something that, deep down, I already knew.

My Dad, despite his dangerous edges, is, foremost, a gentle man.

# V

*A Full - Figured Being Emerges From the Heat*

Daddy told me to go to the car while he settled up. The lady who looked like Roseanne re - committed for our boat ride the next dawn, then honored my father in the highest by doing another flabby armed Gator chomp, and suddenly the whole bar responded likewise, a great honor in that region, let me tell you, their palms all slapping up and down together amidst much laughter and graphic comment. *Na Na NaNaNa – Go, Gators!*

"To the car, Watson – I'll be there in a moment." Dad was totally calm, like nothing had happened. But I could tell he liked being honored by the Chomp.

"Dad, why do we have to leave." I hadn't even had a chance to play 'Don't Be Cruel' yet.

"Go."

It's true, looking back on it, at the time I felt, or sensed, a sort of furtive movement behind me as I went out through the swinging doors. Outside that cypress womb – I'm working on my literary imagery here – the coastal twilight heat was like the opening of a furnace door. That's something about Florida nobody ever gets used to, but it's a feeling that is both good and bad at the same time.

It all depends on what's next on the agenda. I wouldn't want to be a roofer, going back to finish a job before dark, but we were on our way to a nice, air - conditioned motel room. The wet, fiery air just provided a momentary rush, but it really hits you...

Somebody was following me. I turned. I thought it might be 'Darryl.'

"Did I leave something in the bar?" I asked, turning back.

The perspiring shadow, stumbling close behind me, was short, beautifully built, and clothed in shapeless dusty black silk pantsuit, sweat - soaked, and dirty high heels. She reached a hand from her throat shakily toward me, as though fearing me: *well, as for that – right back at you, girlfriend.*

"Hi there. What up?"

*"In the name of God – I need your help."*

In my writing class there was this axiom, *all literature is a damsel in distress.* This was a truly beautiful damsel. Definitely in some kind of distress. I almost recognized her. I was *sure* I recognized her. But I'd recognized every single famous soul in Pauley Vee's saloon, just a very disorienting afternoon, and the August heat didn't help. Maybe I'd even gotten a buzz off the Shirley Temple.

"What's the matter ma'am?"

"Just please hear me out. This is so important. *In the name of God!* My life depends on it. I heard your father say he's going to Crystal Lagoon tomorrow?"

"Yes." I had moved sort of sideways so I was right beside the passenger door of our car, key out and ready. "He's a journalist. He's interviewing Mr. Perkins tomorrow over there."

"Will you be going with him?"

"Uh huh."

"Take me with you. I'll give you five million dollars if you can get me onto that island safely."

Long black hair tied back, shining obsidian - dark eyes, a cobra - shaped head emphasizing the extreme dimensions and planes of an extraordinary, more than beautiful face absolutely designed by God for cameras to love without judgment, that amazing head atop a small upper body with exaggerated, famously voluptuous assets, Hispanic or middle - eastern, and though young, with a quality of exhaustion and even desperation in her demeanor, as she came nearer.

"My name is Kammi Kay. You may have heard of me. I'm travelling *incognito*. What's *your* name?"

She gave me a weary, but blinding smile, and suddenly I was the only person on the whole planet, the bff of a goddess.

"You couldn't be Kammi Kay. Who are you? You're probably a lookalike chick who works jewelry at Wal - Mart in Chiefland." *If you're not her, who the hell are you? Because you couldn't be her. You couldn't.*

"Oh, you recognize me!" Those famous black pitchfork eyelashes stirred a breeze when she batted them at me. "Well, then. I'm sure you can understand: *I'm for real!* I'm more than real. *I'm Reality itself!* And I'm in desperate need of your help."

"I'm Jessica." I stuck out my hand.

"Jessica. What a perfectly lovely name. I'll give you five million dollars to help me. It's imperative."

"Are you in danger?"

"I cannot describe the stakes in play here. Words have never been invented that would describe the danger I'm in."

"I can't believe I'm meeting the world's most famous girl."

Her clothing was obviously expensive, obviously an amazing quality of silk, in perfectly tailored black, but worn and dirty. On her small feet were black suede beat - up Jimmy Choo heels, the thousand dollar kind Mom likes to show off when she's modeling in all the local society charity gigs up in Tallahassee. Mom'd do it for free, but she likes it when they pay her in designer sling - backs.

"Oh, I'm not really that famous. Well, actually, you're right – I suppose I am! Nobody knows the trouble I've seen! When you are as famous as I am, there's no place to hide!"

Kammi Kay looked beat up and worn out, but she wasn't wearing knock - offs. The hems of her stylishly flared slacks showed dried salt - lines, suggesting she'd been walking, or had come ashore, through a salty marsh or at high tide somewhere.

"I'm sorry to mention this – you smell like fish."

"I was kidnapped in a crocker sack that had been filled with oysters. By a fat woman covered in tattoos. And that's not the half of it." A horrified look crossed her Cobra face. "God, that bag – it was so...so *granular!*"

"I think I just met her in the bar." *A short, tough - looking woman resembling Roseanne Barr?*

"That's the bitch. She works for the Perkins' brothers – specifically, the lawyer, my dread enemy."

"Oh, she's not so bad."

"This will sound strange," The self - identifying Kammi Kay murmured, obsidian eyes averted.

"Try me." I was watching the saloon's doors for my father's saving appearance. I try to play grown up, but it's at times like these it occurs to me I'm still a kid, very much so.

"Please. Just hear me out."

113

"I don't have any money." I added carefully. "Maybe enough for a Greyhound ticket outta here."

"Oh, I have all the money in the world," She whispered. "You can have some of it, if you'll help me – you can have a lot of it. A million dollars."

"I thought you said five million?"

"Whatever."

"Okay." *Who do I have to kill?*

"Persuade your father to do something tomorrow."

"Okay – maybe. We'll see. Talk. You're one half of KamYe? You're *really* Kammi Kay, the sex tape girl? Married to Dr. Munye? The Ghost Posse guy?"

I could tell she was flattered.

"Oh, God, that tape will follow me to the end," She giggled.

"You were good in it. You inspired me and my bf. We may make one. Of our first time."

"How interesting. What I need is for you to sneak me on the boat ride back over there. I need to get to that island. That's all. Let me be your big sister..." *Every little girl needs a big sister, don't they?* "Or better yet, your Saudi housekeeper. I can be in disguise. One of the brothers hates me and will murder me if I re - appear over there. He swore he would. It's the other brother I need to see. We're in love. If I can get to him, it'll all be okay." She laughed. "I've so got him by the b—s," She half - whispered.

"Aren't you married to Doctor Munye?"

"Yes, but that's not the important thing right now."

"Do you love them both?"

"Yes, but that's not the important thing right now."

"But you love Doctor Munye?"

"Well, he's got me by the b—s too," She answered grimly. "Put it that way." *We're all in that condition, in one way or another –*

"You'll give me five million dollars to help you get onto the island?"

"I never quoted an exact amount," She answered evasively. "But...But...whatever's in the account – it's yours!"

That blinding smile got her into the back seat of the scorching Toyota, and the next thing I knew we were frantically rolling down the windows. It didn't help.

"My God, the heat."

Kammi Kay, *big sister* – as I would soon be calling her – started complaining almost immediately.

# VI

*The Fabulous Mrs. KamYe*


*Kammi Kay! The real Kammi Kay? The richest, most hated, most beautiful, most talent - free, most famous, hottest, porn star infamous of a whole generation of Reality Royalty in America? Successor to the sexual scepter - bearer, London Astoria, the twin female regents of the dark side of the Reality empire? Wife of the planet's reigning rap star and controversial genius political theorist?* How could this be? The utmost weird afternoon of my young life...

*Will the real Kammi Kay please stand up, please stand up please stand up...*

"How do you know Tony Perkins?" I had asked this strange girl.

"I'm his lover. In fact, we were once scheduled to be secretly married. Before I met um...you know.."

"Black Jeesus! My bf's hero of heroes."

"I still don't know exactly how it all happened. It was during Sweeps Week. My Mom always puts a lot of pressure on me during Sweeps Week. I think I was supposed to make another sex tape. With Dr. Munye. The ratings would have hit the stratosphere. My Mom's really smart about these things. You may have heard of her. Kressa Kay. She's the original Tiger Mom. Well, so anyway, we made the tape, and it's locked up in a vault somewhere, and I wound up married to it."

"You're kidding me. Too many coincidences!"

"The coincidence is that you and your dad are going to interview Tony Perkins. If it weren't for that coincidence, I wouldn't have introduced myself to you. Thus, this coincidence, in such a case, wouldn't have coincided with the other coincidences. Can't you start the car and turn the a/c on?"

"No."

"Tony's wife found us out and threw me off the Cay. I've got to get back and straighten everything out. I love him desperately, and I simply must get him back."

I'd heard that exact tonality before from this individual, although it had been a season earlier, in High Def on Channel 13.

At that time, amidst a fiery carnage of flashbulbs, the stricken Reality diva had been weepily relating to reporters her feelings about her famous four - hour marriage to the black Russian hockey star, and as unconvincing as she was — *there was the language barrier, of course, that was a contributing factor, and since I don't speak his language I never had a clue what he was saying — but more than anything, our schedules were simply too, too incompatible — who knew how far away Russia is? Did Hitler even know how big the damn place is? Like, if he had, he would never have invaded. Like, he was the one who invaded, right? Hitler? That was the guy's name, right?* — as unconvincing as she had been, sobbing about the tragic, incomprehensible annulment during Sweeps Week, she was twice as unconvincing now.

Once I thought she was going to yawn between sobs. But I liked her from the get go. She had the gift, what can I say?

And I needed a big sister like the flowers need the rain.

"You're leaving the Doctor? To go back to Anthony Perkins?"

"We have an open marriage, that's all," She didn't seem eager to explain. "It's complicated. I was with Tony first. We're...bonded. There's a billion dollars in Swiss gold involved, and I already explained: I've got him by the balls. I like that in a man."

While we waited, I had to ask the question the whole world had been asking for the many months since it happened.

"Kammi, is it true – you weren't able to count from one to ten on that Reality Show, 'Counting From One to Ten With the Stars'?"

"I've never been good under pressure," She wept, never shedding a tear, and glancing just once over her hand to see if I was watching her. I hate stating the obvious. But Kammi loved being watched.

Whether she was lying about her fast food catastrophe of a marriage, or f****** some random rapper on a public beach in front of a camera's unblinking eye, or being stuck in front of a hundred million pairs of worshipful eyeballs while trying to remember the number that came after 'seven', content was irrelevant.

As long as we were watching, ratings could go nowhere but up, and if ratings were up, God was in Heaven, laughing hysterically perhaps – and all was right with the world. This much she knew.

I loved her. Maybe not as much as Tony Perkins loved her, or even her husband, the great People's Guerilla General, Doctor Munye. But I loved her.

*(Excerpted from my father's Op - Ed essay in Esquire,
"Kammi Kay: A Study In American Values")*

...Because Kammi was to her hundreds of millions of
fans what a Rorschach ink blot is to a psychotic, not a
splatter of dumb ink filling a rectangle, but instead a perfect
mirror, not of reality, but in a way of its opposite, an image
so remarkably void of any objective content, so empty that
it was capable of absorbing, reflecting and revealing every
Jungian archetype, every Freudian fantasy, mirroring in its
hypnotic vapidity the millions of utterly unique dreams
arising from the vast, hardworking, talentless spectrum
encompassing every hapless secretary and clerk, line
worker, cook, janitor, maid, telemarketer, butcher, baker,
and candlestick maker the planet - wide: *whatever it is before
me that I see, that so arrests my eyes, it is nothing, an illusion, a
cipher, and yet whatever it is I see, just like a Rorschach, in essence it
is me, and thus it is forgiving, and designed to be forgiven — it is
perfect, accurate, truthful, inclusive. And it is famous.*

I loved my big sister, then as now. She's not to be
trusted. But she's the planet's ultimate default selfie.

\* \* \*

She needed a ride. She needed a place to stay.
Nobody knew she was here. She was momentarily broke.
She would explain why later. She would explain everything
later.

The important thing was, she needed to be on that
airboat tomorrow, pretending to be my big sister.

No, wait, even better — my heavily disguised Saudi
housekeeper. Sunglasses, hijab, shapeless oversized Wal -
Mart black tunic...

"Wal - Mart?" She cried in fear. *"Wal - Mart?"*

She needed Chanel, she needed prescription acne medication, she needed this, she needed that. *Pre - emptive,* that's such a pretty word, don't you agree? Use it in a sentence? Okay, how about this: Kammi Kay's personal needs were always utterly *pre - emptive.*

My beautiful, slightly buzzed Daddy came wandering out of the bar shortly thereafter.

"Daddy, there's a girl in our car. A famous girl. A famous - all - over - the - planet girl."

"Damn it, I'm not adopting her. Stop bringing in strays, sweetheart. Particularly humans. No more adoptions." *No more rabbits. And damn sure no more human beings!*

"It's Kammi Kay."

"The girl on the sex tape?"

"Yes. The Reality Queen."

"At Pauley Vee's? I don't think so."

"It's Crystal Lagoon," I explained. "It seems to draw beautiful women like a magnet."

"I don't think so."

"I don't think so either." I shrugged. "But somehow I know so."


*(Jess to Angela, 1040pm Friday)*


*Jess: hi oh dear A, so exctd about this trip..in the a.m. meetin th big boyz..ovr the moon! B's gonna luv ths..This island is gettin biggest media coverage in the state.. B says he's joining the Ghost Posse posse. The ones doing the attack. But they won't let him in.. too young. just as well B is a lover not a fighter..lol! Besides Dr. is using the attack to unify the crips and bloods .. Gonna fly elements of both*

*groups in from LA. that's Abe Lincoln - level thinking. KK*
*promised me five mil. Then down to fifty thou. Now 2 thou. To get*
*her onto the island. ..Kammi wouldn't know the truth if it bit her*
   *Angela: About Barry*
   *Jess: I tell u KK is biggr in life than tv even*
   *Angela: Is her butt as big as they show on tv*
   *Jess: Monstrous...Designed by Pixar...cute tho*
   *Angela: She came on to your dad?*
   *Jess: She said she wished he was black. What does that tell*
*you*

   *Angela:..i've been sort of sad, feel hungover...something to tell*
*u Jess I messed up J .. dont know how to say this*
   *Jess: Kammi would love Barry..A black virgin male. Rare*
   *Angela: have something to tell u J..concerning that subject..*
   *Jess: finally told him i'm in love w/ him..but by txt..that*
*doesn't count does it? lol*
   *Angela:..he told me...we went out last night..spur of the*
*moment..*
   *Jess: u and b?*
   *Angela: Still don't know how it happened*
   *Jess: ?*
   *Angela: still getting my nerve up wait a minute*
   *Jess: ?????????????????*
   *Jess: ok luv*
   *Angela: he showed me yr texts*
   *Jess: ?! not cool*
   *Angela: ik*
   *Jess: ?*
   *Angela: Kammi there in the motel w u 2?*
   *Jess: Cleaning baseboards w one hand, txting her mom with*
*the othr*
   *Angela: Big ass ha I knew it. Secret to her sucess in*
*America. America's a sick puppy. That's why I'm joining peace corps*

*and moving to Viet Nam...feel like leaving Tally today...nxt flight out*

*Jess: secret to her success is you can look right through her and still see yourself... like a motel landscape painting... safe .. no content to interfere with image*

*Angela: u like her?*

*Jess: I love her.*

*Angela: never miss an episode. so sad about the black russian hockey player.. how could she know he was gay? Or that he was already married to a Bolshoi ballerina? He tried to tell her but she doesn't speak Russian.. starcrossed from the beginning like Romeo and Juliet.. Total coincidence it all happened during Sweeps Week...everything always happens to her during Sweeps Week..*

*Jess:. At least dad & me get a look at how the other one fifty thousandth of one per cent lives..when we go ovr....so what the h up*

*Angela: J, I want us always to be the Oscarteers...Swear we wil b*

*Jess: Always grl...?*

*Angela: Its so important to me u feel that way..I love u child*

*Jess: you and Phong should change bodies. u 2 were switched at birth. She wants to be the cheerleader for the Texas Longhorns, u want to muck around in the rice paddies disarming land mines*

*Angela: .. bleak world today*

*Jess: U ok?*

*Angela: not really*

*Jess: like Oscar said, 'youth is the only thing worth having.'..whut up?*

*Angela: ....actually wish i could go back a day just erase yesterday*

*Jess: What happened yesterday..u & b?*

*Angela: trying to think of a way to explain it..wait*

*Jess: Well— But wouldn't all our brand new experiences just get old after being repeated? U can't lose virginity but one time, no matter how long u r 15 — isn't that the best part of being young?*

*New sights, sounds, tastes, touches .. Even if we stayed young our experiences wouldn't .. wouldn't it be awful to experience life like old trogs do one day just walk around hating every minute and snarling at everybody, but still in our hot sixteen year old bodies and faces, all twisted up from the awareness of what reality is really like?*

*Angela: Maybe old trogs are that way because they still love life but feel betrayed because life doesn't love them back — not enough to let them keep living*

*Jess: Everything we study now, friction, gravity, resistance — one day these are the forces the gods send to kill us..fire wld be bad*

*Angela:..J pls believ me i luv u like sister luv u so much...oscateers everything t me*

*Jess: ik sistah grl...got ur nrv up yet?...?*

*Angela: tell me about kk*

*Jess: Somethin on that island has got k absolutely obsessed..keeps bitching about her wrinkles..like her Dorian portrait got out of the closet and stuck itself to her face*

*Angela: Is that what they do on that island — they have a way to keep u youngr longer*

*Jess:.. what's the big news u want to tell me? gtta sign off soon*

*Angela: feel i'm gonna throw up*

*Jess: Who's the new Oscar Wilde fan you mentioned*

*Angela: Barry.*

*Jess: why am i not surprised*

*Angela: need take a deep breath*

*Jess: i already did when u started this*

*Angela: i betrayed u jess. he put something in some wine..my fault I take full fault for it but i think he tricked m too*

*Jess: oh ok.....??! We talkn That Thing?*

*Angela: o god this is the worst had to let u know right away not thru grapevine*

*Jess: ok*

*Angela: the worst*

*Jess: oh*

*Angela; jesu end of th world*

*Jess: Guess i sort of knew it. he's obsessed w/ u..He's mensa smart...smooth too...is that what u wanted to tell me...I'll always love u angel*

*Angela: Oh this is hard...guys gossip..wanted u to hear it from me first*

*Jess: oh he's a charmer..smooth operator lk the song*

*Angela: didn't mean for it to go that far*

*Jess: He's been obsessed w u since day one...'the silver fox'..*

*Angela: u hate me?..he must have put something in my wine...I'd never done coke before...swear to u, once only, never again, never, won't happen again..feel like slit my wrists*

*Jess: it's okay. I love u grl. Chix b4 dix*

*Angela: i love u J...we still the 3 oscarteers?*

*Jess: always..i blame him only not u..u r so sweet..glad u told me..better 2 kno*

*Angela: think he's goin for Phong nxt..he kept talking about her..like a game w him*

*Jess: i leave town for like a day and he goes to work fast and furious..should hav known*

*Angela: warn phong*

*Jess: She hates him*

*Angela: so do i..now*

*Jess: that'll be fun..she'll play him along, then when least expected.. lol..she hates B..she had him figured out long ago but i was blind.. u know what I hate?*

*Angela: forgive me? pls*

*Jess: I hate growing up, angie, think I just did grow up a little just now....it's awful..it's like a sprain, goes thru yr body and soul at same time...and then presto u r older*

*Angela: I feel the same J..it hurts so bad what i did to u. wisdom comes from loss but age comes from betrayal..think i just aged ten yrs..i deserve it..can't think straight today he put something in my drink i just know it..everythin double vision since I woke up*

*Jess: u still the foxiest on the sidelines..don't blame yourself for being irresistible*

*Angela: J please forgive me..feel so hungover, cant forgive myself*

*Jess: dont think twice its alright...chixs b4 dixs. always*

*Angela: always..lemme explain —*

*Jess: dlos must blaze. get some sleep no worries love ya its all a big joke anyway so worn out can't wait to hit the feathers*

*Angela: swear u frgive dearest sista pls...jess.. u there? My Oscarteer? u there?*

*Jess: Love u always dearest. Peace out Jessica out*

*(Angela signs off 1059pm Fri. night est)*


Needless to say, Dear Diary, I slept not a wink the long night. I remember to this moment an image that appeared before me in the half - lit darkness of the motel room, Kammi snoring like a stevedore next to me, having sucked up the mini - bar's entire stock of tequila.

There, by the dresser across the room, fled the ghostly memory of ten year old tomboy Jessica, as spotless and fresh - starched as the white piano recital frock she was wearing as she ran away, as in a dream, running in terror, fleeing a monster, but then tripping, crawling, falling into the dirt rabbit - hole of horrifying adult truth, clawing at the roots, the serpentlike vines and debris that had hidden the trap, struggling to climb back out, to get back to freedom and fresh air, to the piano recital she'd snuck out of, but instead I watched as the ghostly memory of a child vanished for ever, vanished without even a scream.

That was a moment of vivid waking nightmare in a night without sleep. I never have forgotten that one.

So the night passed slowly by.

I lay there, watching my childhood self wave goodbye to what was left of it, felt myself growing up, a little more with every slow tick of the clock, with every laughably absurd endless minute.

Growing up, even a little during the night, was at times sort of breathless – I felt the small bones that had always formed a protective cage around the emotional center of my heart began breaking, one after another, only from the heart outward. Fortunately, in all youth, those twinkling starry places within can only shatter a single time.

# VII

*Hard night, harsh dawn.*

*To be? To do? To have?*
*—Ancient Bedouin Paradox*

Dawn's first streaky moments of pink light appeared over the mangrove marshes to the west of the marina's long, shaky dock where the three of us stood, waiting for Roseanne's airboat to arrive and haul us from the fringe of Spanish Swamp – Old Florida as it once was – to Oz, to Versailles, to the modern barbered Old Florida of the One Per Centers.

Daddy and Kammi Kay looked shakier than the dock.

*It doesn't surprise me a bit that Barry nailed my best friend. He's had a thing for Angela since he first got a glimpse of that long platinum pelt. Princess Cantaloupes. Head cheerleader. 'She's the ultimate kill'. His words. Almost broke us up then. Should have. Congratulations, Charmer. And guess what? I'll bet he'll tell me he's still loyal to me. In his own way. I have to learn to handle any emotion. My parents already broke my heart, it can't happen twice. Maybe my heart will even get stronger in the broken place. Maybe I'll just get bitchier. Like Mom. Growing up is what I always knew it would be – a joke. With a mean punchline that might even be funny from time to time but still hurts your feelings. every time you hear it.*

*Wonder if I was – am – always will be – in love with him? It's a cinch that it's one thing that doesn't matter anymore. And never will again, God be my witness.*

"I have the flu," Kammi complained. We had disguised her in a black hijab and a shapeless burka - like tunic, as our Saudi housekeeper. Black two dollar Wal - Mart sunglasses obscured the cobra - blade of her face right down to the frown. There was a chance it would work.

"Doesn't anybody on this dock have an aspirin?"

"Kammi, I thought you didn't drink."

When caught in an outright lie, her instinctive rhetorical technique was to merely stick out her tongue. A winning riposte.

But this time, instead, she replied with a canned answer that revealed that the cameras had been watching her every move for so long that somehow, way out here at the end of a dock in the Gulf of Mexico when it was still so early even God hadn't woke up yet, she must have instinctively believed that somehow even out here the cameras were on her still.

"I never drink. Drinking's immoral. I try to always be a role model for my fans, especially the kids. The kids are so important to me – and to our future." *It's all about the kids.*

Dad and I looked at each other.

"But, Kammi, how can you even – "

"Here's our taxi," Daddy interrupted, even though the hum of the airboat was as distant as the misty horizon.

"I'll do whatever's necessary. I've gotta see Tony again and get all this straightened out. I love him!"

"What about the Doctor? Didn't he buy you, like, a billion dollar wedding ring?"

Kammi brightened. "Oh, you watch the show?"

"Sometimes," I grudgingly admitted.

"Why didn't you say so!"

"I did – last night. You just didn't hear me." *You were on the phone with your mirror. Touché!*

"Which sister do you like the best?" The puffiness in Kammi's face had suddenly departed, replaced by the radiance of youth and total self - involvement.

"Uh, you, probably. I hate the tall one. She looks like Frankenstein..."

"Kory? I agree!" Kammi laughed in total delight. "I absolutely agree! Never tell her I said so. We think her dad is, uh, not the same guy as our dad, not that it matters. Who do you think is the prettiest?" She smiled widely and blinked her pitchfork eyelashes almost in self - parody. "Be brutally honest!"

"How much do they pay you to let the cameras follow you around?"

"Money isn't everything!"

Then she leaned close and whispered an amount into my ear that caused me to gasp in disbelief.

"Liar!"

"*How* much?"

"That's not counting residuals or some other back - ends I'm not at liberty to discuss," She added primly.

Even Sherlock, who'd been performing his dadster duties of scanning the water for our taxi, leaned a little to catch what she was pitching. Before his eyes returned to the horizon, Daddy and I exchanged a disbelieving glance. I wondered if I looked as dazed as he did.

"Why don't you just buy the damned island, and Mr. Tony Perkins with it. Pocket change to you, Kammi!"

Kammi cast her lovely eyes to the horizon.

"Uh uh. There's money, and then there's *real* money. The Perkins' brothers have the real money. It's almost unimaginable. Money buys people. Real money buys the future."

"Tell me about the brother," Daddy asked, shoving his flask back in his journalist's bag. It brightened him instantly.

"Oh, Tom's the good - looking one," Kammi remembered. "They're both good looking, but Tom's...Tom could be a movie star. He's a lawyer."

"We hear your husband is organizing an attempt to seize this island in the name of Africa America. It's not part of America. This would be more like an attack on Cuba, or some other foreign land. Do you know anything about that? Is any of it even true?"

She sighed. "Believe me, I've tried. I've tried everything. The island really *should* belong to my husband's people. It was theirs till Reconstruction, and it's going to be theirs again. Nothing can stop it, really. The American government is behind my husband's movement all the way to the very highest level. I tried to persuade Tony to just surrender peacefully, and just walk away. I was making progress. But that bitch wife of his has it in for me. Less than a week ago – I was *banished! Me! No longer on the List! Impossible!*"

Island Security had shoved her into a croker sack, onto Roseanne's airboat kicking and screaming, a hell to leather fifty minute bouncing roar of a boat ride, a half - mile walk through the Big Bend's mucky mainland mangrove marshes once she'd been dumped off, and next thing you know, the world - famous but now much - chastened queen was introducing herself to me outside a bar and begging a hitch back to little ole soon - to - be New Haiti.

As President Nixon famously said, *when the president says it, it's true.* KK had the same opinion of anything that came out of her own pretty mouth.

Daddy thinks I'm the best little liar in Florida, but, looking back on it, I couldn't hold a candle to *HMS Kammi Kay.*

"My hair still smells like those oyster bags," Kammi noted bitterly. "Tommy has it in for me. He's protecting his brother from me. It's not my fault that Tony is crazy out of his mind in love with me."

"You could reach Tony Perkins with a phone call. There's something else going on, Kammi. Something about the island."

"I have no idea what you're talking about." Once again, the Diva's eyes started to shift about. "For once, can't somebody trust that I'm telling the God's truth?"

"Have you got money stashed over there? Something of value?"

"I mean, look at me – Tony's wife has reduced me to wearing a Wal - Mart mu - mu, dirty shoes, motel hair conditioner, I feel like I'm coming down with the flu – "

"That's called a hangover, honey," Daddy commented.

"It's the flu! I don't even drink! The point is, that bitch threw me off the island and kept everything that belonged to me, even my favorite Prada!" *Jack, she fluttered her world - famed lashes, thank you for fronting the money to buy another i, what on God's earth would I do without it – had to let mama know I'm okay...*

*I could have been a peacemaker between the Perkins's and my husband. I might have even won the Nobel Prize. That would make my enemies shut it about that silly one to ten business, once and for all!*

"How would you have resolved the conflict?" Daddy asked, as if his question was just idle conversation. "I hadn't realized the problem had reached this...international... level. We were just down here to do a sort of fluff piece."

"Oh, I can resolve anything regarding Tony Perkins. He's so in love with me he can't think straight. I *so* have him by the b****. He'll do anything I ask."

She looked beseechingly first at Daddy, then at me.

"I've just got to make it onto the island. Thank you both so much for helping me. You're not just helping me, you're helping the cause of world peace!"

"Will we have trouble getting on the island?" I asked her.

"I've *got* to see Tony. That bitch wife of his – "

"His wife shouldn't prevent that," Daddy looked at the Reality Goddess very directly. "In fact, according to my information, which I'm certain is accurate, Tony Perkins doesn't *have* a wife." My father's face was impassive, but his beautiful brown eyes stared down our stowaway, watchful and unblinking. "In fact, he's *never* been married."

"I said *fiancé!* I never said wife, never. His *fiancé!* Oh, our ride is here!" Cried Kammi gratefully, distracting us from what would otherwise have become an awkward moment.

Daddy gave me a look of near - amazement that said, roughly translated, *has this woman said one thing since we've known her that contains even a single kernel of Truth?*

I shrugged and we both laughed. We'd mounted the Tiger. It would not be our option now to decide when to get off.

"Roseanne!" I waved both arms over my head and responded to her chomp with another of my own.

"Our pilot. She was at Pauley Vee's," Daddy remarked. "She's as good as her word, thank God." The airboat, aluminum, dirty and flat - bottomed, was bumping against the barnacled dock pilings below us. She held the bow skillfully against the tide. Still, the dock shook every time a gentle wave took the nose of the skiff into it.

"Oh, I know her," Kammi scowled.

"All aboard that's going aboard." Roseanne shouted from below.

"All it's costing us is gas and a case of short Bud. And fifty bucks. Want to split it with us, Kammi?"

The Diva pretended to have missed the question. She was staring down at Roseanne. They obviously recognized each other.

"Just love the tats'," Kammi smiled sarcastically, rolling her pretty, bloodshot eyes… "It's all coming back to me now."

"Hello, Snake Eyes," Roseanne called jovially. "Welcome back."

"This airboat doesn't seem well - designed for the Gulf."

"I ain't drowned thus far," Roseanne gave a raucous laugh that broke the stillness of the dawn. "One other thing — "

Dad was halfway down the rotted ladder.

"Sure."

"The chick don't ride with you two. Wasn't in the contract."

"Why not?"

"Tommy says so. She don't ride."

"She's our housekeeper."

"And I'm Madam Butterfly. It's a no - go."

"You've despised me since I made fun of your tatoos," Kammi Kay hissed at her. "Guess what: *I'm going.* I've got to see Tony!"

Kammi started for the ladder.

"The chick don't ride."

*Chick - chick!*

Kammi and I found ourselves staring down into the twin barrels of a twelve gauge sawed - off shotgun.

And that was that.


As the airboat pulled away into the grey soft waters of the Gulf, I didn't bother looking back over my shoulder at the sad, shapeless black figure on the dock in the receding misty distance. I knew I would see her again.

I already knew my new big sister well enough to know nothing would stop her from attaining her goal. I would see her again on Crystal Lagoon, hell or high water, God be my witness.

> *Farewell and adieu*
> *to you fair Spanish ladies…*
> *Farewell and adieu*
> *To you ladies of Spain…*


\* \* \*


*Diary Memories, Written Years Later, of Kammi Kay and my First visit to Eden, and my First Glimpse of Tom…Memories I Wish Never to Forget…*

One of the Sikh security guys had picked us up by jeep after a pretty hairy departure from the airboat onto a sea - wall at the base of the great limestone hill that rose from the Gulf.

The eventual beauty of Eden was disguised by a barren, pock - marked white walled - off facade, with a thousand hungry - looking sea birds circling in the empty skies overhead...The jeep came down the limestone berm via a series of steep switchbacks. Roseanne skillfully held the bow against the tide; and then we were gratefully on land again...

The trip across the island was fifteen minutes, up an elevator, to an ante - room off the King's office, where we sat, napped, and waited...

"Hello, Jessica," Tommy's soft voice was next to my ear. "Sorry to have kept you guys waiting so long. Tony's been having a melt - down lately. But it's okay now. My brother's ready for his close - up."

*My God.*

We'd been sitting in a small, mahogany jewel - like, sconce - lit ante - room next to Tony Perkins' office on the island. We'd been waiting an hour. It seemed like a week.

"His close - up?" I laughed. "That's from 'Sunset Boulevard.'" I wanted to impress him.

"Maybe you could wake up Poppa?"

"I'm awake." I felt dad sit up fast.

"Well, we're ready to go if you are," The King's attorney smiled. Tommy's good looks weren't exactly friendly, but his manner was beautifully correct. He felt me staring at him and frowned.

"Kammi wanted to come with us but the lady, Roseanne, wouldn't let her on the boat. She said it was your orders."

"That's right. She's a friend of this island. Did you know Roseanne used to teach economic philosophy at Chiefland College? She comes across like a truck - driver now. All part of the proletarian curtain she hides behind. Like the tatoos."

"But why?"

"There's a federal warrant out for her. Back from the radical days. We won't mention that, will we?"

"No we won't!"

"Once she tried to save the world. What's that old Bob Dylan line? *'To live outside the law/ You must be honest.'* A very brave lady, that one. Willing to risk her life for her beliefs. Leave it at that."

"I love her."

"Well, let's go in, then."

As I entered King Perkins' office, I was still combing the Gulf salt out of my hair. The forty - minute voyage from Earth to Oz had been breathtaking, scary and thrilling. I'm quite the little landlubber. Daddy sensed the fragility of our aluminum conveyance, not to mention the beer - swilling skipper who kept yelling at the trailing gulls, swooping down through the mists...

The grey gulf waters had shattered off the forward sweep of the airboat's bow. Heavy, rippling waves, from the white wakes of departing fishing boats, slapped in hard, loud, irregular patterns across the light aluminum hull, causing Roseanne to fight the tiller angrily a couple of times.

The dawn sky was streaky blue red, the contrasting shades of light pulled together by damp, rolling grey clouds of chilly mist. In an hour under the August sun, the mists would have long vanished, against the cry of the birds, the roar of the big fan, the vague stench of fish guts coming from somewhere, and the beating of the Gulf against the boat's thin aluminum skin.

"Crystal Lagoon is Heaven on the half - shell," Captain Roseanne had shouted at one point in the forty - minute voyage. "I hope the brothers can save it. If anybody can, those two can. Never underestimate those sweethearts… that's my advice."

*In time to come I would recall that advice as being some of the best I've ever gotten in life…*

We all ducked under the incoming wet morning wind. I huddled down and wrapped my arms around myself. I glimpsed Dad reach into his book bag. I knew why.

"What's it like over there?" I shouted. "Will we be in danger?"

"That's the purtiest place you'll ever lay eyes on in this life," Roseanne replied. "Maybe Mr. Perkins stole the place, but it was God who invented it. You won't believe it. Straight out of a science fiction movie. Shangri - la."

"I can't wait!"

"That magic tree dominates everything. But if you look closer, you'll see what I'm talking about…Not a skeeter on the whole island! Can you believe it? That ain't Florida. That's Heaven!" She gave that great laugh that caused the birds to fly up. "Strawberries grow wild all over the island – big as lightbulbs. Mangoes, avocados, they grow year round, cantaloupes... We used to try to guess the different continents the melons came from, they was all different, and delicious. Sweet. And the tree - fruit... You don't even have to reach your arm up. Even gardens of corn, the cobs as big as your forearm. And huge golden daffodils, like canaries, frozen in flight, as far as the eye can see. Unbelievable. Man."

"No mosquitoes? Perhaps in the winter – " Daddy started to correct her. He was shouting over the roar of the fan and the smash - slap of the waves.

"My people have lived on this coast three hundred years, Sugar Ray. There ain't no skeeters on that island. Period. It's purtier than Cypress Gardens. And it was like that before Tony and Tom showed up. God built that island. Or aliens. I wouldn't hazard a guess which."

*The Ruminations of Ms. Kammi Kay*

As the previous evening at the motel had progressed, after we'd returned from Wal - Mart and Kammi was attempting to wash away the shame of it all with miniature after miniature of Cuervo from the motel mini - bar, I had an opportunity to study this most dynamic and pre - eminent of Reality Stars....

She was obsessively selfie - ing, sucking down tequila, coming on to Dad, scrubbing the room's dirty baseboards, texting her Mom, reading *People,* and not minding in the slightest as her new little sister studied her every move and moment. She was used to it. The whole planet did that.

Kammi hesitated, and I remembered a look in her eyes I'd not seen previously. She was forming another memory. There was a sudden dark depth in those amazing eyes I'd never before seen, not in person nor on television.

For an eternal child of eternal fame, who'd never had an actual childhood, I thought I glimpsed, just for a moment, an echoing black cave of sadness, of wistful sadness.

Underneath it all, I always had the feeling that, emotionally, and – who knows, even intellectually – another human being existed under Kammi's irresistible surface. How can you feel sadness, unless you possess a soul?

*A glimpse, just for a moment, of her soul secretly searching for itself, resonating inside of my big sister's artificial, almost clownish façade.*

*Emotionally Kammi was all over the map; the camera daily showed her who she must be. She was the ever changing image inside the last photograph taken of her, each image different, each image bigger than life... her soul was a lifelong continually explosively coagulating universe of converging pixelations.*

*But in rare moments of self - reflection, you sensed her trying to gather in the bits and bytes of her incandescent chaotic fame into a coherent reality she could recognize, and love. It didn't happen often; she loved being famous. That was usually enough for Kammi Kay.*

*But sometimes... sometimes, when she was staring into a mirror, you realized this amazing, inexplicably charismatic beauty was studying – no, hunting for something – looking for something more than the age - lines around that miraculously empty smile. I realize now, she was looking for her own soul. Or trying to achieve at least a glimpse of its embryonic formulation...*

"My mom's PR people have done a number on the brothers' reputation," Kammi shrugged.

"The Media makes the island sound like 1938 Germany. That the Perkins' are like the Nazis who ruled Germany then."

"More like Jonestown," I threw in.

"Please call it 'New Haiti'," She quickly reprimanded us. *"As we think, so we become*', that's what my husband says. And he's a genius. He says, '*language corrupts thought more than thought corrupts language*'." She put the palm of her hand over her mouth and burped. "It's 'New Haiti' anyway. Just remember that. It's no longer Crystal Lagoon."

"George Orwell authored that last quote."

"Well, my husband *sampled* it. My husband's almost as famous as me. His name is Dr. Munye. You can't get sued for sampling. My husband has lawyers. He has the best lawyers in Hollywood. Vanilla Ice sued my husband. Vanilla Ice *lost*."

She paused.

"Tom... Tony... Oh, those crazy guys – I miss them. New Haiti is the loveliest, most gentle, easiest world to be in. It's Heaven on Earth."

"Seriously!"

"Oh, I miss that whole place so much! Oh, I can't let myself think that way! Tony – I *loved* Tony. He never cheated on me. Maybe Kressa will let me move back during Sweeps Week." Kammi had shrugged sadly, as if to explain everything weird about her often very weird behavior. "I have to plan everything around Sweeps Week."

Kressa Kay – *salud!*


"Look at this, will you?" Kammi shouted. "Four pages of Kardashians! They absolutely dominate this rag! Me and my shadows!"

Kammi had been angrily slapping through the pages of a two month old *People*, she'd stolen, oh excuse me, borrowed from the motel lobby when we were checking in just before dusk. I could barely hear her curse - filled commentary toward the photo - spread she was now holding up to my face, the magazine folded back, its interior pages crowded with grinning Kardashians.

"Look at them!"

I nodded. "Horrible." *Oh, those fat asses!*

"Exactly! *Look* at this! Four pages dedicated to these epic Biscuits!"

"You're so much more beautiful than she is, big sister..."

"Kim Kardashian! Everywhere I go, she's just a step behind. Oh, and this bitch (inaudible) copies and cheapens everything I do...(inaudible) American way. At least I (inaudible) modeled my career after a *true* queen, London Astoria...(inaudible) Kim worships, copies and underprices everything about that... that vodka - swilling B list trust fund (inaudible) %xx@##* *Hilton!*"

Kammi shoved the magazine in front of my face again.

"Look at this picture," My new big sister's voice echoed angrily in my ear. "The colors of their faces are switched. Annie Liebowitz photoshopped it. *Kim looks like she's black.. and Kanye looks like he's white.* That's exactly my point..."

"Epidermal Regression!" I cried.

"That's what you're *supposed* to think. But it's not Epidermal Regression. It's photoshopping. "She laughed bitterly. "Imagine how they'd look if Epidermal Regression hit them. I'd love to see God switch those two."

"It's not God, it's something to do with some chemical in water sometimes. Black people turn white, and vice versa. The water causes you to swap skin color."

"Oh, I know that. But *God's* behind it. God's behind everything. That's why I'm so famous. It's God's Will. If He made Kim and Kanye switch skin color... l - o - l, little sister. If Kanye was white, he couldn't get a job shining shoes at O'Hare airport. What would a zebra be without its stripes?"

I nodded. I hated them too.

"The Kardashians are incapable of shame. Just like Hillary Clinton. It's almost a form of evolutionary superiority."

"Kim will never overtake me. You think Kris Jenner could ever outfight my Tiger Mom, Kressa? Ha. That's a laugh. L - O - L." *Nobody beats Kressa. Nooo — body. Not even the Perkins' brothers! Probably not even them. And they can fight.*

"You're so much more beautiful than Kim, big sister." I don't mind repeating myself when it's honest flattery. "If you two ever stood together on the red carpet, side by side, all the cameras would focus on you first."

"Yes, that would destroy her. She would be doomed then for eternity. The camera loves *me* more. She would *never* recover."

She finished off another Cuervo miniature.

A self - involved, pleased smile crossed my big sister's face. "Her can is *so* photoshopped. Black or white, it's a bright shining lie."

I laughed at that, and she brightened momentarily. Then she looked sick.

"Oh, God — Wal - Mart."

"It's the only place in central Florida that sells Burkas."

She suddenly brightened. Another miniature landed in a trash can by the bed.

"Did you see what *Time Magazine* said about *my* can?"

"Uh uh."

"I can almost quote it exact, from memory. I memorized their words. Their editorial stated *my* can was as famous in the twenty first century as that other guy's soup cans were in the twentieth. What was his name, Andy..Andy...Andy...Hardy? Warhol? That's it. Andy Warhol. *Time* said his soup cans captured the sadness of America's repetitive consumerist banality. But *my* can represents *this* century's post - industrial descent into the sensual corruption of cyber - image..."

"That's quite a mouthful, big sister."

"I was so proud! Took three days to memorize it! Whoever said I couldn't count from one to ten! I just froze, that's all. *My* can is the nation's prevalent aesthetic icon, better known than the liberty bell or the Washington Monument – imagine that! They took a poll! *Suck on it, Kimmy baby – !*"

*Bow down, all you other fat asses, and despair! Including the Kartrashians, let me add...*

"There can only be one queen, and I am *she*." Kammi added imperiously, tossing *People* onto the worn beige motel carpet and returning to her life's foremost duty – selfies. Typical big sister.


So, this morning as Dad and I had awaited entry into King Perkins's mysterious *sanctum sanctorum,* I had spent the long hour, salty and half - asleep, recounting the previous night's fascinating encounter with the world - famous

Reality Star and the shade her genius threw across my own young existence.

*In the brown motel room, the lightning and the lightning bug – humbling insights, to be sure – invaluable nonetheless.*

Each time Kammi's flashbulb selfies burst in the dreary room, I sensed Time halt, if for a moment.

But like the *Terminator,* Time always rose again from its momentary arrest, and again and again lurched implacably forward.

This was my fifteen year old subconscious working, always a part of me hearing the heartbeat of the clock of my youth ticking away, and suddenly without warning a kind of deep emotional desolation swept over me.

B's betrayal was only a part of it, though I could tell it was a big part; out of nowhere came another memory – one of our favorite teen - aged Oscar - isms, from our formerly so beloved, now utterly shattered, Daughters of Dorian: *friends stab you from the front.*

But I had already known that. Maybe just now I had felt it for the first time. Knowing and feeling are two different levels.


"Damn it, I look so puffy!" I heard Kammi mutter. "I look a thousand years old."

No, it was more than the betrayal of a front - stabbing boyfriend and a once - upon - a - time 'best friend forever' that so suddenly hurt my heart, it was the terrible pressure of time passing through me that had been troubling me more and more, time sliced up next to me by the strobelike intrusion of big sister's i, as she snapped selfie after selfie in the big motel bed, time momentarily frozen and slammed down image by image but unstoppable all the same, time passing through me harsher and more bitterly than any sea wind, stinging my eyes with the horrific truth of immortal Oscar's most damning axiom of all, *youth is the only thing worth having.*

Youth was leaving me already, as a soul leaves a dazed body while still alive, and nothing could stay its departure, nothing could stop its going, not a million selfies, not a million shots of my mother's best Scotch.

I had a couple of thousand days left of pure youth. After that, one outcome only: *Life.* I could almost hear the judge's gavel crash down.

And somehow I understood exactly what that one word sentence meant...

As Roseanne had expertly guided us toward Crystal Lagoon, across the morning on the friendly shoulder of the sea, approaching what we would all learn later on was Paradise itself, and approaching our interview with the two handsome, mysterious young gazillionaires who presided over Eden's stupendous bounty, what should have been one of the most exciting mornings of my whole life, instead had settled upon my heart like a deep aching illness; on this beautiful morning, traveling toward one of the all - time greatest teenage adventures ever available to most girls, I could still barely breathe from a relentless, eery pressure that made it barely possible to swallow, much less choke back further tears down past the heavy lump in my throat... *Slow, deep breaths, slow, deep breaths...*

The sad music of Oscar's immortal words echoed through me, rose and fell with the pitch and yaw of our little vessel, as we approached Eden, Oscar's cruel reminder as softly whispered and as simultaneously as ghostly and all

- powerful as the encompassing wind, the handful of words that said everything, that said it all, *youth is the only thing worth having, the only thing worth having… worth having…*

Tom swung open the door to his brother's office.

Our eyes met. There's a theory that a girl knows within seven seconds whether she wants to make love with a guy she's just met. It didn't take me nearly that long. But I'm fifteen, I still believe in love at first sight. He was stunning.

*My God.*

I would soon learn that both Perkins brothers had beautiful eyes, but when Tom looked at you, there was a hardness, mixed with a kind of crazy humorousness, in his gaze – the grey irises reflected a sort of pitiless gleam, cold as chips of flint, expressing an inner hardness and cynical intellectual caution I had sometimes glimpsed in my own father's eyes.

There was simply no question. Tom had that complicated facial structure that the best looking guys have, half dumb - looking, half - intelligent, kind of reminiscent of the screen actor Channing Tatum. By day, girls want to see the one side of a guy, by night the other.

"Stop staring at him, Jessica!" Dad hushed me, and in we went.

# Part II

# VIII

*The Tree of Knowledge of Good and Evil*

San Simeon castle was the model architecturally for
the great edifice King Perkins had spent two hundred fifty
million dollars building for himself and his legacy of 'right
living' – I'd read that fact amidst the flackery Dadster had
given me the night before.

He got his money's worth. *No doubt.* Frank Gehry
had added silvery, hammered gull - wing wild curving wind
- scoops across the cupolas and battlements, along all its
angled heights, giving the ancient design of the castle the
dancing, jubilant energy of a giant bird about to take flight.
It *so* worked, this blending of old with new...

When we'd first arrived, our jeep pulled to an abrupt
halt underneath the white towers that flanked the big rust -
colored front gates. The gates were twice the size of one of
our famous *Florida Orange Juice* billboards, covered with

ornate religious looking scrollwork, and guarded by a couple of guys trying to act like they were gardening, around the goldfish ponds out front. But even I had no trouble seeing they were armed with automatic weapons.

The fountains, flowers, gardens and fishponds stretched outward from the walls and towers of the castle for vast, sunlit distances, shimmering in the August morning sunlight.

Now, suddenly I understood what Roseanne had been talking about. In the near distance, partially hidden by the castle wall...

That tree...OMFG!

"That tree!"

"The brothers will tell you all about it, Jessica," Our Sikh guide softly explained, his British accent perfectly inflected.

Even the morning air in this magic place seemed twenty degrees cooler than the world of the Gulf of Mexico around us, and miraculously, seemingly completely free of Florida's true state bird, not the Glock Nine, as Barry had insisted – the mosquito.

Then I remembered, *Toto, we're not in Florida any more.* We can't be.

Crystal Lagoon was an island nation, beyond the twelve - mile limit, an island kingdom apparently beyond the reach of FBI and mosquito alike...

I managed to briefly engaged Tom in a chat about the brilliance of the castle's designer, Frank Gehry.

"I've studied all his designs. He's far greater than Frank Lloyd Wright. Maybe the best architect ever."

Now Tom looked at me, impressed. The intelligent aspect of his face projected itself. And he even smiled at me.

"Actually, that's sort of the theme of this whole island. Crystal Lagoon – where the past and the future converge... Where all Time becomes a figure 8..."

"Thanks for inviting us, Mr. Perkins. It's an honor."

"Call me Tom. And I'll call you Jack. And your beautiful young daughter – Jessica?"

"Correct - o," I gave him a blinding smile. That didn't work either.

"My brother Tony is a great admirer of your past writings. Your series on the dog track graft is a masterpiece, well worthy of the Pulitzer. Talent like that deserves special praise. It's why we chose you for this interview and cover. We need your talent. We especially need your integrity. We can't out - lie our opponents. We're getting set up for a beat - down. There's a gunfight side to this thing, and a propaganda side. We have to beat them by telling the truth."

Daddy shrugged again.

"Given the current state of my career, I'm not immune to flattery."

"It looks like my brother's going to be busy a little longer – why don't I give you guys a tour of the courtyard. We can go bouncing around in the jeep some more too. The island is bigger than it looks."

"Great!"

"Yes!"

Down the elevator, out into the incredible courtyard, under the immense spreading shade of the tree of Good and Evil, I believe is how it was described then...

I think I caught the briefest boyish blush in my father's face when Tommy praised his writing.

Nobody's immune to the kind of money and power that we'd observed on our short drive from the barnacled sea - wall to the castle.

The pockmarked white hill, rising high and broad above the Gulf, made a wondrous disguise for the Edenesque environment beyond its lofty crest.

"Ah, here's our limo."

A waiting jeep had sharply tacked its way, back and forth, up the long hill, as Dad and I had sat in the back on weathered canvas cushions and hung on for dear life...

And then, suddenly, from the top of the hill, we had first seen – let me see, how can I put this so it doesn't sound over - dramatic? How about – *Heaven on earth?*

*Yep.*

The jeep with its silent Sikh driver, armed with a holstered pistol, had started down the far side of the slope away from the suddenly distant Perkins' castle. The jeep was bouncing like a carnival ride. We rode around Paradise for what seemed like a few minutes. What struck me was the utter divinity of fragrances within the air itself.

"Every breath on your island is absolutely intoxicating."

"Thank you."

And within a few minutes, we were truly once again in the shade of the gates of Eden.

"Well, let's hope my brother is finished with his work. He's dealing with a scientist, a crazy old guy named Rafferty. Ever hear of him?"

"The guy who did the original design for the neutron bomb? Not him..Him?"

"Yeah. He looks homeless but he's really quite put - together. Maybe you can meet him. Anyway, let's go up. Hopefully all the times will fit in...it's been busy as hell around here since the...the incident."

"Did you see the headline in the Herald accusing us of torturing kittens and puppies?" Tom laughed, as we had entered the courtyard.

"We read it."

"That's when we realized we were going to need some outside publicity assistance."

"I'm here as a reporter." Daddy warned him.

"We just want you to tell the truth."

"America can't handle the truth!" I blurted.

Tom laughed.

"Probably not. But we don't have a Plan B."

The gate doors now stood wide open.

"*And sir, we've got a gift of Grey Goose waiting for you up at the shop.*"

"*Oh, you know I chase the Goose?*"

"*You've been thoroughly vetted, Jack — yes, we know about the Goose,*" *Tommy had laughed. "It's our job to know everything. You could say our lives depend on that.*"

"Wow."

Any way I try to describe this place would just show how inexperienced a scribe I am.

I remember asking Tommy – I was already applying subconsciously the more familiar nickname to him that I'd come to call him by later – I remember asking him the source of the wonderful, blending fragrances that filled the soft perfect island air, and he replied, *'wisteria, gardenias, fields of gigantic black and scarlet tulips, a vast stretch of sunflowers, jasmine, honeysuckle, roses, snapdragons, cilantro, mint, rosemary, I can't remember half of them,'* the list of flowers went on and on. *'I can't really remember them all. There's a kind of ivy that grows here that emits a marvelous, dry sweet note we all really love... We've had perfumists from Chanel take away petals from all the blooms indigenous to this island only, to try to blend them into a scent like what the breezes blow across our shores every day, it would be worth a fortune, but they could never emulate it exactly...*

"My God, it's intoxicating," Daddy murmured. "I speak as an authority."

"On fragrances?"

"Intoxicants."

"Florida means, literally, 'land of flowers'," I could feel Tommy's amusement at the effect the whole overwhelming environment was having on me – and, for that matter, Daddy too, who stood at the courtyard threshold, staring in disbelief. "Helps to explain it."

"But we're not in Florida. This is a sovereign island."

"That's due to an upgrade in satellite technology. Satellite measurements may have altered factual reality, but not emotional reality. Tony and I still think of this rock as old Florida. We think Ponce de León discovered it. We *know* he discovered it."

"That tree," Daddy murmured. "OMFG. That tree!"

*Daddy, that's the first time you've ever cursed in front of your young daughter – even in acronym form. We've crossed a communications threshold ourselves. OMFG! I'm so very proud!*

*And then I looked up... and up...*

*I saw what he'd seen, what had elicited his stunned, unguarded reaction...*

*That... tree!*

In the exact center of the vast, gardened courtyard there stood, surrounded by a low brick wall, the most amazing tree that has ever existed on this planet, more amazing even than the great redwoods of northern California, although this tree, with its spreading foliage and branchwork included, could not have stood more than two hundred feet in height. Maybe taller. Two thirds as tall as a football field is long.

Without exactly thinking it through, I realized nonetheless: *this is the great Magic Presence Pauley Vee had told us about yesterday afternoon in his bar.*

At first glimpse, and from a distance away, the island's undoubted centerpiece appeared only as a really massive oak tree in full bloom, a complex multi - layered creation off the patient pen of the pointillist Seurat, as detailed as it was immense, arching upward as magnificently as the dome of many - colored glass of the poem, yet still of human dimension.

Coming closer, however, what expressed itself foremost was the mood generated by its presence, an abiding, weary, determined quality that suggested its historic longevity – that of a stubborn, immortal giant.

And there was, indeed, a subtle, sad kind of music issuing from the drifting gentle breeze that moved through its limbs... You couldn't hear the music so much as feel it.

"Is that music?"

"We don't know what it is," Tom shrugged. "My brother's really looking forward to meeting you guys. He's been under a lot of pressure. Promise you'll be gentle."

Was it an oak? So it at first appeared, dark, rough -
trunked, thick rooted. But the leaves were more delicate,
multi - colored, dancing with light, fruit - bearing,
protective clusters of tiny rippling leafage, greens, silvers,
golds and pinks gorgeously commingled, thick trembling
downy bursts of moist, almost smiling beauty...

The branches tapered dramatically, allowing the
long, downward curving limbs to nearly touch their own
playful shadows in a coherent visual embrace, mirroring the
spangling play of light and dark that arrived and departed,
upon the great arc of shaded earth below, with every fresh,
gentle wind, distorted only by the relentless whisper of
Time.

In the silence of its presence before us, there was yet
a kind of profound blending of intense harmonies reaching
toward us, from trunk and limb and root and leaf and
shade, eerie as that sounds unless you've experienced it —
the emotional music of silent Time, passing as enigmatically
as the breezes, over us.

Light arising from this colossal being seemed tinted
by first a rosy, then a purplish aura. Though essentially
motionless, the tree vibrated with energy and history. I
thought for a moment I could feel its soul. That a
profound memory was imprisoned within the bark, *timeless
truth, profound memory, captured inside a living tomb.*

I thought for a moment I could hear a wistful
humming coming from it, but that's a kid's imagination for
you. Hearing music that wasn't quite there.

"That's some tree."

"I want to hug it!"

Its majestic umbrella - like reach extended outward,
and outward, releasing an invisible, yet palpably serene aura
of blended energy and tranquility over all the courtyard, its

shade a deep, spectacularly dappled spread of invitation to all the picnickers, from the first souls on earth a billion years ago – from Adam and Eve – to the modern moment, to every picnicker who had ever lived and loved, shared fruit and breath and intimate kisses within its dark protection…

"What kind of tree is this? I've never seen anything like it – you can *feel* it, actually feel it."

"It's so *old*. Older than the world."

"We don't know. We think it's a fruit tree of some sort. The top arborists disagree. They can't identify it either. It's the only one of its kind on earth."

Neither fruit nor vegetation hung from its willowy limbs, just a rich jigsaw overlay of sometimes pale, sometimes golden/green, sometime rosy leafwork that caught the sunshine in a miraculous way, giving the light itself a soft, patient yet simultaneously explosive aspect, as though the dappling gentle interplay of sun and shadow settled through a magnificent filter of crystalline stained glass – eerie, majestic, Cathedral - like.

Another odd, visual sensation – misting rain seemed to glimmer and spark along its vast branches too, causing the branchwork to gleam like human bone, yet not a single drop of water had fallen anywhere.

"I can hear music coming from it – even through the silence? How can that be possible?"

"What kind of tree? Yes. Well, we have come to believe this tree is actually the, the… now don't laugh… the actual biblical Tree of Knowledge of Good and Evil. The tree that Adam and Eve once stood before, just as we are standing before it now."

*…the dappled spread of wondrous shade an invitation to all the picnickers, from the first spirits to the modern moment, all the souls who had ever lived and loved on the earth, even to the first of*

*these — Adam and Eve — the dumbstruck lovers, the first uncomprehending failures, first innocent betrayers of the world to come behind them, the first victims of passion, discoverers of human lust, just as Prometheus much later discovered fire...*

"Adam and Eve? In *Florida?*"

"I know," Tom acknowledged. "It doesn't fit. We can't explain it. But there it is."

"An apple tree?" Daddy seemed stunned. Just as there was no crying in baseball, there were no apple trees in Florida, not even in this incredible island oasis.

"There is no evidence anywhere in the Bible that the tree of knowledge was actually an apple tree," Tom gently corrected him.

"Eve took a bite of the apple – the forbidden fruit. Didn't she?"

"No specific fruit is mentioned. We've had scholars research this, the Bible in every language and formulation. No fruit was mentioned. Yet my brother feels that this is, indeed, an apple tree."

We walked past the great tree, slowly and still in awe. I stumbled on a walkway.

"There's no scientific explanation for it."

"Tom – y'know what it reminds me of?" Daddy was walking forward, but still looking back. "Did you ever see the Kubrick film, '2001 – A Space Odyssey'?"

"Oh yes."

"The obelisk the astronauts discover? God's Tuning Fork?"

"Yes, yes," Tom answered excitedly. "I've heard that one, too. The debate often goes on into the early hours. We'll love to have you two join in."

"My brother is waiting for us, dear people,"

Tommy waved us forward toward a guarded steel door at the far end of the courtyard.

"First Ponce de León," My father mused, "now Adam and Eve. It just gets curiouser and curiouser."

Tommy laughed.

"Just remember the saying from Hamlet, 'there are more things under Heaven and Earth than your philosophy has dreamt of.' Some of those things are here on Crystal Cay."

*I've been here a very long time,* he added softly, *and I don't understand them either.*

# IX

So. Where were we?

"Mr. Perkins will see you now," Tom came out into the dark waiting room. "Just give him a couple more minutes."

*My brother is ready for his close - up.*

We rose and attempted to dust ourselves off. There was no dust, only salt from the Gulf that had dried on our clothes on the way over. The waiting room outside Perkins' office, where we'd been parked for over an hour, was dark and lit with low frosted sconces.

"I'll be right back," Tommy had promised. "I need to be with you when you're interviewing my brother. I have to take a sort of important call. I can't leave him alone with anybody for five minutes. He's spilling his guts. I'm afraid my dear brother is having a nervous breakdown. He's never been the target of an assassination before. He's such a pussycat... So take it easy on him, will you? And until I return, it's all off the record. Good?"

"Just idle chit - chat. Till you return."

"That's right. Nothing but air kisses. Do I have your promise?"

"My dad never betrays a trust," I smiled. I looked directly into his gorgeous eyes. Frowning again, he quickly looked away.

Tommy had said goodbye in his courteous, Old World way. He'd never really looked at me throughout our time together. Except when I'd gone all goo - goo on him. Then he'd grimaced, and made me feel fourteen again.

Half - embarrassed, half - angry with myself, I realized I was jealous for the attention of his eyes. It's natural I know, particularly at my age. But I felt even more stupid than usual. What can I say?

*This man is hell - a cute.*

I'd seen enough of the provocative, far reaching intellect in those flint - grey eyes; I wanted the dumb side of him, the stammering uncertain side that came with the irresistible attraction I wanted him to feel for me. My fifteen - year old hormones never left me alone for long.

*Woman, you've got some kind of sick perv-o imagination. You've known this guy five minutes! Oh, so in love!*

*I'm just as horny as Kansas in August, I'm as normal as a blueberry pie. No more a smart little girl with no heart, I have found me a wonderful guy! If you'll excuse an expression I use, I'm in love I'm in love I'm in love with a wonderful guy! I'm as horny as —*

*Jessica, you idiot! What's happening here? Not even a fifteen - year old can be this butterfly - flirty — where in Heaven's name had that even come from?*

*Last year's Middle School production of South Pacific, those lyrics I had dreamed of after I'd heard them, dreaming of the feel of that rush of romantic emotion, the wonderful purity of romantic love expressed in Broadway musical lyrics like nowhere else, the wonderful unlikely possibility, ticking away in my subconscious, then galvanized more than a year later by one look into a beautiful grown man's coldly averted eyes? He's a grown man! And he's even wearing a pocket - protector like a nerd! Doesn't that prove you've lost touch with reality? Oh, so in love, every five minutes! L - O - frigging L! Come on, child! God be my witness!*

"Stop being so antsy," Daddy whispered, right after Tom had left. We'd sat down for the long wait.

"I'm not being antsy!"

Daddy could cat nap outdoors in the middle of a cat 5, and he was already drifting off when I held up my i. He looked at it, and he just nodded an okay.

"You're being antsy."

"I'm not being antsy!"

"You're being antsy." But what did he care?

"What do you care? You're already asleep."

He was already asleep.

Thus had the hour passed, thus was our audience now granted. I felt for a moment I was in the court of Henry VIII. It was hard not to feel a little afraid.

*Jess to Phong 10:35 am – Sorry I lost u earlier...rough jeep ride..Waiting to meet the King just saw the most amazing garden around this castle like the old pix of Cypress gardens but more like the hanging gardens of Babylon it's almost biblical P., u must see it..2 wrds, secret and serene... oh, and majestic...*

*Phong: u sound amped*

*Jess: feel like i'm breathing in all human history*

*Phong: Her Majesty still there?*

*Jess: Kammi got left in the lurch literally*

*Phong: not on the A list anymore?*

*Jess: lol don't count her out tho. she's relentless. The rentas think she's behind some kind of plot to take ovr the island. Not exactly the most brilliant secret agent*

*Phong: that cant be it*

*Jess: Ik..but still*

*Phong: Still?!*

*Jess: Know who they seem to be afraid of? dont laugh*

*Phong: ok*

*Jess: The Reality people stars of reality shows like Kammi. u know the ones, fancy lace and crab fishermen and Jrry Springer and laury mobitch, daddy calls them rats in the silo of American popular culture..Orca? Money Hoo Hoo? I saw building where Perkins makes all those tv movies and documentaries. It's the biggest thing, bigger than Epcot. evil - looking. I could see why Reality Nation is attracted, it looks like state - of - art. Locked down tho, like everything. this guy Tom (Tony's brother, smart and oh God yummy CUTE) there's an attack coming, didnt say so exactly but he must have mentioned Kammi's mom Kressa enough times to make me wonder*

*Phong: is there a fountain of youth like everybody says*

*Jess; haven't seen it but there's a billion year old tree right in the middle of everything... so incredible*

*Phong: billion year old tree...?!*

*Jess: tree of knowledge of good and evil. u could feel it, something about it, a wisdom.. music coming from it swear to god, music you couldn't quite hear yet i heard it, i felt i was in presence of wisdom. they think it's where adam and eve spoke their vows.. made me want to drop to my knees*

*Phong: in Florida? get a grip*

*Jess: I could hear something coming from it, like music..the wind*

*Phong: from a tree? get a grip*

*Jess: told you not to laugh*

*Phong: didn't the air in Shangra la mesmerize visitors*

*Jess: think ur thinking of the odyssey*

*Jess: just met man i'm gonna marry*

*Phong: u huffin!! ...btw barry keeps hmu...what u want me to do...loathe that dude..he stabbed u jess*

*Jess: i'm out of town 3-4 days and he just had to get busy...my 2 best friends*

*Phong: what u want m to do*

*Jess: what u want to do*

*Phong: u don't want to know..lol*

*Jess: be my guest...think he roofied Angie*

*Phong: Roofie his ass then night night i'll glue his dick to something haven't decided what yet...maybe file a rape charge too. Attemptd rape 'cause he ain't gonna touch it*

*Jess: u such a b when u get started. little ass - kicker...teach him don't kill him..no cops*

*Phong: yes dear. love u*

*Jess: love u too. tell angie its okay okay? we need to stick together..daughters of dorian for always..lets try to hold it together*

*Phong: i'll make sure its all good*

*Jess: love u grl*

*Phong: chix b4 dix...lookin for the superglue right now..itll be the date of his life baby*

*Jess: lol*


*(Jessica signs off 1220pm...)*


"How good it is to meet you both." Anthony Perkins extended both hands toward us.

"Sir, you look just like Elon Musk!" I heard my big mouth introduce itself.

Tony Perkins warmly greeted first Daddy, then me. "You're a very handsome man!"

"And you're a very lovely young woman – Jessica?"

Daddy may have hated that opening, but it was honest, and I could tell my words not only caught him by surprise but went straight to his troubled heart. He too was wearing a pocket - protector. Somehow, at some deep level, I already knew both these powerful brothers. Those pocket - protectors formed our fan club for the Daughters of Dorian back at school. They were always the loneliest, and appreciated true friendship the most, as long as you didn't let them get too attached.

And that was easy to control – usually.

Tony Perkins didn't seem shaky to me, at least not at first. It would take him a few minutes, and a few shots of Goose, to come unglued, and prove to me once again what a genius journalist my Daddy is in getting the truth out of a very loveable Mook.

The three of us were alone in a big sort of study - like room, not the office I'd envisioned, but dark and rich with low lights and leather furniture. Louvered shutters gave the room an almost *Godfather* feel. As you may have guessed, that's my favorite flick.

"Glad you could make it down from Tallahassee on short notice. This shooting business seems to have accelerated everything." Tony gestured to a couch where we sat down beside him. "We need to get our side of this conflict out to the world – "

"Good to meet you too, sir. It's an honor." My dad can be incredibly ingratiating. "I never thought I'd have this opportunity."

"Tom and I love your writing."

"You and your brother are the first geniuses I've actually ever met in my career. Other than my daughter, of course."

"My dad tends to exaggerate a little, sir."

"Jessica? So you're a prodigy?"

"Well of course, my friends all say I have extraordinary – "

"We're teasing you, daughter."

"Well, you *look* smart," Tony Perkins spoke to me directly. "That's half the game."

During the preliminaries preceding what were supposed to be the first of two or three 'conversations' – not interviews – we realized we weren't alone in the big office. I could tell Tony was waiting for Tom to join us.

"Who's that?" I asked.

"Aha!" Tony laughed. "Now we're talking *real* genius. I'd introduce you to Dr. Rafferty but he doesn't like to meet new people. But that guy is the real deal."

An older looking, strange - behaving guy was bent over the big desk in the corner. He looked homeless and wild. His grey hair was sticking out everywhere. He had a beard about halfway down, grey - white and wildly untrimmed. *Rasputin! He looks exactly like the Russian madman, Rasputin!*

He was wearing a long dirty grey overcoat, odd in any season in our region, incomprehensible in late summer for Florida. I expected him to have crazy eyes too, but when I got a look into them, behind their Lenin - esque wire - rimmed glasses, Rasputin's eyes were cold, clear, analytical, predatory, and Scandinavian pale. He had a wolf's amoral gaze, and that gaze did not linger long in any one direction.

"Who's that?" I blurted. "Who's Dr. Rafferty?"

"Rafferson," Daddy corrected me. "Except for his politics he'd have won the Nobel Prize. Doesn't he look like a mad old genius scientist?"

"He's the man who created the Hubble telescope. And the neuron bomb. Other than that, not much."

"He's just leaving."

"Is he homeless?"

Mr. Tony Perkins chuckled.

"No. He's a scientist who works with us sometimes. He handles the difficult stuff. He's got a challenge ahead of him right now, that's for sure." Perkins carefully approached the big table where Dr. Rafferson was bent over, studying some charts.

"Are you almost finished, Doctor Rafferson?"

"Finished."

"Goodbye then. I'll listen for your call. This is so important, okay?"

"Okay, boss. I understand the importance. Thanks again."

When Dr. Rafferson had closed the door behind him, Daddy laughed.

"That guy reminded me of Columbo – the dirty overcoat."

"I was a big 'Columbo' fan. Doctor Rafferson's a scientist, but I guess you could call him a kind of detective too. He looks crazy. But he's not. He's one of the smartest men on the planet. He used to practically run the Ukrainian secret service. Did you see his eyes?"

"Like a wolf's eyes," I blurted.

"Exactly. He could write a book about his life – it would be a best - seller. He's seen it all. We're lucky to have him on our side."

Papers were scattered all over the desk in the corner. Like the Godfather's study. I even looked for that white cat. No cats.

"That tree in the courtyard," I couldn't resist, "It's like the eighth Wonder of the world. It took our breath away."

"God put that tree there. Nothing can remove it."

"I can see where you'd want to protect it."

"No – it doesn't need our protection. I'm saying the tree is divinely placed. It is immortal. When we were first building this castle, we were all living in tents out on the periphery of the construction. By an enormous mistake, the tree got bulldozed down late one afternoon. An incredible, soul - destroying error. We were catatonic. Tom will tell you, we even considered abandoning the island. That's how iconic, how central – how *religiously* we viewed that ancient giant. Drank quite a bit that night. Fired the 'dozer driver, and almost shot him. I wept. And then I slept. As the moon rose, I looked out at the huge hole in the earth where the tree trunk had been ripped out, down to the smallest root... It sat atop a limestone cave. The oddest placement. The crater was as big and deep as a swimming pool. There was no question. This made it impossible to re - root."

"How in the world did you manage to repair it?"

"We did nothing. At dawn the next day, the tree was exactly as it had been before, down to the last majestic branch, beautiful leaf, mystical throw of shade. Even the sort of silent music you hear, that we all hear. The limbs, that look like human bones, and the mists gathered along them, like tears trying to form. Nothing short of divine magic could have achieved that resurrection, not even mass hypnosis. We at first assumed mass hypnosis was responsible for what we were seeing...

"But no. We're convinced the tree is, divine, immortal. I'm not religious, but once I was convinced what I was looking at was in fact real, I dropped to my knees. And I wept. That was a surprising response. And I prayed. I literally prayed. Talk about fear and trembling! And I'm an atheist.

"My heart was transformed that morning. The tree will preside over this island until the last syllable of recorded Time. I located the 'dozer driver, re - hired him, and asked his forgiveness. But when he saw the tree again, he backed away, and fled the island like a murderer attempting to escape judgment. Tom and I were both kneeling. We kept whispering to each other, *we're home, we're home!* I cannot articulate the transformative power of that moment. My brother and I had already been granted certain... special powers. But at that moment we both became fully human."

A few moments of awed, awkward silence fell across the office.

"I've never related that before," Admitted Perkins. "To anyone. What's happening to me?" He gave a melancholy laugh. "Honestly? I think I'm having a meltdown. Why did I even tell you that?"

"It touched my heart," I added. "That tree! I can believe it. I was overwhelmed, just looking up at it. It was like looking up into the... well not the heart, but the memory of God."

"I know Kammi," Mr. Perkins waved his hand to indicate a change of topic. "Did you throw her out of the boat?"

"Roseanne had to hold a shotgun on her to keep her out," Daddy said.

"She was begging to be allowed to see you." I couldn't resist blurting out. As Daddy is fond of saying, *Jessica, you've got a mouth on you.* "She said you guys were lovers."

"Really? What did she say about me? Probably nothing very nice." Mr. Perkins tried to sound disinterested, which came off as slightly high school, which is where I spend so much of my time I didn't have trouble noting the little catch in his voice.

"She – "

"Wait, don't say anything just yet – are we on the record?"

"That's up to you."

"Off the record, we – may I have your word, Jack – off the record, here?"

"Of course."

"I have enormous respect for your integrity, and your talent, as a journalist," Mr. Perkins remarked. "You got my letter about the job?"

"I got it."

"You don't accomplish what you've accomplished without integrity."

"My dad's the best."

"So – off the record, Ms. Kay and I got to know each other last year in California. The truth? She absolutely blew me away. I still feel that way about her. She told me there was absolutely nothing between her and Munye. A month later she was married. She lies about everything. I don't keep up with the tabloids. I made the mistake of inviting her to Crystal Lagoon. All very innocent at first... um. I thought we would be married. Such a happy time in my life... Biggest mistake of my life."

*I knew it!* "Don't feel bad, Mr. Perkins," I consoled him. The subject was closer to me than to Daddy, who kept respectfully silent. "Kammi's incredibly sexy."

"What Kammi wants, Kammi gets," Mr. Perkins looked down at his hands. "Usually. Always. Almost always. First she wanted me. But then she wanted him."

"Is that why Mrs. Perkins left for Europe? When Kammi snuck back to see you?"

"Did she blame everything on Mrs. Perkins?" Tony asked angrily. "There *is* no Mrs. Perkins! Never has been!

God what a liar she is – I can't believe I love her so darn much! Still! Even now!"

"She's gorgeous," I said.

"She really is," Daddy agreed.

"Her booty defines her."

"She always hated that," Perkins interrupted. "Jessica – what did you think of her? You couldn't have known her long. Neither did I! It was love at first sight! Did you like her?"

"I love her too," I shrugged. I wanted to hug this tired, lonely - looking man. "She has the magic. You forgive her anything. Some people are like that. The truly innocent ones. It's like she never had a childhood. She's just making it up as she goes along."

"She's not at all innocent. She's a spy for the rapper Munye and for her mother – for that blasted Reality Network they're forming."

"Kammi is all id," Daddy tried to comfort our host.

"Romance is all about treachery." I said. "All about betrayal." *In a way it's the best part.*

This is the only time since Angie's text when I almost lost it. I took a deep breath. "I just found out the boy of my dreams stabbed me in the back. I broke up with him. It hurts so much I don't even feel it yet. So, anyway sir, I'm right there with you. What we want from life is a sense of control of our circumstances, and then love hits you like a bowling ball – Emotions are just anarchy, flying ten pins."

"You're babbling, daughter."

"No, no," Mr. Perkins interrupted. "She's telling it exactly like it is. Age isn't even a factor. We're all vulnerable."

I could tell, our mutual misery had bonded the unhappy King and the frontstabbed teenager at a special level, not by our pain but by our admission of it.

"I'm separated too," Daddy threw in. His was an infected emotional wound, I happened to know, that my father was fighting every day of his life. We were all silent a moment in the aftermath of these odd, rather personal romantic confessions. It was a strange moment in the conversation...

"I haven't known you two for five minutes. Why are we even discussing this?"

*Because it's about hot girls and high school emotions! Who cares what else is happening in the world, compared to that? Who cares if somebody just tried to shoot you two weeks ago? Who cares if your island is about to be attacked by a paramilitary arm of the U.S. government? It's all about who takes Kammi to the dance, who she's making out with, is she pregnant? I heard she's pregnant! Who's is it? Once we all start breathing hard, nothing else matters by comparison. The whole herd is watching, the whole hive is buzzing... And Kammi's queen of the hive.*

There was a light tap on the door, and a saffron - gowned orderly pushed in a silver tray silently across the plush pearl carpet. On the tray was.... *everything.*

"You guys help yourselves. Caviar? Krispy Kreme? Grey Goose? Jack?"

"Seriously?!" *Krispy Kremes?!*

"I want you to be happy," He smiled, watching me stuff my first Krisp, since the trip down, past my own bright teenaged grin. Fresh! Well, fresh enough!

"I'm feeling better already," I laughed. I was imagining some of the places where my creative bff might be planning to slather on the Super Glue on poor Barry. I was already wondering where Tom had disappeared to — that was a good sign. And suddenly I was smiling.

"When you're young you heal fast," King Perkins said happily. My smile seemed to give him a lift.

"How did you know about the 'potato wine'?"

"Your family has been vetted. Well - vetted. It's my job to know everything. Everything. In my position, it's pretty mandatory." Perkins gave us another sad, nerdy smile. "Sometimes more than I want to know. How could I have been so blind when it came to her? I never even checked her driver's license!"

"But – Krisps?" *You knew that? How could you know that! What are you, the NSA?*

Tony laughed. It was though he could read my thought cloud too.

"We let the NSA monitor everybody else. Then we monitor the NSA."

"Krisps are yummy good."

"All better?"

"Getting there," I laughed, reaching again. Daddy had selected a frosted bottle of Goose on ice. The silver tray was a great relaxant.

"The code words to my heart are, *'off the record.'* I virtually never speak to anyone off the record, not even our Foundation's attorneys. There are always stenographers present, seems like."

Mr. Perkins joined my father in a shot of Goose.

"Go Gators."

"Go Gators."

*Gulp.*

*Aaahh.*

"Jack – I know enough about you to trust you. That's why we made you the offer."

Very oddly, I thought, Mr. Perkins, aka King of the World, reached for and once again shook my father's hand vigorously, then softly. "See, it's like this: other than my brother, I don't really have a friend in the world."

Dad and I looked away from him, not knowing what to say.

"Isn't that amazing?" Perkins asked. "To have all this, and to be so lonely"

"It's a friendless world," Dad said finally. "I'm in the same boat – a million acquaintances. Not a single friend. Not really."

"Where's Tommy now?"

"He's mad at me now." Tony's face showed, first embarrassment, then shame. "Kammi wrecked everything. He'll be in shortly. He has to be in attendance during our interview. I guess you'd call it an interview. I wanted it to be a conversation, that's all. Tommy's my personal attorney. The best."

"Oh." I paused. Teenagers, because we're always running our mouths, can get away with asking anything. "Why's he mad at you?"

"Because I gave away a secret I shouldn't have..."

"What kind of secret?"

"A big secret. The biggest secret on this island. And I gave it away to a bitch. A *bitch!* Because I was in love!"

"Go Gators."

"Go Gators," the glasses lifted, then down the hatch.

"I usually never drink this stuff." He admitted. "But it's good. I've been under a lot of stress." Fatigue held down the corners of Mr. Tony Perkins' smile.

"When do you want to go on the record? We can do this interview at your convenience. Do you want an attorney present? Does it have to be Tom?"

"Tom is my attorney."

"That's perfect. He's a big part of the picture here."

"Well – any way you guys can stay another day? We have super comfortable accommodations. I'm a bit busy. Did you hear? I almost got shot... *Can you believe that? Twice?*"

"We heard."

"Go Gators."

"Go Gators."

*Aaaahhhh.*

Tony was loosening up by the swallow. *This is just how they do it in the movies.*

This time Tony Perkins wasn't interested in reading my thought cloud.

"It's really quite nice having you two here. I have a good feeling about you," Mr. Perkins admitted, looking down again. *This guy is like a shy nerd, like the shy boys at the Nerd table in the lunchroom, just like them, only older – a lot older. Fatigue is like age. He's young looking, but so tired it makes him the oldest person we've seen on the Cay so far... The same quality possessed by the wonderful tree below, that of patient, stubborn weariness, a dry rain always a moment away from falling... The misting quality around the tree's bonelike limbs... the old saying, the saddest tears are those that are never shed.*

"Oh, that god - awful racist rap music! My God, I gave her my heart. I gave her all the secrets of this island! I can always get a heart transplant, but those secrets – ah! Oh, no! Can't get them back!"

"What secrets?" I sensed Daddy's change of personality from The Dads to Sherlock Holmes...

"I'm still in love with her. See?"

"She's lovable. What did you give her?"

"Oh. The keys to the kingdom. That's all. Nothing more than that."

"Off the record, of course." Daddy quickly added. "What secret?"

"You know this island is about to be attacked?" Perkins mumbled.

Once I'd begun to view him as King Nerd instead of Capitalism's Devil Ambassador, it was hard not to feel sorry for him. I could tell he had little experience in tossing down shots.

"There's sure to be an attack." He repeated.

"Attacked?" I blurted out. "By who? Who would attack this place? It's Paradise!"

"Exactly."

After another shot of Goose, Tony had half - persuaded us to stay a couple of days, rather than for just a single interview.

We could tour all of the facilities at Crystal Lagoon. *Carte blanche.* He would take us around himself, chauffeur the jeep, show us through the great research laboratories for which Crystal Lagoon was justly renowned, the monstrous television and recording studios that were the envy of the mainland - based cable television industry.

Or we could bicycle the miles of trails, through gardens, forests, beaches. We would have our choice of about forty different sailboats of every size. We could sail to Key West and back, time provided.

Or we could just lay around like beachcombers, bust up coconuts, and watch the sun slip behind the ocean every evening, *or raise our hands in the air like we just don't care...* with every Goose toast, the world Tony offered became just a little more beautiful.

Perkins' Industries had its own satellites — *thirty - nine* of them, he noted. And there would soon be nine more. He and Tom had been considering launching their own financial network.

"The real geniuses who work for me are the financial guys. It takes up so much of our time."

"Are there any other trees like the one in your courtyard?" I asked.

"No. That's the only one like that. Anywhere on earth. Did Tom tell you what we think it is?"

"Yes. I believe it. I've never seen anything like it." *Go Gators! Another Krisp, down the hatch... ahhh. Potato wine or Krisps, it's all about the sugar.*

"It's lovely here," Daddy nodded. "It reminds me of the old Cypress Gardens. Back before the Mouse arrived."

"I'd love it if we could just pal around," He was almost pleading. "Jack, it would help your story too. I'd be able to give you a better perspective of my world. You have a deadline on this?"

"Not a hard deadline. They don't want me down here getting drunk night and day with Jimmy Buffet. Or Warren Buffet."

Although almost all the dues - paying guests had by now fled the island, there were at least four distinct bungalow villages scattered peacefully across the gardened, forested immensity of Crystal Lagoon.

"Our make - up and prosthetics facilities are mind - blowing, even to me. Our specialists could turn Adolph Hitler into Roger Rabbit in about three hours."

"He's not on this island, is he?"

"Who."

"Hitler." *Big Media kept up the drumbeat that the island was hiding Nazis all the way up the line to the top dog...All part of Kressa Kay's relentless propaganda campaign, softening up the target...*

Tony laughed in disbelief. "Hitler? God, no. The last anybody heard, he was still in Paraguay." Perkins laughed.

"Running for his life. Working in the last place anyone would think to look – a kosher deli. Twelve - hour days for a man his age? Karma's a bitch, ha?"

Briefly Mr. Perkins hit a button under his desk, and a wall opened, revealing a kind of Command Center. I just got the briefest glimpse in there. It was packed with flat screen monitors, a room the size of a basketball court maybe, but with a low, warmly - lit ceiling, its dozen or more jumpsuited technicians tasking without evident oversight.

"Most of what's going on in this room is buying and selling commodities and currency trading. It's an enormous pre - occupation."

"It looks like a room straight out of a James Bond movie!"

Tony laughed. "Everything on this island, every design, was taken from some American movie or other. Everything but the Gehry touch - ups above the castle walls. Those are original. The main thing is, keeping the architecture from interfering with the natural perfection of this Paradise."

"I love you!"

Another touch of a button, and in a moment the command center had vanished behind the somber oak wall.

Before the doors glided shut and became an oak wall again, we'd gotten just a glimpse, beyond the warm welcoming smiles, into the hard - edged, complex technical world of Crystal Lagoon. Tony Perkins must have trusted us to show us even that much. Tom had put it accurately, *that shooting has really accelerated everything.*

A friendship between the three of us, sitting on the black leather couch in his office, that ordinarily would have taken five years to cultivate, had reached a kind of intimate maturity in five minutes. And four quick hits of Goose.

"Go Gators."

"Go Gators."

*Gulp.*

*Aaaaahhhh*

"Damn," Tony Perkins looked around, as if seeing his environment somehow for the first time. "Where did all the stress go?"

Tony Perkins sat down between us and put his head in his hands for a moment. For all the non - stop hum of electronic activity I knew was going on only a thick oak wall away, the soundproofed room was so utterly silent now that I thought I could hear his heart beating.

"What is extraordinary is how Dr. Munye and Kressa Kay have turned history on its head. They've achieved a complete alteration in the Narrative. Now Tom and I are considered slave - owners, Capitalist exprorionists. Now we are the hunted ones. All because of the island. All because of one secret I gave away to a girl I was in love with – "

"But what secret – ?"

"Their narrative insists this is a political question, a question of justice. It's not. It's about the island. There's a good reason why they want it. I wish I could explain more. They'll do anything to get control over this world of ours."

"Can I see that diary you mentioned?"

"It's in London. Being carbon tested. Again. It's authenticity keeps being called into question. We're like everybody else – we are desperate to get to the truth."

"And the point of the diary is – ?"

"That it wasn't an evolved parliamentary democracy at all, when the ex - slaves ran this island. This doctor kept a diary of the place during his captivity. Slave Island was a pirate island, in perfect position to predate on vessels between Cuba and Mobile Bay. How could you blame them, the runaway slaves of that time? It's how they survived. It was the Somalia of its time. But who would believe us, if we published that information?

"And more importantly, who would care? *It was over two hundred years ago!* How long can we feast on the bones of the past without choking on the consequence?"

"It throws a monkey - wrench into the Narrative," Daddy commented.

"Before this conversation," Mr. Tony Perkins stated expansively, a tone of voice I knew only too well from my beloved father, *a three shot of Goose tone of voice, the fourth hadn't even crossed the goalposts yet,* "I had felt the need to get to know you better," Perkins was basically apologizing to us – expansively.

"With us two," Daddy laughed, very relaxed, "What you see is pretty much what you get."

"We know so much about you and your family already, but, I don't know – it's an intuitive thing... I want to offer you this position with our organization – the office of public relations director for the entire Foundation, the job I mentioned in the letter – a position of great power, authority, responsibility, and financial reward... will you automatically say 'no'?"

"I have my daughter to think about."

*Not to mention the likelihood your little bump of limestone is likely a Gulf of Mexico version of Dien Bien Phu. You're asking me to swim onto the Titanic in order to help the billionaires with the bailing...*

King Perkins took my father's hand between his. A clumsy, Mookish, endearingly heartfelt gesture...

"Jack, we have a school on the island with private tutors, the best in the world. After finishing high school, she could go to any university on earth, admission guaranteed, completely free of charge. Oxford? Harvard? Sorbonne?"

Tony gave us that same sad, brittle, Elon Musk - like technocrat's smile, corners downturned.

"I was going to offer you this job at the end of our visit. That Goose really hit the spot I guess. I never do anything till I know it's the right thing at the right time... Jack, Jessica... Join us!"

We were both staring at King Perkins.

I'd already seen a couple of times on this trip when a few pops of Potato Wine or Cactus Wine changed the flow of the narrative completely, as when the night before at the motel, after about a half dozen of the miniature Cuervos, Kammi started raving about Munye's physical attributes, *I tell you Jess, so often I'd like to be free of Felix, he's kind of a jerk and he constantly cheats on me, but when he's inside me, it's like the key that unlocks the door to my soul, all I can do is go with it, and his rap music is booming all around the room, I feel like I'm being stretched to the limit inside and out, and that's why I'm his bitch, I hear his genius, see it, feel it — it's not because of the publicity, which is what everybody thinks, that I'm only about the pubbly, that's Mom's department, she hates him but loves the pubbly, y'know? My mom's such a bully, such a soul dragon, I'm his bitch, her bitch, everybody's bitch around here, I think I'm gonna puke... There's a lot more to me than a big ass. I'm in lust, not love. Being in lust is worst. Your mistakes are always for the wrong reasons. There's a lot more to me than a big ass... You'll all see... Felix knows how to open me up, but only physically, and I'll miss that for a little while when he's gone... but... Felix is gonna find himself kicked to the curb... Some day...*

Now here we were, being offered the key to a vault of a different kind?

"What about it, Jack? We'd love to have a Pulitzer Prize winner on staff. Join us?" Even though King Perkins was slurring his words, there was no doubt the offer was clearheaded, and had been planned in advance.

"I wouldn't say no offhand."

"You'd be perfect for the job. You and your beautiful daughter have already been vetted, extensively vetted, by the most in - depth process of background checks and psychological evaluation this side of the Israeli *Mossad.*"

"I'm surprised," Daddy admitted. "Amazed." *I didn't think anybody even knew I was still alive.*

"Your agents really freaked out my Mom," I admonished him.

"I'm so sorry."

"Oh, that's fine anyway," I laughed. "It's good to see her freaking out from time to time. Keeps her to the real. She can be a real witch."

"Be sweet about your Mom," Daddy warned. "Loyalty matters most — witch or otherwise."

"My experience with Kammi taught me, once again, how important it is that we in positions of great trust must be careful who we trust."

Tony Perkins was still holding onto my father's hand. But he looked directly at me.

"Here's the important thing — the secret of the island you must never divulge to anyone. Can I count on that?"

"We're still off the record."

Daddy now reached for Perkin's hand, and grasped it comfortingly between his own.

Priest and penitent, the two men, already obviously fond of each other, took turns switching roles.

"It's okay, Tony. I can tell, you've been needing to unburden yourself. It's okay."

"Oh, God, Tom's going to be so mad..." He gripped my father's hand more tightly. My dad would have made a great therapist.

"Tom tells everyone I can't keep a secret. Damn it, he's so right!"

"Tell us!" I commanded. *I know how to handle nerds.* "We'll never tell a soul."

I assumed it was more juicy gossip about the delectable Madame Munye. I was about to receive the surprise of my fifteen – going on sixteen – years to heaven.

"Just between friends?"

"Of course."

"Join us, Jack... Join us! Your ability with words could help save this island! Money's no object. We've got more money than God. Just name your price. One million dollars? Two million? A year? Just name your price!"

"A year?"

"Sure." Tony slurred his concurrence. "Anything. We don't care."

"But first – The secret you referenced? Absolutely off the record?"

"Yes.." King Perkins was struggling within himself. Thanks to the Goose, the struggle was shortlived.

*Confess!... Confess!..... En nomino Patri.... Confess!*

"This island holds the... the secret, the secret..."

"The secret?!" I used my sternest voice. This was no time to let some nerd Mickey Mouse us around. *"Please continue.* We're waiting." *Cute girls don't like to be kept waiting!*

"Well, that's the secret. That's it, the Fountain of Youth," Perkins whispered. "Yeah. Well, we found it. The

Fountain of Youth. It's ours. You can't tell anybody. Don't tell Tom I told you. And we think this island was once the Garden of Eden. You can't tell anybody that either. Either of you." He paused. "But it's the, the uh, the Fountain of Youth that will change everything for you two."

Tony then jerked his fist up to his mouth and bit his knuckles hard, nearly to bleeding.

"I can't believe I just gave that up," He mumbled through his knuckles. "Friendship starts with trust. And trust goes both ways."

"The what?"

"That's what Munye and Kressa want. The Fountain of Youth. That's all Kammi ever cared about... She never gave a rip about me. Eternal Youth. That's it for Kammi."

"The what?"

After a long pause came the still – unbelievable, whispered confirmation. And yet Daddy was yet uncertain he'd correctly heard the terms of endearment.

"The what?"

Tony realized he'd have to dumb it down a scintilla.

"Join us, and you and your daughter will never age another day for the remainder of Eternity!"

*And also a million a year tax free and full health and dental, and a month's paid vaca every year, month of your choice...?*

Daddy's eyes widened in disbelief.

"Full dental?"

Tony Perkins pulled his other hand away from my father's, then clumsily extracted a handkerchief from his pocket and wiped the suddenly heavy film of sweat off his lip and forehead.

"There," He almost gasped. "I've said it and I'm glad! Welcome aboard. Now you've got to stay! If you tried to leave now we'd have to kill you. Not really – but it's important you become friends of this island. So important."

Tommy walked into the office just then, took one look at his brother, whose fist was still stuffed in his mouth, and exhaled deeply, almost whistling. I was watching his eyes closely. What I saw was anger, but softened greatly by tenderness and understanding and resigned acceptance.

"Damn it, Tony. You've just given away the Secret of Eternal Life to an alcoholic reporter and a fifteen - year old teenage girl with a mouth the size of the Mississippi River. Could you have picked two more secure sources? These two make Kammi look like the Sphinx! Damn it! Here we go again. *Damn* it."

"Sir, with all due respect, my mouth is nowhere *near* as big as the Mississippi River!"

"Full dental?" My father repeated incredulously.

# X

*All the love*

"Well, brother," Tom remarked, hiding his anger in a soft, thoughtful laugh, "We probably ought to just buy you a bullhorn, and turn you loose in the streets like a prophet of some sort."

"I told them you'd be mad. I can't stand it when you're mad at me."

"We didn't take Tony seriously," Daddy smiled. He was looking at the bottle of Goose on the serving tray as he spoke.

"We've been drinking."

Tommy, too, was evaluating the half - empty quart bottle of *Goose*.

"My brother covered all the details about what makes this island special?"

"You had us at 'eternal life'," I blurted out. These brothers were fun. They were like my nerd buddies back at school. They needed a big sister as much as I did.

"As usual, my daughter is to the point. We were just flattered to be offered so much money. Believe me, the salary and benefits would have been sufficient alone."

"But you really had us at 'eternal life'," I added. "Perhaps you could elaborate?"

"How much did my visionary of a brother offer you?"

"Very low seven figures."

"Will that be enough?"

"Yes. But as my bar tender friend pointed out, this island is getting hairy."

"Pauley Vee?"

"You know him?"

"We know of him. A very serious man in his chosen profession, shall we say."

"Well, as for our chances of survival – We may still have a speck of a chance. We're not quite out the door yet."

"We're not?"

"Kammi is the worst military scout since Custer's 7th Cavalry."

"You think?"

"I know." Tommy smiled. I could tell he was still furious with his brother. "I suppose you guys would have to have been brought aboard at some point. The Water is free when you work here. This isn't the kind of offer we make very frequently."

Tony Perkins was not the only Trog in the room making snap decisions because of the encouragement of the high - end potato wine.

"Okay. Done deal. I'll stay." Daddy cut in. Just like that. Must have been the full dental. "But my daughter will have to return home to her mother, at least for now."

"No way!"

"Way."

"Oh, this blows big - time!"

"And we can keep a secret, Jessica?" Tom was looking at me with his very shrewdest face. "When you go home, and your friends ask about us: A very big secret?"

"I know how to keep it zipped," I answered irritably.

"Can she stay another few days, at least?" Tom asked my father.

It was the first time I'd heard him sound awkward. He was looking me over. This time with his dumb face. His grey eyes met my eyes. Right then I could tell that he could tell that I could tell. From *West Side Story – Somethin's comin', somethin' good – if I can wait...*

"Is the island safe?"

"We think so. At least for the next week or two. We'd have heard otherwise."

"Sure. Through the weekend then."

"Let me stay, Daddy. I can shoot an M-16 almost as well as you can."

"Damn it, daughter," Daddy laughed, "No women in combat!"

"Prehistoric trog."

"Can I give them a sip, Tom?"

Tom shrugged, rolling his eyes in absolute exasperation. Then, finally, he nodded.

"This thing my brother mentioned to you about... the Water... would you like to try a first sip?"

"Of course."

Daddy and I both nodded eagerly.

"Proof's in the pudding."

"You'll have to sign a confidentiality agreement later. It's stringent. But it's the planet's best - kept secret. The reason? Self - interest pure and simple. The one emotion you can always count on. The people who share this Divine secret are not fools. Of the hundreds who pay great fortunes for a sip every six weeks, we've only sprung one leak in all the years."

"Kammi," King Perkins bit his fist again.

By my father's reaction I could sense absolutely that he, like me, had at least half - believed Tony's earlier admission about the island being the home of the Fountain of Youth – had half - believed his earnest, sweating, knuckle - gnawing confession.

It was impossible. But so was that crown of Heaven's majesty in the courtyard four floors below, the Tree of Knowledge of Good and Evil, impossible also. Yet with good reason we had believed in it. The island was full of subtle magic, I could sense it with every breath I took of the miraculously fragrant air, with every radiant glimpse of garden, forest, sea and sky...

*Full Dental!*

Mr. Perkins rose and took a small glass container from the tray. It looked like a syrup pitcher from IHOP, the kind where you pull the metal lid back with your thumb. It too looked half - filled with vodka. Raspberry vodka.

"No, no, this is just our Water, but it makes a good chaser. May I recommend a toast with this? I think you'll like it."

"I'd like some vodka," I stated firmly. "Like the rest of you guys."

"Jessica, be still."

Then Daddy looked up.

"Water? No additives?"

"Don't ask me for a scientific explanation," Tony Perkins spoke softly, almost reverently. "We think it explains the longevity of the tree you were so impressed by. Perhaps this Water provides nourishment for every living thing on Crystal Lagoon. We don't know."

He held the mini - carafe up to the recessed light in the room's ceiling, as though looking into the glass in search for an explanation to satisfy himself.

"Oh, my God! Why did I have to tell that bitch about this," Tony muttered under his breath. "...jeopardized everything..."

"Hush, brother. This is a sacred moment."

"Yes. And now a shot glass for young Miss Jessica."

The shot glass was cut crystal, weighed about a pound, and he poured three shots into our elegant glasses, barely a finger of liquid into each glass, scarcely even a half - swallow.

The water, and perhaps this is only my imagination, looking back on it, but there seemed an almost amethyst tint to the sparkling downward splash from the IHOP carafe, a feeling rather than appearance of effervescence – like the almost uncanny vibrational dynamism I'd felt while nearby the great tree in the courtyard, this water gave me the deepest momentary visual sense of peace and energy as Mr. Perkins carefully filled my glass to a little over a quarter inch.

And there was a fragrance – like flowers – drifting lazily upward from the glass.

"This water looks almost purple."

"It does, doesn't it."

"Is it safe?"

"To our Eternal friendship," Tony Perkins raised his glass. He swallowed his sip first, to show it was safe.

"It smells like roses," I smiled.

"To our Eternal friendship."

At that moment, I felt the love. All the love. Before even sipping it, the unique fragrance of the water triggered an amazing rush throughout my chest, caused by the sudden racing of my heart. Then my lips touched the fragrant liquid – all the love. *Oh. All the love!*

I started to hug my dad. I'd never felt a rush like this go through me in my life, not sexual, not spiritual, not emotional. It was as primal as birth must be, only accompanied by the highest pitch of psychic clarity and alertness.

Another moment passed. *All the love.* The sense of all consuming energy, tranquility, power and calm embodied the highest qualities of every best emotion in my entire life, magnified and intensified a thousandfold. *All the love all the love all the love.... I want to hug my Dad!*

I started toward him. All. The. Love. *All the love!*

"God, Daddy – this is *wonderful!*"

"DON'T TOUCH HIM!" Tony Perkins shouted. I hesitated. "Nobody touch ANYBODY!"

"But I want a hug! I want to *give* a hug! Oh, I want to hug my Daddy! I've never in my life felt this way, felt this."

"Please, *please! No hugs! No touching!*"

"That effect only lasts for about ten minutes," Tom interrupted, his voice calm and re - assuring. "It's an effect that comes with the water. Just trust us. All will be well, just a little patience."

"But *why?!*"

"NO TOUCHING!"

Just at that moment, Tony Perkins actually stepped between Daddy and me. In my thrall, I almost reached out and tried to hug him too.

From his pocket protector, ever - present, Mr. Perkins produced what appeared to be a solid gold ballpoint pen, so much more elegant than Pauley's jacked - up fat barreled gift to Daddy.

With his gold pen, Perkins nudged my shoulder, almost antiseptically, guiding me, easing me back away from my father, as well as from himself.

"Excellent. No touching. No touching whatsoever." Tom quickly fronted Daddy and repeated the maneuver with a second gold ballpoint pen, further separating daughter from father, pushing us back away from each other by more than a yard now, then stepping away from us both, backward toward the bar - tray. "Just be a little patient, dear friends, and there'll be plenty of hugs all around..."

"But why?"

"We should have mentioned this ahead of time. It's a phenomenon called 'Epidermal Regression' that our Magic Water makes us susceptible to – it's rare, but it's the only downside to the ingestion of this water. Basically, it causes a swapping of skin pigment from one subject to another. Even though you're related to your father, Jessica – you probably don't want his forty year old skin."

"Thirty nine year old skin," Daddy corrected him.

"We've got your records, Jack."

"I've heard of this, I know about it!" *Allthelove!* "I read all about Epidermal Regression on the internet. Those African women – "

"Yes. That's the most recent case. They were all touching just after they drank from that mysterious purple stream.. We sent a team of scientists to that village. You see, we've had it happen here on the island too. We've had the top scientists on earth studying this, using every resource money can buy... the top epidemiologists.. We've just learned to respect it. It is a relatively rare occurrence. But it happens. And it's irreversible. To this day those African women are treated as Albino lepers in their own village. We send them money. It's caused by touching skin during ingestion. Different races are especially vulnerable. There's a ten minute sanction. Then we'll be safe."

"About six more minutes," Tom smiled, "And then a great big old group grope, eh?"

"Till then, it's like an eighth grade dance," Tony sighed, betraying a rarely witnessed sense of irony. "No skin to skin contact...or there...will...be ...trouble..."

"So now we live for ever?" Even Daddy was having trouble catching his breath. *Whew*. This exhilaration, this energy – it feels almost like a heavy steroid. An amphetamine injection. Both. Except that it's making me calmer. I feel a calmness at the center of my heart."

"You can still be killed – run over by a truck, say. But as long as you're breathing, you just won't age. You'll stay just as you are. Cease the water, you begin to age again at normal rate. Start the water again, aging ceases. Really, it's ideal, and it seems almost planned. You need a small sip of this water every sixth week. That's the purpose of our Communion services. We're barely able to collect enough water to keep up with the demand. The secret's been so well - kept... except for recently... because we all understand what is at stake. Eternal life. Which can be snatched away in a blink, once the information is in the wrong hands."

"I'm so sorry," Tony said again.

"It's behind us brother. Don't look back."

"She has snake - charmer eyes. They say this is a political conflict. But it's not. It's all about this Magic Water. That's all they care about. All those Reality people, the Kay daughters and that awful mother. To never age, that's the great Thirst that has come upon them..." *And who can blame them? Every war that's ever been fought, every Dream that's ever been dreamed, all to achieve the outcome of our few sips of Paradise on earth.*

"And Munye just wants to sell it. He thinks it's just a placebo."

"How old are you?" I could barely keep my hands off Tom.

"So very old."

"I don't care. I trust you. Tell us what to do and we'll do it." *Yes I will I said yes again I will Yes.*

"I'm reeling, daughter. You too? I can't imagine what it would be like to have this kind of luck when you're just fifteen years old." Whew. *Whew!*

*All the love all the love all the love. All. The. Love. Oh, yesyesyesyesyesyesyesyes... All the love... All the love.*

"Me too." *Fifteen – going on sixteen – for ever.*

My first thought: *We've got to find a way to get Mom down here.*

"We have to find a way to help you guys save this place."

*And that's why we charge our clients five million a year, in Euros, up - front, with a waiting list stretching from here to Saudi Arabia...*

"We trust your discretion, of course." Tom replied. "But it's like with literature, there comes a point we could no longer *tell*. It was time to *show.*"

"Yes," Daddy nodded, his voice soft. "As to your credibility – this takes it to a whole other level."

"This wonderful water, this fantastic amethyst nectar that fuels the beauty and perfection of our island," Tom confessed to us then, in a gloomy, almost grim admission, "This is the daily, unrelenting Promethean burden of our lives."

"Amen, my dear brother. And again, my deepest apologies."

"I love you, Tony. We'll get through this. Nobody's beaten us yet. And we have two new friends."

I stood apart from the three adults, my heart pounding. Whatever was occurring within me, racing through me, converged in a nexus of truth, beauty, wisdom, divinity, innocence, forgiveness of others. Most of all – Forgiveness of self.

In a single moment's wave of breathless, terrified disequilibrium, I felt the chains of my mortality falling away from me, a confining inner heaviness far greater than the weight of gravity itself, and in its place the equally frightening, equally breathtaking sense of the weightlessness of my soul's true freedom.

"About three minutes left, Jessica," Tom smiled at me, his smile radiant and reassuring. "Think you can make it?"

"Hope so." I gasped.

Although my bare feet remained firmly affixed to the plush pearl carpet, I felt myself rising above the others in the room, lifting upward, the essence of youth itself, like Peter Pan, *sans* theatrical guy - wires, *sans* green feathered cap, *sans* every thing – half - child, half - woman, suddenly never needing to look at another day behind me in the long progression. *Never growing up nor old, hovering utterly in the Present,* ahead of me, above me, below me, the past a heap of rusted chains, the future – formerly a narrowing Time – road reaching guaranteed immolation just beyond some unknowable but certain horizon – now, instead, a span of perfect, spreading, all encompassing light, erasing all linear mythology about human decay, now all the moments of eternity, as buoyant, glimmering and as purple as a child's bottle of soap bubbles, were bouncing happily along through the ether beside me, *say hello to my leetle friends, do you believe in magic, boys and girls,* Tommy watched me clapping my hands super fast, and laughed affectionately, the moments lighter than soap - bubbles, floating wondrously upward, all the moments and the months in eternity, shimmering soap - bubbles bursting amusingly at my pleasure, *for ever and ever, amen. God be my witness!*

"Dad, I can say, at least once – *whew!* – I experienced a moment of perfection."

*"Whew! Whew!"* He replied. *"Perfectly summarized. Oh,* God!"

*I'll never have to carry those cards that have expiration dates that only reminded me that I have one too... No mas! Never have to wear shoes all the time, never have to learn how to drive a damn car... All the love. Scarf Krispy Kremes, go to the Mall — travel the planet, memorize the libraries, learn to thank my luck in every language, all the love. Mass and energy identical. Then, with the crack of an invisible whip, the lacquered ponies of History's brutal carousel now fled away at the speed of light from their brass tethers, the deathly cconfines of their circular entrapped Destiny, of decay, regret, error, mortality; meanwhile, as I gasped for breath and fought back sudden tears, ringing down from the Heavens, I heard a great tuning fork in the form of ten thousand cathedral bells announcing the first cosmic explosion of pre - Time, the Big Bang's first moment synchronized with mathematical precision to the individual beat of my own heart, held now ever so gently and lovingly in Eternity's hands while the small girl's emergent soul grew, breath by breath, beat by beat full and wise at the almost orgasmic precipice under and within those loving Hands; the Peace that surpatheth Understanding — the Understanding that surpatheth Peace. Above all, as I gasped for air between bursts of tears, my voice impossibly silent — those gentle Hands gave my soul the protected sanctuary to forgive itself the fatal flaw of its own mortality, and to arise within myself as innocent and eternal as in the sunlight of Eden, perfect and patient, with Time now to perfect every flaw, to make immortality the wondrous norm...Forgiveness of all things, forgiveness of self...Love for all things. All the love.*

"I can't breathe," I cried out. *"It's perfect. I can't surive it."*

"Always remember this moment, Jessica," Tommy whispered softly, reassuringly. "This will only happen once. You are crossing over."

I was flawed. I was perfect. I was human. All. The. Love. *All the love, all the love, all the love.* I could touch the stars at midday. I could drink the wind, and live from its burning, chilling, sublime roar inside me, Eternity's breath nourishing and sustaining me, breathing for me all the rest of Days; God's hands held my heart so gently, squeezing my blood, beat to beat, with the metronomic patience and guarantee of eternity, the pleasures, challenges, gifts, the forgiveness and perfection and deepest peace of a world without end. I could feel it happening. There's simply no way to articulate the all - consuming patience of these few transformational moments... *God be my witness* —

Every heartbeat another soaring, brimming, breathlessly beautiful star in an infinity of stars, a beautiful, glimmering limitless uncountable infinity of stars, stars I could leap across like silver pavingstones, effortlessly pirouetting from heaven to earth and back again... *To dance beneath the diamond sky, with one hand waving free...*

The dark, softly lit room reached its intimate embrace all around us. We stood, looking at each other with these big stupid grins on our faces, like for ever. Like. For. Ever.

"Okay," Tommy laughed at last. "Time's up. Epidermal Regression window's closed. We're safe. Big hugs, everyone."

\* \* \*

*My little island, in the Pacific* — Daddy sang softly — *Where everything that happens is Terrific!*

*"We're not in the Pacific, Daddy,"* I laughed, tickling him back for once. *"We're in the stupid old wonderful Gulf of Mexico."*

A village of thatched roof bungalows became our next stop on the Magical Mystery Tour.

"You guys ok?"

"We're ok."

"And how."

"And you did say – 'full dental' – right?" Daddy teased himself, and we laughed and laughed.

We were breathless, dazed, victims or beneficiaries of a Wondrous Dream. Tony drove us in smiling silence to our bungalow. The world and the skies above it were bathed in the fragrance of azaleas and rosemary, and a thousand other blooms commingling. Even with all human history breathing for me, I had trouble catching my breath through my almost surreal excitement.

The village itself was like Sandals on Steroids, with two - dozen or so bungalows. The bar, cafe, restaurant – even a bowling alley – meant to attend them, had been built along all four fringes of a wide, sandy plaza – unoccupied at the moment. *Lights on, nobody home, honor system, help y'all selves...*

"One thing I couldn't help noticing," I'd asked Tom as we were leaving Tony's office. "The whole island seems almost empty." *All this lonely beauty, even the perfect island breezes seem to have echoes...*

"Yeah," Daddy confirmed, "Other than security and maintenance people, we're pretty much all alone?"

"For the safety of the flock, we put them on jets. They'll be back the day after all this is settled."

There was an unforced, leisurely quality to the architecture and outlook of the village, not exactly ramshackle, but if a hurricane took it all away, this address would not be difficult to replicate... a series of indoor and outdoor verandas, two huge living rooms crowded with big comfortable furniture –

Tony Perkins himself dropped us at the gate of the bungalow's low picket fence, waved a friendly goodbye, and went roaring off in his old jeep. Our future itinerary was a little uncertain.

*Well, daddy — so what are we going to do with the rest of our lives, do you suppose?*

"Feel like a nap?" Dads left the front door to our bungalow open behind us.

"I never want to sleep another wink."

"You're still a growing girl – "

"No! I've never felt more energy in my entire life!"

"The Krisps were that good?" He teased. I could tell, he felt the same way too. "So you don't hate Tony Perkins any more?"

"You know, Dad, it's very trog - like to remind a teenager that she is often an idiot." I laughed and hugged my beloved Daddy. "Never pre - judge. And I never will again. Those guys...they're like.. like children, somehow."

"I just wonder how old they are."

Whew! *Whew!*

"My God, what was in that water?!"

"I'll get us another glass." Oh, did I bounce, reaching the stainless steel kitchen sink in two teenaged strides.

"I don't think this is the same."

"Have you tried a sip?"

"I can tell by looking at it." I held the glass up to the kitchen window. It looked like nice, normal water. "Uh uh. I can sense it. Not the same, Dads."

"Try it."

I'd seen wine connoisseurs testing a new Merlot or whatever. Mom was some kind of a connoisseur. I swished the water, down the hatch, Jessica...

*Aaahhh.*

"Nope."

Daddy made another note on his omnipresent pad.

"Wonder what the difference is – "

"Well, this is just water. Delicious water. But water."

"I noticed a water tower on the edge of that forest we came through...and every building, even this bungalow, has rain barrels all around the back...We're getting water from the sky to drink or bathe in." I went back to the kitchen and looked out again.

"Yep. Rain barrels. You don't miss much, do you, Sherlock?"

"I don't remember ever feeling this way, Jess – maybe in childhood. Maybe Eternity is like childhood, the best day of childhood endlessly repeated. It caused me to focus on the potential source." We looked at each other.

"What a place!" We exclaimed, together, and laughed.

"Jinx on coke."

"What?"

"Oh," He laughed, seemingly surprised at himself, "it's just something we used to say, a phrase in high school, when two people say the same thing at the same time... Funny to hear it come out of my mouth, from so long ago."

"The gardens, so beautiful and unique..."

"The grass, the glades, the flowers... not a mosquito nor sandspur, even the Spanish moss seems to exist for aesthetic effect..." *There's a tree thick with ripe tangerines by the front gate, and strawberry vines in full fruit running through the yard; and coconuts, clustered in that low - curving palm, in the corner of the fenced side - yard... You could just reach out and pull 'em down with one hand!*

"And that incredible tree!"

*"Jinx on coke!"*

We both caught ourselves exclaiming together, once again, same subject, same emotional level, and this time I shrieked in happy surprise. *I can't believe we're on the same wavelength like this! Wished for it a million times, never thought it could happen, not for even an instant!*

"Jinx on coke!" He roared with laughter, and I got a glimpse of my father in high school, jock, student council guy, pimply, flaky teenager – like me.

"I love you, Dad."

"Me too you, crazy wonderful daughter."

I snuggled up under his shoulder, and we sat on that couch for what seemed to be a million years, in perfect silence gazing through the broad veranda windows as warm sunlight graced the lime - bright waters of the Gulf of Mexico in the distance, its glittering surface broken infrequently by tiny gull - shaped whitecaps.

Much closer, a slight breeze moved the roses, wisteria, honeysuckle, magnolia, mint and ivy in the garden by the front picket fence.

Only briefly did I wonder how big sister Kammi Kay was doing. Mom would be happy here. *All it is is heaven on earth.*

I laid in my dad's lap with my arms around him. Usually he was so relaxed, so laid back, so pre - possessed – it was quite unusual, to feel him inside the circle of my arms, suddenly begin to tremble at the overwhelming secret we now shared.

"Daddy, you're trembling – you're shaking like a leaf!"

"No I'm not."

"It's okay. I am too."

"It's just that....This island feels like – like where it all might have actually begun," I heard my father murmur, almost to himself. He was shaking like a leaf. "Jessica, this is the most unbelievable thing…"

I began to cry, tears of wonder. My tears, at least in memory, had a lovely, salty purple flavor. Each sweet tear drop contained within itself a ghostly whispered word from the memory of Oscar Wilde:

*youth..is…the…only…thing…worth…having….*

# XI

Two days would pass before we would again encounter King Perkins. He called our bungalow frequently and apologetically postponed the tour and interview.

Sherlock and I used the time to walk this fantastic island, which seemed to stretch out to infinity, a land without time or borders.

Every hour another jet would land, and shortly thereafter, depart, but such was the magical balance of all elements of sight and sound on Crystal Lagoon, even the shriek of jet engines seemed muted and distant, although the unmarked silver bellies of the aircraft often passed just over our heads as we walked.

The last of the island's billionaire trust fund babies were jetting off to sanctuary. The coordinated efficiency of the refugee transfer was remarkable. But I had a feeling the departing jets were carrying away now, not just people, but money. And maybe something a lot more important than money.

Magic Water.

About a half - mile southwest of the castle, and inland by about the length of a football field from the sea - wall that held back the Gulf, stood the massive Perkins' Media Center. This was the mausoleum that Reality Nation was planning to most happily occupy, once the island had been surrendered to Dr. Munye's mini - army. It gave enhanced meaning to 'state - of - the - art.'

This Gulliver of a structure rose above its Lilliputian neighbors by about a factor of twelve to one. Bigger than the biggest airplane hanger ever envisioned, Great Gulliver was capable of housing a couple of Spruce Gooses, and its altitude loomed lofty enough to be able, like the Superdome, to create its own inner atmosphere.

Gigantic, corrugated, ugly, the blue steel barnlike building was nearly the size of the castle itself. Its brutalistic architecture featured broad metal roll - down doors interrupting each of its four heavily buttressed walls. To either side of each great door bristled telecommunications antennae and supporting electronic paraphernalia, giving the monster edifice a kind of sharp - edged, blinking gingerbread; in fact, atop the brow of the great box, the antennae spread like a crown of metallic thorns, from whose steel barbs you expected, in storms, a demonic lightning to arise.

There was such a sense of brooding technological indifference expressed in the theme, scope and feel of the structure that it was my only unfavorite place in our otherwise gentle, pacific world.

Sometimes when we were on an afternoon stroll nearby this place, a brief afternoon shower would provide a sense of humanity to the structure's competent face, its immense undulating contours shining from the rivulets of glimmering moisture. The raindrops, like tears, gave you the impression Great Gulliver knew what it looked like and was daily saddened by its own ugliness, if only for a half hour.

Rain fell for a little while daily on Crystal Lagoon, yet only enough to refresh the streams, ponds and central lagoon itself, wash the face of day, and remind us all that into every life a little rain must fall.

Scattered about in the shadow of Great Gulliver were a number of low, mirrored research buildings, giving the compound a sort of feudal sense, and the afternoon showers polished the walls and solar rooftops of the modern silver facilities to a dazzling gleam.

It was the part of the island I cared for least. But like the others, I accepted it. The compound was a brutalistic triumph of function over form, as Daddy said, and, contradicting classical feudalism, in this case Great Gulliver fed the pretty little mirrored serf entities surrounding and enskirting its ugliness instead of the other way around; the research on aging, cold fusion, cancer, even epidermal regression were all fed by revenues generated inside the cold, sterile blue mountain that wept for itself a half an hour a day...

Great Gulliver was where massive revenues and positive propaganda for the island were generated; movies, documentaries, talk shows, political commercials, public service ads, and so forth.

This temple was the Heart of Darkness that so drew the fascinated gaze of Reality Nation, because, down to the last baby spot, it had all the technological prowess necessary to rule the world's electronic media.

"It's a necessary weevil," Tommy teased me. "We could have filmed 'Gone With The Wind' in there. There are enough sound stages to get it done all at once."

Both Perkins brothers acknowledged the crucial necessity of this workplace to the lives and fortunes of everyone in or near its shadow. But Tony and Tom hated it too.

"Next time Gehry designs the whole island, Media Center included," Tom remarked irritably once, but then he shrugged and let it go.

Between Great Gulliver, as we started calling it, and the sea, stretched a beautifully graded smooth bare limestone field, onto which had been crowded row on row of enormous silver metal saucers – satellite dishes, each one big enough to sail to Cuba on, row after row after row guarded behind barbed wire and pointed upward on a southwestern axis.

Contrasted with the gloom of Great Gulliver, into which their information was fed, these lovely dishes fascinated me by their function, cleanness, efficiency.

"Daddy, let's say that, hypothetically, some day we're not here any more, and aliens come upon this place – do you think that when they're looking upon these dishes, that they'll be as puzzled as we are by Easter Island?"

"Or Stonehenge?"

"No. Not Stonehenge. These dishes are standing like guardians by the sea, looking upward like those sculptures on Easter Island."

He gave me an odd look. If I didn't know better, I'd have said it was a look of pride.

"Have you started to grow a brain in that pretty head when I wasn't looking, daughter?"

"Not a chance, mister," I growled and elbowed him violently for teasing me.

Dad and I were holding hands as twilight approached, just like in the movies, daddy and daughter together... *just like in the movies...*

But deep down, I think I already knew, it was too good to last.

Maybe only a fifteen year old can appreciate the value of eternal life, but it seemed so obvious that an island with such gigantic, even immeasurable qualities of wealth and value was in the gentle guardian hands of the losing side.

What little I knew of History showed this, and so did my personal experience.

My dear Dad was simply too far down in his own emotional life, and the Perkins' brothers simply too innocent, too sweet, to do what was necessary to forestall the barbarian invasion lurking beyond the island's temperate shores.

I remembered how the lunchroom tables had been allocated in my high school, the nerds had occupied prime window space until a group of jocks had simply picked up their chairs, with the cursing, pleading, kicking, complaining nerds still seated in them, and moved them across the lunchroom to a table by the kitchen door, depositing them there and advising them to there remain.

Until semester's end, seating arrangements in the lunchroom altered not. The jocks kept their views, the nerds kept their lives. High school might not teach you much else, but you learn all about future reality there.

*Enjoy your time in Paradise, Jessica. Nothing lasts forever, especially Eternity...*

One afternoon early in the visit, especially dear to my heart in memory, Daddy gave me a little lesson on modern American jazz – alongside motion pictures, the art form Americans can lay most honest claim to creating.

Daddy let me read a column he'd written about a jazz concert he'd attended, and then we spent the afternoon in silence, listening.

"In my opinion, this guy – Pharoah Sanders is his name, Jess, and he plays horn, most frequently tenor sax – you can hear the memory of the Nile river in his music, Jessica, he reaches back into a primal emotion in history that is unrivaled, he's the best of a great many geniuses of the form. John Coltraine, Miles Davis, Wes Montgomery...just listen..."

And while I listened, I read what my father had written...*their last piece, a recessional began with a stabilized melodic narrative introduction, a conventional structure, melody, chorus, compressed lyrical control over the music, lovely, rhythmic, unsurprising, supper club dance jazz, modest, to the beat perfectly up - tempo, yet with the crash of a single pair of cymbals, the smooth fabric of the performance was interrupted by, followed by, ripped apart by, then utterly exploded by, the magnificent improvisational comet's tail of shrieking saxophone riffs of indescribable power and originality, with frightening surging suddenness the convergence of maracas, congas, tambours, saxophones recreating the passion and brutality, the helpless screamed cries rising as though from the barred cages in the holds of slave ships, the howling loneliness of isolation in a foreign world filled with terror and courage and survival, the woven notes borne by angels clawing, then soaring upward to expressive infinity with every breath from the artist's genius soul, rounded to patient, masterful understanding, and the concluding transcendence of true soul, suffering, catharsis, even forgiveness, or at least eternal patience, twenty minutes of uninterrupted, volcanic interpretive anger and redemption from the chaos of the slave memory, in memoriam, the wild*

*perfection of deepest human truth in the only music capable of*
*capturing, articulating and forgiving it:*

*The Creator has a Master Plan*
*Peace and happiness through all the land...*
*The Creator has a Master Plan*
*Peace and happiness*
*Through all*
*The land...*
*Through all*
*The land...*
*Through all......the..... land.....*
*Peace*
*and*
*Happiness*
*Through*
*All .......the.........land.......*
*All........the.........land....!*
*All.........the.........land.....*

My father had concluded his column this way: *In its*
*intellectual breadth and insight, and in its anguished emotional depth*
*and resonance, this music equals anything in the human experience*
*that Michelangelo ever created...*

# XII

*Of these three, which matters most —*
*To be? To do? To have?*

*Ancient Bedouin Paradox*

*All the love.*

Even now, as much time as I've had to think about
it, there are simply no words in any known language to
capture the miraculous essence of the single sip I had held
in my hand — only glimpses of inarticulate truth in the jazz
of the genius Pharoah Sanders that I'd come to love, or at
the opposite end of the spectrum, the profoundly silent
music that came from the wind that trembled in the leaves
and branches of the immortal tree of Knowledge itself: *The
Tree of Knowledge of Good and Evil.*

Above all, even more than Time, was the gift of a
kind of divine patience, a self - awareness so complete that
the utter forgiveness that came with it reached to the
deepest place in my soul. A single sip.

In spite of every flaw, I was perfect. I was human.
All the love all the love all the love, the love that passeth
understanding, the peace that passeth understanding, the
radiant angelic perfection of self - understanding and

forgiveness, all this flowed down into me, not as a drug, but almost like heaven's mirror.

Everything became possible, nothing was necessary, forever was this moment. *All the love.*

"This is as good as it gets," Daddy had whispered, an understatement for the Ages.

He too seemed healing at last. I know he missed my Mom so much a part of him had been daily dying, for the several years since their separation. I could feel it every time we were together, that emotional undertow he was always sort of swimming against when he thought of her.

But as he hugged me, I could sense it: He'd begun to swim free, in the embrace of an amethyst - tinted rainbow of water droplets that were the emotional opposite of tears. But he and I both knew he'd never really be completely free of her. That's just how their love was.

*This stuff could really help your Mom,* his eyes told me. He was so in love with her he wanted eternity for them both, and both together. Realizing that was what was in his heart jolted me physically, like another sip of magic: *all the love.*

We were in Tony's office. They were expressing enthusiastic approval for Daddy's work. The steel - wheeled Welcome Wagon sat nearby the sofa where we were most comfortable being together.

"We love your latest press releases. Clean and to the point. All we can do is tell the truth."

"Thanks for staying, Jack. Thanks for letting your lovely daughter stay too."

"I'd have to stuff her in croker sacks and dump her on *Gator Rosie*. Short of that, she stays."

"Damn straight," I threw down. "Time to fix bayonets."

"Her mother gave permission for her to stay another two weeks."

"She had to finally accept the fact that I'm a grown, adult woman now," I intoned. I held both fists dramatically to my breast. "Able to make my own decisions. Courageous. And able to face the world courageously. To rely on no one but myself and exercise responsibility as an adult."

"That's so admirable, Jessica," Tom said.

"My body matured quite early. I guess everything else just followed."

"And you swore you'd clean your room as soon as you got back." Daddy prompted.

"That too."

"And no texting after ten at night."

"*And* that."

"And no more calling her 'mommy dearest' – "

"Yessss." I turned dramatically toward my three admiring elders. "I've come to realize, at the threshold of adulthood, that complete integrity, combined with self - forgiveness, form the basis for real character."

Daddy, remembering something, interrupted again.

"And you've got to promise, Jessica – no more skateboarding through the City Cemetery, especially on Sunday, during their outdoor services."

"Dad, you are putting a Trog stake right through the heart of my adult moment!"

"Apologies, daughter." He blushed with embarrassment. Then we both laughed. Ultimate proof of how much daddy and I love each other deep down. After every quarrel, no matter how fierce, we always start laughing at the superficiality of it all.

"You'll make a great adult, Jessica," Tom said. Our eyes met. That gaze had trouble untangling.

"I never want to grow up completely."

"Luckily, you still have that existential option. We don't."

We were sitting on a long couch in the dark room, our feet up on the coffee table, as the conversation drifted easily around all the important aspects of our visit. I was barefoot, beside me I looked down at Dad, and beside his old Topsiders, two pairs of Hush Puppies, Tom's and Tony's.

"What's our strategy?" Tom laughed. "It's all up to the lawyers. The attorneys decide which wars are to be fought and how to fight them – they do everything but bleed. We'll have to leave it in the hands of the lawyers."

"You can't be serious!"

"We've never been threatened like this before. Everything gets run by Legal first."

"Kressa Kay has bought up our entire security force," Tom pointed out. "No matter what we offer, they offer more."

"Sure," Tony added. "They promise them their lives. I don't blame anybody from jumping ship."

Hush Puppies! I would have loved those guys for their Hush Puppies alone! Nerdware. Gentle souls, custodians of Paradise, perhaps against their wishes, but so contradictory to the public image of the malefactors of Crystal Lagoon, the Capitalist, racist satans who ruled the world from behind these castle walls.

Nothing could be further from the truth. Pocket protectors, bad haircuts, ill - fitting albeit expensive casualwear. Tom and Tony were better suited to play roles in *The Big Bang Theory,* long in syndication. I loved them both, like big sister Penny would, almost...

About ten days after our arrival, we found ourselves in Tony's office again. The brothers asked Daddy to come by. They'd been working on a new pr initiative. Now Daddy's input was necessary. We'd cancelled a sailing junket and returned to the castle. Ten days of perfection, each happier than the one before it.

I'd learned to open a coconut with a single wallop of a machete. I was learning to sail. Ghost Posse, Barry, Princess Cantaloupes, all painful but fading memories in a fifteen - year old mind. I missed Mom so much. But I always missed her, even when we were in the same room, yelling at each other...

"Maybe it's almost time for another sip?"

"I think they just need company."

When we arrived, Tommy and Tony were alone in the office. They were quarreling, calmly as always, about strategy. Tommy waved without turning.

"... I just found out about it yesterday. She knows how this island works."

Tommy was glaring at his brother.

"Stop looking at me that way. I was a fool. Fine. But they don't know where the Water is. They don't know how to get to it. I never told her that."

"I have a question," My father interrupted.

"Yessir."

"I'm working on this press release. But I'm having trouble analyzing their angle. Munye and Ghost Posse have a plausible political motive for moving against this island. What in God's name have this Confederacy of Dunces –

this so - called Reality Nation – got to do with any of this? What's their interest? How do they benefit?"

"Munye's wife, the incredible Kammi Kay, is the queen of that Nation. Start there."

"It's the perfect convergence of politics and culture, really," Tommy explained further. I could tell he was thinking as he was talking, trying to get deeper into the converging motivations of the two powerful interest groups.

"Nitro? Meet Glycerine. White America is choking on Dr. Munye and his Separatist ambitions. So Kammi and her company of idiots are being brought in to beard up Munye's splendid little war against us.

"Munye's mug will be on every reality screen – from Jerry Springer to Orca. Once she gets out of that mental hospital. Big smiles, everyone – cue the Applause sign. The American public must really approve of what Dr. Munye believes in. Look, they're applauding. Stand and Cheer. Look, they're standing and cheering, on every program, on every channel, people just like us, just like trained seals. Aaarrkk! Aaarrkk! Can't you just see the headlines already?

\* \* \* \* \* \* \*

*MUNYE POLLS IN STEADY RISE,*
*SOURCES SAY*

\* \* \* \* \* \* \*

*MUNYE TROOPS FLY OLD GLORY*
*OVER ISLE'S MYSTERY*
*MOSQUE; AL QAEDA LINKS FOUND,*
*SOURCES SAY.*

\* \* \* \* \* \* \*

*POTUS, MUNYE HUG AT KID'S CHARITY*
*FETE,*
*GHOST POSSE UP FOR EIGHT GRAMMYS,*
*GP COLONY BID GETS POTUS OK,*

SOURCES SAY
* * * * * *

"And what will Reality Nation get out of it, other than an island full of ready - made, state - of - the - art electronics and a planetary satellite capability, already up and running?" Tommy grinned, palms up in a rhetorical gesture. "With the power and technology to rule worldwide cable television? What else will their payoff be?"

"Just the Water," His brother added.

Daddy stretched, relaxed, and put his arm around me again. Perfect.

"Thanks, guys," he laughed. "Now it's clear. I needed that."

"You guys aren't linked to Al - Qaeda, are you?" I asked in alarm.

"No. But it's easy to think that because that's what the Narrative will say. We tend to think the way they want us to think. What the Narrative lays down."

"The mother – Kressa Kay – is behind the whole thing. That's one smart lady."

"Kammi and Doctor Munye want to install a cultural autocracy once they've taken over the island. It's sort of unclear, but they know we have immense studio capacity, and the bandwidth and licensing access with which they will create a separate Reality Super Network that would give them communications power to their supporters – to the millions, the idiots, the morons, the cretins, of planet earth."

"You mean the voters."

"Uh – huh."

*And there'll be a new Reality series soon, right after we're finished off – 'Africa America: The Fourteenth American Colony – Is It Time?', real time video verité, brought to you by ORC (Orca Renfroe Channel)... It's already in pre - produc...*

"In a sense, we're swimming in a sea of mortal enemies. It's true, we contribute a boatload of money to politicians in Florida and Washington, but nothing can compete with the electoral power controlled by Munye and his network, growing exponentially in the fourteen largest industrial states. They're paralyzed in Washington by this... this *interior nation*. Africa America – it's descriptive."

"Now you sound like Lush Rimbaud."

"He's a comedian," Tommy said to me. "But when we laugh, it means he's hit a nerve. Have you noticed how scared he's been sounding lately? He's braying like a deflating balloon. Always on this one issue."

Tony took a rare shot of Goose.

"Easy on that stuff, brother."

"Once they've got the Magic Water – Kressa Kay's KayKable Channel One will be up and running from our facilities here. Money Hoo Hoo can stay four years old forever. *Even Judge Trudy will never die.* Oh, the horror. Tommy and I get tried on terrorism charges out in Kansas and wind up serving Life Without in a Supermax somewhere. POTUS is re - elected. Munye addresses the U.N. Checkmate. Applause. Cheers. Fade to black."

"Some Narrative."

"The Narrative is everything."

"My brother tends to the dramatic. That's an extreme analysis. In any case, our position is dangerous."

"Maybe the drama comes from the fact I was almost shot to death *twice!*"

Tom turned to Dad and me.

"They're also trying to buy a Bomb now."

"What kind of bomb?"

"The only kind that matters."

Daddy looked at the two of them with disbelief.

"An A - Bomb?"

Tony nodded, his face equally mixed with puzzlement and anger.

"If they can't have the island, they want to be able to threaten to blow it."

"You've gotta be kidding me."

"Kressa Kay is negotiating with the Chechnyans. She's functioning as the agent for Ghost Posse. Ten - kiloton minimum. You'd be amazed how cheap the damn things are going for. I mean – it's as though they're just laying around on the ground over there. Really cheap."

"How cheap?"

"Cheaper than a new Buick. For one bomb. But one is all they'll need."

The brothers were both becoming more agitated. Soon the office would be too claustrophobic and we'd have to take another island tour, a walk to ward off panic attacks.

"Think about it. If this idiot racial colony, Africa America, comes into being, they'll be the seventh or eighth independent nation to have their own nuclear capability! Intolerable."

*And we've got Kressa Kay's texts to her daughter Kammi, over a hundred of them, laying the whole thing out. Not to mention the intercepts our people have put on their phones. Fortunately, Dr. Munye is not taking us too seriously, None of them are. This island is considered low - hanging fruit.*

"You tap their phones?"

"We tap everything."

"This is hard to believe," Daddy replied.

"We couldn't believe it either. We considered it a theoretical problem. Until however many months ago, when Kammi got cut off from the Water. Then everything accelerated. Kressa's driving the train now. You can just sense it: mother and daughter don't want to lose any more time."

I remembered our night together in the cheap motel, and how Kammi had kept running every five minutes to the hall mirror, obsessively checking the laugh - lines around her mouth. At the time I'd thought it was no more than her enormous narcissism. Now it made perfect sense. She was watching Time eat her alive, meanwhile knowing there was a way to stay Time's appetite. Now it all made perfect sense.

Tommy and Tony liked showing us around their jewel box of an island, its secret grottoes and hideaways. I think it helped them get away from their problems. They knew I adored them both. Perhaps they liked that too.

By now I was sort of major crushing on Tommy. *Fifteen going on sixteen, okay? What can I say? Don't give me a hard time. Want me to sing another Broadway romantic tune to more deeply explain my subconscious attraction to this man?*

*Look – he's awesome. Harvard Law, a hundred pushups a day, the best sailor and massage giver in the hemisphere, builds sailboats and plays keyboard, and more and more I was seeing the dumb side of him, off - balance and stammering, when we're together... Physically, he's – oh, man.*

*Gorgeous grey eyes and he always makes me laugh. Who cares if he's probably five hundred years old? What's that in dog years? And what's time got to do with a dog anyway? Tom is one of those rare people who've learned to give Time meaning, every moment. Both brothers were brilliant, with centuries of experience to bolster their intuitive intellects.*

*And Tommy was crazy sexy. It was just in his nature. He kept his behavior, even after a few drinks, absolutely correct, courtly as Old World royalty – but it was always there all the same. Teenagers notice these things.*

Mostly we walked the seemingly endless expanse of Crystal Lagoon. Roseanne had been right; the strawberries that grew wild along the trails and throughout the forests of the island were as large as lightbulbs, and overhanging them, tangerines, mangoes, lemons, limes, oranges, the limbs of their trees bending with the proliferation of delicious beauty, the forest floor at every turn pregnant with melons so exotic we seemed to find a new one to experience on practically every picnic...

I had an escort when I wanted one, sometimes my wonderful Dad, sometimes the proper but increasingly attracted Tommy, and sometimes all three, when I got to be Dorothy in perfect Oz...

Goats and peacocks and pigs and key deer drifted through the forests, they'd come up and eat out of your hand, a marvelous balance of sufficiency and trust that seemed to rule all the beings lucky enough to have reached this place...

We walked through the rich high soft grass – I felt like running, somersaulting, making grass angels in the soccer field's lush lovely field of grass.

Trolley tracks, currently unused, ran outside the bleachers that overlooked the soccer field. Recently some odd construction had occurred on the soccer field itself, which lay directly outside the castle's front gates. The brothers had ordered a series of culverts to be installed vertically and covered by turf, side by side by side, a row of man - sized concrete culverts stretching from one sideline to the other at midfield, a truly inexplicable addition to the pristine soccer field that stretched out from the castle's front gates, like a huge swath of emerald carpet, and flanked by the low, almost ceremonial bleachers.

The location of the soccer field, with one of its netted goals hard athwart the castle's front gates, was aesthetically fortuitous, pardon the big words – the flat turf surface and low flanking bleachers only emphasized the huge, lofty presence of the castle's walls and gates immediately above and beyond.

The field led right up to the castle's front doors, so to speak. But the addition of the culverts were odd. And the brothers were never particularly forthcoming when it came to their various madnesses, nor of the methods behind them. I asked once, got a couple of deflected comments and a shrug or two, and let it go.

I say 'odd' because it was the only construction work happening anywhere on the entire island. I guess the concrete culverts had been successfully buried, the field re - landscaped.

I liked to walk ballet - style on the steel rails where the trolley had once run, my arms stretched outward, while my three admirers watched. I was Shirley Temple sometimes, Dorothy in Oz sometimes, sometimes Elizabeth Taylor in *National Velvet,* sometimes merely me. To my amused adult admirers, I might as well have been Queen of the Roller derby…

To be the queen of anything was wonderful, especially with such an appreciative and gentle court of adult male admirers. Tom remained forever correct, courtly, Old World, and I could always tell when he was watching me, thinking I was unaware…

*Oh, that this summer might never have ended…*

"None of us think we're ever going to die, anyway. Jester," Tommy had pointed out once. "You might not want to be fifteen going on sixteen for ever. You might want to be eighteen, or even twenty one someday..."

"I like fifteen," I said to myself.

I was only fifteen. I was already immortal! What a great birthday present, better than a vintage Mustang, which I'd never have received anyway. Mom had troggily attached the requirement that I clean my room before she'd buy the car for me.

Have you even seen that room? Of course you haven't. Anyway, the Mustang wasn't going to be happening anytime soon. Immortality was twice as good, and there was no place to drive on the island anyway...

*No way those racist trogs are taking this world away from us. Time to fix bayonets!*

Run it by legal? I wasn't even really sure what that even meant.

"How old are you guys?" I interrupted. "Tom – how old are you? I'm almost sixteen...."

"Time doesn't mean anything on this island."

But it was the little things that gave me an insight...

I remembered catching Tom reading by candlelight one evening...

"How can you even see anything in here?"

"Old habits die hard." He had laughed. "Even after all these decades, electric lights still bother me.

"How old are you?" I demanded.

And then he had kissed me.

"You taste so good," He said.

"Keep kissing!"

Just one kiss before he pulled away, in the beauty of the candlelight, touching my shoulder before he slipped out of the room. It was as gentle and as pure a gesture as the grace notes of the silent music that came from the Tree of Knowledge of Good and Evil, but in this case, it was good, all good, all so good, and for the next week I thought of little else.

Now, several weeks later, sometimes Tom and I held hands on our walks, and Dad never objected when he was walking with us, performing the unconscious task almost of a chaperone. We four fond friends were walking along under the soft sunlight, graced by a gentle breeze filled with island fragrances, perfect in the moment.

The chemistry among us was perfect, hard to understand, but perfect somehow. Even as the island had emptied, the Perkins' brothers were daily very busy in a world far beyond anything we understood. From private phone calls and video - conferences, to visits that sometimes occurred inside the jets that still arrived and departed, theirs was another world still.

But somehow, through all this, Dad and I had become their friends, and they had become ours. And our afternoon walks were treasured.

"For whatever reason," Tony had mentioned once, "Jessica, you and your father are the most wonderful de - stressers…"

Flattered, my father had only nodded.

"Well, we'll always tell you the truth. When you're as rich as you guys are, truth is a hard commodity to come by." *Every smiling face around you hides a lie or at the least a contrary self - interest that can destroy you just as quick. Truth, honesty — the most important commodity we can provide.*

I wanted to ask each of them, over and over again, if they felt as I did, that life under heaven could ever have been imagined to be this wonderful...

"Will it get really crowded on the island, when the war is settled, and the guests come back?"

"Not really," Tony laughed.

"Perhaps half stay on the island anywhere near full time. Most fly in for their sip and fly out again. These are busy people. The rulers of the world." *The only place they can get even a drop of the Water is here, on this island — it can't ever be beyond our control. We maintain a twenty - four hour buffet, a jet arrives every third day — it's pretty smooth, actually.*

"I'd love to meet Madonna sometime," I said. "I heard she comes here on vaca...she's my heroine."

"There's every chance of that, Jessica."

But then the world itself, and our lives in it, changed frighteningly in the next moment.

Once before in recent memory, Death had sent an oven - sized razorback as His random warning ambassador. *Horseman, pass by.*

Daddy had skidded us out of that one. From time to time I still daydreamed of the terrifying moment and his coolness under fire, and framed it in another Hemingway quote he'd urged me to commit to memory, *courage is grace under pressure.*

This time, Death intruded from the beautiful blue sky.

I'd just wrapped one arm around Daddy, the other around Tommy, and we'd cheerily emerged from a little wood onto a sandy walkway that led back past glum Great Gulliver toward the castle. We'd planned to go sailing later.

*Whupwhupwhupwhupwhup!!*

Just above the tree - tops we glimpsed the giant minnow shape of a helicopter racing across the sky, an ugly storm of diesel power preceding it, whup - whup - whup - whup *whupwhupwhupwhup* WHUPWHUPWHUPWHUP!!

*"Down! Duck down, daddy!"*

"They're not that close – it's okay!"

*"Look out!"* Tom shouted. *"Jessica!"*

Not that close, but still we dropped to our knees, all four of us, as a moment's bleak shade passed over us, then with a sharp starboard turn, the thundering silhouette of the low level airborne trespasser had suddenly curled upward, and, trembling violently, had ascended behind the pines and was gone...

*WHUPWHUPWHUPWHUPwhupwhupwhup.* It was as though a cloud had just flown over the future, and taken the future with it in its indifferent departure, leaving a lingering imprint of helpless anger on each of our faces.

After a moment of shaken silence, Daddy spoke first.

"What the hell was that all about?"

"Part of the recent harassment." *Ghost posse recon.* "Third overflight in ten days."

"How come I haven't heard them?"

"You and your dad are usually out sailing, sailor," Tony shrugged.

"Maybe that's just a tourist ride," I answered unconvincingly. "Everybody on the mainland is fascinated by this place."

"The Vietnamese had a name for helicopters," Daddy was as startled and shaken as me by the incursion.

"They called them, 'stuttering death.' This is the first time I've understood..."

"Damn it!" Tom said. "I've had enough of this."

"Brother, this is the third time this week."

We felt the stricken sense of danger that passed between the two brothers as their eyes searched the horizon.

"It's intimidation. They want us to just run off."

"We should shoot the bastards down and be done with it!"

"They're photographing again — we can't shoot people for taking pictures." *Legal would kill us for doing something like that. When the lawyers start yelling — that's when it gets ugly... Depositions... Subpoenas... Writs... Blood all over the walls...*

"I thought I saw Kammi riding passenger." *I'm pretty sure it was her.*

"I hate her," Tony cursed. "I hate her with all my heart. I've never hated anyone the way I hate her. I'm amazed the emotion could go so deep."

"They're getting ready to attack. They're getting ready to kick our asses! It's like fourth grade school recess all over again!"


"Time for you to go home to your mother. Give her my love. And clean up your room. I'll keep in touch."

"Well, I'm not going."

"Jessica, this time you're going to have to actually obey an order."

"I don't obey trog orders. It's like – it's an illegal order! It blows like never before! I thought we were a team here."

"I have legal custody. I'm expected to act like an adult. You've got to go home. We're putting you on the next plane out."

"I *am* home. I do your word processing! Your editing! And I know how to shoot." *Damn it, I'm one of the guys!*

"She *is* one of the guys," Tommy backed me, having read my thought cloud without so much as moving his beautiful lips.

"I feel so old," Tony said. "Older than Tiresias."

Tom gave his brother an affectionate hug.

"Oh, come on – Age is all just a state of mind, or hadn't you heard?"

\* \* \*

"This room is like being inside a submarine," I commented to Tom. We stood at the threshold, in deep carpet, looking into what appeared to be a miniature version of the communications center of a network like CNN, only with low ceiling, recessed lighting, paneled walls, and the dozen, or two dozen, techies in pale jumpsuits, socks and slippers. It was as antiseptic a world as a surgical amphitheater. This was the room Tony usually kept hidden behind the thick false oak wall next to his own office.

There were clocks for every time zone on earth, at the far end, old - fashioned round clocks, not digitized numbers.

I think we all understood our afternoon's sailing lesson was cancelled, and there might never be another sailing lesson on Crystal Lagoon; and we'd very calmly moved into crisis mode.

It was so flattering to have reached the island's top administrative echelon in just weeks after arriving here. *The brothers are not looking for more professional support. They've got all of that they need. They're looking for friends, and somehow, we've become friends to these poor, beleaguered geniuses. I'm like the girl in The Big Bang Theory. And Daddy knows how to fight. I love these guys. They're deeply lovable, and like Kammi — only for diametrically opposite reasons — very sad.*

Shortly after Death had danced its shadow across the lovely afternoon sky, Dad and I found ourselves following the silent, fast - moving brothers through a series of rooms and halls before arriving at the mega - lift, and up we went. And now here we were.

At the center of the world, behind the fake oak wall in Tony's office, which opened with the touch of a button to reveal – the War Room.

I've never figured out which of the two brothers was actually in charge. Tony was more the dreamer, the big - picture visionary, neurotic, insecure. Tom got things done. Tom was the pragmatist. He knew how to laugh, and how to make us all laugh. Leadership between the two brothers sort of went back and forth. But whenever either of these two prodigies had a gut feeling, it was always acted upon.

Now Tony had his hand on the shoulder of one of the controllers, whose screen showed the image of the gorgeous green gulf waters, and in the foreground, the solid black silhouettes of the palmetto, scrub pine and coconut palms, all the beauty of the natural foliage that meandered along the island's southern shore. Cameras covered every square inch of the island's immensity, on screen after screen after screen, in the low - ceilinged, somber, endless room. You could hear yourself breathing in there.

The sunshine off the Gulf was blinding - bright. Everything back from the blazing Gulf, every shape in the foreground, became black shadows on the HD screens.

"Is that a boat? That's a big boat."

"Cruise ship, sir. We spotted it last night. Nothing unusual. We left a note on your desk. And on your phone."

"I forgot to check it." Lately we'd all been happily oblivious to all threats foreign and domestic.

Slowly the camera image panned across the distant bow of what was obviously a cruise ship, only it wasn't cruising, but stationary on the horizon, a great banner stretched across its port hull.

"Wait a minute. Go back."

"Probably just a tourist cruiser."

"Go slow. Pan across the banner."


## THE REALITY THAT IS AMERICA (CRUISE)


"What the hell?"

"Get the image as close as possible."

Upon the screen, the mercifully indistinct deck images revealed dwarves being tossed into trampolines, Money Hoo Hoo one of the presumed tossers, Judge Trudy leaning on a crutch with a shawl across the dowager hump of her shoulders, and there, the distinctive Spanish moss chins of the Goose Garrison boys gathered close in conversation, pointing at the helicopters, and leaning against the railing, facing our island though very far away, there was Methanny's gremlinesque silhouette, easily observable not because of her emaciated body but for the way she was flashing her schoolgirl's skirt up and down, obsessively showing her unclothed lower half like an obscene parody of the Japanese fleet semaphores in *Tora! Tora! Tora!*

Once we focused on it – clearly, the deck of the cruise ship was swarming with Reality royalty.

"This cruise boat is packed with the top tier of Reality Nation. One accurately aimed torpedo, and we'd have television worth watching again –"

"The chopper that just overflew us is landing on the deck of that cruiser."

"It's not the Cobra that worries me. Look again. It's like an airfield on the foredeck."

"Three Chinooks."

"What's a Chinook?" I blurted.

"Troop carriers." Tom laughed. "Of course, that's just a guess."

"You could get a hundred armed men onto those birds. Fifty Crips. Fifty Bloods. Scarier than Green Berets. Pretty well - planned."

"Good planning means Kressa's involved."

"In a military attack?"

"Don't underestimate her."

"I can see three, maybe four other Hueys on deck too. War surplus."

"It's starting. I don't think we can keep kidding ourselves."

"It's them," I heard Tom mutter angrily.

"I'll call Legal." Tony muttered, reaching for his i.

"What's Legal got to do with this?" Dad asked sharply.

"Everything has to be run by Legal."

"Guys, we're going to have to deal with this." Tommy took Dad and me by our elbows and started guiding us back toward the lights of the office beyond the world of screens and fear. Already there was an uptick in the sense of urgency among the techies overlooking the world of glimmering screens. Terse murmured commands issued over mouth - mikes, and laptop texts started flying out of the room.

"Who was that in the helicopter?"

"Somehow I thought... I was naïve enough to think they might leave us alone."

"Is the island being attacked?" Daddy asked. "Are we under attack?"

"Mr. Perkins?" I interrupted my father. "Tony? Are we in danger?"

Tony's eyes glistened with tears.

"Never gave a damn about me." He wiped his eyes angrily with the palms of his hands. "It was just the Water." He gave a bitter little laugh. "That's the male ego for you – bat - blind."

"She told me she loved you," I tried to make him feel better.

"She did? She told you that?"

"And she meant it. From the heart. I could tell." *Kammi's got a soul. It's in there somewhere.*

"Jack, you and Jessica need to go back to your bungalow." Tom advised us quietly.

"Guys – what's going on? Is our bungalow safe? Do we need security? Do Dad and me need guns? Because I can sure as hell shoot one! If necessary!" *Our little island*

*Alamo! Oh, who wants Eternity to last for ever anyhow! Grace under pressure, that's what counts...*

Tommy took a deep breath and spoke to me softly and directly. He was staring intently at one of the screens.

"The Chinooks are getting ready for lift - off. Let's get you two out of here."

"Tell us what's happening!"

"Go back to your bungalow, dearest. We've anticipated this. You must trust us. Whatever you think is happening, you must trust us. We love you two. No matter what it looks like, no matter what Legal tells us to do, you simply must....*Trust us.*"

As commanded, Dad and I headed back to the sanctuary of our bungalow.

But we kept taking detours, visiting corners of Paradise I think both of us realized we might never see again. The bungalow could wait.

In the castle's courtyard, we paused a moment nearby the great tree, the massive iconic centerpiece we'd come to regard unquestionably as the Tree of Knowledge of Good and Evil.

We watched a strolling couple pause by the mighty tree, then kneel reverently in a pose of homage recognized universally as The Tebow. And then they moved on.

"I want to say a prayer to it."

"We need to be praying for some good lawyers. I wish your Mom was down here."

"Oh, if only Tebow could come and save us. Like he did last time. Against Oklahoma."

"This time we may have to do it for ourselves."

The great tree's broad, misting branchwork seemed yet more stubbornly patient, stauncher, more everlasting in its profound abiding dynamism than at any time in the weeks previous.

*This magic Presence is greater than the Rock of Ages. It breathes. It will always breathe. It will always live here.*

*And, God be my witness, so will we.*

"What are we going to do, Dad? I never want to leave here."

In the twilight distance, the curving wall of palm trees defined the faraway island shore, and beyond it, the sparkling Gulf of Mexico. You could just barely glimpse the tiny silhouette of Reality Nation's cruise ship, a black bump on the edge of the Gulf's horizon, as we walked, the castle receding behind us.

From the castle, we walked through emerald grass fields that stretched out toward the sea.

A pine forest surrounded our tourist village, with blazing red roses, elegant black and lavender tulips rising as tall as sunflowers, violets, an indigo universe, thousands it seemed, wisteria, hyacinths, azaleas and ivy spilling across the white picket fences that surrounded every structure, the sweet faint resin pine scent that rose and fell with the breeze, the solar roofs and rainbarrels that were so much a part of the island's architecture – images I'd already taken into my heart and knew I'd never forget, natural perfection spread out in tropical harmony as far as the eye could see in all four magic directions.

I inhaled it with every available sense and instinct, like a tourist preparing to go home from any magic place that might never be re - visited.

My heart already ached for the future of my new home, a home I hadn't even envisioned three weeks earlier, an eternity ago, when all I had was my i, an insincere, treacherous boyfriend, a golden trinket hanging off my navel, a pressure cooker of a high school, a crazy diary, two bffs who turned out to be only one — and a sad, split - up family.

And then a series of questions began to form, popping up out of nowhere, the oddest thoughts, just as the oddest gems form from the greatest pressure: *Maybe the Water is only the designed fuel, designed by aliens, or designed more likely by God for his newly created playmates, Adam and Eve.... maybe we have discovered the Garden of Eden. All the love.... Peace and happiness through all the land — let it be so. If we could achieve it — ever — maybe the Creator would forgive us at last? With all his Omnipotence and Immaturity, is He really even capable of true Forgiveness? There was no justice in Eden last time around. Rely on the kindness of a Stranger? Really?*

*The best we can do now is rely on the kindness of the Absentee Landlord of this Paradise? This Mysterious Stranger? Rely on Him? What about ourselves! Perhaps, ashamed of Himself, for the childish cruelty of his crime in the Garden of Eden, He has moved on. To do His mischief and learn His own lessons in some galaxy far, far away. Left it all in our laps. The problems, the solutions, the whole damn clusterf\*\*\*...*

*No, IMHO it's too late to rely on the kindness of any Stranger. Too risky. I've got too much to lose now. Eternal life requires absolute personal, moral, relentless commitment. Our only chance is the Gods within ourselves. Pray for salvation from the Gods within ourselves. They're all that matters, all that can save us now.*

*Love The Gods within ourselves — Start with that. Go from there.*
*See where that takes us.*

"I don't want to leave either," Daddy quietly replied.
"I know how to work an M - 16. I'll give them a hand.
Who knows how many security people they still even have
here? You never see anybody with a weapon, on the entire
island, not even personal bodyguards! What do these
brothers know about small arms combat?" He shook his
head angrily. We were approaching our bungalow. "This is
one battle their lawyers *can't* fight for them. Damn lovable
goofballs. Those pocket - protectors say it all."

Our village's rectangle of bungalows had been built
along the four edges of a great, sandy central plaza, and our
walk back from the castle took us behind a row of
bungalows and out of the line of sight of the three olive
drab, unmarked helicopters — the Chinooks we'd seen
warming up an hour earlier on the Reality ship — that had
landed there, on the sand of the plaza, only a few crucial
minutes earlier.

They must have come in low, from the direction of
the cruise ship parked off the island's south flank. They
settled onto the sand, silently.

At least we never heard them. As usual on Fantasy
Island, Dad and I were living out the afternoon in our own
happy dream.

All the other love shacks looked empty. Even the twilight breeze through the pine tree - tops seemed to echo abandonment and a warning tension.

"Loveable, wonderful, innocent.... How would Pauley put it? The brothers? *Goombahs!*"

I laughed. "You sound just like him."

"No soldiers on this island at all. Just a half - dozen rent - a's."

"I can see the lights from that cruise boat. Out on the Gulf. Look, through the trees, you can just barely see it... It'll be really pretty, once night falls."

"Yeah. Like a little twinkling star, resting on the horizon - line." He laughed bitterly. "Harmless and sweet."

"It's all part of this?"

"I'm afraid so. We're running out of coincidences." Daddy's hands were stuffed in his pockets and his shoulders were slumped in contemplative sadness. "The way they were partying on deck, it's like they think they've already won the battle. Before the first shot was even fired...."

"Did you leave the front door open this morning?"

"No."

"Maybe I did." I was first onto the porch, barefoot and bouncing.

"You left the lights on too!"

Daddy was behind me at the threshold to our little home away from home when we first heard, from inside, that unforgettable, slightly nasal, slightly mid - Eastern, high - pitched, fluttery, falsely cheerful female voice.

"Come on in, neighbor, and sit a spell! Haven't you missed me? Missed you more!"

"Big sister?"

"Baby sister!"

And behind her, in the smoky darkness of the bungalow, a restless crowd of tribal enemies.

# Part III

# XIII

*Return of the Emperor Jones*

The livingroom was slightly dark, or as the *diva* herself would have put it, 'shady' after the warm light of day outside. I was instantly sick inside. But yet excited to see my big sister again, to be in her magic presence.

"And don't even think about running. We'll shoot you down like dogs. Ha ha, just kidding. Not. Love you lots. Love you more."

I also recognized Doctor Munye's rough, low voice.

"These are the two you told me about?"

"Yes, Daddy." Kammi snuggled closer to her doctor.

"We've got the wrong address," My father apologized. "We were looking for a friend. Excuse us. Goodbye."

"Come visit a while."

"Sorry – we're already running late. Thanks anyway."

*Chick - chick.*

"And bring the chick."

Behind my father, I stood a moment just inside the threshold, reluctant to approach the shotgun that was leveled at us. My eyes adjusted to the lower light in the big, crowded living room, heavy with *ganja* smoke and tension. Massed throughout, there were dozens and dozens of armed, bandanna - wearing 'soldiers of the Revolution', the Crips and Bloods Kammi and Barry had foretold, spilling out into the kitchen and onto the screened patio. Thinking back on it, I realized they remained separated into two wary groups, defined by their colors.

But it was the Reality star - power, scattered throughout the big room that drew my astonished gaze. Orca, Money Hoo Hoo, Fancy Lace, Springer, Povitch, Dr. Pill, Goose Garrison, Jersey Bores, Beverly Hills Shepherds – I was looking now at a phalanx of very famous people I had always subconsciously assumed were actually no larger than eighteen inches in height – the size of my bedroom tv.

*My God, I've walked in on the Daytime Emmys!*

"Come on in, Polar Bears. Kammi's little sister will always be welcome in our home. Get your asses in here. Right now."

And those were the first words spoken to me, personally, by the great Cultural Leader of the Ghost Posse, the Emily Dickinson of the Revolution Upcoming, the Magic Man with the Magic Plan himself, the future Sam Houston of the future Africa America – the iconic rapper and visionary Giant of *People* and *US* magazines, the huge - headed Fuehrer Lush Rimbaud so often referred to in his daily broadcasts, at times sarcastically, at times fearfully, as Dr. Dumbday, future Emperor of Africa America...

I would know this man for a single night only.

On television and in print, I felt I knew him already, shrewd, charming, mean, loud, generous, funny, visionary, bitterly angry, wild, articulate whether speaking in either white or black dialect, professorial, boastful, confrontational, thugged - out, self - reflective, and charismatic.

Above all, charismatic.

What little of these qualities I saw in Ghost Posse's Fearless Leader on this well - remembered eve, are overwhelmed in memory by what now confronted me: an arrogant, drunken braggart, at times funny, yes, at times insightful, but — on the verge of his greatest triumph, the seizure of the island and the immortality that would come with it — a leader whose central defects preceded him onto the throne, coming from an uncertainty about himself, an inferiority complex, even a sense of shame about what he'd achieved, that haunted his presence even before he'd ascended to these new, transcendent heights.

Like my father's stories about Richard Nixon, or like *Richard III* before him, a play I'd actually studied, Dr. Munye was a guy who wanted us to know who he was, he wanted to tell us — he just didn't know how. He had risen too high too fast. Tonight the altitude sickness showed.

"More yak." Dr. Munye. That explained part of it. He was drunk.

"Comin' right up, boss."

"Who's the beauty?"

"My daughter."

"That's the child I was telling you about, Doctor. My little sister — honorary."

"And you — you the publicist for these cracker brothers?"

"Right." My father gave an ingratiating laugh that grated. "Unless you need a publicist." *I'm a laptop for hire.* By my father's verbal maneuvering, I realized the trouble we were in.

"We'll see. Their press releases have improved lately."

"My dad won the Pulitzer Prize."

"These two tried to help me, honey. It wasn't their fault I wound up in an oyster sack."


Dr. Munye on this night spoke almost exclusively ebonically, specifically to communicate with the two groups of thug warriors he'd brought with him, in a brilliant gesture of symbolic unification – to symbolically enter Perkins' castle – Crips and Bloods, flown in from Los Angeles, by separate charter, but at last united in the larger struggle.

I mention this because his linguistic style, so effective, so brilliantly powerful when you're in the room with him, doesn't translate well to the page. So with few exceptions, I'm recounting his words using academic syntax. Yet, there are exceptions...

"I want to introduce you to the next President and grand Mojo of New Haiti." Kammi couldn't restrain a giggle. "The honorable Dr. Munye, e...s...q.... You may now approach him and shake his hand."

The livingroom, as my eyes adjusted, was crowded by armed men in blue and red bandannas, all flying their colors, and separated by those colors into two distinct, glaring groups – You could sense that, despite their momentary historic truce, these two gangs of guys really hated one another.

Some were wearing what I now know were *bandoleros* of ammunition criss - crossed over their chests, their cigarette smoke already causing the room to grow hazy, passing several bottles of cognac around.

There was a party going on.

*So the attack has already started. Tony and Tom had used us as bait, knowing my father and I were the weakest link, the obvious entry point, to coordinate the rest of it... The brothers knew that the Brothas would start first with us...*

Perhaps from the accumulated tension of knowing my recent taste of Eternal Life, not to mention happiness, was about to be erased, along with our presence on the island itself, I felt suddenly ready to vomit; maybe the cigarette smoke alone caused that. The commingling ganja smoke helped settle things down a little, but also made the dark, crowded gathering glimmer like a dream, a hallucination....*Fancy Lace! Dr. Pill! Orca! No way, José!*

"Yo' little sister ain't half - bad, Kammi. Add a little booty, she might just qualify."

"She's fifteen," My father said sternly.

"I don't give a damn."

"Doctor's just teasing," Kammi interrupted.

*Going on sixteen,* I thought to add. Long after, looking back on it, I realize now I was – even staring at the double barrels of the shotgun – I was *still* half - crushing on my idealized fantasies of Doctor Munye.

Soon enough to be erased by reality.

Oddly, throughout the long night ahead, I never felt a sense of personal fear for my life, nor for Daddy's. Banishment from Paradise would be worse than Death anyway. Soon enough I'd be the girl clambering up the castle walls, a net freshly draped over me, just as Kammi before me.

The ominous sight of these armed, silent, glowering thugs made the nausea just that much more special. You really had the sense the two groups were a single subtle insult from opening up on each other.

Doctor Munye's amazing personality was all that made it possible for the warring cadres to even share the same air.

A subtle golden light seemed to flow, as powerfully as electromagnetism, around Dr. Munye. How interesting it would be to go back in history and see if Hitler, Caesar, Martin Luther, Napoleon, drew, or merely emanated, that same kind of spectral, surreal aura?

He seemed to sit about four feet taller than everybody else. And, toward the rear of the livingroom, I got my first glimpse of a group of Reality Royalty, arguing aesthetics in the shadows.

"Little sister, where do you keep the Water?" Kammi whispered. "We tried the tap. It's not the same. Did the brothers give you some for safe - keeping?" She turned away from me and marched to a mirror on the livingroom wall. "Oh, Jesus Christ, can you believe it? I have another wrinkle!"

"Money Hoo Hoo needs to go potty," came the unmistakable childish cracker holler of the diminutive Reality star, from somewhere behind one of the sofas.

"Oh, of course you do," Kammi replied solicitously, turning from the mirror. "Minion, take care of the child's needs." There was movement, and the problem was resolved, two nurses scuttling off down the hallway, through the crowds of armed bandannas, with the child genius.

"This air is making me ill," Another familiar voice complained. It was an old lady's voice, and she pronounced 'air' *a - yuh*. It was the NaziJew Judge Trudy, worst of the infestation of popular culture referred to as 'Reality Stars'...

"Somebody turn on a fan," Kammi ordered.

"Why don't you all come in and sit down and make yourselves comfortable," My father interrupted sarcastically.

"Thank you, honkey paperback writer," The great Doctor answered. "We will. We lu' yo' southern hospitality. Just like back on the plantation."

\* \* \*

"They were naïve enough to try to help me, these two," Kammi whispered to her Master. "They tried to sneak me on the island, three weeks ago." She was wrapped all around him. He kept pushing her away. The shotgun had been set aside.

"You crowdin' my action, baby girl."

I was on the sofa next to Kammi. The doctor's eyes were on me, far more in hatred than lust. Dad put his arm around me. Kammi kissed the Doctor.

"I told them Tony Perkins was my secret lover. That you and I have an open marriage. But it was just to get their help."

"Oh, I know you f***** that rich cracker. Think I'm blind?"

"Kammi – big sister! You're telling me you betrayed us after we risked everything to help you? My Daddy put his job on the line for you!"

"Why is everyone all of a sudden getting on my case?" The diva returned fire with fire.

"I can't believe – "

"Okay, sure. So I repeatedly committed adultery. I may have possibly lied. Several times or more. And so I betrayed dear people who had taken a huge chance just because I'd asked them to. But let me put it this way – if any of you – *any of you* – had been thinking only of yourselves first, would any of you have necessarily behaved any differently?"

It was as though she sensed the cameras were on her, and drama, any drama, only increased the ratings. Her job was to jack the ratings. Kammi was really good at her job.

"Can't argue with a woman," Dr. Munye shrugged, after a long contemplative silence. He took a couple of swigs straight out of the Yak bottle, before someone replenished his ice.

As for me – how can I explain this to anyone, even myself – but I could never help but love my big sister.

Our bungalow, now expropriated, featured a really large living area with plenty of chummy, clubby furniture, but as we entered, it was quickly obvious every seat was taken as well as the arm of every chair and sofa.

The floor was crowded too, not only by the armed, bandanna - adorned Revolutionaries – separated into glaring, mean – mugging contingents divided implacably by squares of differently colored cloths, haters each of the silly flags of the other despite Munye's politic effort at unification.

"Get them rags off your heads, gentlemens. There's only one color that counts in here."

"We keepin' our colors, Doc," A voice stated from one group, and every bandanna nodded agreement.

"Colors make us strong, not weak." The other group asserted, and gathered closer.

"There's only one color that matters on this island. This is New Haiti!"

But the Doctor argued the point no further.

"We've....got.....*CRAWFISH!!!*"

Everyone fell silent, as the huge, waddling figure came from the hallway, entering the livingroom, hauling her little red wagon behind her.

Everyone understood that Orca, queen of all Reality, had suffered recently a psychological meltdown of significance, and seemed at times to have lost all touch with reality, small r, in another of this narrative's ironies. Now she was constantly accompanied, at all times, by two white suited psychiatric attendants.

What could anyone say to this massive *UberDiva* who had made fame possible for so many other of the talentless hack beneficiaries in this very room? She had recently lost another hundred million dollars investment in a weight - watching scam; since then she'd been eating even more obsessively.

"Her brain just needs....to...*rest*," A voice unmistakably phony, southern and unctuous, solicitous and self - involved, had evaluated The Mother of Them All. *Fancy Lace, ex - prosecutor and Red Queen — in tha house!* "Orca has made...America, which we love so...*what* ...*it...is...today!*"

"Let's hear it for Orca!"

"The Mother of all Reality!"

"God, Daddy, what's that smell?!"

"Orca's little red wagon," Daddy whispered.

"Orca...has helped...so…many...of…the...*children*," Ms. Lace butted in. She was used to an audience's undivided attention. She did not suffer other voices lightly. "And isn't...that...what...matters? *The kids? The kids? What about the kids?!*"

Ms. Lace tried her hardest to ignore the presence of the wagon.

Everywhere Orca went, she bore behind her the burden of her seventy pound lard - filled red wagon, reeking of decay now, the brewing stench of rotting lard parting the crowd long before The Orca, as she was known industry - wide, came into actual view. She stood there now, and the crowd in the semi - darkness behind her, backed away.

"We've ... got....... Tom......*CRUISE!*" She cried loudly.

Orca had reputedly lost a great deal of her fortune in a series of catastrophic restaurant and cable television investments. And after years of cosmic Sisyphean struggle to keep Lindsey Lohan "faithful to her sobriety," our nation's massive daytime Mentor — her endless reservoir of self - regard and certitude finally drained dry — had simply gone crackers.

The worst would occur when, periodically, she would reach back into the reeking wagon, scoop up a pawful of gross drippy slurry, and lick it down as a form of expiation. And no one said a word.

"Oh, Orca," suicide blond ex - prosecutor Lace put her chubby, manicured fingers to her face in homage and horror, all at once. "You're the reason we're all here tonight. You made it all possible for the rest of us! *You opened....the....doors....and...we all...came...tumbling...out! Just... as Seinfeld... said — you... proved...a culture...a culture... about... nothing... could... succeed... beyond... our wildest... dreams!*"

Fancy's southern drawl dripped off of her mouth like the warm grease smearing down Orca's chops, the unctuous artificiality of her expression embarrassing even to the others throughout the bungalow who likewise earned their daily bread from hypocrisy and routine public ass -

exposing. Among them all, Fancy Lace was considered the most loathsome of the species.

Even worse than Judge Trudy. If that is possible. What is it about lawyers?

"Make room for Lady Orca," the bearded troll from Goose Garrison insisted.

Orca reached back into the wagon, and with two fingers scooped up a tasty soupcon of the reeking, viscous glut. Around her, her friends and former worshippers averted their eyes. I could hear someone in the rear of the room retching.

Orca put her grease - covered fingers slowly and lovingly in her mouth.

"*Mmmm*. Tastes like Nineteen Ninety *EE - EEEIIGGHT!*"

There was a distant, glazed look in Orca's eyes, an attempt to gather, or sort out, a past memory. *Top of the world, Ma – 1998, top of...of....uh, where was I? Where am I now? Am I still in Hawaii? What have I become? Lindsey? Lindsey? Put down that tumbler!....uh...*

"*Good news, everybody – Today we're giving away.......* PONTI - *AAAAAAAAAACCCSS!!*"

But it was hopeless. Eventually, she turned, and slowly lumbered back down the hallway from where she'd come. Two attendants followed. Everyone she passed nodded reverently, but none could take their eyes from the little red wagon's sloshing, slowly liquefying lard, the part of herself the former talk show queen could not bear to leave behind.

All of us have that part, but ordinarily it's more effectively internalized.

"Tony and Tom knew we'd have a greeting party," I whispered to Daddy. "They knew, and they still sold us out. I'm a teenager. I know all about betrayal."

I could feel Dr. Munye looking me over.

"I might find a place for you in the typing pool," Dr. Munye leered.

"I'm not a good typist."

"It ain't that kind of pool."

"Why is Reality Nation accompanying you here tonight?"

Munye thought about his answer a long moment.

"Flavor," Munye took his time with the word, savoring it, almost tasting it. "When we take the keys to the castle, little Money Hoo Hoo gonna give this N**** a great big kiss. Our numbers will rule the Nielsens for the whole week – just that one sweet little kiss! Validation. All eyes on me. Money Hoo Hoo's benediction – it's better than the Pope."

"The whole world will embrace the Doctor's Revolution," Kammi added. "Money Hoo Hoo. Wisdom from the mouths of babes!"

Mixed among the silent, heavily armed black men were central elements of the whole glittering universe of Reality TV Royalty. It was as surreal a juxtapositioning as that of the cartoon figures next to real human beings in the old classic, *Who Framed Roger Rabbit?*"

There, like a long - lost friend from my own bedroom 23" Sony, Jerry Springer, the ex - Mayor and hog - caller from Ohio, I could almost hear the ghostly voices of his guests swirling around him as he grinned at me, *you don't know me, you don't know me!*

Attached to the ex - mayor's belt hung the Taser that Huffpo had reported he was never without since being attacked by his drooling, wild - eyed, celebrity - crazed audience, almost torn to pieces before his own Security could save him...

On a stool next to him, I instantly recognized the sour frowning aforementioned Shrunken Head of shrieking cronester Judge Trudy, Janus - faced NaziJew. Beside her, the manipulative, gremlin - headed speed freak Methanny, going Commando again in the shortest schoolgirl skirt allowable on cable; *that was her shtick, I'll make them look at me, I'll make them make me feel good about myself, look at me, you scum, I'm uncrossing my legs again;* and at her bony shoulder, the wise and sorrowful Doctor Pill...

And there, all four of them, the vacant, overlipsticked grins of the wine - throwing Trophy Wives of Amarillo, gulping Ambien, and Enovid, and STD medication by the fistful, and there, passing the jug provided by the bleary - eyed brothers of Korn Kookers, were the Spanish - moss beards of Goose Garrison, and at least a dozen others, more of the endlessly expanding metastasizing horror known as Reality TV – Dad would like the way I just used the word *metastasizing,* proof of developing literary technique!

Anyway, there they all were, the brain - dead, breathing reasons that all my teenaged friends, had stopped watching television and lived on YouTube. I was staring into the dark heart of the current Daytime Emmys.

"Where's your Mom?" I asked Kammi.

"Still on the boat, waiting for the 'all clear'..."

"What boat?"

"Our cruise ship. Haven't you heard about it? Everyone's heard about it." *You can see its lights offshore from here. That's where my Mom and all the others are...*

"Gimme dat jug, Amos," The Crips and Bloods were at it again. The two groups had separated off, one from another, gathering in opposite parts of the livingroom, mean - mugging each other, but letting it go no further. Munye held them apart, like two pit bulls on separate leashes, by the remarkable force of his personality, his charisma.

"When I ready, Andy, an' don' grab."

"Knock it off, n*****," the people's Poet snapped, and instantly they did. There was never any question as to who commanded this brooding, ominous crew. Nonetheless, the two gangs were fractious, restive. The tension ebbed, then flowed again. "And knock off that Amos and Andy BS. Have some respect for yourselves. We're building a new nation. This is New Haiti. Our capital! Not the Balkans…"

"When we run this island," One of the safari - clad warriors of *'Gator Wrasslers'* announced – to the last two people in the room who didn't already know it – "we are just goin' to form the world's network – a Super Network – and produce it all from the Perkins' brothers studios right here on Crystal Lagoon! Our own network! A gigantic empire, the most powerful on earth, run from right here. Crystal Lagoon *über alles!'*

"New Haiti," Somebody mumbled.

"Right. Sorry. New Haiti." *The New Haiti Reality Super Network! The beginning of the New Order.*

"We'll rule television, and whoever rules television rules planet earth," One of the Housewives proclaimed, braying and gulping champagne. *Kressa Kay loves Pubbly, but these random bitches just love Bubbly...*

"The last piece of the puzzle," Kammi shrugged. "Mom's got it all figured out. Between her and my husband, the two smartest people ever." She hesitated. She lowered her magnificent eyes. "Maybe even smarter than the Perkins brothers."

"Nobody watches tv any more," I shot back.

I felt the guns in the room, and the angry eyes behind them, lift and point toward me.

"My daughter's young. She's got a mouth on her. Please disregard." Daddy leaned over in front of me and extended his hand toward the great Doctor, who switched his "'yak'" on ice to his left hand and reached back. A handshake and a nod, equally brief.

"So you want a job, Mr. Jack?" Munye was staring straight through me.

"Sure." *I don't need a weatherman/ To know which way the wind's blowin'*....

In the face of this scary display of firepower, Dad's immediate acquiescence confirmed the fact of the brothers' defenselessness. In Ghost Posse's dark, smoky, dangerous HQ, I suddenly realized he and I were both tiptoeing through a minefield.

"You want to work for me? Then take us to your leader, bitch," the People's Genius smiled.

During the hours till complete darkness, the Revolutionary forces continued to party on the prodigious liquor stocks they'd expropriated from our kitchen and from the empty island saloon nearby.

I stayed silent and sulking, while Daddy slowly ingratiated himself into the good offices of the Revolutionary leadership – aka Dr. Munye.

Hip hop music thundered from the stereo, polluting the gentle skies above and around our compound, and I could almost feel the gardens of sweet - fragranced blooms surrounding the bungalows beginning to curl and die a little...

*I got a Nine by my spine,*
*Feelin' so fine*
*Bust a lick*
*An' what's yo's is mine*
*Got a Nine by my spine*
*Shut up bitches*
*Snitches get stitches*
*Cut dat phone line*
*Got a Nine by my spine...*

"Genius, baby, sheer genius," Kammi whispered, kissing through the stubble on the Doctor's massive black jaw.

"Look, I'm just a journalist," Daddy kept trying to persuade the Leader to trust his objectivity. "It's my job to get the story. We'll take you to the castle as soon as it's dark. But I want a story out of it. I'm a journalist, I go where the story takes me. I don't have a dog in this fight. The nerds that run this place now aren't going to be able to stand up to you and your forces – they know the U.S. government is backing your play!"

"They are? The American Government? POTUS? I knew he'd come through. Kressa never tells me anything!"

"I just want the story. We even have a video - cam. It's VHS, but it'll work...Why don't we cover it like a documentary? Like *The Battle of Algiers...*"

"VHS!" Kammi snorted. She was back and forth between Munye's shoulder and the wall mirror at least five times. "Adds twenty years to my smile - lines."

"VHS," the Doctor grumbled to himself. He waved for a Yak re - fill. These guys were so confident of victory they were already celebrating it. In advance.

"I don't like VHS."

"Why didn't we remember to bring our own camera people?"

"'Cause I forgot it."

"You always forget when you've been drinking. Just like with my birthday."

"Shut it."

"VHS makes me look a hundred years old," Kammi wailed.

"It's all I've got. But we'll do it like they did with Castro. You'll be a hero, riding a jeep through the castle gate. The rougher the images, the more authentic – like 'The Battle of Algiers'. Victory of the proletariat, all that. I just want the story, the back story, and the interview." *I want a second Pulitzer,* I could hear my father pleading between the lines. That was hard for me to hear him say.

It would have been harder had I believed him for even a single moment. My Daddy would have made a great therapist, as I may have mentioned. And he could even out - lie Kammi.

Well, maybe not. But close.

# XIV

Even after darkness fell, there was a kind of radiant afterlight spreading out over this remarkable island, a light that rose up slowly to meet the light from the full, golden moon as it ascended. The Forces of Racial Equity had to wait for this afterlight to dissipate before striking at the castle.

Tony had called us twice, just to make conversation it seemed. It was normal for Tommy to call me, but not Tony. Not before tonight.

Before I was allowed to answer, Munye's thumping hip - hop masterpiece opera 'Whip That Ass' had to be turned down, and the loud arguments, shrieks of laughter, and the aesthetic quarreling of the Reality *auteurs,* debating techniques of video *vérité,* Truffaut and the French New Wave, Fellini and whether relentlessly prolonged farts improved audience ratings or ultimately harmed them – all fell slowly quiet.

These idiots I had come to realize, all considered themselves to be great *artistes,* right up there with Orson Welles and Tarantino. It was best not to laugh at them, given our circumstance.

Only when silence was eventually achieved was I allowed to pick up the cordless.

"You guys okay?" I could hear the anxiety in Tony's voice.

"Sure. You want to talk to Dad?"

"Just checking in. Anything unusual happening around your scatter?"

"Unusual? Uh uh. Not a thing."

The good Doctor held the barrel of his weapon in front of my young nose.

"Everything A - ok."

"Well, maybe you should lock your doors tonight. That cruise ship that has stationed itself just off our southwest shore...ah, well. Nothing to be worried about. Probably just more nosy tourists..."

"It's a wonderful island, Tony. Thank you so much for all you've done for Dad and me. You've helped him so much."

"Sure you two are okay?"

"Not at all."

A brief pause.

"You have guests?"

"Yes."

"I want you to give Munye a message. Can you do that?"

"He's right here."

"I don't want to talk to that mangy bastard – that *cuckolder!* I want you to tell him we're ready to cede control of the island to him and his people. We've run it by Legal. There's no chance. The U.S. Defense Department is ready to move in once Munye takes control. We don't want to fight. I'll come over after dark, and escort them to the Water. We're out of options. Above all, no bloodshed."

"Oh, Tony, please – "

"It's a legal matter, Jessica. We're listening to the attorneys. There can be no bloodshed. And Tommy and I have to be allowed to leave the island unimpeded. We've got a chopper parked in the courtyard. We'll just fly away into the night. Tommy's an expert pilot. Maybe I can persuade Kammi to let you and your father stay. And that's the last requirement of the deal. I have to be allowed to see Kammi once more."

"Hold the line, Tony."

I relayed the Perkins' brothers' terms of endearment to Dr. Munye.

"That's more like it," Munye answered, this time switching effortlessly from ebonics to white dialect. "We want a show of force. We don't want to kill anybody, just that we could kill everyone on this island if required. And my wife wants to visit the Water. Pronto."

"Why am I not surprised," Tony gave a bitter laugh. "I'll take her to it."

I reported Tony's reply to the Doctor.

"As soon as it's dark," Said Munye.

After a moment, I looked over at the Doctor and nodded.

"Tony says a key component of his legal position is that there be no bloodshed," I explained back to Munye. "The brothers simply want to vanish. That can't happen if there are active warrants. Up till now, it's a straight corporate takeover." *They're ready to hand over title in return for their lives and freedom...*

I was starting to grow weary of being a ping pong ball between the two warring paddles...

"Nobody will be injured," Munye gave his assurance. "Just some shooting up in the air, some flares – that sort of thing. For the six o'clock news." He smiled pleasurably. *"Fo' FLAVAH."*

Munye knew about Perkins' 'War Room', an almost comical appellation, I remember thinking at the time. *War Room. Oh, yes indeedy.*

It was quickly negotiated to chopper the personnel therein back to the mainland. No arms, not even sidearms, to be allowed.

All the island's logistical personnel would leave with their lives. The brothers by then would already be long gone.

Doctor Munye, inebriated or not, quickly grasped that the Perkins' brothers predicament – they had nowhere to hide. They'd be scooped up quicker than Saddam Hussein. They could fly their super Chopper from here to Hell. But ultimately there were no holes left, anywhere in North America, for my former sponsors to hide in.

Whatever Bail requirements the Federal government established, let them run *that* by Legal...

My heart was broken. It was hard not to break out in tears. These beautiful Wonka brothers, so out of their league, and my father and I had placed all trust in them. Live and learn. Dad and I had been used as bait. Even Tom's affection for me seemed so phony retrospectively. A bitter, angry tear ran down my cheek, the only evidence I allowed of the depthless turmoil going on deeper down.

So then I gave the Doctor a great big sexy smile.

*Say hello to the new Boss. Same as the old Boss.*

"Kammi says she'll allow you to kiss her ass goodbye."

"That's what I thought." Tony sighed into the receiver. "Just a last kiss. Then I'll take her to the Water."

"Tony – You shouldn't have hung us out to dry. I thought we were best friends."

"It's kind of important that you continue to trust us to do the right thing."

"Yeah." I hoped he could hear the anger and betrayal in my tone. "Nothing like trust." My anger caught in my throat. "We know you set us up. Why did you even need to do that? We're just a couple of pawns. Why? To give you more time to get out of Dodge? We walked right into it."

I heard Munye laugh.

Tony hesitated.

"I'll talk to Kammi about helping you two to stay on the island."

"I don't know whether we'll even want to stay."

"They ain't takin' a dime on that chopper with 'em," Munye made clear. "Those Polar Bears leave with the fur on their backs. Nothin' else."

"I'll come by in my jeep just after dark." Tony seemed to agree.

"Perfect."

"Any tricks," Munye added, loud enough to be heard, "We'll paint this house. Know what I'm sayin'?"

"Yes. No tricks. Right at dark."

*Click.*

"He's coming over when it's dark. He'll be alone. Promise me you won't hurt the brothers."

This plea I directed toward Kammi. Although kept hidden carefully from sight, sometimes she actually seemed to have a soul – and a heart. *It's in there somewhere, I know it is. Somebody so false has to be true, deep down.* She was my big sister. My big sister had to have a heart.

"Kammi – promise you'll help them get away. Make sure."

She was standing at the mirror again, pulling up her eyebrows.

"I don't know – my husband handles the politics."

"Kammi! Big Sister! Won't you even consider saving human life?"

"Damn it," She had found another wrinkle.

"Those brothers are dead meat," Dr. Munye muttered into his glass of yak.

"Why kill those two when they're worth so much alive, at least for now?" My father asked.

"They ain't worth the shotgun shells," Doctor Munye seemed to agree. "I go back and forth on what to do. Yak brings on the rage. Not good in a leader."

"Let 'em fly away." Daddy added. "The Feds will hunt 'em down in days."

"I just want the Water!" Kammi cried, proving she'd been listening despite the rapturous self - involvement she'd thrown at the exhausted mirror.

"What water?" Somebody asked, out of the smoky darkness. "What water does she keep talkin' about? You want water? Go in the kitchen."

"Doc," Daddy soothed the progressively inebriated People's Leader, "face it, what's the hurry? You're the man with the plan, with the Nine by your spine – what do the Perkins brothers have? Pocket protectors and solar calculators? Who wins that shoot - out?"

"I wins," Dr. Munye gravely acknowledged. "That's my finest lyric – "

"Y'know why it's so good, honey? Because it's true!" *You do have a Nine by yo' spine!*

"And there you are!" Daddy proclaimed. "Genius will out every time!"

"Perkins is coming when it's dark?"

I nodded. "You guys win. Without even firing a shot."

"Money Hoo Hoo has to go potty," The diminutive diva demanded once more.

"Help me put on my face, Jessie," Kammi half - asked, half - commanded. "I want to look good when that geek sees me. I'm the best thing that ever happened to him. I'll make him take us to the Water. He never let me see where it comes from. I'm going to drink a gallon as soon as I get to the source. Drink enough of it, I'll bet I'll be eighteen again – a kid like you."

"I don't think it works that way."

"Sure it does. The more the better – just like with everything."

"You're beautiful as you are, Kammi," I replied. I was still desperate to have a big sister. In Kammi, I knew I had a big sister – in there somewhere. *She has to be in there somewhere – she just has to be.*

"Younger is always better. Right, honey?"

"Unnhh?"

"I'm going to bathe me and my husband in the fountain, just wash every pore – and then we're gonna have the hottest sex you can imagine... We should video it – but not VHS. I look ancient on VHS."

"That's not true. It's your imagination."

"Can't you see the genius of this whole thing? Once we have access to the Water, we'll be locked in, season after season..."

Kammi's dark eyes were big and bright with happiness. *It's the first time,* I realized, *I've ever seen her happy – even on television.*

"My whole Kay family will never age – we'll never be cancelled! Reality Nation will be a permanent fixture on the airwaves of our nation. My mother Kressa Kay is the true genius here. To save our brand from Time itself.

"That's always the problem, us mega - stars always age out of our greatness... Look what happened to the

Olsens! To Alyssa Milano! *Even Shirley Temple.* Look where she wound up – at the U.N.!"

"But not this time, baby. We're going to own an island full of eternal youth! We'll broadcast all day for our new All Reality Network and f*** our brains out all night. Right, honey? We'll rule cable America! Right, honey?"

"Unnnhhhh?"

"It's okay, he's just had a little too much to drink. He'll handle the politics side, I'll handle the reality side, and my Mom Kressa will handle us both. We've got another company of killers on that cruise ship, waiting for the signal to join the attack. Even if we don't have to kill anybody, there's got to be a full show of force. Put fear in their hearts – all their hearts."

"I'd like to interview your mother, too, Kammi – at some point," Daddy asked.

Just then I did a double - take. Shows you my youth. A more acute group of captors would have noticed my stunned, drop - jaw reaction. My dad saw what – I should say *who* – I saw, in the same moment, the exact unmistakable dirty long grey overcoat, and Dad didn't so much as blink an eye.

Fortunately, our captors were not Mooks, but Gourds. My jerky reaction passed unnoticed.

"Doctor Rafferson? Is that you?"

Once again, a hallucination had appeared from the direction of the kitchen.

I compounded my error.

"Sir? Mr. Rafferson? Doctor Rafferson? Is that you?"

Dr. Rafferson was dragging a gigantic leather steamer - style trunk into the livingroom. From the effort, it was as extremely heavy as it was outsized.

He wasn't letting anybody help him move the trunk. it was a tedious, slow, laborious process. A couple of the Crips – the blue bandannas, right? – grabbed the back strap and helped him.

"Be careful. Don't drop."

"Doctor Rafferson?"

"Be *still*, Jessica!"

At the unfortunate third mention of his name, Dr. Rafferson looked reflexively around at me. Then he looked quickly away.

It had to be Rafferson. Could there be two men as crazy - looking as him, in all the earth? Those icy, wolf's avaricious eyes, behind wire - rimmed glasses? The crazy old man from Tony's office, the long, dirty grey topcoat, Rasputin's crazy wild tangled grey hair, from that first wondrous morning, so recently, yet so long ago? The morning I had taken that first purple sip of Eternity?

It was him or his twin.

"But Dad – "

"*Be...still...Jessica.*" Daddy repeated in a whisper.

The wild grey hair, long grey - white beard, the dirty grey overcoat in the eighty - degree island night. I clearly remembered him from Tony's office the first day we'd all met. I had to be sure. Jessica's retinal scan was failsafe. Behind his intellectual rimless glasses, those cold, pale, amoral Scandinavian blue eyes – it was Rafferson.

"You done, Rasputin?" Munye's tone was friendly and respectful. "Almost done?"

"Okay." Dr. Rafferson nodded, and maintained eye contact, only with Dr. Munye, his current contractual employer, so it seemed. "Device ready. Remote control detonate. I write down steps. You follow exactly. Don't take tape off Remote button until ready to use."

"Just like a DVD player?"

"Five double A batteries. I include. No charge. Include in final price."

"That's what I like about Europeans," Munye smiled appreciatively. "No nickel - and - diming. Americans would stick me for the batteries."

"Dr. Rafferson!"

"Be *still,* Jessica," Daddy whispered low and sharp. "Stop being so antsy!"

"That's my boy!" Munye exclaimed. "My dawg Rasputin. From Chechnya. N******, come meet my boy. He got me my bomb. We failsafe now."

"Your boy?"

"No Chechnyan ever called me N*****!" Munye paraphrased Ali.

"I meet no one. I go now. Good business do with you. Be careful. Don't go bump with bomb! I leave fifth battery out. Don't put in till ready to use. I tape to remote. No see you again. Most important. No further contact."

"Ah, ha ha ha!" Munye loved that. "Don't go bump with bomb. Or bomb go bump with you. Is that it?"

"This is one half of bomb. Timing device. Other half in trunk already on boat. Put two side by side when ready to use. Wiring folded inside both trunks. Connect by colors. All steps clear on diagram enclosed. Follow exact. Okay? Payment already confirmed. All good. Best luck. Finished now. I go."

"*But that was Dr. Raff –*"

"*Jessica, damn it – be still!*"

Dr. Rafferson was out the door, dirty grey overcoat flapping behind him. But Munye, as was his wont after a dozen drinks or so, had to brag a bit more about the interchange we'd just witnessed.

"My dawg just sold Ghost Posse a ten kiloton piece of work. No more doomsday gap. Things go wrong tonight, we blow the island, that's all. There won't be so much as a seagull feather left, after it's over. By then we've long since choppered outta here."

"Can't blow up the Magic Water, honey." I heard Kammi whisper in a frightened voice. "Anything but that. We can't blow up the Water!"

"As long as we have the threat, we won't have to use it. It's called MAD. I wrote my Master's thesis on the psychology behind it. Mutual Assured Destruction. We've got 'em by the b***s now, baby."

"No! Please! No! You can't blow up the island!" *You can't blow up the island! Don't you undersand me? You cannot do that! No matter what!*

"I never said we'd blow up the f****** island. Did I say that?"

"Promise me, honey. Swear to me! That's the one thing you CANNOT do!"

"It was yo' Momma first hooked me up with that crazy mf - er."

"How did she know him?"

Munye shrugged. "She knew him. She paid him. He pulls weight for both the Iranians *and* the Israelis. Highest recommendation. Yo' Momma's got more connections than the Clintons."

Munye took a long, pleasurable swallow of yak and wiped his mouth with the back of his hand.

"Ten K. Hope to God we don't have to use it."

*"Just don't do anything to hurt the Water,"* Kammi pleaded. "You just can't. You CAN'T!!"

"What the hell does she keep talking about – the water?" Somebody mumbled through the thick, roiling smoke and booming rap music. "Just go in the kitchen and get it out of the goddamn tap."

# XV

Tony drove up alone, cut the jeep's motor and headlights, and offered no resistance when two soldiers of the New African Brotherhood stepped silently out of the darkness and poked automatic rifles in his face.

It was hard for me to overlook that 'Pontias Pilate' look the two brothers had exchanged just before they'd sent us home. *The brothers have to have been using us, pawns in some independent series of events they had already worked through. It would have been nice to have been included in plans that included us. They have handed these thugs two valuable hostages, at the least. How could the brothers dare to do that to Dad and me, without even giving us a warning? They just threw us away.*

My father and I awaited orders to go get in the jeep.

"If they intended to use us as bait, they should have left my daughter out of it," Daddy said angrily. "That's not easy to forgive."

"Don't ever trust no white man, Jack." The Doctor laughed softly. He liked giving us advice. "You're around 'em all the time. Ought to know that by now."

"Right back at you, Doctor."

"Yeah, I made that mistake. I thought if I kissed enough white ass, I could pass. Never happen. Even got a Masters' Degree. I was still black. The worst fate of all. Live and learn."

One odd thing had happened while Daddy was inside interviewing the future King of Crystal Cay. He'd gone to his shoulder bag, which caused several of the less inebriated weaponized thugs to react suspiciously, their rifles swinging around.

"We already checked the bag," Dr. Munye waved them off.

"Somebody took my flask?"

"So if we did?" The Leader barked out a laugh.

"I need to get my pen. Is that okay?"

"As long as you don't pull out a sword." *I ain't worried about no ballpoint pen.*

The odd thing was the size and shape of the ballpoint pen Daddy pulled out. I recognized it from the same night Daddy had been in the beef at Pauley Vee's. I had asked him about it.

"That's the oddest looking pen, Dad – why did Pauley give it to you? Does he want you to sell those for him at the flea market?"

"And all you have to remember about this pen is one thing, Watson..."

"Which is?"

"Never touch it. Never."

Now the fat odd ballpoint in my father's hand attracted Dr. Munye's slurred attention.

"What kind of pen is that?"

"It has an endless supply of ink. Solar - powered. It's a prototype. Awkward to hold, but it's my lucky pen."

"Gimme."

"Sure."

"The damn thing is vibrating," Observed the future Emperor Jones. From dewy - eyed fan worship of this powerful and admittedly remarkable leader, I had pretty quickly converted to a direct loathing of him, which I disguised by a sexy, admiring teenaged smile. Like so many guys, pour enough liquor into him, Mr. Hyde appeared just as Dr. Jekyll vanished.

"That's the solar component." Dad explained. "It never runs out of ink. That's the pen I used during the Pulitzer series I wrote. It's my lucky pen."

"This pen is totally whack. That's why I like it. I want it."

"Why don't I give it to you at your coronation. Let me use it for our interviews and for this story..."

"At the coronation." By his gold - toothed grin, I could tell Dr. Munye liked the sound of that.

"And maybe you'll give it back when you hire me as your publicist for this island. It's so big nobody can write with it but me. I'm used to it."

"We'll see."

"Coronation, baby?" Kammi kissed him. "Like the sound of that?"

"I likes."

"Baby," Kammi sounded near to crying, "Swear to me you're not going to do anything *stupid - o* to our island."

"Stop harping on that, god damn it. I've heard your goddamn opinion!"

"Doctor, please listen! It's got so much history! It's going to be the capital of the re - unification of the African diaspora in America. The island is so important! An atomic bomb would be the end... the end of everything"

"You just worrying about your smile lines." He laughed at her. "That Water's a placebo, believe it."

"It'll be my honor to present you with the pen," Daddy was staring at its swollen, unwieldy surface. "But I need to start making notes if we're going to do this thing."

"It feels like a bomb."

"It's not."

"But it's getting hot!"

"That's normal. When there's no sunlight."

Dr. Munye forked over the pen reluctantly.

"Okay, where were we?" Daddy asked gently.

"The mean streets. Where my destiny was first revealed to me – in a jail cell, being beat down by four white cops. Just like Rodney King."

"The unauthorized biography – that you were the child of two Sociology professors at Howard – that you went to boarding school in Switzerland... that's all..."

"White man's lie," Munye waved it off, and glared at the fat pen that might write down another lie about him. "White man's trick."

"You've got a Master's in Political Theory. From Yale?"

"So?"

"Doctor," Came a soft call from one of his troopers, from the porch. "We've got the dweeb. No resistance. We're ready when you are."

Money Hoo Hoo took center stage just then, arms akimbo, tiny fists pressed against her already oversized hips. She looked angry and in need of adulation.

"Money Hoo Hoo's got to – "

"We'll alert the media," somebody muttered irritably.

"Choke on it, porkah," Judge Trudy snarled, slamming her gavel hard on the Formica countertop; and the livingroom broke out in general applause.

"You guys okay?" Tony asked anxiously.

He was alone. Twisting around from the canvas driver's seat, he looked back, guiltily, at Daddy and me. His face was distorted, even in the starlight, by apology and regret.

The jeep rolled slowly across the grass toward the freshly re - sodded soccer field that stretched out from the forefront of the King's castle.

Low - lit rectangles of solar halide lighting cast down a soft, lonely definition over the distant contours, and across architect Gehry's aluminum swooping gull - wings, and the distant, magic spires of Crystal castle, as we slowly approached.

The jeep rolled silently toward it. We were about three minutes from the gate.

"Jack? You okay?"

"Never better," Dad answered him coldly. "So appreciative you asked."

The Doctor laughed. It was a beautiful, star - filled night. He was feeling good. Kammi was snuggled close.

Other than a rustling breeze, and the steady shuffle of dozens of pairs of unlaced Timbs on both sides of the jeep behind us, the island seemed overwhelmed by emptiness and silence. Ranks of armed men fell into line behind us strictly in accordance with the colors they were flying. Bloods to the left, Crips to the right, in ragged parallel formation. In distrusting, wary silence.

"Jessica?"

"We're okay. We're great. Wonderful." *You knew they were coming, didn't you? You used Daddy and me like staked goats. And what for? What good did it do you?*

"Shut up. All you honks." Munye was shotgun, backed up by a truly brutal guy in a blue bandanna next to me in the back seat. Tony didn't look back again. Kammi was in the Doctor's lap, her arms around his neck, to his annoyance.

The armed B/Ms in their red and blue bandannas must have watched enough war movies to know to form single columns to either side of the slow moving vehicle, red bandannas flying to the left, blue to the right, halting under the shade and shelter of the pines as we approached the darkly shining silhouette of the great castle, and the darkened wide soccer field that lay before it, the whole dreamy landscape moonlit and somber, as though already sorrowfully anticipating the approaching change of leadership.

"Glad to see me, Tony?" Kammi had teased him, when we'd been climbing into the old jeep. Her plunging black billowy silk jumpsuit, she informed me, was original Gautier – tacky without being sexy.

"Like it?" She'd asked me, as she tucked down in the front of the jeep beside the knees of the Great leader.

"It goes without saying." *I still can't believe how you're screwing me, big sister. I guess when it comes to water in the desert, all bets are off. Some sister.*

When the jeep reached the far edge of the soccer field, our security contingent halted, remaining concealed under the pines, awaiting Munye's next order.

The jeep followed its low beams across the length of the soccer field toward the gates.

The night was black, the stars tiny and glimmering behind the castle spires. I wasn't breathing anymore. I was crying in fear, biting my lip in anger, anything but taking a breath. *So they're just going to hand these jerks the keys to the kingdom?*

Where were the guards, the usual security? From a guard shack by the front gate, illuminated by the golden lamplight, a single silver - haired Trog in tie - dye, flashing the mandatory peace sign – sometimes they'd give us a Gator chomp – manipulated the security panel, and the wide, massive front gates began slowly swinging open.

*It can't be this easy...Tom, Tony, dear Mooks, I understand you're afraid, it's why you did what you did – I'm afraid too. But...but at least put up some kind of fight, you don't even have to win, just fight. Show me you can, and I'll claw my big sister's bitch eyes out before she kills me – if we're going down, please Gods, let us go down fighting...*

"They're letting us in!" Kammi hissed in alarm. "Look out for a trap."

"They recognize me," Tony answered without turning. "After all, I own the place."

"You used to own the place," Dr. Munye seemed to have regained his faculties, his anger, his paranoia and egotism. He sucked on a fresh bottle of yak. "Been down so long this looks like up to me. Way up."

"Are the front gates closing?" Kammi hissed. "What about your personal guard? They're still out there!"

She reached over and pinched Tony.

*"The gates are closing! Answer me!"*

I looked back. Munye's bandannaed platoon had halted at the edge of the soccer field, under pines, and had faded now into shadowy invisibility, waiting.

*"Leave the gates open!"*

"Walter," Tony called out to the wheezer in the guard - house. "Leave the gate doors open."

"Roger that, Tony."

"There's no trap, dearest. We don't have the skills."

Tony turned and looked down at her. His voice was that of a high school boy, either very frightened, very in love – both. I couldn't identify any distinction.

"Water?" Kammi asked, her voice soft and small. "Show me? Like you promised? Where it is?"

"Don't worry. I'll take you to the Water. It will be smarter if no alert is sounded. Tom and I don't want anybody to get hurt. We've discussed this. We're ready to let it all go. I can't have people shooting at me all the time." *I'm having a nervous breakdown.*

"I just want the Water. I don't care about the rest of it."

"You asked if I'd missed you," Tony whispered down at her. "Yes. I've missed you. Every day."

"Awww," Kammi replied. "You're sweet. Is that billion bucks still an honest offer?"

"Of course it is."

"She married, honkey," Dr. Munye lifted his head a little, cursing the jeep's pale, distressed, so - in - love driver. "Tell you what, peckerwood – I'll let you watch me f*** the bitch. You only have to pay a million bucks for that." *Only when the Feds haul yo' ass out of here tonight, you won't have a million to spare. You be too broke to bail out. We takin' it all.*

# XVI

There were two sets of controls necessary to open the huge steel tunnel vault door, a conventional alpha numeric keypad, and beyond that, an old - school, conventional dial - type combination lock in the steel door itself.

While Tony navigated us through these impediments, he was giving non - stop instructions on how to run the island after the now - disgraced brothers had departed, lifting away by polished, state - of - the - art chopper, to oblivion, running partners soon to be a mile high in the night, in the flight of their lives.

Tony spoke to Kammi only, although Munye hovered nearby, listening carefully.

"It's important that you honor all the current contracts with our paying clients. The secret of the Water must be kept; otherwise the boats slamming into these shores and seawalls will make Dunkirk look like the Kayak Pond at Disney World. You'll have a million people – or more – trying to swim the twelve miles. Chaos. Keeping this secret is our greatest challenge – Use your imagination."

"Who's Dunkirk?" Kammi asked.

"Those sheeple are welcome to stay. As long as they pay," Munye broke in, also speaking directly to Kammi. "But they have to pay more."

"Don't be a damn fool," Tony was urging Kammi. Now she was playing ping pong ball between the two angry paddles. She looked exhausted. She kept feeling her face, as though every second counted. It was really all she was focused on; the rest was noise, clutter.

"You want to play you got to pay," Munye insisted. "It costs money to build a new nation."

"Wrong. At least not at first." He was spinning the combination again, having missed it on his first try. "You've got to remember that your clients are the richest and most powerful people on the planet. They can be dangerous. Very dangerous. This goose will lay golden eggs – forever. Show restraint. *Especially during the transition!*

Munye whispered something to my mean big sister.

"We'll have to see your books," She then replied.

"Our law firm has been given instructions to cooperate with you fully. You'll be paying them, starting tomorrow. I left you the particulars, but it's that Orlando outfit, the best in Florida – *Canwee, Robbyall & Howmache.* We got their name out of the book and have never been disappointed yet. They are thieves. And in a thieves' market, you'll want the best."

"Thank heavens you guys chose the civilized approach to this," Kammi tried to smile, but I could sense her emotions were in taut conflict. I knew her awareness of the existence of an atom bomb was a new, mortal fear. Doctor Munye had an impetuous, unpredictable side, and he'd been putting away Yak – the second bottle since we'd all met, under such interesting circumstances.

Tony only nodded.

"Everything gets run by Legal. We're out of options." He was all business now.

"You're lucky I'm in an accommodating mood." Munye muttered.

"All the corporate paperwork has been signed and notarized. It's a straight business transfer. No problems there...

"But I have another suitcase of paperwork, critical, secret documents, stuff you can't run this place without. We'll turn those over to you just at the moment we fly out of here. This is for our protection, not yours. We're not fools. Well, maybe we are, but..."

"Will you guys be okay?" Kammi actually seemed concerned. She was speaking into the jeep's windshield so Munye would have a hard time hearing her. "What will you do for Water?"

"We've set some aside." Tony's face, as he looked at her, was a portrait in emotional torture. I always had the sense, now as then, if he could have had Kammi, he'd have been willing to give up all the rest of it. "We've saved some back."

"Enough?"

"For a while."

"Maybe I'll see you again then – someday."

"Maybe one day we'll be clients of this island."

"You got the price, we'll talk." Munye interrupted. "But tonight you leave here barefoot."

Tony's face was a mask.

*Click...click.*

"Okay, we're in. Let's go down."

"Don't worry, little sister," I heard Kammi's voice whisper, as she reached back and hugged me impulsively. "I'll try to look out for you and your dad. As much as I possibly can. Doctor's calling the shots now. But I'll do everything I can."

"Dad and I love this place so much, big sister."

She nodded. "It's a magic place. A perfect place to not grow old together."

\* \* \*

The descent through the limestone tunnel was gentle and lit along its base by Christmas - tree lights.

That was a typically whimsical Perkins' touch. The dangerous, shadowed underground canal, where you'd expect to trip over the bones of some of the pirates that had no doubt fought over this island and its precious treasure in previous centuries, was lit instead with cheerful, happy little flame - shaped bulbs, in all the generic Wal Mart colors, red, blue, green, gold, white.

The clustered strands of Christmas lights merrily scampered beside the tunnel's left baseboards, guiding us downward, placed there almost as an afterthought by the brothers who had always lit their way downward in the past by torches or flashlights, till one Christmas eve years, or perhaps decades ago... *Hey, brother, I've got an idea....*

"Hurry, hurry." Kammi kept urging us on, almost panting. I could see her feeling her face and forehead for new wrinkles. *"Hurry!"*

As with everything else on this long, sad, crazy, dispiriting, uplifting night, leaping, frightening shadows seemed to dominate and distort the light. It was hard saying goodbye to eternal life. I knew Daddy felt the same. I didn't like him so quiet. Neither Daddy nor I wanted to say goodbye to this island now. Or ever. We'd both known it had all been such a dream, but who wants to wake up from the best dream ever? *The best dream in all the world, ever?*

The light during the tunnel descent was all claustrophobic and asymmetric, the air wet and breathless, the Glock at my back almost like another human presence in the narrow, Christmas light falseness of our short journey...

"How much further?"

"We're here."

"We are?" Cried Kammi. "I want to dance naked, wash my whole body in the Water..."

The chamber containing the Fountain of Youth wasn't much bigger than a child's small bedroom, a sort of arched, damp, shadowy space with a low shell roof lit in its irregular close corners by more handfuls of clustered Christmas lights.

"Well, here we are." I tried to sound like a tour guide. "It's been fun. Okay if Daddy and I leave now? We'll be upstairs if you need us!"

"Oh, little sister. You're so funny! Such a mouth on you. Now shut up."

"Well, I – "

"No. I mean it. Shut up."

Perhaps we'd been expecting a Disney - like, enchanted water spill. With maybe carp, swimming above an underwater rock garden with gold coins glinting everywhere, the fountain floored by gold - flecked slabs of *lapis lazuli* scattered aesthetically, shattered flat chunks of the rare, gold - flecked ore interrupting the spilling swirls of purplish Immortal Water in their surging, cascading, sparkling progress across a cobwebbed tomb of memory, a Dreamworks created fantasy of a magic world that Indiana Jones, not a couple of nerds from Spain five hundred years ago, should have stumbled across on a routine military patrol...

That's what I had expected, anyway. A cool world, a heavenly grotto, exploding with dry ice and snakes crawling out of crevasses in the limestone... I'd fully expected it.

But instead, before us there was only a tiny little room carved out of the smooth limestone rock, and a small aperture, not much bigger than a bullet - hole, its central and only irregularity – a narrow little opening in the limestone, bigger than a dime, maybe the size of a quarter, located at about waist - level in the curved, utterly featureless pale wall.

"This is *it?*"

"This is it."

Gently spilling down the pocked white surface of the limestone, Heaven's thirst - quenching Secret – the gleaming, sparking, purplish narrow trickling promise of Immortality itself..

The endless tears of Eden.

From this vertical cut emerged – sometimes dripping, sometimes gurgling, sometimes spilling in little bursts, actually – sometimes droplets, sometimes a tiny stream of water dripping slowly downward, meandering a few inches down the limestone curve of the wall, running vertically for a few inches, and then falling steadily, with an audible *drip drop drip drop tick tock tick tock,* and underneath it, nothing so glamorous as a fountain.... yet there was no disguising the dynamic, purplish effervescent aura that seemed to vibrate, trembling and almost alive, from the several clear, incredibly powerful, silently vibrating, lavender gallons of liquid gathering in its dull green container.

Looking down into the Heart of Forever, I felt myself scarcely able to breath. *Drip drop drip drop tick tock tick tock… the ticking of Eternity's clock,* neutralized by the perfect, royal dynamic purity of the Water, gently gathering, its surface moving hypnotically, almost of its own volition…

"A plastic tub?" Kammi put her hand to her mouth in horror or disgust. "That's how you capture the Water? You cannot be serious!"

"Why?" Tony replied mildly. "Is it leaking?"

"And – let me guess. *You bought that tub at the Chiefland Wal - Mart!*"

"Right you are. How did you guess?"

"A Wal - Mart tub! What is it with you people and Wal - Mart?"

"We got it for less than twenty dollars, five years ago. The Fabergé and the Tiffany crystal both leaked like a sieve. And, we felt, were pretentious. Our lives are already pretentious enough. Nobody ever came down here before. Not until tonight." Everyone else was looking at the gathering eternity in the tub pushed against the limestone. But Tony was looking at Kammi. He couldn't take his eyes away from her.

"But yes, the main reason is the tub doesn't leak. We can barely keep up with the demand as it is. We don't dare waste any. And it's got wheels. That's important. It's a steep haul up to the lift."

"Oh!" Then Kammi expropriated my favorite word in the world, and I'll admit it, Diary, I was flattered. "Oh! Oh….you….*Trog!*"

*Tick tock, tick tock, tick tock, tick tock.* The tub, as we approached and stood over it, was a third full. *Drip. Drop. Tick. Tock.* The purplish, trembling Water seemed to almost physically stretch, as though embracing organically each arriving dollop as it struck the vibrating, wondrous surface.

Each descending drop seemed to fall with the power of railroad hammers. I wanted only to touch my fingertips to the gentle, purple, magically immortal surface..

But I didn't dare move. Munye had his Glock pointed at the three of us. Kammi rested her beautiful black hair on his shoulder, her perfect white arms around his waist.

"Knock a hole in the wall, honey. Make the water cascade down! I want us to make love with the water pouring down over us – "

"I wouldn't do that," Tony warned.

"That's reason to do it right there, honk." Snapped Munye.

"Why mess with a good thing?"

"To make it better," The Leader of Future Masses answered. "And because a dumb - ass white boy like you said not to mess with it. Reason enough. Baby, cover your ears."

*POW!!*

*"Too loud!"* Kammi cried out.

The blast from Munye's Glock shook limestone dust down off the roof of the little chamber, and a flint - like spark that flew amidst the leaking water, suggested the bullet had accurately ricocheted off the limestone.

That was a big pistol, square handle, square barrel – *Undoubtedly Barry's favorite, a Glock Nine, Florida's true state flower –* and it seemed impossible the limestone wasn't fractured.

A black powder burn appeared and spread a little where the bullet had struck and harmlessly ricocheted away. But that was all.

Daddy, Tony and I had covered our ears the instant Kammi had covered hers, but there was still a monster echo from the pistol blast, inside my poor head and reverberating all the way up the tunnel behind us.

"What the hell? Not even a mark!"

"I see a mark, honey – do it again!"

Both Kammi and Munye went to the shallow mark the bullet had chipped, and ran their hands together over it.

"This Water is full of some awful magic," She explained to him, when no other explanation was possible. "That's why that tree in the courtyard is so freaky."

She reached down for the ladle that rested under - water in the tub.

"That's okay, honey. There's plenty already collected. We'll do it this other way. Tilt your beautiful head back and let me drown you in this love."

"Lemme mix it w' some yak," Munye brightened.

"No, honey, you'll see. Pure love."

"Huh?"

We watched their faces press close together in the shadowed chamber, the purplish spilling stream cascading down into their mouths, the lovers kissing each other with affection, then relish, the splashing explosions of magic now dancing in rivulets down their faces, their mouths, their necks and onto their clothing, as she dipped the ladle deeply into the tub, the next wondrous waterfall from the ladle soaking their hair, their clothing –

"Not so much, Kammi!" The forcefulness, the fear in Tony's voice, caused the hair to stand up on my neck, not a cliché – I felt it.

"You jealous, white boy?" Munye laughed, already sensing the power of the Water.

"It just takes an eye - dropper's worth. That much Water is unstable…"

"Jealous, Tony?" Kammi teased him. "I'm getting so excited – can you see my nipples?"

"I can feel 'em, honkey. They full of love, those sweet pretty babies… Just like this island, all mine."

A third ladle was raised high as Kammi and Munye, ever the Reality stars, were French - kissing by now, pressed close together, as much for the audience's entertainment as their own – as always – and the mighty promise of Eternal Life splashed downward, Kammi gulping, and then Munye too, their erotic distraction becoming progressively focused on themselves and indifferent to their captive audience.

"Oh, God, baby, it's never been like this. I ain't believin' these rushes!"

"Put your tongue in my mouth again. I can't breath."

From mouth to groin, the lovers were truly *KamYe,* a single being, its two halves grinding forcefully each against the other, the bubbling, explosive purple flow spilling over them both, a unifying, irresistible, stupefying verification of their narcissism.

It may have been wishful thinking, but I could see what Tony had warned about, beginning to happen, all the more beautiful because of the Christmas lighting flickering amidst the cascading purple baptismal force flowing over them, enveloping them...

"What happens when they're drinking so much?" I whispered to Tony. Dad leaned in.

"It's never certain," Tony was staring at his once - beloved's rapturous lovemaking. He couldn't take his eyes

off her. Other than Tom and me, and of course my love -
mad parents, I've never seen a guy in love like that.

He spoke to me without looking away from the
lovers.

"It doesn't happen every time. But they're playing
with History."

"Epidermal Regression?"

"Stop it! Stop it, you two! You don't know what
you're doing!"

Kammi giggled. "Don't worry, Mr. King Perkins. He
knows what he's doing! I promise you! Does he evermore
know what he's doing! He's amazing! Oh, he's so shady!
He's Slim Shady!"

Now Mr. and Ms. KamYe had forced their mouths
fully up against the narrow cut in the limestone – *again,
instinctively, for the invisible cameras they were certain watched their
every move worshipfully* – sucking the richness from it, showing
off, their tongues touching, then pressing again upon the
slit in the limestone where the world – where all History –
had begun.

In only a moment, that single sip of Water I'd tasted
weeks earlier, was now whispering the secret, melancholy
truth of Eden – I was able to clearly visualize Adam and
Eve, naked at this wall, billions of sunsets ago, their perfect
innocence enjoined at this somehow almost vaginally
narrow oval.

I could see it so clearly, almost in slow motion, *I
could see it whole* – that here, in Eden, the lonely Creator had
first conjured these two divine, innocent companions, His
pals, history's first bffs, granted youth and immortality at
the dawn of human Time.

God's perfect playmates.

And these two innocents, having already been granted by their Creator eternal life, and youth, had in the course of divine, endless summer, discovered lust together.

Our Creator, stunned, enraged, found Himself odd man out, an excruciating emotional rejection most of us have known at least once... to be the unneeded, unwanted, disregarded Third... *Oh, why won't you just go away and leave us to this wondrous feeling, Humanity's first, first love? Oh, God – Please just <u>Go away and let us be together alone!</u> Give us this endless moment in the emerald glade of Eden, this splendor in the grass of Always... We don't need you any more. We have each other.*

One problem our Creator seems to have experienced throughout History was the inability to correct a mistake once He'd made it, else how do you explain what our world has become? And I don't want to hear about arks and floods and rainbows, everybody knows now that was global warming.

Perhaps the Creator had stumbled, unexpected, upon the lovers here, in the limestone bower. Perhaps His Mighty jealousy of their lust's mindless preeminence over Him, proved the true serpent, slithering lethally in Eden.

In the deepest place in my heart, I could sense it. I could feel it. And hear it in the sad, silent music that whispered through the wind itself, all across Crystal Lagoon, but most perceptibly in the branches and leafwork of the magic tree directly above this tiny limestone chamber – the endless whisper of the lovers' disbelief.

For after jealousy had worked its wicked poison, the Creator had turned away from his own thunderous rage, vengeance, madness, jealousy, rejection, and then... blind, childish punishment.

*Heaven's first sin was His own – Our Great Father, Our Absentee Landlord, The Mysterious Stranger Who Art In Heaven –* now sorrowful, wiser, but too late to wisdom, realizing His horrific punishment of the Innocents was irreparable, His curse upon Eden's first children irreversible. They had only been doing what comes naturally.

Too bad. So sad. *Your Dad.*

Adam and Eve had not been forgiven. None of the rest of us have been forgiven either, but the first two out of History's Gate really took it in the neck.

And Eden had been left silent for all the intervening millennia. Our Creator had turned away from Paradise, never to return.

One single tree rose overhead – directly above us. When I realized its exact proximity to us, that's when I knew. Don't ask me the source of the momentous insight. I expect it was the Water, its silent song echoing, whispering to me.

The single sip of Water I'd taken, weeks ago, now illuminated my consciousness with the dark fable of Eden. I actually lost my breath for a moment.

For Adam and Eve had not been forgiven.

The tree of Knowledge of Good and Evil had become the enduring crypt for the world's first doomed lovers. The great tree formed their breathing oak - hard, immovable prison – their home, yesterday, tomorrow – their forever.

For they had not been forgiven. Their Creator simply did not know how. In a moment of bitter jealous rage, He had buried them alive. Paralyzed within a breath of each other, their lips within a teardrop of being able to whisper another word of love, ever share another kiss...

Theirs were tears that could never fall, never cool their burning, paralyzed, agonized near - embrace — except for the few divine drops trickling downward daily into this narrow limestone cut. Their sorrow was all the proof of the perfection and innocence of Eden that yet remained...

The eternal tears of the world's first lovers, the gift of their unending anguish, became the origin of eternal life for those of us lucky enough to taste their supernatural innocence. Their sorrow, formed into pure, purple droplets and sweetened with the fragrance of roses, now provide a lucky few souls access to the truth of Eden — of Eternity.

Weeping tears of mute uncomprehending sorrow at the cruelty of their Fate, Humanity's immortal parents, for ever young, for ever only a kiss away, for ever frozen motionless — they for ever guard Time above us.

The beautiful tree is their tomb, and always will be.

Watching KamYe cavorting under the terrible truth whispering within the Water, we stood staring at this smirking mockery of the world's first lovers — a blasphemy beyond expression against the sacrifice of Humanity's long - ago, youthful father and mother, condemned now to eternal paralysis for the crime of innocence, History's very first Knockout Game — and one further thought struck me most forcefully, Dad's quote from that old Russian trog Marx, *history repeats itself, the first time as tragedy, the second time as farce.*

It was hard to watch Kammi and Munye mock History, harder still to look away.

Munye had stuffed the Nine in his unbelted pants. One huge hand was around Kammi's waist, the other balancing both of them against the limestone wall. It still wasn't safe to run for it, although all three of us were thinking exactly the same thing, I'm sure...

"Did you hear something behind us?" Daddy whispered just then.

*Wishful thinking.* I was merely trying to catch my breath, and to shake off the terrible empathetic anguish pressing down on my heart from the near - whispers, the almost - echoes, the sad music drifting silently from the lovely tomb above us....

Our Creator at least has a long memory. The lovers will live forever trapped within that memory. My heart broke for them; but, and I am ashamed to admit this, at the very moment, my thirst for their immortal tears had never been greater.

"I think I hear Munye's troops, coming down the tunnel."

"We should have fought back, Tony." I said. "We've made it too easy."

"Trust us."

Yes, I thought I had heard rowdy voices above us in the distance, coming down through the tunnel, but this was a world full of echoes, and these two by the Water were making such a prolonged spectacle of themselves, who knew where the sound was coming from?

Besides, Ghost Posse was in process of capturing the castle above militarily. A lot could account for that racket.

"Shouldn't someone warn These Two Reality Stars?"

"I tried," Tony kept staring. "But I don't think it's happening with these two. The Effect is never certain. It doesn't happen in every case. It's not happening here."

"I don't see anything happening," Daddy acknowledged. "Except she'll be pregnant in about two more minutes of this."

"I love you so much, baby," Kammi kissed her husband again, her tongue all over his mouth and face.

"Don't *do* that!" Tony shouted.

Tony was watching his beloved very closely.

"Nothing's happening."

"Oh yes it is," I whispered almost to myself.

"No, Jessica, it's not," Tony gently corrected me.

"Tony! Listen! Look!"

"No, sweetheart. Look a little more closely. It's the light in here."

"They're *changing*."

"No," Tony smiled at me, insistently, wisely and sadly. "Not this time. I know all the symptoms of this. There's simply no Regression. They're not changing."

"*Oh yes they are!*"

"Spit some of dat juice in my mouth, sexy," Munye ordered her.

*Wishful thinking?* There was definitely some commotion far up the tunnel behind us. We could have made a run for it right then, and succeeded, I'm sure.

But I simply couldn't tear my eyes away from the miraculous transformation beginning to occur under the spilling, cascading, sluicing amethyst power of the moment.

"OMG," Daddy whispered, his eyes half - dollar size.

"OMFG," Tony agreed, more forcefully. "Oh, my beautiful Kammi!"

Daddy and I were looking at each other. I was nodding *yes, let's run.* He was shaking his head *no, let's watch.*

Tony was staring so hard at his beloved it was as though he was looking upon the moment of his own death... or birth.

"I can't believe it. I think... I think... Jessica, you may just be right," Tony murmured to himself.

"I can see it. I know I can."

"I don't think so," Daddy said. "It's... I don't think so."

"There's a Regression occurring."

"*I know!*"

"Oh, my God," Daddy interrupted. This was no time for acronyms. "It's... *Yes!*"

"It's full blown. It's occurring. *I've never actually seen one before!*" Tony wiped his eyes. "She's becoming..."

*My darling. Oh, my beloved Nubian darling!*

The tunnel seemed a long way behind us. I was younger and faster and ready to flee. *Not so fast, my friend,* Daddy kept shaking his head, his eyes big and very trog - like. I was momentarily distracted by an approaching, echoing commotion behind us in the tunnel...

"......What the hell is this on the steps, is that Christmas lights? Is f****** Christmas early this year?"

It sounded like gravel being poured out of a concrete truck and rumbling down the long, crazy – cheerful corridor, a voice you'd recognize if you heard it in the pitch black of night, and would be so glad you heard it – unless you were in the trunk of a Cadillac, on your way down to the river.

"Christmas lights!" Pauley Vee's rumbling voice was disparaging. "This whole island is like a doll's house."

"I dunno, Pauley," A second heavy male voice, also a wise guy's Joisey accented flavor, carefully contradicted his boss. "I sort of like it. Gives a rich feminine flavor to the limestone, sort of a cool touch of seasonal irony to the summer outside this tunnel...Eh? Eh?"

These wise guys weren't pulling up to the wagon train wearing ballet slippers. Their four hundred dollar two tone wingtips fairly thundered down the tunnel toward the bizarre scene occurring below their voices in the limestone water closet.

"Ask Vinny," I heard Pauley Vee call. "See what Vinny thinks."

"Eh? What can I say, Boss. I like the lights. They project a harmonious, deflective quasi - floral eclecticism. I like 'em. What can I say?"

Pauley Vee snorted angrily.

"I'm canceling *Home and Garden.* To hell with the bar's free subscription."

In the tunnel far above us, there was a moment's silence.

"Check the GPS," a woman's gruff voice ordered. "How much further?"

"We're right on top of 'em!"

Although the windy upper reaches of the tunnel caused the voices I was hearing to commingle indistinctly, nonetheless I felt a warm instinctive reaction toward the quarreling conversation approaching from far away.

A very warm, very relieved reaction.

I remember what Daddy had said about Pauley Vee, *if he's giving you a ride to the river, it probably doesn't mean you're about to go swimming...* words to that effect. I loved him.

"Hey, Jack — you down here, buddy?"

"I've never been so glad to see anyone," Daddy was white - faced with relief as the tunnel gave up its fresh human bounty.

"Pauley Vee!" I strangled a screech, and managed just a whisper. Why interrupt the lovers, at least just yet?

I looked past Pauley.

"Roseanne!"

"Who'd you expect? Tim Tebow?"

"I wouldn't have minded," I laughed in pure joy.

"I don't blame you," She laughed back.

"But this is even better!"

"Well, at least we brought shotguns."

"Them two look like they have a history," Roseanne laughed, and that ribald Gator laugh at last alerted the French - kissing, sexed - up revelers that their protracted water orgy was now rudely concluded.

"So your pen worked after all, Pauley... I thought we were gone gators."

*That stupid pen was actually a GPS beacon, emergencies only?*

"Life and *Death* only," Pauley corrected my thought cloud like he could read my mind. "We wouldn't have broke our necks gettin' over here otherwise. Jesse James, I can always count on yore dad never to push the panic button without good cause. He's a pro. We left the bar open and here we are. There are some happy crackers in Pauley Vee's tonight. I told 'em not to try to work the blenders. Straight shots only."

"So glad to see you," I could barely whisper.

"Like they'll be able to keep their hands off them blenders. Once that Parrothead music starts, all bets are off."

Pauley Vee gave that mirthless gravel laugh. "And my new girlfriend can drive a damn speed boat like beatin' the band. Close call, all the same. They almost wouldn't let us on this island! What the hell kind of password is 'Heisenberg'?"

His shovel - face turned toward Munye the way a wolf would eye a rabbit.

"Hello, Big Head. Hello, Idaho Ass."

"Honey, what's happening to your hands?" I heard Kammi asking Munye in a half - whisper of alarm. *"Your hands!"*

Only then did I notice the sawed - off shotgun in Pauley Vee's own huge mitts, and three more sawed - off shotguns held tenderly by the wise guys backing him up, their Hawaiian shirts adding a festive touch to the moment. Just like the Palm Tree shortsleeve dad had been wearing when we'd started out, so many centuries ago...

Munye started to reach for his Glock. The two barrels of the shotgun immediately leveled down at the soaking wet silk boxer shorts spilling over Munye's empty belt loops.

*Chick - chick!*

"Try it, Thug Boy. Just try it. Make my night."

"Please, please – no bloodshed," Tony pleaded.

"How come the dude ain't wearing a belt. His panties are showing."

"Don't shoot the girl," Tony urged Pauley Vee, and the panic in his voice was compelling. "I don't care what you do with that d***."

"Where's Tom?" I asked. I wanted to kiss everybody in the tunnel entrance, but Tom for a different reason.

"I'm here." Tom was out of breath. "I heard about the party – didn't want to miss it."

*Where had he come from?*

I didn't notice it at the moment, but he too was armed, with what he's explained to me since is a .45 automatic. Looks a lot like a Glock, only steel - barreled. Equally scary.

"Tommy, I know the secret of the Tree," I told him softly. "I'm so glad to see you! The tree whispered to me its secret. The secret of the Water."

"Tell me later, Gator."

Knowing Daddy was staring at The Lovers obsessively, I kissed Tom full, if briefly, on the mouth.

He looked stunned.

"You're only fifteen years old!" He whispered urgently.

"Well, I won't be for ever! Well, maybe I will be... but not really...oh, you know what I mean!"

"I don't care anyway. We don't have those kind of laws on this island."

I kissed him again. This time I'm afraid maybe Daddy noticed.

"Are they attacking the island yet?"

"Not yet. It doesn't matter." *It's already over. It hasn't even started yet, but it's already over.*

"Hands up, Big Head."

"It's okay, baby." Dr. Munye snapped at Kammi. "Stay frosty, we come out ahead later tonight. I got a little army to take care of us. And a bomb."

"*Honey! No bomb, okay? Okay? Oh, God! Look at your hands!*"

Munye and Kammi angrily raised their hands, behaving as though they'd been interrupted by the Sheriff in the middle of an erotic by - the - hour motel encounter, debauched, distracted and angry, faces dripping, panting noticeably.

"Daddy – I know I'm not mistaken. They're starting to switch colors."

I noticed Kammi was still licking the Water off her chin, arms and wrists. The wise guys, I could just feel, were checking out the super hot reality star, and they weren't thrilled by her choice of boyfriends.

The terrible miracle that Tony had tried to warn them of, now began to transpire, slowly, subtly, but...*very* noticeably.

I thought I had noticed it earlier, but now there was no doubt, even in the dim, multicolored Christmas lighting in the small room.

"Now what!" Shouted Dr. Munye, looking down at himself, holding his arms forward, looking at his arms and then starting to brush at them with his hands. Then something about his hands caught his attention. He stared at first the palms, then the backs of his hands. He repeated the gesture, then repeated it again.

"What the hell? NOW WHAT!"

"You're getting lighter," King Perkins tried to explain. "It doesn't matter how much you consume. A single sip is sufficient to trigger a Regression. More is less when it comes to this Magic Water. You're both going to be changed."

"Well, Doctor. You're becoming white. At last you'll have an equal chance in life."

"Tony," The frightened diva cried. "Make it stop. It's happening to me too."

Tony shrugged, speaking only to Kammi.

"I tried to warn you, dearest. I'll love you, black or white. What does color matter? I love you. It can't be reversed. I tried, I tried to warn you..." *Oh, my lovely Carribou queen!*

"What the hell!" Shouted Munye. "Get me back THE WAY I WAS!"

Pauley Vee's frog - eyes narrowed, as though not believing what he was witnessing. Munye started brushing all the harder. Now he was clawing first one forearm, then the other, with his long fingernails.

"WHAT THE HELL!!!"

"It's the light, honey. It's the light in here?"

"Yeah?" Munye looked at her. It's the first time I ever glimpsed the slightest uncertainty in his eyes. "The light in here is bad..."

"It's just the light, honey. Oh, God, it's just the light..."

But then I heard Pauley Vee's deep gravel humorless laugh, this time betraying the slightest amusement. You could trust that laugh. It was the laugh of a man who had seen everything, who had thrown enemies into rivers. He had seen everything. Well, not everything. Not till now.

"That thug is changing teams," He said over his shoulder, and the wise guys backing him just cracked up.

"WHAT... THE..... OHHHH MY GOD..... NOOOOOOOOO!"

"My lord, honey....I think you're..."

Dr. Munye said nothing, just sat down by the tub, began ladling the gorgeous Water on himself, and started to scrub and claw his arms almost violently.

"No! No! No! No! NO! NO!"

"Slide that Glock over here, Whitey," Pauley Vee roared with that same dark, gravelly, mirthless laughter.

Munye stopped trying to wash the emerging whiteness away long enough to obey the command of the sawed off twelve gauge, and since I was closest and quickest, I grabbed up the heavy Glock and handed it to our frog - eyed savior.

*Will the real Slim Shady… please stand up? Please stand up? Please stand up?*

"OMG," I heard Kammi whisper to herself, and realized that she had realized that even given Dr. Munye's changing appearance, that at least they would continue to proceed through the world, and the Nielsen Cable Ratings, and the all - important Sweeps Week, as an interracial couple – for she too was changing, darkening by the moment, her perfect porcelain skin still perfect, but no longer porcelain.

Uh, no. Nowhere near porcelain.

Golden for a moment, then tawny, then merely deeply tanned, then even more deeply tanned, then brown, first shoe - leather brown, then mahogany brown, and then…. as she watched Munye changing, and watching herself changing, and responding not by trying to wash herself as he kept obsessively doing, but instead merely holding her breath as though fighting off the moment before drowning, she began to glow in the uncertain light with a new beauty, alabaster replaced with obsidian, her eyes if anything more luminescent than before.

Kammi Kay was gorgeous in any color.

"What's the scientific term for this?" Roseanne asked.

"Epidermal Regression."

"No doubt about it, the bitch is black as the queen of Spades," One of the wise guys remarked.

"Don't use that word," Kammi warned him softly.

"Which one?"

"There go the ratings," Roseanne guffawed.

"Not necessarily," Tony Perkins argued angrily. "BET would love her. Handled correctly, this could make her bigger than ever. She'll be like Obama, both black *and* white." *Biracial. Not biologically biracial. Sequentially biracial!*

"OMG. OMFG." The newly minted soul diva whispered, also like Munye, halfway between a chant and a prayer.

"Cuff him up," Pauley Vee ordered his assistants. "Thug boy has got a date to make. A very important date."

"How long does dis last, mfers," Munye demanded. "How long I got to wait before this goes back to black? I got the army to lead."

"It's irreversible."

"Irreversible? What does that mean?"

"It means what it says. It means if you decided to join the Klan five years from now, nobody in the recruiting office is going to object."

"WHAT DID YOU DO TO ME?" At last he understood. Munye leapt to his feet, thrusting his arms out toward his bride. "BITCH, WHAT DID YOU DO TO ME WID' DAT FOUL WATER?"

"Don't call me bitch," Kammi snapped, staring down at her own ebony arms and feeling her face, her neck, her still - straight jet hair.

If there was any doubt that what we were witnessing was fact and not hallucination, it was confirmed in the next exchange between the two former lovers.

"You f****** BITCH! Turn me into a HONKEY!"

"I told you, MF******, you don't call me no BITCH!"

*Wham!* And Kammi took a roundhouse swing at the wise doctor that started at the right field bleachers, and, due to the size of his immense, now chalk - white, stubbled jaw, the blow landed hard and solid. His giant head spun back, and he staggered. Kammi's posture of obedient deference had vanished with her pale flesh.

"Bitch!"

Kammi slapped him again.

*Wham!* "I warned you — You no - talent *punk*. Dime Bag a far superior lyricist to you. Who you think you foolin'?"

"Dime Bag? You crazy! Dime Bag? Dime Bag can't touch my words!"

And then, in a single scathing up - and - down, Kammi coldly noted her ex - bf's pale flesh, sandy brown 70s dandruffy over - the - collar haircut, so oddly contrasting with the gold gangsta chain, gold teeth, blooming silver silk pleated boxer underwear that billowed out over the sagging belt loops, and then she glared at his tattoos, now so oddly flabbily misplaced on his scrawny, middle - aged white arms...

Kammi spat out the greatest, most evil and wicked epithet available in all the culture:

"Who you think you are, Munye? *Malibu's Most Wanted? YOU F****** POSER!*"

"The unkindest cut of all," Roseanne barely breathed.

*Wham!* "And that's for forgetting my birthday. Jerk."

Before Munye could respond, Pauley Vee gave him this advice:

"Thug Boy — you have the right to remain silent."

"My God, she's magnificent," King Tony, sighed in absolute worshipful reverence. "Carribou Queen!"

"I love that song!" Kammi batted her eyelashes.

"Look at Doctor Munye," My father observed, to no one in particular. "Why, he's starting to look just like ...M&M?"

"No way that's M&M," Vinny interjected. "I got a crew that runs security for M&M when he's in Miami. Not even close."

"My God?"

"My God — "

*"My God! It's Dick Clark. He's been turned into Dick Clark! Only breathing!"*

"The breathing part is easily repaired," Vinny remarked. "Eh? Eh, Pauley?"

"Say what?"

"Want me to push the button on this jerk?"

"Eh? Naw. Let him live life as a middle - aged white man for a while. Let him learn what true suffering is all about."

"You know, Jack? You're right. Jerk boy's a spitting image for Dick Clark. Whitebread Dick Clark. Now by God, that's irony. God has a sense of humor after all – a good sense of humor."

"Who's Dick Clark?" I asked innocently.

# XVII

*Time is Nature's Way of Keeping Everything From Happening All At Once*

So. What happened next on the night when everything did actually – or so it seemed at the time – Happen All At Once?

Dr. Munye had been fitted with flex cuffs behind his back – Pauley Vee always said flex cuffs were like American Express – *never leave home without them.* They came in handy now.

And Kammi kept asking me if I had a mirror on me. I let her take a Selfie from my i, which nobody had bothered to confiscate, that's how important I was.

Kammi glared at the selfie, and took a long time frowning and studying it carefully. She squinted. Frowned. Glared. Tilted the screen left, right, up down, and at every angle in between. Finally she shrugged.

"I can't believe it. I'm definitely black. But I don't look half bad."

I gave Tom another hug. He hugged me back, and I could just tell. Right then, I could just tell.

If love was possible between a fifteen year old girl and a five hundred year old guy (and I'll bet you this is one kind of sex the state of Florida hasn't yet gotten around to outlawing) – this was the real dope – soda shoppe two straw Magic, high school letter sweater, let's exchange class rings and wear them on our neck chains, I'll get us a motel room with my brother's credit card Magic.... Besides, he doesn't *look* five hundred, and although I might always look fifteen, going on sixteen, in a couple of years I'll be legal enough.

Of course on this island we don't have those kinds of laws, and besides, I'm engaged to one of its owners. *Ha. What a Mook I am! Isn't that just like a fifteen year old girl – going on sixteen – getting distracted from the story still ahead by the silliest most fascinating stuff?!*

There wasn't any question after that brief, incredibly intense hug between us, in the scream - filled, crowded, eerily lit tunnel, the Magic Water dripping down again into the Wal - Mart wheeled tub, *tick tock...tick tock...tick tock...* Tommy wanted to hold my hand, just like in that old Trog song...

"I'm still beautiful," I heard Kammi announce shakily, albeit with real relief in her voice. "Black skin hides the acne *much* better."

We were being marched to the surface, Pauley Vee and his guys bringing up the rear. Tom had two guys with him too. Where had they come from? Munye seemed in shock. He kept muttering to himself, almost as if performing a catechism, *I have the right to remain silent. Anything I say can and will be used against me in a court of law. I have the right to an attorney...*

Kammi knelt, again and again, next to clusters of the multicolored flame shaped Christmas bulbs, carefully studying her face glowing back at her from the selfie in the dim lighting. The tunnel led very gradually upward.

"Wrinkles don't show up on black skin quite so much," She observed with evident surprise. "Jessica, my hair's still straight. Will you give me braids?"

"Sure."

"Should I get a weave?"

"Lawyer!" Munye shouted. "Lawyer!"

Now we were at the tunnel mouth, emerging into moonlight and the sweet warm breath of the courtyard, when the first shotgun blasts broke out from the wide soccer field, flares lighting up the whole island like the fourth of July, and the whup - whup - whup of a half dozen or so helicopters settling, tail - first, one after another, at the far edge of the soccer field.

We all stood in the warm night air just outside the vault door that led from behind us back down into the tunnel.

Tom had to use both hands and all the strength in his handsome shoulders to slam the industrial - sized combination vault door shut, and closed over it the professionally disguised work door with its sign, _Janitor's Bathroom Out of Order!_

I'd passed that door a half dozen times. The subterfuge was perfect. The brothers always entered the tunnel from an office lift anyway. This was the emergency access. I laughed.

"Godfather," my father shook Tony's hand, then Tom's. Pauley Vee was grinning like a teenager.

Roseanne hugged Kammi, then whispered an important confidence.

"Don't worry, honey. We like black people. We really do. Y'all have made such great strides. We just don't like thugs."

"My mom will have a cow," Kammi giggled, studying the Selfie like it was a map to the future...

"_Lawyer!_" Dr. Munye shouted to a merciless Heaven...

From where we stood, the big open castle gates about half a football field away, to the south I think, gave a partial but scary view of the war for the future of Crystal Lagoon.

Forget New Haiti. Now that would never happen. Without the Doctor's leadership, his forces seemed almost spiritually adrift, capable of fighting, weaponized, angry and aggressive, but strangely directionless. I could tell by the way Tom and Tony were shaking hands with everyone that we were about to witness the *denouement* of one of the Corleone family's sagas.

Admittedly, Daddy helped me with the foregoing passage. Daddy also said the Corleone movie saga he was most reminded of, by the way Tom and Tony were acting, once Munye was in cuffs and the flares started soaring, was the movie that ended with a lot of bowing and ring - kissing. I think that was the first one. With Brando, Pacino as Michael.

*Godfathers. We underestimated these two every time.*

Not a war, but a battle. A quick battle. I watched it later on dvd, and understood far better what was going on, when Tom and I watched it together on a dvd at an intimate little post - wedding party, in our bungalow...

\* \* \*

The Great General and Rapper Munye probably wasn't in the greatest focus at the moment the battle actually began.

He'd been first transmogrified from ebony to ivory, and then bitch - slapped by his ex - slave of a wife, now black, proud and free at last... then handcuffed with a sawed - off at his spine, held by a very serious, shovel - faced wise guy, and lastly had been mocked by everyone but me for looking almost exactly like a big - headed version of Dick Clark, whom I know now was once, a long time ago, emcee of *American Bandstand* –

No, I think it's fair to say that even more than Napoleon's hemorrhoids at Waterloo, Dr. Munye probably had his own reasons for not being in the greatest focus at the outset of the Great Battle of Crystal Lagoon, the facts of which – except for that single dvd – seem to have been lost to history entirely.

*First:* Napoleon said, the battle is decided before the first shot is ever fired. One small glitch is often what dooms the whole enterprise...

*Pants on the ground!*

Who would ever imagine that such a small detail in the formulating of Dr. Munye's brilliant guerilla battle plan would foil his seizure of the island, and its guarantee of immortality, at least for the King and Queen of Reality itself?

Immortality in *the palms of their hands, they had it, absolutely... well, at least the fight would have been closer...*

*Pants on the ground!*

I watched this comedy of errors later, as mentioned, and it's hard to see a lot of coherence in the running around of the shadowy shapes racing and stumbling all across the soccer field. The term 'fog of war', as Daddy has often said, is the greatest understatement in history.

It was absolutely crazy, even small as the spatial dimensions of battlefield and numbers of combatants were, above everything else was a sense of colossal confusion...

Watching the dvd later, we were able to better track events, as the attack proceeded from where the helicopters first landed, near the far end of the field, and Munye's forces, now minus their now boyishly pale - faced leader, began sweeping across the wide empty soccer field toward the castle's wide - open gates, under the soaring, unearthly pink glaring illumination of flares arcing everywhere, and the helicopter rotors, now powering down.

"Time for you dropouts to die, DIE," I was able to hear one of the attackers screaming – only they were all shooting at their own people!

Something had set off both angry, half - inebriated crews.

"You MFers killed Biggie!"

"Naw, f*** you, *you* MFers killed Biggie!"

"Step up then Big Playa – !"

"Oh, yeah? I got some medicine to apply on yo' ass!"

*Popopopopopopopopop!* A gracefully curvilinear row of bullet - holes carved an instantaneous, inky squiggle across the white stucco masonry across a low portion of the castle's front wall as the AKs, already set on rock 'n roll, started cranking out rounds with pent - up enthusiasm.

And although you couldn't see that many colors in the flare - light (at least on the dvd), it seems obvious, the smoldering anger between these crosstown 'brothas' had, over some real or imagined slight, burst into actual small arms combat, noisy, frightening, yes, but due to the lighting, confusion, yak, and panic, little damage was done, except to the tree - tops of the surrounding pine forest.

"We may die, but you die first, b****", and another set of AK - 47s commenced lighting up the warm island night.

Reinforcements spilled from the choppers – like my military slang, Trogs? – and despite the aggression the warring cousins were directing toward each other's colors – enough of the company, now a ragged wave of confused but well - armed attackers, seemed to start moving forward relentlessly across the broad flare - lit ground, toward the open castle gate.

Every sixth round was a tracer, so the wildly arcing AK fire could be tracked, even at night. It was almost like watching lasers at a rock concert...

Long, erratic spattering rows of bullet holes raced *ratatataratatata* across the front of the castle walls, chunks of stucco shattering wildly, just as the top row of soccer field bleachers exploded in a shower of splinters; burst after burst of automatic fire shredded tree - tops. *Ratatatatatatatatatatatatatatatatat!!! Ratatatatatata!*

*Whoooooooosh!!* Two more flares soared high above the shadowy fray, intensifying the battlefield's shadows and irreality. Warriors looked ten feet tall and running at impossible angles in the hot distorted light. Divots of the manicured soccer lawn flew up in great hairy - looking tufts of grass - filled dirt. Several warriors had dropped to earth and were low crawling, squirming toward the open gate, meanwhile foolishly continuing to blast away.

"Get to the castle," We could hear somebody yelling. And again:

"I got some medicine for yo' ass."

AK rounds skipped like hard - thrown stones across the lily - scattered *koi* ponds nearby the castle walls, the pond water lifted by the hot lead bursts like a succession of steamy little waterspouts white and black; and tracer rounds bounced around and soared through the summer night air, hissing as they cooked down in the grass like lit cigarettes, the whole potentially deadly carnival even seeming for just a moment to be celebratory.

But then the attack seemed to stutter, and began to slow. Cousins in blue, cousins in red, blasted away recklessly at each other, hitting little but night sky.

But as the warriors moved more slowly and awkwardly, trying to pull their trousers back into place and tie their unlaced Timbs, the danger for serious bloodshed actually increased significantly.

You can't see us on the dvd, but through all this commotion our group, including white Dr. Munye and black Kammi Kay, stood motionless and essentially helpless, at the rear of the castle courtyard, watching History unfold through the wide - open, distant front gates.

"This way, my warriors! THIS WAY!!" Screamed Dr. Munye.

He was acting like he was watching a ballgame on tv, and with about the same impact. Even his voice seemed to be changing, a little above baritone to a little below tenor. Once again, Dad and I exchanged glances, two blood relatives who happened to have become the bestest of buddies, in the crucible of historical catharsis, each of us realizing we were witnessing the most amazing night that either of us would ever experience...

*Pants on the ground!*

That's what was slowing them down! A little thing, a problem with attire, not so noticeable, not so much a problem if you're standing around on the corner handing packets through car windows and collecting cash, not so much of a problem if you're chillin' on the stoop and suckin' on a fawty, countin' a roll of twenties and steppin' up on Shawty, but under sustained automatic weapons fire from your hated enemy the cross - town gangstas, you try to run, you can't run, because your pants are around your knees by now, and ain't nobody wearin' a belt, and even if you are wearin' a belt, by now you've forgotten how it works...

You struggle to pull 'em up, try to run holding 'em up and shoot with one arm and hand just like John Wayne in *The Green Berets,* everybody's aim thrown off that much more, limping along, cursing, shooting, not realizing that the genius leadership of Doctor had been placed in severe arrest.

If Dr. Munye had shown foresight enough to merely have confiscated all the colors, blue and red alike, perhaps the soldiers of Africa America would have realized that in their struggle, which was certainly historically valid, only a single color mattered, a color every one of them shared.

Live and learn.

But not to be dissed, my brothers. After all, white Europeans spent the better part of a century merrily slaughtering one another based solely on the color of the flowers they chose to pin into their lapels...

Live and learn *not.*

"Where's *OUR* side, Tommy?" First time I'd called him by nickname in front of Dad, who noticed, and I regretted it and hated it. I felt my face go beet - red.

But, where *WERE* they?

"Patience, Prudence. They'll be along."

"Yo' day is comin', Honkey," Munye cursed Tom, then Tony, unsure who was who, turning his attention away from the faltering approach of his platoons to rage at his captors, and, not last, the satan - ette Delilah that had led him to this Fall. "And yo' day, is comin' too, bitch!"

Kammi looked at me and sort of shrugged in a way that said, *'dis polar bear jus' don't learn,'* before stepping up and slapping her former master sideways – again.

*Wham!*

"Oooowwwww!"

"And that's for my birthday – *Last* year. Jerk."

"Please, honey, don't hit me no mo'. I be good. I get you somethin' special for Christmas."

"I ain't handcuffed," Kammi told him. "You might try remembering that." She was rubbing the back of her karate - chopping hand. "Say 'bitch' again. SAY 'BITCH'

AGAIN! I dare you! *I double - dare you!* SAY BITCH AGAIN!"

She must have seen *Pulp Fiction* more than twice too.

Kammi's transformation was fascinating, and I couldn't resist watching. Munye was desperate, and although my guess was this was impossible, nonetheless he seemed six inches shorter already, and his voice kept getting higher.

But she said nothing. It took Kammi a while to process even offers that benefited her, and I think she was beginning to see the positives of her recent shape - shift.

"Okay, Jester," I heard Tom's lovely voice alerting me. He used my special nickname. I was suddenly blushing again as I sensed Daddy's surprise and disapproval. "I think our team just took the field."

# XVIII

If an attack fails in the forest, and nobody hears it, can the political party currently in power in Washington be held to blame?

Ghost Posse supporters in charge of Public Relations at the U.S. Justice Department, the CIA and at the Pentagon, their interests politically hard - wired to those of the White House, were already electronically prepared to alert the American mainland's media of a magnificent regime change just outside our nation's territorial waters.

The Narrative was in place and ready to rock.

The whole official Federal propaganda hive was preparing to announce a small yet significant and courageous paramilitary victory against the pirate Monopolists of Crystal Lagoon, now re - named New Haiti on behalf of the popular military triumph achieved here.

Dr. Felix Munye's writings had loosely formed the ideological framework for a projected future internal separatist colony within American borders often nominally referenced as 'Africa America.'

This Narrative, for dissemination nation - wide, merely awaited word that the island of Crystal Lagoon *aka* 'New Haiti' had rebelled successfully against its fascist masters.

Release of the Narrative in its various modalities awaited only word that the target was sufficiently secured so that American troops and civilian authorities could arrive and provide assistance in establishing legal stability on the island for the safety of its citizens – just as the CIA and Pentagon long ago had salivated at the opportunity to provide similar stability at the Bay of Pigs, until that brilliant plan too inevitably went south.

The entire military propaganda apparatus of the United States government awaited an outcome to the battle we were now watching, on a beautifully barbered, freshly re - sodded soccer field in a not - too - distant land.

"Why are our guys wearing turbans?"

The Battle of Crystal Lagoon was being played out, as we ate wedding cake, on a big flat screen in our bungalow...

"Turbans?" I repeated.

"Because they're Sikhs. Real fighters. If we'd lost, they'd be identified by the boys at the Pentagon as Al - Qaeda. The press releases had already been written and were just waiting. But the Sikhs are mercenaries. The best in the world. Completely non - political. They don't give a damn who they're shooting. It's why you can trust them. They were on a jet back to Kashmir by dawn after the battle ended. And they'll be back here in ninety - six hours if we need 'em again. The best fighters on earth."

"Shotguns?" Daddy asked. "That's what your soldiers used?"

"Pump action twelve gauge. That's a weapon that instills fear. Look how the good Doctor reacted when your friends showed up down in the tunnel?"

"Yeah. It's an unmistakable sound. Like a Doberman growling. *Chick - Chiiiick!* Times forty."

"All our guys had for ammo was rock salt," Tony admitted proudly.

"You're kidding!"

"Legal said we couldn't risk hurting anybody."

"Look at that! They keep falling down! Their pants!"

"Pants on the ground," Tommy shrugged. "Who would have thought?"

"I always thought that was a sort of an idiotic style," Kammi added. As we watched the dvd, months after the actual battle, Kammi had divorced Munye – *in absentia,* since no one could say for sure where he was, of course, or even *if* he was – and she had remarried the *true* man of her dreams, her billion dollar baby.

"I love you." Tony whispered dreamily.

"Love you more."

Kammi was, as always, seated close to King Tony, and as always, she made sure her gorgeous, ebony hands were fully visible either on her lap, or with at least one of them resting proprietarily on her new husband's thigh.

That way it was hard not to notice her wedding ring. Tony wanted to make sure Kammi understood she was well - appreciated, and that he would do anything on earth to keep her happy. Freshly on the ring finger of her left hand was a twenty five million dollar chocolate diamond as big as the Ritz.

Beautifully invisible, twenty spider - holes had been dug nearly shoulder to shoulder about midfield on the soccer field's playing surface, and in each of these five foot deep cylinders crouched a sharpshooter with a shotgun loaded with rock salt. *Well, I guess that explains the pile - drivers and stacked culverts in the middle of the soccer field. Well - played, Godfathers...*

The captured texts between Munye and Kressa had laid out the exact plan of battle. That made it easy. Piece of cake.


The bearded Sikhs waited until Munye's two - platoon - sized attack had swept by over them, rushing toward the invitingly open castle gates, sort of an inversion of the Trojan Horse stratagem, as Dad later pointed out.

What slowed them so was the struggle to keep their pants in place, but since it was happening universally, at least the attack remained raggedly coordinated, just fatally slowed.

Once Munye's guerillas were caught between the spider holes and the castle moat, now electrified, the holes popped open, and twenty pump action shotguns locked and loaded in terrifying unison. Shotgun barrels were trained down on the suddenly hesitant attackers.

*CHICK - CHIIIIIIIKK!*

Meanwhile, on cue to the stunning appearance of the formerly hidden, spider - hole snipers, another rank of shooters, these snipers stretched out prone under the lowest bleacher bench on the north side of the field — forming the long arm of the L — now locked and loaded in tandem.

The single rank of shooters hidden under the bleacher seats — only another twenty or so — retrospectively proved a far larger force than necessary.

Forty barrels cut loose virtually simultaneously, the L forming a scorching ambush, both arms of the L achieving a stinging interlocking field of fire.

Aiming from the waist down, the Sikh infantry produced a terrific fiery spread of rocksalt that ended the attack within about ten seconds. Interlocking fields of fire achieved a saturation effect, literally scalding the attackers into quick submission.

Whatever the Perkins' brothers had paid this Sikh infantry, they'd gotten their money's worth.

"When your pants are around your knees, there's simply no protection from the rock salt," Tony mentioned. "Comic, really, if it wasn't all so sad. I've never seen a military event so arrogantly misplayed. And those guys were tough. If they'd been led properly, they could have caused us trouble."

"Those guys were all wearing too much gold. Gold makes the wrong fashion statement anyway," Kammi murmured, meanwhile studying her wedding ring in the various aspects of light in the bungalow. "Sometimes my people be so evil."

She looked up when she realized we were all staring at her.

"Oh, come on, Nerds," She remarked irritably. "It's a song lyric. And I can speak rap when I feel like it. I've paid my dues. I may not have lived the Streets – but I've *seen* the Streets! I've driven *on* the Streets. My taxes have fixed potholes *in* the streets. So stop staring. Show some respect for my struggle. Nobody knows the trouble I've seen." She gazed down at the vast crown of the rare, dark diamond on her left hand. "Nobody knows but Jesus."

"I love you," Tony whispered.

"Love you more." Kammi smiled. She'd just signed a forty million dollar deal as spokesperson for *EverTan Cosmetics* and she was feeling feisty.

The battle for Crystal Lagoon ended bloodlessly and in a hurry.

A last, lonely flare soared above the soccer field, with its huddled, defeated groups of Munye's soldiers, bereft now of gold grilles and heavy figaro chain, but hanging onto their identifying bandannas to the bitter end, their hands atop their heads, fingers interlaced, wondering what had happened to Dr. Munye and the brave new world that they had been promised, their forty acres, their mules, their seventy two virgins – wait, different lies, same outcome.

None of these defeated young guys had the slightest inkling of the existence of the Water of the Fountain of Youth, dripping again into the Wal - Mart tub ten minutes' walk below ground, nor of the fact that they'd transgressed the actual, biblical Garden of Eden itself, its emotional and physical perfection fed by the Magic Water, yes, but embodying a far greater truth.

*Money will always outsmart greed, I remember Tommy observing once... Up to a point.*

Three giant Sikorsky cargo helicopters were already approaching the soccer field, great nets descending from their bellies as they halted overhead, hovered, and then quite slowly began to descend on the now silent battlefield...

We were watching Dr. Munye frog - marched, metaphorically, out of the castle courtyard and across the soccer field, cursing, and, reflexively we assumed, demanding his lawyer and one free call, as he was guided, stumbling, toward the nets...

Whatever curses he flung back at us last were lost in the *whup whup whup whup* of the cargo choppers, turning slowly southward for their ten mile flight out to the cruise ship from where this doomed attack had first originated.

POWs in blue and red bandanas were being stacked horizontally three - deep in the nets, laid in as comfortably as possible. Occasionally a pack of crushed Kools or a random unlaced Timb would work its way down through the nets, and fall from the sky onto the quiet grass of the soccer field, where the Sikhs, per contract, were already policing up the lonely battlefield. You could have set your watch by it all.

You could also hear shouting from the nets, moments before the first giant chopper lifted away on its fifteen minute trip back to the cruise ship.

"*Who the hell is this ugly white man?*"

"He stole Doctor Munye's chain. I know that chain! What you do to the Doctor?"

"He have the Doctor's gold grille too!"

"I *am* the Doctor, god damn it – *your leader!* Shut up and listen, you bastards. I'll give the orders, you take the orders – got it? *We can still win this thing!*"

"You the Doctor? Oh? That right? How come you so white?"

"And ugly."

"He say he the Doctor? Where you been, Doctor? You look like you seen a ghost!"

"You look different somehow, Doctor!"

"Well, if he's the doctor, let's get him to the hospital!"

"Yeah, whitey, we got some medicine to apply to yo' ass —"

"God damn it, listen to me! *I got a Nine by my spine! That's my lyric!*"

But the fists were already flying, inside the great net, now full of struggling fish wearing red and blue bandannas and feeling very betrayed. These hard young men were at last unified by a common enemy, and now converged upon him.

Fists were flying, and the huge net started shaking and swinging violently, even as the Sikorsky powered up, lifting toward the stars.

\* \* \*

Late that night, after the battle of Crystal Lagoon had successfully ended, Daddy and I sat up together for hours. We were so torqued. We were so happy.

We knew about the Bomb. Once or twice I even remember glimpsing, at the corner of my awareness, the Death Stare in Doctor Rafferson's pale eyes as his eyes had met mine, in that fearful moment earlier as twilight was giving way to the darkness ahead.

But, really, after the miracle of our own personal survival, we weren't thinking about it just then.

We listened to jazz and looked out into the night, watching the moonlit Gulf, and the tiny twinkling lights of Reality Nation's cruise ship, still apparently at anchor just above the darker, starless line of the sea. We wondered, only half - curiously, about what the stragglers would do next. What could they do?

"Nothing." Daddy laughed. "Absolutely nothing."

"What if he blows everything up?"

"You mean Munye?"

"Uh huh."

"He could do that, I guess. If he makes it back to the boat alive. You think either of those gangs would take orders from Dick Clark?"

Daddy and I sat on the sofa together and listened to Mr. Pharoah Sanders together, a while.

You wouldn't think jazz that frenetic, with horns shrieking to the heavens, the giant African drums and tambourines, and the sad, historic chanting voice of a race of people proposing relentless faith and optimism in the face of all the suffering and adversity visited upon them, would give to the night a perfect historic counterpoint to that which we'd just experienced... *The Creator has a Master Plan, Peace and happiness through all/ the Land.... Through all/ the Land...... Through all...the Land...*

*This is the music appropriate for Paradise.*

"Daddy, what if they decide to attack us again?"

"They won't."

"I wish I could be so sure."

"I talked to Tony. They've been monitoring the Pentagon, Benning, Justice. CIA. You've heard the NSA monitoring the privacy of every American citizen? Guess what. Crystal Lagoon Corp. LLC *monitors the NSA!* These Perkins' brothers are tough. Don't let the pocket protectors fool you."

"I learned that tonight."

"To your point – the second Munye's assault fell apart, a couple of things happened. The airborne alert was quietly cancelled. The publicity releases connected to this whole Ghost Posse initiative were not only trashed, but removed from the Pentagon and Justice department computer hard drives.

"Effectively, none of those documents exist any longer. The attorneys and colonels have all quietly been reassigned. And this has happened within hours of the failure of this stupid assault."

Daddy hugged me hard, tousled my hair in a way he knew I loved and hated, and gave a deep laugh of great and heartfelt relief.

"Oh, I forgot. Your question was – ?"

"Are we safe?"

"Yes."

"Thank God." *Now if we can just figure some way to rid Reality of those who would claim to entertain us in its soiled name...*

A moment of peace and silence through all our land.

"Oh, dad – "

"What?"

"One thing would make it perfect?"

He gave a smile that I recognized indicated he was in possession of a happy surprise.

"What would make it perfect?"

"You know."

"Do I?" He wasn't hitting the Goose any more, but he was as playful as ever. "I don't think of you as reticent, Jessica. You've got a mouth on you. What would make it perfect?"

"Mom."

"Mom what?"

"If Mom was here. I hate stating the obvious."

He paused a long time.

We looked at each other.

His poker face needed some work.

His smile broke wide and youthful.

"Click your heels three times, Jessica dearest..."

"*Daaaaa - aaaadddyy! Seriously? Really?*"

"I just put down the phone. You were outside, busting up a coconut. We've been waiting to see — to see how things would turn out down here before I'd let her come down."

"Let me read her text!"

"Are you trying to be funny, or just mean? Machete don't text. And neither does Mrs. Machete."

"*This is the best day!*"

"She wants to come down and start fresh — as a twenty eight year old." He laughed happily. "She's getting a facelift first. Vanity, thy name is Woman."

"Vanity is our strength." I shot back. "It's why we're the ascendant species. We just had to wait for the way the world produces things to catch up with us. Now everything's nice and tidy, clean and tiny. That's how we like it — not some dreary old, noisy assembly line. Now we'll leave you Trogs in the dust."

He looked at me in shock.

"*Tú – Feminista?*"

"*Sí!*"

"Oh Princess Dancing Thumbs – I'm so proud!"

"She's smart to do that. The facelift I mean. She's turning back Time. Even we haven't been able to do that."

He paused, cleared his throat, and added shyly, "She asked if we would be able to forgive her."

"What did you say?"

He paused a long time. I started nodding like a dashboard ornament.

He laughed at me.

"DAD! WHAT DID YOU SAY?!"

"*Hell...to the....yes!*"

The timing was perfect. *The timing was perfect! Mom's coming home! Our family, together after a thousand nights of tears, after a thousand nights of prayers. My reaction? To go momentarily blind from the sudden shriek of arc - light that turned darkest night to brightest day.*

How could a fifteen - year old momentarily blind girl ever forget exactly such a profound moment in her life?

Never forget it, that's sure. Phosphorescent white light silently ripped heaven wide open, from seam to seam, at the very moment I got the news about Mom.

A blinding light etched my face, silently sweeping like molten silver fire across every window in the bungalow's living room. How could the timing be more perfect?

*"DADDY! DADDY! They're hitting us again!"*

*"COVER YOUR EYES JESS! HERE! IT'S NOT AN ATTACK! GET DOWN!"*

I dove for his lap and he threw his body over me as I grabbed him and hung on. Outside, the world was as bright as a thousand silver suns, and absolutely silent – that's what threw our instincts so far off about what might be happening, such a murderous volume of light, but unaccompanied by the slightest sound!

A great carbon arc light blazed, invading our air, windows, walls, blazing with a silent blinding incandescence, glimmering relentlessly, for what seemed more than a half - minute.

The light was so fierce, so intense, I could almost see my father's facial bone structure under his flesh. The world

around us went black and white. There was no third color
in the spectrum. In my Dad's lap I tried to shield my eyes.
There was no third color. Outside, night turned into day.
And day turned into ten minutes that were a thousand
sunrises combined into one melting furnace of light.

Fully thirty seconds passed, as Daddy and I hung on
to each other in absolute fear and astonishment – I'll bet I
clung so hard to my father that his ribs were bruised –
before the thunderous roaring rumble of what we now
know was at least a multi - kiloton atomic blast, swept
across Crystal Lagoon.

The shockwave shook the bungalow. The oak beams
in our livingroom rattled like trailer park plywood,
*whhhhaaaaaaaaaamm,* throwing bric - a - brac off the shelves,
dumping books and CDs onto the floor, lamps falling over,
glass crashing, doors and windows shaking so hard it
seemed certain they'd fly off their frames, the silhouettes of
the palms outside black against white, bent back with their
fronds blown back like human hair in a high wind, tiles
bouncing down off the bungalow roof, we could hear the
tiles splashing into the rainbarrels in back, four or five
moments of pure terror. *Bambambambam.*

"Hand grenades." I shouted.

"Coconuts." Daddy answered, but held me all the
tighter. "We're ok."

Daddy had his arms around me, and mine around
him.

"Holy God, what now?" Kammi had raced into the
livingroom, her gown half covering her voluptuous ebony
body. There was the *Playboy* cover pictorial to prepare for.
Now that she was black, Hefner would have to pay her five
times the price – that much we'd all agreed on.

Daddy had trouble looking away from the uncovered half. Black, white, green, you could even paint her paisley — Kammi was gorgeous. Enough so that, for a moment anyway, our attention was pulled away from an actual massive atomic explosion.

Kammi blinked away sleep and squinted, as we all did, in the direction from where the light, and then the thunder had come racing at us. Then she looked down at her arms.

"Oh, well, I'm still black. That's all that matters. I'm going back to bed."

From another guest bedroom, Pauley Vee and Roseanne now emerged, both incongruously attired in Disney pajamas. His pajamas honored Goofy, hers Minnie. They looked like typical middle - aged Mouse tourists, except of course for the shotgun.

"What the hell was that, Jack?"

"I think the Reality cruise may have ended prematurely."

"Their boat blew up?"

"Well — Dr. Munye was bragging about having obtained a nuclear weapon he was going to booby - trap our little island with, once he owned it. Y'know — like Dr. Strangelove. A Doomsday gap. So nobody could take a chance on messing with him, y'know?"

"You think he tried to assemble it by himself?"

"It's the only weapon Dick Clark had left. He may have been mucking around with it — trying to figure out how it works"

"They print warnings about that on the box."

"Yah. Only they're probably in Russian."

"Not no more," Roseanne laughed, and gave a sleepy, emphatic Gator chomp of goodbye to all that. "We'll check it in the morning."

"Damn, it's still bright outside. That was some bomb." Pauley Vee said admiringly. "I remember this time down in Little Italy – "

"Come on, honey, let's go back to bed. Too late to do anything about it tonight. It'll be on all the news shows tomorrow."

Pauley Vee and Roseanne returned to their guest bedroom.

"I want to watch this a little longer," Daddy murmured. "This is history. It's the journalist in me."

"Mind if I stay up with you?"

"I'd like that very much. What a night."

We played jazz softly, and watched the fire in the sky ebb with the hours...

"Daddy?"

"Hmm?"

"I'll bet it was Dr. Rafferson."

"Who?"

"That crazy – looking guy with the steamer trunk. The guy Munye called Rasputin. We met him at Tony's office once. I remember. That first day."

"What's your theory?"

"That he was working for the Perkins' brothers all along. He detonated that steamer trunk by remote control. Once he was sure they were all aboard again."

"You should write detective stories, Jess. That's devious."

I was still staring hypnotically at the blast's afterlight.

"That's how the Godfather would have done it. That's all. That's all I was thinking. That's how Michael would have gotten rid of Barzini, under similar circumstances."

Daddy thought about that one for a moment, then nodded despite himself.

"You think the brothers are that smart?"

"Yes."

"And that ruthless?"

"Yes. They were betting the farm."

"If there's mercy in Heaven, we'll never know for sure."

And a night with one more poignant human moment.

"Kammi?"

She was standing in the bedroom doorway, her face an almost comic twisted mask of self - awareness.

"Honey, go back to bed."

"That was the cruise ship blowing up?"

"Chances are good it was. Ghost Posse had a nuclear weapon on board."

*"I just realized – My Mom was on that boat!"*

Kammi raced across the livingroom, grabbed her shawl from a hook by the screen door, and flew out into the night, running toward the still - bright, shimmering afterlight of the mushroom umbrella spreading across the horizons, to the far distance of eyesight, in the hot Gulf night.

For a few hours only, the blast had eaten the stars –
both kinds. The stars in the sky would return. If there's
mercy in heaven, the other stars won't be seen again, even
in re - runs.

I started out the still - banging screen door after her.
Daddy reached for my arm.

"Let her go," He advised me softly. "You can't do
anything now. She's been through a lot of changes today
and tonight. She'll still be on the beach tomorrow morning.
By then she'll have begun to learn the true nature of
loneliness. With loss comes wisdom. Maybe she'll grow a
brain. She'll need you then. She'll need a hug. Maybe for
the first time in her insane life, Kammi will really need a
hug. And a sister."

That long night I might have slept five minutes.
Dawn came, and I was out the door. Daddy was still asleep.
I could hear Pauley Vee snoring like a cement mixer.
Perhaps that was Roseanne. They were so perfectly
matched.

The path down to the beach led first across our
deserted village, then through a lovely little wood floored
by the miracle colorations of bloom that seemed to change
aspect and intensity in the morning's first gentle breeze as I
walked by them, the forest floor ever - beautiful, ever
changing no matter how often I strolled there.

I bagged a bunch of wild strawberries from the
winding vines that ran everywhere in the forest, and a
couple of ripe tangerines too. And a mango. I tied them all
inside a cloth that had been holding my hair together. I'd

forgotten to bring a knife. We liked to eat mangos like apples anyway.

The slope beyond the forest gently descended toward the *hush hush* of the dawn's chasing surf, where I knew I would find her.

At the crest of the slope I halted and looked a long few moments from horizon to horizon. Just a straight, unbroken line. Not a smokestack, nor a lifesaver ring.

Like Dr. Munye himself, the sea had returned to first principles. Dozens of news helicopters, at least a dozen big Coast Guard rescue planes, hundreds of gulls and the shadows of other sea birds, shrieking and circling closer to shore, all hunted high and low across the empty Gulf, looking for something they would never find.

In a low saddle between the sugary dunes below, reposed a small, lonely, isolated, familiar silhouette...

"Oh – big sister."

Kammi was sitting on a sea - shell tangled mound of seaweed, her arms wrapped around her knees.

From some distance away, I could see her shoulders trembling under the shawl, as though from the chill off the surf.

But coming closer, I realized the trembling figure was instead wracked by dry, silent sobs, slow and measured and from the depths of a dear, sad girl who'd never, in the past, ever been accused of possessing depth. Live and learn.

Wisdom came from loss, more than any other thing.

"Big sister," I hugged her.

"Little sister," She wept, and we embraced on the sugar beach a long time.

"Are you going to be okay?"

"So much has happened since this time yesterday. So much has changed. Everything has changed. I may be a widow."

"You look good in black."

"You have a strange sense of humor, little sister." she laughed. "Mmm. I'd forgotten how good the fruit is here." She paused. "It's true. You can't see my acne at all. My fame...it's just beginning."

She started crying again, not a tear, but again from the depths, dry heaves instead of tears, an attempt to rid herself of something inside that didn't want to let go.

"I miss my mom," She gasped. "Evil, insane, controlling soul - dragon that she was, it'll take time to get over this. Thank God I'm a strong black woman. We know how to handle suffering." *Nobody knows the trouble I've seen. Nobody knows (but Jesus.)*

"I was thinking the same thing exactly. How about a morning frap? I'm buying."

"I think I'll just wait here a while longer. Maybe she'll come swimming up. My Mom's so tough. Maybe she thought of a way to save herself. My Mom's so smart..." She wiped her face with her arm, never taking her eyes from the horizon. We both knew better.

I hugged her.

"My family – all good swimmers. And we were good, too." She wiped away the tears. More fell. "One Halloween Mom designed mermaid - tail costumes for all of us. Before our family became rich and famous, and she went crazy, Kressa tried to be a good mom to us..." Another pause. "God, to be normal. Just to be normal. We used to be like that. We were a good family..."

"Wisdom begins with loss, big sister."

"Oh, then, please God – I hope I can stay stupid a while longer."

"I love you, big sister."

"Love you more." She began sobbing again, the same deep, dry - heave desolation, memory and love trying to escape her heart, but her heart nowhere near letting go.

"You're all I have, Jesse James. My sisters were on that boat too. What a gift, to go quick like that. Death comes in a flash of light…"

*We may never know, big sister, with a little luck we'll never have that experience at all,* I almost said, but it would just have made everything hurt worse just then.

I left the folded cloth on the sand underneath Eden's fresh island fruit, and watched Kammi picking through the giant strawberries a while, before kissing my big sister goodbye and returning to our home.

*We'll get the full story of the cruise ship explosion in the papers and on tv tomorrow morning. The full story will appear with the first editions and the early morning tv chat stories —*

Only it never happened.

The cruise ship, and its famous citizenry, were vaporized so completely, that no single hair, nor fiber nor bulkhead plate, were ever found. The ship's giant anchor and three hundred foot long steel chain — annihilated to a molecular level.

Not to mention Judge Trudy's prized mahogany gavel, Fancy Lace's one - of - a - kind handcuff necklace, Jerry Springer's 12 volt Taser, no longer needed to protect him from either his slobbering audience or guests, Money Hoo Hoo's authentic antique porto - potty, the harpoons and spears and hand grenades the various charmingly eccentric backwoods families of animal and fish killers used in their slaughter, the clay jugs of the moonshining Korn Kookers, the wigs, wines, girdles and Morning After pills of the various warring Housewives, the stupidest of women from the stupidest of cities…

Oh, the horror, the indescribable loss! Whole museums full of potentially soul - enriching cultural ephemera, gone now, all so tragically gone, and will they ever return, no they'll never return, and their fate is still unlearned...

And that was the problem for America's ravenous social media, not to mention the professional journalists, unwilling to write off the vanishing of a whole generation of unquestioned Reality genius as the work of the Bermuda Triangle.

How could the Bermuda Triangle be responsible? Had it moved mysteriously hundreds of miles northward? How could the Bermuda Triangle be issuing detectable radiation for months after the Great Eery Reality Disappearance (GERD)? *Oh, the cruelty, the horror, the humanity! Fancy Lace, never again to pass erroneous, screamed, spit - flecked judgment upon some poor innocent wretch who had come within her crosshairs! Oh, Judge Trudy! And Orca, poor mad Orca, with her little red wagon filled with the viscous globs of reeking lard that represented memories with which she could not bear to part, now gone, gone with the radioactive wind!*

*How can we make fun of these idiots, even on the coroner's slabs, when we can't even find them?*

How could that many famous people, the matrix of modern American television culture, go missing all within one five thousandth of a second of one another? A second question arose: How would we manage another day without them?

Did the Martians or Venusians, desperate for quality television entertainment, vacuum up the whole cruise boat and teleport them across the universe to a kinder, gentler, less commercial video environment? Were the Reality geniuses kidnapped somehow and taken to Cambodia to entertain villages of heroin - producers, along the lines popularized In *Tropic Thunder* and its equally talented comic genius, Simple Jack?

These were only two of many instantly debated theories, filling some of the vast gaps that suddenly appeared on nighttime television. Late night talk - shows chattered the hours away. *Gunsmoke, the Beverly Hillbillys, Lawrence Welk,* all these re - runs helped, taking us back, along with *Bewitched* and *Gilligan's Island,* to a kinder, gentler, more honest vision of the American empire...

Like it or lump it, America was forced to reach back with both arms to embrace *The Great Wasteland,* and to give it a great big kiss of inner recognition.

Miraculously, the huge, deadly radioactive wall stopped exactly five miles beyond the pristine shores of Crystal Lagoon. That left us plenty of room to go sailing. Whatever else you may say about him, Our Absentee Landlord had left the Gates of Eden well - protected.

For weeks thereafter, the gentle surf lapped at the sandy reaches of our island's main beach, disgorging no memory of the previous season's Neilsen's rulers, no evidence of the cultural loss, only, very occasionally, washing up a dripping glob of reeking, rotting lard, which no amount of radiation would ever obliterate, and which could have come from anywhere.

\* \* \*

# XIX

"Are you going to the luau tomorrow night?" This time I was braiding Kammi's long hair in front of the bathroom mirror. New Year's Eve had arrived at Crystal Cay with clear beautiful skies and seventy plus temperatures, a slight breeze with heavenly fragrances, and a sense of peace and happiness that was, to use one of Daddy's five dollar words, *palpable*.

What kind of luau would it be?

If Gatsby and Truman Capote put their heads together, set an unlimited budget, and hired Wolfgang Puck to cater and the Rolling Stones to headline – *that* kind of luau.

"Let me ask you something: did Tony ever mention anything about this island being... The Garden of Eden?"

"The Garden of Eden?" She seemed genuinely surprised. "No. I never heard that. Come to think about it, I've always been so happy here... I'm not aging."

"Prometheus is immortal. But he isn't happy."

"Who?"

"Never mind. You know who I hope I'll meet tomorrow night?"

"Who?"

"Madonna."

"I've met her. She's a bitch."

"Love her music."

"Love it more." Kammi looked away from the mirror, indicating she was in process of formulating an independent thought. "Wouldn't it be the tops if this turned out to be the Garden of Eden, after all? And the Water is just the fuel that feeds it all? Wow."

"You're so beautiful, black sister."

"I'm liking this new Kammi."

"You've matured so much, even in the little time I've known you."

"Could I have gotten any dumber?" She gave an ironic smile into the mirror. "Maybe I've learned something from the suffering of my people."

"It's going to be a big party tomorrow night. The Stones are playing two sets."

"Your Mom's so pretty!" Kammi said out of nowhere. "She's the one who looks like your big sister – so young! Gorgeous red hair. Long legs. She's got a model's legs. You've got her legs, Jessica. Bet she's a forest fire in the sack."

"*Kaa - aammii!*"

"Sorry, little sister. It's just the ghetto in me coming out."

"You're gonna make the best U.N. envoy, Kammi. You'll represent everything that's good about this island. We've established diplomatic relations with everybody now. Even the American government loves us. Do you suppose POTUS heard about the Magic Water?"

She laughed. "You know damn well he has."

"You're smart, charming, gorgeous, *sequentially* bi - racial. *First* white. *Then* black. By *choice!* Your willingness to undergo a voluntary Epidermal Regression shows where your heart is in the matter of race relations in America. It proves you're all in."

"Thanks for keeping my secret, Jess. My new fame depends on the Regression being voluntary, not like... not like it was – "

"Sshhh."

"I love having you as my white stepsister."

"I only pray your sacrifice will help build a better, more racially harmonious America." *Dear big sister, America's foremost default selfie, now in black AND white... Our future as a Nation is at last to be unified by the dominant image of this fiery, sequentially bi - racial, famous, starbright, big - assed Reality supernova. Our last hope.*

*Our best hope.*

"Me too, little sister. My wish too."

"It might just help your self - esteem too."

"But my God, Jessica, you know better than anyone – I'm a serial adulteress, probable bigamist, habitual liar, shameless exhibitionist, forger, greedy double - dealing user, only caring about myself, stabbing everybody in the back, doing anything to maintain youth, beauty, wealth and fame – "

"Big sister, when America looks at you, it sees itself. You're pure. That's your magic." *America sees itself, low - information, horny, aggressive, grasping, gullible, self - obsessed, ruthless, trusting, innocent, sad, courageous, relentless, cynical, believing, religious, patriotic, hypocritical, quietly desperate... most of all, unapologetic. So you've got a couple of minor character flaws. Don't we all? That's why America loves the Dream of Kammi Kay – a Rorschacht that may resemble De Kooning's 'Woman II' but yet somehow allows for ultimate forgiveness, our post - modern Virgin Mary – the final, most horrifically forgivable, inconceivable Mother of all forgiveness.*

*You are She.*

*Blame the Absentee Landlord for Humanity's every other shortcoming.*

*Don't blame us.*

"I'm going to lead America to a better day." Kammi set her jaw in a determined, even patriotic, expression. "I'll show everyone that we *can* all just get along, like that guy said, after the riots – Rodney what's his name?"

She hugged me with all her heart and soul.

"Remember, Jessica, a long time ago, when I told you one day the world would learn about me, that there was more to me than my physique? That someday I would soar across the sky like that famous comet? I forget the name. Maybe that someday is now."

"Big sister, you're even brighter than Hailey's Comet – remember that old Paul Simon song? *You're America's new Joe DiMaggio, Kammi – a nation turns its lonely eyes to you...*"

*Hoo hoo hoo. Hoo hoo hoo...!*

\* \* \* \* \* \* \*

*FBI LAUDS NEW CRIME STATS IN DETROIT, 800 CARJACKINGS IN JAN. A 25% DROP, KAMMI KAY, BI-RACIAL U.N. ENVOY, VISITS MOTOWN IN ARMED CONVOY*

\* \* \* \* \* \* \*

*DETROIT MAYOR CARJACKED, BEATEN IN MANSION DRIVEWAY; MAYOR THANKS ATTACKERS, 'AT LEAST THEY DIDN'T SHOOT ME', ARRESTS UNLIKELY, SOURCES SAY*

\* \* \* \* \* \* \*

*NEWARK MAYOR CARJACKS OWN SECRETARY, FAMILY AFTER BIZARRE ROAD RAGE INCIDENT; CHARGES LIKELY, SOURCES SAY*

\* \* \* \* \* \* \*

*KAMMI KAY MULLS CHICAGO MAYOR RUN;*

*'CAN'T DRIVE, NO FEAR OF BEING*
*CARJACKED', BIRACIAL DIVA BOASTS,*
*PROMISES MORE PLATFORM DETAILS*
*AFTER OSCARS*
* * * * * * *

*LIFETIME OSCAR TO KAMMI KAY FOR*
*RACIAL EFFORT, LEADERSHIP,*
*'BRAVE SACRIFICE';*
*KAMMI 'WALKS THE WALK'*
*BUBBA TELLS OSCAR CROWD*
* * * * * * *

*KAMMI THANKS VOTERS FOR*
*LANDSLIDE WIN,*
*VOWS TO BE CHICAGO'S GREATEST*
*MAYOR, 'AND I NEVER LIE'...*
* * * * * * *

*DREAMPERKS OPTIONS DIVA'S STUNNING*
*LIFE STORY, BIG SCREEN BIO EPIC LIKELY,*
*SOURCES SAY...*
*WILL KAMMI PLAY HERSELF?*
*SEQUENTIALLY BIRACIAL*
*DIVA, MUM ON EARLY OSCAR BUZZ...*
* * * * * * *

*POPE RAGENDICHER BESTOWS*
*HONORARY SAINTHOOD ON*
*KAMMI: 'SHE'S WHAT IS BEST IN*
*HUMANITY'; DIVA WEEPS, GOES SHOPPING*
*FOR 'CUTE CRUCIFIX PENDANT'*
*WAVES TO VATICAN THRONG OF*
*HALF MILLION WORSHIPPERS*
* * * * * * *

*IN WAKE OF NOBEL WIN KK MULLS WH*
*RUN, POLLS SHOW LANDSLIDE LIKELY,*
*KAMMI PROMISES TO BE 'BEST PREZ EVER*

*AND I NEVER LIE'*
*\* \* \* \* \* \* \**

*MT. RUSHMORE SPOT FOR KAMMI KAY*
*PASSES CONGRESS*
*OVER POTUS VETO, WORK TO START SOON,*
*SOURCES SAY...*
*\* \* \* \* \* \* \**

*HAMPTONS' HOUSEWIVES TO CHASE*
*GREASED PIGS; TOUTED NEW SHOW*
*LEADS NBC FALL LINE - UP, RATINGS*
*BONANZA PROJECTED, ABC FOLLOWS*
*WITH NUNS SELLING VIRGINITY FOR*
*'SISTER THERESA' CHARITY, /*
*CONTROVERSY DOMINATES LATE NIGHT*
*TALK SHOWS, SUNDAY PULPITS...*
*RATINGS SOAR...*
*KARDASHIANS RENEWED FIVE MORE*
*YEARS, KANYE AGAIN DENIED BAIL*


"...And I promise," Mom hugged me as we walked along the beach. "No more listening to Lush Rimbaud."

"...And I'll give up the Rev. Jeremiah..."

"Oh, he wasn't so bad. Actually, sometimes he made a lot of sense."

"I'm amazed they weren't on that Reality Cruise that got so mysteriously vaporized," Daddy said.

*Don't worry, Dad. We'll get 'em next time.*

The sugary sand crunched under three pairs of bare feet, Mom carrying her thongs in one hand, holding onto Dad with the other. She had a crown of purple wildflowers holding back her waist - length, wild red hair.

"Purple looks really sexy against your hair and eyes," Dad noted.

"Oh," She laughed, pulling him closer.

Even Daddy had a rose tucked behind one ear, only emphasizing the dumb silly grin on his handsome face that he didn't seem to be able to get rid of.

As twilight approached, I waited for exactly the right light and selfied eternal Jessica, wearing denim cutoffs, a paisley halter, Jimmy Buffet straw hat and Lolita sunglasses – *fo' flavah.*

Sometimes, even now, I scroll up that selfie, which I've labeled *Daughter of Dorian* in honor of my dear bffs from those never - to - be - forgotten high school days. So long ago.

All these many moons later, sometimes I find myself standing before my bedroom mirror, holding the selfie next to my face, in order to visually unify person and portrait, the selfie from so long ago – yet still we are twins in eternal youth. I see a mirror within a mirror, an exact visual echo – a daily miracle.

Technically I guess I've never passed fifteen, but a wisdom has come upon me, a wisdom that I cherish. Perhaps you can see it in my prose.

*Or not. lol.*

Still can't write like Daddy – but I'm working on it. That's just a little retroactive twist in the narration, Trogs. *Immortal Oscar would be so very proud –*


The sun was setting. My i was in hand. I was about to prove to the Dads that these days, there was such a technological miracle as a phone with a camera inside...

The beach stretched before us wide and gently arcing behind a little mangrove island, palmettos, coconut palms and a field of hibiscus, all moving very gently in the twilight breeze, the whisper of the Gulf splashing upward onto the sand.

Entangled in the black maidenshair of seaweed, a child's treasure of seashells, sand dollars and exotic bonelike driftwood all spilled out of the surf, to be swarmed by this laughing, excited trio of beachcombers, gravely examined, listened to, studied and remarked upon, before being fed laughingly back into the foamy twilight tide...

The light around us, like Time itself, seemed to halt in a rosy glow.

"Thank you for coming down, wife," Daddy smiled.

"Oh, dearest, thank you so much for *inviting* me – husband. For forgiving me. For everything."

"You've never looked sexier, not even on our wedding day. And that's saying something."

"I'd like to give the credit to my surgeon. But, honestly, a lot of it may have to do with the fact this is the first time in years I remember being happy."

I jumped out in front of these two lovebirds, the soft bloated golden moon just starting to appear behind them, and got a great i pic.

"Now kiss."

*Click. Click. Click. Click. Click.*

"Okay. Got it. You two really *are* in love. The moon makes a perfect backdrop. Night and day in one."

"A couple more." Dad had his arms around her.

*Click. Click. Click.......Click.....Click.*

"Okay. Got it. I said I got it!"

"Couple more," Mom laughed. "Mmm..."

*Click ....Click...................Click................*

"Okay. Okay! Cut! Enough, you two! Get a room!"

Before taking our evening stroll, we'd stopped by Pauley Vee's Frappuccino Salon, for a ganja frap. Pauley and Roseanne were in love too. It was a good season for it.

It had been a while since I'd seen Old Shovel - Head without his shotgun. Roseanne was wearing a Gator T - shirt in honor of our upcoming Sugar bowl appearance. She was replacing napkins in the steel containers at every marble table in the quaint little soda shop/fern bar that had become a sort of hip celebrity hangout on this island where there weren't many places to hang out. Celebrities love wise guys too. Roseanne and Pauley had actually *met* Madonna. "She was nice."

"Kammi said she's a bitch."

"Nah. She's just hungry all the time. I know the look. It's one thing to live for ever, it's another thing to live for ever and not get fat."

Pauley looked funny wearing a tie - dye t - shirt. He is one scary hippie. But Daddy always vows Pauley has a heart of gold, and heaven knows, without his timely arrival in that tunnel last August, I wouldn't be writing this now...

Pauley Vee was glad to be out of the booze business.

"I got tired of all the fights over point spreads," He laughed. "Nobody could ever figure 'em out. The half - point thingie."

Phong had brought two - dozen Krispies, so we had a snack – I think they used to call them 'munchies' – after celebrating with these wonderful ganja fraps. We grow our own in this region, I'm proud to say, and fed by the Immortal Water, the results are radical. Just say it in two words, Jess – *Purple Bud.*

Only once had Phong and I discussed B.

"Well?"

"TCB," She had shrugged, ever the Elvis fan. Then she gave an evil little laugh. She'd reached up for a high - five, happily delivered. "Put it this way: three cheers for Super Glue."

We high - fived.

And never mentioned my first love again.

Phong had gone back to the bungalow for a nap before luau, and a family, at last healed, walked slowly along the sugar highway under perfect moonlight. Twilight was waving us goodbye underneath a diamond sky.

I walked between my mother and father, all the way to where the beach broke off at the mangroves. I felt them holding hands together behind me, and you could hear our laughter up and down the beach.

"The Rolling Stones?" My mother giggled like a teenager. "They're actually performing at this party?"

"Luau."

"And they're actually still *young?*"

"Just like 1971."

"No!"

"It costs five - million per year per Stone to stay that way – why do you think they're still touring?"

"The make - up people here are magicians," Daddy confirmed. "The key is to make people appear to be aging very slowly, subtly – not like the movies. Then, when they've finished a tour, they return here and the make - up people peel off the special effects that create the illusion of the forty years between then and now. It takes a couple of hours. You've gotta be careful with all that latex and adhesive... The cornstarch is tricky..."

"You should see Barack Obama without grey hair. He looks like he's still teaching law school."

"I want their autographs!"

"That can be arranged, dearest."

The moon rose, and its golden light traced the slow, lazy surf.

We turned back. You could hear, in the near distance, the tuning of electric guitars, and view the glow of firelight from the luau, faintly outlining the tips of the serrated pines and coconut fronds, the hibiscus, wisteria, rose and palmetto grottos stretching away from the sugar beach toward the lofty, lighted minarets of the castle.

I had a portable jar of Pauley's iced ganjafrap, in case I got thirsty during the concert. Not to worry. On this island, there are no pat - downs.

With every breath I took, happiness and excitement rose up in my throat, and I had to fight hard not to start crying with an absolutely exultant joy. Every day since Mom came down, even better than the last, every moment impossibly more perfect – with every breath, steady, patient, controlled exhilaration.

Daddy's heart had healed, Mother had come to her senses, and our family had become whole and bonded in deepest love once more, something I couldn't have expected in my profoundest, most prayerful dreams when I first began these diary entries...

Furthermore, Tommy had promised to throw away his pocket protector on my eighteenth birthday. I'll choose when that is. Anyhow, I'll believe it when I see it, and when I see it, I'm going to marry him.

*Tall and tan and young and lovely, the girl from Ipanema goes walking, and when she passes, each one she passes goes –*
*Aahhh....*

The wet sugar sand squished between our toes, and the incoming tide came racing up the beach to give us a warm foamy explosive kiss, before reluctantly sluicing downward again into the roaring near - darkness. *Rinse and repeat.*

We chased the silver hem of the retreating sea till the tide reached our knees. Impulsively I grabbed my Mom, and clung to her a very long time before I realized we were both crying.

"Love you, Mom."

"Oh, thank God. I love you, Jessica."

"We all made it home."

"Yes. Your father's favorite quote – We healed strongest at the broken place. It's happening. I can feel it happening."

"Huggsies," I cried, laughing, "Can't get enough."

"Me neither, daughter. Me neither."

And for the next few minutes, listening to my mother laughing and crying, I do believe she was much more the teenager than even her crazy daughter.

Emotionally, she had turned back Time, and it was a wonderful thing to see.

I would always have my Mom. But suddenly I realized I might just have another big sister too.

I remember the first time I decided I would live forever. I was about nine then, walking one bright black winter night with my parents on a beach at Alligator Point, up in the panhandle. The sky was just like tonight, a diamond night sky.

Somehow, like every nine - year old, I knew my life *must* last forever – *must*. The secret to it lay hidden somewhere among those billions of mystical fragments spilling down out of the arcing black heights, their dusty silver signatures dancing off the silver grains of sand crunching underneath our bare feet –

The shore ahead curved timelessly, simultaneously mirroring the Heavens while leading toward them – a sugar shoreline, then as now, back - lit by galaxies of starlight descending all the way to the edge of the sea. I remember thinking I could almost reach out and touch the miraculous, milky starfall lighting the carbon curtain of night in front of me, the starlight glimmering off the grains of icy sand where we walked. *As above, so below.*

I remember how happy my parents were together that night.

*Either I use my great big gigantic nine - year old brain to solve the puzzle of the night sky,* I remember thinking then – or maybe I might just have to get lucky. Either way I planned to live forever. I'm not the only nine - year old who ever had that plan.

I've never thought of the night sky as a distant, impassive or lonely place. I think of it as a Pandora's vault of Hope, where the solution to our predicament awaits.

Sure, Time is racing away from us always, but Heaven is yearning to yield to us its eternal secrets, from the first moment of Eden to the infinite swath of cinnamon moonlight tonight on this very beach.

Every night, the dome of eternity opens its arms, waiting to invite us in. Every step the human race takes should be following that singular starlit shore, leading right to the edge, and then the heart, of Time; nothing else really matters. We've conquered the skies, the seas – why not our Great Predicament next? Purpose, identity, mortality – even immortality?

Here I am, already fifteen – nearly sixteen, which is when I stopped counting – and I *still* haven't been able to solve the mysteries of the stars.

Ridiculous.

But...well...gosh...did I forget to mention this? I *did* get lucky.

Miraculously, Powerball times a million lucky...

So, so lucky.

*Kammi Kay lucky.*

And you don't get any luckier than that.

And who's to say that one day you might not get this lucky? If it happened to me, it could happen to anybody.

Someday, when I'm absolutely certain it's safe to do so, I'll gather together and publish this narrative, these diaries and texts, sexts and emails, covering the months up in Tallahassee and down here at Crystal Lagoon, when my life changed so much, when I took a weekend trip with my father, at vacation's end – the magic, long - ago summer when I got lucky.

Forgive me – I'll be changing some names to protect the guilty, particularly those in Reality Nation who vanished in that single wonderfully scrubbing flash.

I hate stating the obvious, but I'll be changing the name, and geographical location of our beloved island too. Obviously. Suffice it that we're out here somewhere in the Gulf of Mexico, waking to the sunrise, happily chasing sea shells. They rarely escape. I'll bet Daddy will keep helping me with the intricacies of literary technique too. He's still working on that second Pulitzer.

*We'll get there, Pop. We'll get there...*

Meanwhile, what more could any fifteen - year old immortal girl wish for from this moonlit, shining world? Krisps. Obviously. *Peace and happiness through all the land...*

Yes.

To be? *Yes!* To do? *Yes!* To have? *Yes! To dance beneath the diamond sky with one hand waving free...* Yes. God be my witness –

*The Gods within myself.*

*Yes.*

Peace out, Jessica out.#

# ABOUT THE AUTHOR

Other novels by V. S. Cawthon available on www.amazon.com in
Kindle and Paperback:

In The Thieves' Market
Facing Paralysis
Quarterback Jesus
The Women of Berkeley
Berkeley 1974
Eden, Then and Now

V. S. Cawthon is a business owner, jeweler, and writer. He currently resides
in Tallahassee, Florida.

Made in the USA
Columbia, SC
07 May 2020